THE UNSEEN

THE UNSEEN

by

Mike Clelland

BENEATH THE STARS
PRESS

The story is fiction,

yet the emotions are real.

Prologue

I was frustrated. I was hoping to find a little solace, but it wasn't happening. I wanted to draw and told them so, and they brought me a box of crayons. They've been keeping me on a suicide watch, and that means no pencils and no pens. I've always hated crayons, even as a little kid. There's something about the wax that never truly gets on the paper. Even if you press hard, it's never more than a muddled smear without any real color.

I was trying to capture something subtle, and the red crayon was horrible. The color wasn't right. It was too normal, like a cherry stop sign. They brought me paper, but I was drawing on an old brown paper bag, and pressing lightly meant the tan of the paper would show through and cut down the garish red. I used the white crayon to create a little bit of sheen in the image. I was trying to capture the magic of her hair.

Yesterday they told me I would be seeing another doctor. They never said it, but I could tell by their tone that he didn't work here. I figured they had come to a dead end and didn't know what else to do. I knew this other doctor was in the building. I don't know how I knew, but I did. The staff here was probably overwhelming him. There must have been all kinds of formalities and briefings to fill him in on my case.

The staff told me this new doctor would be giving me an evaluation. I wasn't sure what that meant because I'd already had a lot of them. They did psychological assessments, physical exams, took blood, and ran tests. I sat patiently while they asked an endless list of questions. I evaded some things and answered others. When they ran out of questions, they taped little wires to my head to read my brain waves.

Seems they were baffled about what had happened, so they got on the phone and called in one more doctor. I can understand their confusion. Me on the other hand, I feel like I've got a pretty good grasp on how I got here. Not at first, mind you.

I was sitting up when they pulled the sheet off me, and the look on their faces would have been funny if I knew what was going on. All I knew was I was cold, and two men in hospital garb were staring at me. It was only a few seconds before they were all over me, trying to get me to lie down and asking a lot of questions. I could hear it in their voices, they were scared.

I tried to push them away and demanded, "Where am I?"

They were yelling for help, and the room was filling up with people—doctors, nurses, and attendants, all of them were acting the same way, they were freaked out.

A big guy in a uniform rushed right up close to my face. He looked at me and asked, "Daniel, what do you need?"

I had no idea who Daniel was, but I was cold and said so. He brought a blanket and wrapped it around me. It was then that I realized I was in a morgue.

That was three days ago, and I've settled down, but everyone else is still on edge. They explained I was dead when they found me. I had killed myself here in this hospital. They only told me a little bit, but I eventually remembered the rest of it. I used my shirt. It had long sleeves, and these were long enough to make a clove hitch. This is a knot I knew nothing about and couldn't tie—but Daniel could. Anyway, it was the perfect knot. Once it's snugged in place, it only gets tighter. I looped it around my neck, tied the sleeves together, and hung it on the doorknob. All I needed to do was lie on the floor until I passed out, and that's what I did. It was easy.

And now I was back and trying to draw. When I heard the guard talking in the hall, I knew it would be starting soon. There was about a minute of muffled voices, then a soft knocking, and the latch slid. The door opened, and the doctor I'd been expecting stepped in. He politely thanked the guard, and the heavy door closed behind him.

The doctor seemed perfectly average. Not tall but not short, a little overweight, and a bit balding. He carried a drab leather briefcase, wore glasses and a brown suit with a light blue button-down shirt. He wasn't wearing a tie. I figured he'd arrived with one, but they made him take it off before meeting with me. They were worried I'd grab it and choke him, but that would bring in the guard from the hall, and then a bunch more. They didn't need to bother, because I was done with all that.

He introduced himself and sat across from me at the table where I'd been drawing. He told me he'd been called in because what had happened had left the staff challenged. I was still for a moment, then said, "They called you because you have some sort of specialty."

He nodded and said, "That would be fair to say."

That was a fuzzy kind of non-answer, so I stayed silent. He smiled blandly and said, "I have an interest and previous experience in cases that are out of the ordinary."

"You mean like mine?"

He nodded and said, "Yes."

He opened his briefcase and took out a folder, a yellow legal pad and a pen, and set them on the desk. Then he set a small voice recorder between us, but didn't turn it on. He asked if I needed anything, and I said I'd like a cup of coffee.

He smiled and said, "Good, I could use one, too."

He stood up and opened the door, then asked me how I wanted it. I said black. He politely told the guard to bring two coffees with sugar and milk on the side. Then he added to bring them in ceramic mugs.

The guard looked past the doctor and eyed me with concern. This was the big guy who'd brought me the blanket in the morgue. He knew Daniel, but he obviously didn't know me.

The doctor repeated himself, asking again for two coffees with sugar and milk on the side, and to bring them in ceramic mugs. This was a change from the paper cups I was used to in here. The staff is concerned that heavy mugs could be broken and used as a weapon. His little gesture seemed nice enough, but it felt a little showy. He wanted something.

He sat back down but didn't say anything. After a bit, he calmly arranged the few things on the table, lining them up so they were neat and tidy. I broke the silence and said, "They called you in because they're all stumped about me."

He smiled and shrugged his shoulders as if it wasn't that interesting. "Well, that's one way to look at it. How it was explained to me was that some of the staff here felt it would be helpful to get another opinion."

He asked what I had been drawing, and I said it was nothing, just some doodling to pass the time. He didn't ask to see it, and I didn't show him. I pushed the paper bag to the side of the table and started putting the crayons in their box.

He asked how I'd been sleeping and I said fine, and that was true. He asked how I had been feeling since the event, and I said my neck had been sore but it felt much better now. He asked a few more things, and I answered as best as I could. All this chit-chat seemed breezy and pleasant. I put the last crayon in the box and set it on the paper bag.

There was the metal sound of the latch, and the guard came in with a tray and set it on the table. The doctor thanked him, and he left and latched the door closed. The doctor poured a little milk in his mug and held it for a moment, as if judging the color. I picked up the other mug, took a sip, and noticed right away this was much better than the crappy stuff they had been giving me. I sensed he had arranged this on purpose.

I looked at him and said, "You're here to ask if I went into the light and things like that?"

He sat back and asked, "Did you go into the light?"

His question was simple enough, but for some reason it seemed funny. "Well, yes, I did. But that's not really important." I corrected myself and said, "I guess it might seem important, but it's more complicated than that."

We sat quietly for a bit, then he said, "I was told that Daniel always drank his coffee with sugar."

"You're correct, he did."

He took another sip and set down his mug. He casually asked, "What do you remember of Daniel?"

I said, "The other doctors, they've already asked me that, repeatedly, and you must have talked with them and seen all the files, so you know I remember everything."

He stared at me without emotion and waited. I went on, "Look, Daniel had a hard life. It was very sad for him, and it's not easy for me now, to have all that in me. I don't really want to look back on it —his life."

He said, "Daniel killed a young woman."

"What are you asking?"

"When he was arrested, he explained he was told to do it because she was being controlled by demons."

I said, "Yeah, that's in me, too. The other doctors asked a lot about that. The meds that Daniel was on helped quiet those voices, but it was still in him, the memories and the shame. I can answer the same questions again if you want, but I really don't want to. It's too dark."

"I saw the photographs the police took of her body." He said it in the same untroubled way he'd been saying everything.

I said, "Well, I saw it, too. As it happened. It's horrible, and that's in me."

"In you? You mean like a memory, or like you could do it again?"

"It's his memory, not mine."

The doctor picked up his pen and held it with both hands. He rolled it slowly between his fingertips, but didn't say anything. I said, "Look, Daniel knows what Hell means. And not some abstraction or distant idea, he was swallowed up and trapped in it."

The doctor asked, "It's my understanding that your medications have been discontinued since the event. How is that going for you?"

"When you say since the event, you mean since killing myself—my other self, right?"

"Yes. How do you feel?"

"I feel like a bug in a glass jar, but beyond that I feel okay."

We looked at each other. I could hear the incessant rain on the bushes out the window behind me, and could smell the disinfectant they used to mop the halls. I wasn't in any hurry, and neither was he. I looked down at my hands and arms. They were hard and gnarled, tightened by a life of grinding stress. My old arms were thin and lithe, and I tried so hard to achieve a sort of grace with those other hands.

Eventually, he said, "The staff here told me that you now want to be called John."

"Yes, my name was John. I actually had two names for a while. One was a pseudonym, and that's how I signed my paintings. My real name was John."

"Good, I'll call you John."

We talked for a while, and he nodded periodically as I shared little bits about my other life before arriving here. His pen hovered about an inch above the yellow pad, but he never wrote anything. He wasn't really asking much directly. Everything was framed in this vague sort of maybe realm.

We went round and round like that until I said, "You want to hear the story don't you?"

He set down his pen, looked at me with a new clarity, and said, "Yes, I do."

"They called you in because they needed someone to ask me about the white light and stuff like that. You're here to ask the weird questions they weren't asking, right?"

He raised his eyebrows and said, "Pretty much, yes."

I looked at him for a long time, took a deep breath, pointed to his little recorder and said, "You might want to turn that on."

PART ONE

1

THE FIRST TIME I SAW HER, she was down the street from the gallery. It was at night, and I was sitting alone on the curb. My straw summer Stetson was on the sidewalk next to me. It was upside down with the brim facing the sky. There's an old Western superstition that the luck will spill out if it gets set brim side down.

I wore cowboy boots, Wrangler jeans, and a white pearl snap button shirt. From where I sat, I could look across the street and see all the people through the big window. My name—my fake name, anyway—was printed on the glass in tall, elegant letters. I'm no cowboy, so I was wearing a fake outfit and looking at my fake name. I hated this part, the show of it. The people were standing around my paintings and waiting for me. I saw Ted. He was looking out at the dark street from the big window of the gallery, and I knew he could see me.

There wasn't much traffic on this block, especially at night. All the restaurants and bars were around the corner and down towards the town square. Right then, things seemed unusually calm. All the nice cars were lined up along the sidewalk, and all the nice people were inside, standing around my paintings.

Ted stepped out of the gallery and crossed the street. He walked to where I was sitting on the curb and stood next to me. He took both hands, pinched his khakis above his knees, pulled them up about an inch, and sat beside me on the curb.

He told me, "You have to go in there, you know that."

"I know, I know."

He asked, "Have you been drinking?"

"No, not yet."

We sat in silence for a little while. All the stores were dark except for the gallery, and the light from the white walls poured onto the sidewalk and out to the street.

He said, "Don't worry, you know most everyone in there. They're all here for you."

"I know."

"Are you all right?"

"I'm fine. Sometimes I don't feel up to this part."

Ted looked up and down the street, and said, "It's really quiet tonight." I had lived in this town for eight years, and he'd been here maybe a decade longer. He was right. There was an odd stillness. What I wanted to tell him was the sky and the silence were achingly beautiful, but all I said was, "Yep, quiet."

Ted was waiting for me to say something more. After a bit, he said, "John, please, c'mon in with me. You can sneak away into my office if you need to."

"Give me a minute. I'll walk in on my own."

"Good, there are people in there who'd love to see you." Ted stood up, touched my shoulder, and walked back inside.

I looked at the crowd in the gallery and thought to myself, "They're here to see Arthur, not me."

Every once in a while, I get a sense of how I am, really am, and this was one of those times. I was sitting on the cement curb with my feet on the asphalt, all drooped over like some gloomy drifter. I recognized the drama of my sullen pose, and thought about drawing myself. I'm well aware of my skills and knew I could capture the mood. I could show solitude in the wrinkles of my shirt, and anguish in the shadows on the ground. These thoughts weren't helping. Eventually, I stood up, put on my hat, and started toward the gallery. Sometimes I can walk in a slumped kind of shuffle, and I was doing it right then.

I was about halfway across the street when I saw her. She was on the sidewalk down at the far end of the block. I took off my hat, and I'm not sure why, maybe out of politeness. I stared at her. She was so tiny, and it was hard to see her in the shadows. I waited for her to move, or for her parents to come around the corner, but nothing happened. She was very skinny, and her head seemed odd, like she was wearing a big old-fashioned hat.

Yet what I was seeing was so still that I wondered if some store owner might have left a cut-out silhouette on the sidewalk. It could be nothing more than plywood, but there was a kind of emotion. I felt something. I stood there waiting for her to move, and it was like I got all seized up. It wasn't pain, but more like a kind of dread. Or maybe sadness.

I bowed my head and closed my eyes, then heard a whisper. It's not so much that I heard it, more that I felt it. The quiet voice said *now is the time*. With that, the feeling of dread dropped away, but not completely.

I lifted my head, put my hat back on, and walked the rest of the way across the street. I looked back and she was still there, standing in that same unsettling pose. As corny as it sounds, I nodded and touched the brim of my hat, like a well-mannered cowboy in an old western movie. I stood a little more upright as I entered the gallery. I was an actor stepping onto a stage.

I had done this plenty of times, arriving at my own opening, but I'd never gotten used to it. The people were always nice, but I never really knew what they were thinking. They would compliment my work, and their kind words left me feeling awkward. Everyone called me Arthur.

I said hello and thank you, and smiled politely, but my eyes were on the bar. There was a young woman with red hair moving through the room. She was dressed in the starched white linen worn by the catering service, and I stopped her as she walked past. I whispered, "Be an angel and get me a glass of tequila, would you?"

She was bright-eyed and asked, "Do you want a lime with that?"

"No. No lime, no salt, no ice." She smiled, and I watched her walk toward the bar.

I looked around the room at my own paintings, all tidy on clean, white walls. These were smaller than the huge canvases that have come to represent my work. I was trying to read the expressions and body language of everyone in the room, and that can be disheartening. A few were looking at the paintings, but most were talking with each other. I never cared what people thought. Well, that's not quite true. I cared, I wanted people to like them, but all this work wasn't for them. I did it for myself.

I've painted the same desert landscapes for years. Some were a little more orange, and some a little more purple, but these were all windows. Windows in adobe homes, and windows in weather-beaten cabins. Most were windows at night, with the yellow of lamplight inside. They were painted in the same bold colors as the mesas and sunsets, but they had none of the bigness. Fragments of dialog surrounded me, whispers and murmurs, indistinct and hushed. I did my best to block it all off, and that was easy, because it all felt terribly distant.

She came back and handed me a glass. I thanked her and took a sip. She didn't leave but stood looking at me. She cautiously said, "You have the bluest eyes I've ever seen."

I tipped my head toward the floor and hid my eyes with my hat. It was a sort of reflex. I drank a little more and waited for her to walk away.

2

LATER THAT NIGHT, the girl came back in a dream. I didn't remember much, but it was her. We were standing in some empty place, facing each other. I worked on and off as a house painter in my early twenties, and got called into a film production company in Las Vegas. They needed me to paint what they called the limbo room. Carpenters had built a three-sided set in a big sound stage. It was three tall walls, like an open-ended room. There were no sharp corners, everything was elegantly rounded. The floor curved up smoothly into the walls, and the walls curved around into each other. I painted it all flat white, the walls and floor. When I was in the middle of it and the bright stage lights were on, it felt like I was floating. It was a strange sensation, and it made me dizzy. I needed to turn around and look out at the rest of the stage to orient myself.

That's how the dream felt, like I was in the limbo room with the girl, except there was nowhere to look to get my bearings. The whiteness had a weird silence, and there was the same feeling of sadness I had on the street. It was familiar, not just from the street, but from another time. I remembered something, or I thought I did. It was so frustrating. There was *something*, yet I couldn't bring it up to the surface.

The girl was right in front of me, and she wore the same big hat, but I still couldn't see her face. I had a funny thought, that maybe this was some kind of mannequin or statue, yet I knew it was the same little girl. Then I was hit with this weird sensation, a kind of knowing. It was like my whole soul was feeling a message. I knew, I absolutely knew—*this is important.*

Then someone said, "John?"

The girl moved. She was real.

"John?"

It was the voice again. It was loud and calm, "John. Wake up."

I opened my eyes. The room was full of light, and I was looking at the wall across from the couch. I sat up and saw Ted at the screen door behind me. When he saw me, he let himself in and said, "Good morning, John."

I said, "Oh God, at least call me Arthur. Please."

Ted smiled and said, "Good morning, John. You look like hell, as always."

He held two cups of coffee, one in each hand, and set one on the low table in front of me. They were in paper cups from the little cafe around the corner from his office downtown. He sat across from me and waited.

I sat up and faced him over the low table between us. He knows I'm not much of a good sport in the morning, and was polite enough to wait until I was ready before talking. I straightened myself up and sipped the coffee, which was very good.

I asked, "How did I get home last night?"

Ted smiled and said, "I drove you."

"How was I? Did I embarrass myself?"

"Not so much. You're aging well and moving beyond the fool."

I asked, "Did I bother the girl?"

He gave me a sort of sideways look and asked, "She had red hair? With the catering staff?"

"Yes."

"Not that I saw. You were pretty quiet, and got quieter as the night went on."

I looked past him, and stared out the window on the far wall to the bright blue sky beyond, then asked, "Why are you here so early?"

"First, it's not that early, and second, as your beloved agent, I've come with good news."

He was acting sort of smug, and I said, "Okay. What is it?"

"This morning, I found out that your painting, *The Dream*, sold for a million dollars."

I had to think, then said, "What?"

Ted explained, "There was an auction last night in Santa Fe, and it changed hands for one—million—dollars." He emphasized each word of the price with a staccato clarity.

I said, "That painting? I gave that thing to a gallery years ago."

Ted said, "Yes, I know. That was before you met me. I would never have let you just give something away."

"That's absurd. It isn't worth that much."

"Maybe not, but someone wanted it bad enough to pay an awful lot."

I said, "I won't see anything from that sale, will I?"

"Nope, not a penny."

"Who was fool enough to spend all that money on me?"

Ted said, "I'm not sure. The buyer was representing someone else, but I'm very curious."

I took a long swallow of the coffee, and tried to think, but it didn't make sense. I asked, "What happened?"

He said, "From what I know there was a go-between at the auction. The buyer is unknown. It's all very mysterious. I made a few calls this morning and got nowhere. I can't figure out who would've wanted it so badly."

I said, "I don't know if I ever told you, but I was tripping on peyote when I painted that."

Ted replied calmly, "You did tell me, more than once. That was during your misguided youth at the feet of that shaman, wasn't it?"

"I've never called him a shaman, and neither does he."

Ted shrugged in a way that told me this wasn't important. I said, "His name's Donnie, and I got a lot from that guy. My paintings got very colorful because of him."

Ted went on about the money, and how the news of the sale could generate some buzz. He said, "It might help sell some of your work and turn things around, which you need."

I said, "I have a photo of that thing."

I got up and took a few slow steps to a tall bookshelf along one wall of my studio. I looked up at a row of three-ring binders, each with a year written on the spine in magic marker. I've tried to keep photos of all my paintings. I pulled a binder down, opened it, flipped through a few pages, and there it was. I set the binder down on the low table between us and slid an eight by ten photo out from a glassine envelope. The picture was black and white, and couldn't convey its bright colors.

I never understood that painting. It was frustrating when I made it, and it was still a mystery that morning. The image was of a thin, scruffy tree with a blue ball of light centered in the branches. The tree, or maybe more of a bush, was surrounded by a bunch of psychedelic lines, some with little dot patterns, others with swirling colors, all radiating from the glowing point in the center. The background was a sort of claustrophobic rainbow, with the tree positioned on a low mound. The twisted roots were done with vibrant colors, and you could see them reaching down, like an X-ray view into the earth.

Ted picked up the photo and asked, "Why is it called *The Dream*?"

I sipped the coffee and then said, "Because I dreamed it. I had a really vivid dream, and I guess it made an impression on me."

"And the peyote?"

"I made some tea that day, after the dream. I went out back and barfed my guts out, then painted all night."

I flipped through a few pages in the binder, found another photo, and showed it to Ted.

He asked, "Is that you and Donnie?"

"Yeah, it was taken out in the desert somewhere. I think it was on the reservation."

The image wasn't much, just the two of us standing side by side. The photo had aged. That and the harsh sunlight made it seem so bleary. I was young and skinny, and Donnie was looking right into the camera with that blank expression. He was funny and kind, but his face was always the same, like he had resigned himself to some grim duty.

Ted asked, "Whatever happened to Donnie?"

I said, "I'm not sure. We lost touch when I started to get famous."

That wasn't entirely true. I got fed up. I was impatient and tired of all his riddles. I'd been searching for something, but didn't really know what it was. I was asking for help, and he never gave me a straight answer. He would always turn it around and ask me questions. It got pretty annoying. I wanted to be an artist, to really give myself over to it, and that wasn't easy. There was a point when my work started selling, and I turned my back on a lot of people so I could paint more, and Donnie was one of those friends. Thinking about that now made my heart sink.

I pushed it out of my mind, then turned around the photo of *The Dream* so it faced Ted. I pointed at the signature in the lower right corner and said, "That was the first painting I signed as Art Amiss."

"Well, well. So that was the one that started you on this undercover artist thing."

"Yep. Before that, they were all unsigned."

Ted lamented, "Those old unsigned ones have been selling for a lot. People seem to dig the mystery."

I said, "I think no name is more mysterious than a fake name."

Ted laughed and said, "Well, it sure sounds fake. And I'm the lucky one who protects you and your pseudonym from all the troubles of real life."

I took a sip of coffee, and used the short pause for effect. Then said, "Art Amiss. I liked it at the time."

Ted was having none of it, "Fake though it is."

"Signing 'em with my real name wouldn't be very interesting. I don't think anybody wants that kind of honesty."

Ted said, "You know Artemis was a Greek goddess, right?"

"Yes, you've told me before, and I didn't pick the name because of her. It's from Artemus Gordon. He was a character on a TV show I loved as a kid."

I was hungover and bleary. I took another sip, set the cup on the table and rubbed my temples. Ted asked, "You doing okay?"

"I'm fine."

"You look lousy. I was worried about you last night."

"Did any of the paintings sell?"

"Everybody loved them, at least that's what they all said, but nothing sold. I'm not worried about that. I'm worried about you."

"I know you are." I wanted to tell him more, that I was worried, too. The joy I'd sought in my work wasn't the same anymore. I was blank and uninspired. I sipped my coffee and didn't say anything.

Ted said, "If I can help, just let me know."

I asked, "How are my finances?"

He rolled his eyes in a way I expected, then said, "Let's talk about something else."

"Is it that bad?"

He smiled weakly and said nothing. I got the hint and didn't bother to press him. He tried to sound cheery and said, "Your lonesome cowboy act works. People love it."

I could tell he had more to say, and I asked, "Yeah, but?"

"I think the people there last night were expecting to see your big landscapes."

"You're saying they didn't much like the window series?"

He smiled and said, "I'm saying people love your landscapes."

I let out a long sigh and said, "Jesus, I've been painting the same goddamn orange sunset over the same goddamn red cliffs for nearly two decades."

He smiled, raised his eyebrow and said, "John, those orange sunsets and red cliffs got you a nice house."

I snapped, "I'm hungover, and you're telling me what to paint. Sorry if I sound annoyed."

I held my head in my hands and my thoughts raced back to the frog pond. We talked a little more about nothing at all, and then he left. From where I sat on the couch, I could watch him through the screen door. He got in his car and drove away. I trusted him. I knew he cared about me and wanted to help, but everything felt so empty.

3

I DRANK THE LAST OF THE COFFEE while looking at the photo of Donnie and me. I held it in my hand for a long time. I flipped it over, and there was a phone number written on the back.

My jacket was on the floor, and I dug through the pockets, looking for my phone. It wasn't there, and I looked around each side of the couch. I saw the white charger cord under some papers and followed it to my phone. It was on the floor between the couch and the end table, and I pulled it out and set it on the coffee table in front of me. It was the new iPhone 3G. It cost me over six hundred dollars, and I barely understood how to use it. I got it over the winter at Ted's urging, and the thing baffled me.

I stared at the screen, and couldn't remember what to do. I tried a few times and eventually managed to dial the number. I waited, heard ringing, then listened to the canned recorded voice, "The person you are trying to reach is not available. Please leave your name and number after the tone."

It beeped, and I said, "Hello, I'm trying to reach Donnie. This is —this is—John Wilson. I worked with him years ago. I wanted to say hello. If this is still his number, please let him know I called— and—and that I'm thinking of him."

I left my number and hung up. I put the phone back on the table and picked up the picture of Donnie and me.

My studio wasn't much, but it was so pleasant in the morning. It was an old converted garage with thick adobe walls, so it stayed cool for most of the day. All the windows had screens, and it let me smell the sagebrush. At night I could open the big doors, and listen to the coyotes as I worked.

I did a self-portrait over the winter, and I could see it from the couch. It was leaning against the wall on the far side of the studio, and it was a lot bigger than it should be. It turned out okay, but I didn't think anyone would buy it, and that was fine because I wasn't really interested in selling it. I did it using a mirror, and it showed me wearing a paint-splattered work shirt. I compared that big image of me across the studio to my face in the little photo with Donnie. They were both me—but these were two different people.

The last time I saw him he had just become a father, and he needed to change his life for this new role. He was trying not to drink, and I on the other hand was drinking a lot and wasn't going to change. I was a terrible influence on him, and I hated that feeling. I held his daughter a few times, and saw myself in his shadow. Little Connie was so tiny, and he was both proud and overwhelmed. I didn't see him much after that.

I stood up and looked outside. The morning was bright and still. The mirror I used for the self-portrait was on a shelf next to me, and I looked at myself. I was tired and needed to trim my beard. I eased closer and looked at the few gray hairs on my chin. They'd been there for a while, but I wasn't used to seeing them. I'd used one of my tiniest brushes and titanium white to paint them on that oversized canvas.

I slipped my feet into flip-flops and stepped outside, into the sunshine. I grew up in Wisconsin and have been out west for almost a quarter of a century, but I still marvel at the power of the desert sun. It can be like getting hit with a booming noise, and I never quite recover from its force.

There was a path from the studio, and the gravel crunched with each step as I made my way to the house. I walked in the side door off the kitchen. I poured a little tequila in a glass and got a bottle of water from the refrigerator. I carried both to the second floor and out to the veranda. The house was in the foothills, and the deck hung out over the steepest part of the property. The view was nice, it was two views really. Looking downhill was the sprawl of town. During the day it seemed bleak and washed out, but the lights were pretty at night. Looking uphill past the studio was the desert, and from the deck I could see the line that divided the two. Someone had drawn it on a map, and surveyors had laid it out on the land. They built stuff on one side, and left the other side alone.

I had given myself over to accountants and offices down the hill. I'd become a product of that place. I put bright paint on canvas and handed it off to someone else to sell. This process made it possible to walk into the grocery store with my credit card, and walk out with food. I'd walked into real estate offices and car dealerships, too, and that meant putting more paint on more canvases.

I sipped the tequila and drank the water. I wanted a slice of lime and probably had one in the fridge somewhere, but didn't bother doing anything. Looking uphill was the dividing line, with the empty desert beyond. Dear God, how I wanted to turn my back on *this* world, and how deeply I felt the need to lose myself in *that* world.

From here I could see my truck, the studio, and the other houses in the neighborhood. All these nice homes were lined up against the wilderness boundary. Maybe wilderness isn't the right word. It was federal land, and there was a lot of barbed wire and beer cans out beyond that line. There were water tanks for the cows and trails for the ATVs. But mostly, it was emptiness.

After getting hit with some success I bought this house. Not that I wanted to. Ted, and pretty much everyone else, put the pressure on, and I caved in. Ted gave me this talk, and it felt like the ravings of a faith healer. He was trying to make a blind man see through sheer force of will. There were real estate agents, title company officers, and people at the bank, and they all made it so easy. It was like getting sucked down the bathtub drain. I signed a lot of documents and in the end, I had a four thousand square foot faux-adobe palace.

If you walked a ways past the studio, you'd find a few metal survey stakes marking the property line. Beyond that lay a vast expanse of scrubby bushes and sand. It was tough to walk around in all the thorns and cactus needles, but it felt beautiful knowing it was there.

I never much liked this house, but I loved the old garage behind it. It was part of the original property. There was a house here, too, but the developers tore it down because they didn't think it was big enough. I don't know why they kept the garage out back, but I'm forever grateful. This had been my studio. When people came in for the first time, I could see the look in their eyes. They would do their best to act polite, but they were appalled by the chaos. I got used to that reaction.

Painting is work, and it's messy. The cement floor was covered in little dots of oil paint, every one a different color. I loved that floor. I'd spill a drop, then step in it, and it smeared in with the other drips on the cement. The colors and smells and madness of it lit a fire in me. As the years crept on, that floor became an evolving testament to my role as an artist. The paintings themselves seemed less important than the struggle in that space.

It wasn't the *noun* of a completed painting that I cared about, it was the *verb.* The act of touching the wet brush to the canvas was everything. I never really cared much about the finished work. All I wanted was the effort.

The paint, the linseed oil and the turpentine all combined with the sage-soaked desert air—that smell was glorious. It was a guiding light, and it spoke to me. It said *create.*

That studio had a little second-floor loft I used as an office, but I rarely went up there. I usually slept on the couch in the middle of the room, surrounded by the mayhem. When I was really on a roll, I would paint all night and sleep all day. If I worked during the day, I'd try to sleep outside at night. I had a flat spot in the sagebrush a short walk behind the studio. I would carry a camping pad, sleeping bag, and a pillow out there and sleep under the stars. That dusty spot was a holy place, and I always slept well there.

These times of strong creativity came with an urgent energy. It was solitary but wasn't lonely, and if I lost myself in the work, I was happy. But that spark was fleeting.

I looked uphill from the driveway and north into the open flats. There was a trail out there that I'd always wanted to finish. I had hiked sections of it but would end up cutting off from the main route and taking another trail that looped back to the parking lot. It would take most of the day to hike the full length of the trail, and you'd end up at a different parking lot. People around here all knew what it meant when someone with a backpack was hitchhiking at a trailhead, so thumbing a ride back to your car was pretty easy.

The trail ran roughly east to west, with a bunch of secondary trails that looped around off the main route. I had hiked in, starting at the east end, but never made it to the west end. I tried it a few times, and ended up bailing well before the halfway point. I'd turn around and walk back to my truck.

It was a little disheartening to come home without doing the full length. Looking out to the north I could see a distinct butte on the horizon, and the locals called it Portera Rock. It wasn't much to see from here, but I knew from the map that the trail wrapped around that site. It was a clear spring day, and I could tell it wouldn't get brutally hot like later in the summer. I stared at the empty landscape. It was a calm morning, and it would be a nice day to finish that hike.

My backpack was in the truck, still there from when I came home after my last attempt. I wasn't sure what I had in it, but it was sitting there ready to go.

I drank the last of the tequila, and finished the water, then carried the empty glass and bottle back in the house and down to the kitchen. I looked in the cupboards and found a box of crackers and a tube of Pringles. I opened the fridge and got an apple out of the bottom drawer and a full liter of unopened water from the shelf. I put it all in one of those thin plastic bags from the grocery store. I took my keys from a hook by the side door and walked outside.

I had an old truck that I loved, and it was long gone now. I got a new one last year, but it never felt right. It was bigger, with plenty of room in back to haul around oversized canvases, but I always did fine with my little pickup. If I ever painted anything really big, someone from the gallery would come over and pick it up in a van. This new thing was expensive and smelled like plastic.

I walked across the gravel driveway, opened the topper window, yanked down the tailgate and sat. I kicked off my sandals, reached behind me and found my running shoes.The dirty socks from my last hike were stuffed inside, and I put them on. Then I tugged the shoes on without bothering to untie them.

I slid my backpack next to me, put the bag of food and the bottle of water inside, and pushed it back. Then I stood up, closed the back, and took the few steps to the driver's door. When I tried to start it, nothing happened. This had been happening a lot, enough that I didn't bother to get frustrated. The way the driveway lined up meant I was looking out at the open desert through the windshield. I was facing north, with the lonely orange bluffs in the distance. I had looked out across this sagebrush ocean a thousand times.

I tried starting the truck again. Nothing. I probably should have been angry, but all I felt was a dull emptiness.

I leaned over and shuffled around the mess on the floor in front of the passenger seat. I found a bag of candy that Ted had left in the car. I think he'd either gotten it for his kids or he'd taken it away from them. These were Gummy Bugs, and I remember his kids ate everything except the grasshoppers. I crave sugar when I'm walking, so I set the bag in my lap. There was a half-empty bottle of water in the cup holder between the seats. I drank it and tossed the empty bottle on the floor. I put the keys in the cup holder, stepped out, walked around to the back, and got my pack.

I stood there and looked out at my own unfinished business. I could walk from here, with Portera Rock as my bearing point, then turn west and get to the parking lot before sundown. I could thumb home and be done with it.

The plan seemed fine, but I didn't move. Something felt wrong. I tried to run a mental checklist, ticking off the boxes of what might be bothering me. Art, fame, work, motivation, fears, worries, ego, money—I'd had a messed up relationship with all of these. I'd spent my life either rejecting or obsessing about these issues and more. I was outwardly proud of my stance. Yet that lonely world out at the horizon was goading me on. Whatever I was feeling, it wasn't me. It was beyond my own sense of self, and it scared me.

The first few steps off the driveway and into the sagebrush were a kind of panic. I wasn't quite running. It was more of an urgent stagger. I was rattled, and the truck was the least of my concerns.

It took a while, but my lurching cadence eventually settled into a normal walking. Trying to move on foot through this kind of brushy terrain was problematic. I couldn't make a straight line. All I could do was snake around the bush directly in front of me, then the one after that. It would be nice to avoid all the spiky branches and cactus, but there was only so much I could do. There was a path ahead somewhere, but right then I needed to quiet the anxiety of the morning. I needed to walk.

4

WALKING CAN FEEL SO SLOW. Yet for me, this steady movement through the landscape is somehow important, like moving forward is an emotion all its own. I know walking isn't an emotion, but it can feel that way. There was plenty behind me, and it felt good to walk away from it—all of it. There was a mess of anxiety that could, hopefully, get released with each step deeper into the emptiness.

I've walked away before, so this wasn't anything new.

I lived out of my truck for a while, and slept outside almost every night. I rented studio space, but it was pretty small. It was a hassle at times, but for the most part, I loved it. After that I lived in an adobe hut for nearly a decade, and I'd walked away from a lot before arriving there. That place was tiny, not much bigger than a shed.

During most of those years, I didn't use a washing machine. There wasn't one, and for a while I'd drive to the laundromat in town. Eventually, I started washing my clothes in a bucket on the back deck and used a clothesline to dry everything. I did that for years, and it was easy. I went a full year and made one bag of trash. I guess I cheated a little because I had a wood stove and burned a lot of paper and cardboard and stuff like that. Most of my clothes and furniture came from secondhand stores. None of this was a big deal, and I loved the simplicity.

The world around me generated all kinds of pressures and expectations, and I did my best to ignore its ever-present voice. This spartan lifestyle allowed me a singular focus, and all I cared about was creating and the smell of paint.

My pace slowed. I walked steady in a way that let me think and connect with the dry grass and sky and sand. The travel hadn't been too bad, and the only issue so far had been snagging my pants on the thorny bushes. I thought about turning around, but knew I would eventually get to the trail, and from there I could walk to the parking lot. From there I'd hitch a ride through town and then back home. This was a tidy thought, so I kept walking forward.

At some point I stopped, pulled out my water bottle and drank. I looked for sunblock while the pack was open. I dug around and checked the pockets but couldn't find any. I was pretty sure I had a little tube with me, but it must have still been in the truck. I would need it and thought again about turning back. I put on the pack and kept walking.

It was about then that I realized I'd slept in my clothes. Except for my shoes, I was still wearing my formal cowboy getup from the opening last night. I've hiked in jeans a lot, and they offer pretty good protection from all the sharp things growing out here. I had a leather belt, but it didn't have one of those big gaudy buckles. My white long sleeve shirt was nice in the sun, and so was my white hat. Parts of the route would be in the shade of the canyons, so I wasn't too worried about getting burned, at least not badly.

I didn't like the sunblock I thought was in my pack. Something about it stung my face. I needed a brand that wouldn't irritate my skin, so over the cooler winter months I'd been asking around. I probably only asked three or four people, and they all said the same thing—Neutrogena-45. I got the message and stopped asking. Since then I'd been looking for it, checking the grocery and drug stores, but hadn't found it anywhere.

I had been walking gently uphill for hours and eventually crested onto a wide empty plateau. From this vantage point I could look down into a narrow basin peppered with rocky outcroppings, all standing upright like a mess of toy soldiers. Centered at the far end of the valley was the imposing shape of Portera Rock, maybe two miles away. What had been a mere bump on the horizon from my driveway now stood before me with an unexpected majesty.

Its sturdy barrel shape and flat summit reminded me of the Capitol Records office in Hollywood. I had driven by it the one and only time I was in LA. I found out later that it was designed to look like a stack of records on a spindle. The big rock seemed about the same height as the building, but I had no way of knowing.

The trail I was looking for was hidden among those standing blobs of sandstone. From up here, I had a good view of the terrain, but once down in it, the route finding would be tricky. I took some time and studied the landscape.

I knew from the map there were two trails. A smaller one would come in from the west, turn north, and eventually join the main trail at a T-intersection. My hope was to find the first trail and follow it to the junction at the far end of the basin, somewhere close to Portera Rock. From there I'd turn right, or east, and should be in the parking lot by sundown.

I started downhill. Entering the valley of tall rocks meant losing my wide open view. Without the mammoth target on the horizon, I needed to slow down and carefully pick my way through the maze. It felt menacing, like giant chess pieces staring down at me. After about a half hour of snaking my way around this haunted landscape, I saw the smaller trail. It came out from between two tall pillars and curved north into my line of travel. I stepped onto the thin path and kept walking. I figured I'd hit the main trail in about a mile.

After a long stretch of winding through the rocks, the trail led to an open area, and looking ahead, I got my first good view of Portera Rock from within the basin. It loomed above the pillars around me and was a lot closer than I expected. The trail soon curved back between some rocks, and the view was gone.

Walking on a well worn path means zoning out. I can let go and get lost in thought. The repeating motion of step after step is a kind of meditation. I wanted this feeling and tried to let it happen.

The sadness of this morning's dream came back to me. Facing that girl was like a weight on my soul. It was the same feeling I had when I saw her on the sidewalk last night, and it bothered me. The silhouette was too still, so it must have been something else. It didn't make sense that a girl that tiny would be out alone, but the memory was real, I'm sure of that. I kept mulling this over in my mind, what I might have seen and how we ended up in the limbo room.

There was a real event and a dream, I know that, but both had the same weird power. Maybe it was more of a feeling, something unbearably sad. Last night she said, *now is the time*. I heard it plainly, but I shouldn't have been able to hear anything. She was too far away, and whatever was down that street couldn't have been a girl anyway. But what I heard was heavy with emotion, whether she said it or not.

I stopped walking. The maze of standing stones were behind me and I was looking up at Portera Rock. The trail junction was right in front of me. I stood facing the sign for barely a second, then looked down. There was a bottle of Neutrogena-45 leaning against the signpost. The bottle was set in the sand with a gentle tilt, like it was posing for a picture. It didn't seem possible, yet it was there. My immediate thought was, *it's them.*

I looked right and left, and there was nobody. If someone had left it here, they were long gone.

I picked up the bottle, and it was full. It felt cool in my hand when it should have been hot from the sun. I squeezed a little dab on my fingertips and put it on my nose. It felt so good. Then I put some on the back of my neck and on my ears. As I rubbed it in, I looked at the sand in the trail. I was trying to find any bootprints that might give a clue to how it got there. There was nothing to see. I closed the bottle and put it in my back pocket.

There were two arrows on the sign, pointing left and right, and these gave the mileage to the west and east parking lots. Both were about the same distance from where I stood.

I had enough water, and now I had sunblock. There were two choices. I could walk to either parking lot, but I could barely think. Finding that sunblock left me reeling. I'd been asking and looking for months, and now I'd found it—right when I needed it.

I stood at that sign, facing the huge rock, with all those ominous stones standing behind me, staring down at me, judging me. I looked right and left, and gradually realized I had a third choice. I stepped across the path, past the sign and into the dust.

At first I walked normally, but this wasn't normal at all. Then I moved faster. I was stunned by what happened, and I needed to walk and not think. The trails and sign were now behind me. I was heading uphill, and it didn't take long before my pace slowed. The easiest travel took me close to Portera Rock. I walked for a long time along its western edge. At times, I was close enough to drag my fingertips along its rough surface as I moved through the dry grass.

There was something I couldn't shake. When I saw the bottle against the signpost, I thought, "It's them." This was almost a voice in my head, but not quite. The statement was pragmatic and blunt. But I didn't know what it meant. Who was "them" and why did I think that? I tried to push it out of my mind and kept walking.

I moved past the tower of rock, and for a while I could walk in its immense shadow. It felt nice to be out of the direct sunlight, at least for a few minutes, especially walking uphill. I soon left the shadow and continued on in the bright heat of the day. My pace slowed. The meandering curves of the land funneled me to a wide, gentle pass, and the high point allowed for an amazing view to the north. I stopped, humbled by the immensity of the terrain.

My phone rang. I took it out of my pocket and fumbled trying to answer. I said hello and a voice asked, "Is this John Wilson?"

It was a young woman, and she spoke with the distinct tempo of a local native. I said, "This is John, yes."

"You called earlier and asked for Donnie. I'm his daughter." She paused, took a breath, and said, "I am sorry, but my father is dead."

It felt like I'd been hit in the gut, "Oh God, I didn't know. I'm so sorry. I used to work with your father."

She said something else, but I couldn't make it out.

I said, "Connie, I knew you when you were a little girl."

The signal was breaking up, and I desperately tried to listen. Then it was silent. After a moment, I heard a soft beep that meant the call had ended.

I stood there for a long time. The heat and silence were so empty. I eased down onto my knees. Without thinking, I set the phone on the ground and smashed it with a rock. All that did was crack the screen, so I hit it a few more times. The pieces were all sticking together, so I got a bigger rock. This helped, but it wasn't enough. I crawled forward and set it on a flat area of exposed sandstone, then hit it hard with the bigger rock. It took some work, but it broke into sections. I pounded these into smaller bits and didn't stop until my hands started hurting.

I took off my watch and smashed that, too. I took out my wallet and tore up all the bills. Then I started on the credit cards but couldn't tear them. I tried bending them back and forth to get a fold started so I could split them, but that didn't work either. Finally, I rubbed the folded edges of the cards against the exposed rock, scraping away enough plastic to break them apart. I did the same thing with my drivers license, ATM card, and insurance cards. I had a few business cards. They simply read: "Arthur Amiss, painter" with nothing else but my phone number. I tore these up, too.

I dug a hole in the sand with my hands, pushed all the bits and pieces in, and my wallet, too. Then I filled it back up, found a big rock and rolled it on top of the mess.

I pulled the map out of my pack. It was a big glossy trail guide from the outdoor store. I tore it into little pieces and let them blow away in the wind. They skittered across the gravel to the north. I watched them glide away and muttered, "Map bits."

I started walking north, following the speckled trail of torn up pieces. I felt bad about the map. It was litter, and I had defiled this beautiful place. Some pieces were getting stuck in the brush, and others drifted along with me and the wind. It wasn't long until they had all blown away, except for one. This small fleck stayed a few yards ahead of me as I trudged forward.

Connie was just a baby when I pushed him out of my life. He let me hold her, and she started crying, her attention totally on her father. She stopped crying and smiled when Donnie took her back.

I would drink with him before she was born, and he was a mess in those years. This was when people started buying my work, and I was getting pulled into a different crowd. I gained so much from him, but he needed to be a father, and it was easier for me to run away and keep drinking.

It was hot and lonely, and that little rolling piece of the map had disappeared. I knew I should turn around, yet my feet kept moving forward, and I did nothing to stop myself. I walked for hours.

The sun had crossed a long stretch of the sky before I found water. It was in a sculpted hole in the slickrock, about the size and depth of a kitchen sink. I drank what was left in my bottle, then knelt down and filled it from the pool. I held it up to the sky, and it was tinted slightly green. There's some awful water out here, but this seemed pretty good. I sat and drank. These deep dishes are called potholes, and without running streams they might be the only water source.

I finished most of a liter, then topped it off, and continued on. It was a relief to have found water, so one warning light on my instrument panel was off, but plenty were still flashing red. I ignored them all.

I kept walking north. I didn't have a compass, but earlier in the day when the sun was higher, I could follow my shadow in front of me. And now, with the sun getting lower in the west, I still knew my direction of travel. I'm certain I wandered a wavy route, but it was mostly north.

More than once I stopped, and thought, "What am I doing?" I'd turn around and face south, staring into the full force of the sun. My home and truck and paints, they were all out there, just beyond the horizon. I tried to weigh out my feelings and actions. If I let myself think about it, I'd confront something, and it scared me. I'd say, "This is madness. I should head back." And that statement was true.

Walking toward my home was the only choice. Logically, I should turn around and head back. But I didn't do that. Something in me, something beyond logic, was guiding me. Turning my back to my home and walking away felt correct, and as dumb as it must sound, I trusted that feeling and kept walking north.

I looked at my left wrist a few times. There's a way I'd sort of snap my arm to move my sleeve back an inch or so. I wanted to look at my watch, but it was smashed, and all the pieces were in a hole in the sand miles behind me. I would stare at that empty spot on my wrist. For the most part, I could avoid facing what I'd done. Yet, when I replayed it in my mind, burying all those seemingly essential things in a hole, it felt good. Not good in a happy kind of way, but good in the way you feel when a fever breaks. Or like taking a deep breath while standing upright with your shoulders back, free of any constriction.

5

I PAINTED A MURAL a block off the main street in a little New Mexico town. It was on a wall that faced a parking lot, and the owner of the building let me do pretty much what I wanted. This was one of those times where I lived out of my truck and slept outside at night. I was maybe twenty-five, and this was a nice place to spend a few weeks.

The building had an ice cream store in the front and some kind of community outreach office in the back. I painted a collage of desert imagery and sandstone buttes. It was simple and bold. I put a bunch of animals in the scene, things like roadrunners, jackrabbits, and mule deer. Plus a lot of cactus and flowers.

I had two kids from the ice cream shop helping me. I'd mix up some paint in a quart-sized yogurt container, outline a big section in a color, like orange, and have them fill it in. Then tan, then blue. It seemed fun for them. I'd go back in and add a little tone to some of those sections, and the whole thing was turning out nice.

It had been a long day working in the sun. The kids had left, and I was on a ladder when I heard a voice say, "There are no people in your painting."

I looked down, and there was a big native guy facing the mural. I said, "I didn't want to put anyone in it."

He asked, "Why not?"

"I was worried if I painted a cowboy, some hippy would whine about it, and if I put in a hiker, some hunter would complain."

"Okay. You know people live in this country."

I twisted myself on the ladder to face him. He was probably about my age, maybe a little older, and I said, "Yeah, I know. I wanted to put some native imagery in this, but I'm not from around here, and if I added anything I'd be making it up."

He heard me but didn't say anything. I turned back to the mural and kept working, adding white highlights to the light blue clouds up near the roofline. The wall was brick, and that's a horrible surface for painting.

Eventually, he asked, "Why did you put the owl and coyote together?"

The bottom right of the mural had an owl and coyote sitting side by side. They were both simple, painted like something out of a children's book.

I kept my face to the wall and worked as I explained, "That spot down there seemed empty." I pointed to the lower corner below my ladder where I had painted a dead, crooked tree near the right side of the wall, and it cast a purple shadow across the rust colored sand.

I said, "I added them in because the colors seemed to fit." That was true. I thought the yellow of the coyote and the tan of the owl would look nice against the purple shadow.

He said, "You shouldn't put those two together like that, not around here."

I said, "This ain't the Sistine Chapel. It's just something colorful on the side of an ice cream shop."

"The owl is bad medicine. It shouldn't be there, not like that."

He stood there and watched me until I ran out of paint. I climbed down the ladder. My plan was to refill the yogurt container with white paint, move the ladder and finish the clouds and call it a day. This guy just stayed there, staring at me.

I had my paints and supplies in a cardboard box on a folding table. I tinkered with things, washed a few brushes, and laid them out on newspaper to dry. He never moved. I set the empty yogurt container aside, then dug around the box and found a tube of purple, and squeezed some out on a styrofoam plate. I added a dab of gray and a dab of light blue. I mixed in a little water, and swirled them together with a brush. Then I sat cross-legged in front of the wall and painted over the owl.

I said, "This will need a second coat. It'll be dry soon." I dropped the brush in a jar of water and set the plate along the wall.

I asked, "Could you help me move this stuff? I need to put it in the back of the shop for the night."

I carried the box of paints, and he folded up the table. I opened the back door and showed him where to set it. We carried the ladder together, but I could've easily moved it myself. I locked the back door and sat down in the same spot, facing the wall. The paint had dried, but you could still see the owl. I added a second coat, rinsed the brush with water, and threw away the plate. I tossed the brush in the open window of my truck, and we walked two blocks to a bar on the main street. We took turns buying bottles of beer and left after midnight.

That was how I met Donnie.

That night he told me a story about his elementary school on the reservation. He said, "We had a white woman who taught there. I was told she volunteered to be there. I liked her, and I could tell she wanted to be a good teacher. I was a little boy, and at the end of the year she decorated the classroom with cardboard cutouts of owls. They were cartoon owls with little black graduation caps, and they were thumbtacked all over the room. When the parents found out, they were very angry, and they came to the school and told her to take them all down. They told her to get them out of the building. She didn't know, but for my people, owl is not a cartoon or anything fun. Owl is bad medicine."

It would be a couple of years before I got a sense of Donnie's role in the tribe. He hinted at things but never came right out and said them. For some reason, he paid attention to me and what I was doing. Part of me was intrigued, yet I never quite knew what to think. He saw something in me, and looking back now, it fed my ego.

He implied he was next in line to be the medicine man in his community. I had no idea what that meant, and if I tried to ask, he would deflect my questions or turn them back on me as some sort of riddle.

He presented himself as a spiritual wise man, so I'd ask things like, "How do I proceed forward in this world when people want art, but nobody wants an artist?"

That was a real question. It felt like my lowly presence as a creative type bothered people, and I struggled with it. He told me some long-winded story about a hummingbird meeting a porcupine, and how one would try to outsmart the other. When he was done, I told him I had no idea what it meant.

He said, "All the creatures must play their roles, and each is sacred."

He said things like that a lot. It came out in this lofty way, but I never understood it. Most of the time I figured he was making stuff up to mess with me. But the next day I saw a porcupine on a bridge over an *arroyo*, and it was getting harassed by a little hummingbird. When I told him, all he did was nod like he knew something I didn't.

About a year later, I took Donnie down to Tucson. He said he had family obligations there and needed a ride. I drove him because there were galleries and murals in the old part of the downtown that I wanted to see.

The sun had set when we arrived, and the house was on a big lot in a neglected corner of the city. There was a steady buzz of young people coming and going, and something about the scene made me uneasy. It was a rough crowd, and hardly anyone seemed to know Donnie. He introduced me to a handful of what he said were his cousins. Everyone seemed suspicious of me. I was a skinny white guy from Wisconsin, and I stood out. I didn't feel welcome but wasn't much worried about it. They let me park my truck in the backyard, and I slept under the topper.

Donnie didn't leave the house much, and I spent my days downtown, looking around the galleries and bookstores. I had a sketchbook and I'd draw—things like store fronts, old cars, and street scenes. I didn't really care what I was sketching. I was more concerned with finding a good place to sit. I drew whatever was in front of me, and this felt good.

After a few days, we headed back to New Mexico. I asked Donnie how his visit was, and he didn't say much. I got the sense that something bad was going on with the people there, and I doubted they were his family. They might have been friends, or something else. He wasn't talking and I didn't press it, but they wanted him for something. I wasn't sure what to think, and part of me assumed the worst. There were a lot of drugs coming over the border, and the gang scene was violent. Maybe that's what was going on at the house. That they wanted Donnie's help could have meant some kind of protection spell for their safety, or maybe a curse on a rival gang. I didn't know, but I could tell he was relieved to be heading home.

I wanted to spend a night in the Superstition Mountains on the drive back, and Donnie wasn't sure that was a good idea. I'd never been there and heard it was beautiful. He agreed, but I could tell he didn't want to go.

Donnie said, "The Pima call it Crooked Top Mountain, and the Apache would never go into those hills. The Yavapai once lived there, but not anymore. The Apache say there is a hole in those hills, and it leads down to the lower world." He added, "That would be what you white people call Hell."

I didn't want to disrespect someone else's land and suggested we could get some tobacco as an offering. He seemed uneasy and didn't say anything.

We stopped in Apache Junction, and I got a pouch of pipe tobacco. I also got a bottle of cheap whiskey. We ate dinner and drank beer at a bar in a strip mall. It was filled with retired men, and a golf tournament played on huge TVs. The sun was setting as we left town and drove into the foothills.

I slowed down as we approached an established campground. It was crowded with long white RVs, and I figured we could find a better place. I kept driving and eventually left the asphalt and turned onto a well graded gravel side road. It was dark when we passed a single lane dirt two-track. I stopped, backed up, and turned the truck onto it. I had no idea where I was going, but I hoped we'd find a nice spot to sleep.

Donnie and I were passing the bottle between us as I drove. The road was terrible, and I needed to creep along to avoid the bigger rocks and potholes. There was a steep rock face above me on my side and a drop-off on the right. We gained elevation slowly, and more than one jackrabbit darted across my headlight beams.

Donnie was giving me a hard time, telling me that my culture didn't have traditions for honoring things. I took the bottle from him and said, "Pay attention." Then I lifted the bottle a bit higher, looked right at him, and said, "Cheers to you, Donnie." And I took a sip. Then I lifted the bottle to the night in front of me and said, "Cheers to you, Crooked Top Mountain."

My head was tipped back as I drank, and I heard a sudden thud on the windshield. I stopped the truck and watched something roll off the hood. I asked, "What happened?"

Donnie said, "I think I know why we are here."

He got out and walked into the hot glow of the headlights. He was looking down at something in the road. I shut off the engine and went out to see what it was. There was an aqua green blob in the sand at his feet.

He beckoned me closer and said, "*Mescalito*."

I stepped nearer and saw it was a lumpy cactus. I asked, "What does this mean?"

"The *mescalito* called you here. It chose you."

We stood still for a long time, and I eventually asked, "Can I pick it up?"

He said, "Yeah, sure."

I carried it to the driver's side headlight. It was about the size of a cantaloupe, and I turned it over in my hand. The top part was a waxy blue green cluster of knobby balls, maybe a dozen of them. These were all connected to a root stalk that looked like a stubby carrot. There were thin, hairy roots still clotted with sand and pebbles, like it had just been pulled from the earth.

I asked, "Is this peyote?"

"Yes. It's a more powerful teacher than I am."

I pointed to one of the segments and asked, "And these are the buttons?"

He said yes and stood back to look up at the cliff. There wasn't much to see in the dark. The terrain above was stepped and lumpy, and it looked like the steepness eased off about thirty feet above the road.

He looked down at what I was holding in my hand and said, "This is a very big peyote cactus. I didn't know they could get this big."

He never touched it, letting me handle it. I put it in a brown paper bag and set it behind the truck's bench seat. We got back in and continued up the road. He stared at me as I drove.

I asked, "What?"

He said, "You don't realize it, or admit it, but you are connected to some powerful medicine."

I didn't say anything. I kept driving and tried to avoid the bigger holes in the road.

We found a beautiful place to sleep out that night. There was an open area at the top of the hill where we could turn the truck around. I found a gallon-sized Ziploc plastic bag, filled the bottom third with sand, and stuck a candle in it. I set it on the ground between us, lit the candle, and said, "There, our campfire."

We finished the bottle under that magnificent sky. We counted twelve shooting stars before laying out our sleeping bags on the ground.

In the morning, I got the tobacco out of the glove box. Donnie was still asleep as I put a bandana on the hood of the truck, and poured the tobacco from its plastic pouch into the center of the fabric. I tied the corners into a tight bundle and walked away from where I had parked. I found a cluster of black basalt rocks and slid the bandana in between two upright boulders. It was hidden but would be easy to pull out. I said, "We are visitors here. We both thank you for this beautiful spot to sleep."

During the drive home, I needed to tilt my head a little bit. There was a waxy smear where the cactus hit the windshield. It was centered in my line of sight. I loved the magic of it and wanted to keep it there, but Donnie washed it off when we stopped for gas. He said, "It's okay to think you are special, but you need to be careful driving."

That's how I got the peyote I used to paint *The Dream*.

6

THE AFTERNOON WANED, and I stopped looking at my wrist. My watch was gone, and I didn't feel bad about it. The travel was mostly flat and wide open, allowing me to feel the mighty emptiness. I tried to let go and give myself over to the landscape, but I was uneasy. This kind of clear, calm day can make for a terribly cold night. It's one thing to put on a sweater after dinner on a restaurant patio in Santa Fe, but it's something else alone out here. Walking onward meant being dangerously cold, and there was nothing I could do.

There's a beauty beyond description as the sun sets in the desert. The oven of midday slowly changes to a riot of color. The shadows get longer, and everything softens. The whites turn pink, and the tans turn orange. I looked left, and without sunglasses, I was forced to squint. The sun was almost touching the horizon.

I was in the open moving through waist high juniper bushes, so there was nothing around me to block the grand circle of magnificent views. The low mesa to the west would soon hide the sun, and I stopped walking and looked around.

The rocks and bushes and sand were now beautiful in a way that's hard to describe. A magic filter was descending over everything. It wasn't just the light, but the smells changed, too. Minutes ago, it felt like my nostrils had been switched off because of the dry heat, and now I could take in the perfume of the desert.

Something happened when the sun finally dipped below the horizon. There was a momentary bit of wind that I'd felt many times before. One valley further west was still hot in the sun, while another valley off to the east had cooled off in the shade. The colder air contracts, and warm air gets sucked across the landscape to fill the void. The breeze was a mix of balmy and cold.

I felt a gentle chill. Right then I realized that I had no way to start a fire, and without warm clothes or a blanket, the night could kill me. This should have been frightening, but there was no emotion at all. I was lost in the colors and smells. I stood there, knowing the approaching night was a threat, even though the world around me overflowed with beauty.

The light faded slowly, changing from pink to purple. I was motionless as I drank in the deepening colors, and in a matter-of-fact way, I said aloud, "I'm doomed."

Then I sensed something behind me.

I turned and was smacked in the face by a big black mass, and for a second everything was dark. The wind carried it past me, and I watched a wadded up black clump roll away across the terrain. I was startled enough that it took a few seconds to realize what had happened. Then I was running, trying to catch the rolling blob. Running in sand is awful, but I didn't have to go far. It got stuck in some prickly bushes, and I grabbed it.

It was a tattered synthetic tarp, and I held it open in the breeze. The thing was old and brittle. It must have blown out of someone's truck and been rolling around like a big plastic tumbleweed for who knows how long. It would have measured about eight feet by eight feet, and I folded it, then rolled it into a tube and carried it as I walked.

The twilight turned to night, and the hot sand turned cool. I walked in the starlight until I found a small island of exposed slickrock. This would hold some of the heat of the day. I put on all my clothes, took off my shoes, and stuck my feet in the backpack. I wrapped myself in the tarp, and used my shoes as a pillow. The stars were beautiful, but I was tired enough to be content and fell asleep within minutes.

I was there again. It was night, and I was alone on the path to the frog pond. I knew every twist and turn, moving smooth and quiet. Like always, I was walking away from the pond, toward the gate.

Then it changed. I was running, or trying to. It was dark, but there was a weird glow in the trees behind me. I desperately wanted to move faster but couldn't.

Something had happened. I didn't know what it was, but I felt it and knew it was bad. There were blue lights. They were blinking, they were in front of me and then all around me. I didn't understand why I was here, and I had this awful knowing. I had left Katie, I had abandoned her, and now I didn't know where she was, and I hated myself. Something terrible had happened, and I couldn't help her.

My back was against the fence. I was on the other side of the gate, trying to hide, and I could look up at Katie's window. It was her room, and there were shadows in there. Something was looking for her. I was in her backyard. It was dark, but the light from her window was shining down on me from the second floor. I shouldn't be here. I knew they'd find me, but I didn't know where she was or why I was so scared. Something was right there, something big, moving slowly toward me in the dark—*it knew I was here.*

Then I was looking up at the cold, gray sky. Everything was still. I was wrapped in the tarp, lying flat on my back in the sand. My hands were tight in my armpits, trying to keep my fingers warm.

I sat up and looked around. It was still dark, but there was a purple glow in the sky. The landscape around me was immense and black and quiet. It was like being on a tiny raft in a calm, endless ocean.

I've had this dream, over and over, for most of my life. The feelings are always heart-wrenching, and it never gets better. I know something terrible happened to Katie, but I don't know what it is, and I couldn't save her. I always end up trapped in her backyard, under her window, and there's an awful feeling that I shouldn't be there. Something is wrong, I don't know where she is, and everything is flooded with fear and shame.

My water bottle was next to me, and I drank the last of it. I couldn't think about the dream. I couldn't let myself.

I put on my shoes and stood up. I ate the apple as I watched the sky turn pink. I got down to the core and was about to toss it away, but I ate it all and spit out the seeds.

I didn't drink last night, and by "drink" I mean liquor. As the years marched on, I drank less and less. When I was home by myself it wasn't really an issue. Most nights I'd sip a little tequila, and not much more. Time had lessened the madness. The gallery openings were something else. Those events dredged up every insecurity, and it was easy to cross a line. I'd gotten used to embarrassing myself, and nobody called me out on it.

Coffee was a bigger issue. I felt the craving, but there was nothing I could do about it. Walking and the silence of the landscape helped lessen the worries of things I couldn't control. I had this beauty all around me, and I was grateful.

This dream has always been weighed down with such heavy emotions. Katie's bedroom window faced her backyard, and I've spent years wondering if something happened when I was a boy. I'm worried I did something wrong, and the dream might be about some buried guilt. I know how I was at that age. I was a good kid, and I never would've tried to look in her window, or anything like that. It's been nerve-racking because the dream feels so important, but its intensity is nearly unbearable.

I found another pothole and drank as much as I could. It was wide and shallow, and the water was still warm from yesterday's heat. I topped off my bottle and kept moving. Before long, the sun was brutal and my pace slowed. Even though the sandstone walls were high, the canyon floor was too wide to offer much shade. The dry river bottom snaked between jumbled boulders choked with thorny bushes. That forbidding mess meant getting up to the canyon walls would be a struggle. There were some overhangs against the cliffs, and I wanted the shade, but didn't have the energy to fight my way up there.

There were barely any shadows, so it must have been about noon. My superstitious grandparents would whisper about the witching hour, the darkest time of the night when demons would have their power. Yet I've heard in desert cultures, the spirits come out at noon, in that searing moment of helplessness under the sun.

Ahead of me along the dry river stood a tall, crooked boulder. I looked up at the wall behind it, trying to fit the big blocky shape into the sections of the fractured vertical terrain. That huge chunk of rock came from somewhere, and I tried to visualize how that giant puzzle piece might click into place in the grand expanse of sandstone. I've played this little game a lot over the years, but never once managed to figure out how any big rock on the ground would fit into the wall above. I've scrutinized and hoped, but that isn't enough.

I got closer to the rock, and there was something nice about its shape and how it stood. Walking past, I saw the side that had been hidden from me. It was slightly overhanging and stained with a dark patina. It was a deep, warm brown, almost black. This was a nice example of what gets called desert varnish.

Then I saw the petroglyphs. I moved closer and stood in the small pool of shade. There were antelopes, spirals, and a tortoise. Each image was a rusty orange against the darker surface of the stone. I've seen a lot of ancient rock carvings, and each time I felt the same sense of awe. Someone had used a simple stone chisel and carefully tapped away the dark, shiny surface to make these little images. They stood right where I was standing and created something beautiful. I understood this.

The rock was quite a bit taller than me and about the size of a backyard shed. The little carvings were a bit below my eye level on the overhanging north side, and had been protected from the sun for maybe a thousand years. I stepped back into the sunshine and slowly walked around the boulder, looking for any more images. There was nothing to find, and after circling all the way around, I sat in the shade and marveled at the artwork.

I took off my pack, lay down on my back and faced the rock. I set my hat on my stomach and slid my pack under my head as a pillow. It was a relief to be out of the sun, and the sand felt cool under my hands. This was a magical spot, and whoever created the pictures before me must have felt it, too. I was lying in a sacred place.

I said, "Thank you."

Archeologists would say the rock art in this country was done by the Anasazi, but I never heard Donnie use that term. He simply called them the Ancestors. I've listened to people who claim they can decipher the images, like an Egyptologist reading hieroglyphs. Some make a pretty good case, but I really don't know what to think. I do know what I feel, that this is art and it's beautiful.

Lying in sand is comforting, and I was drifting off to sleep when a sound broke the silence. It was a steady tink, tink, tink. At first I thought it was a bird pecking at something. There was no wind, and I heard it clearly. I listened for a long time. It was hypnotic and seemed close. I was curious, and when I sat up, the sounds stopped.

I got up and looked around, but there was nothing. I scanned the area to find an animal that might have been digging, but everything was so still.

I put on my hat, stepped out of the shade, and walked around the rock again. When I got to the backside, I stopped. There was a little petroglyph about three feet above the sand. I knelt down to see a small image of an owl. This didn't make sense. Minutes before, I had searched the rock for any other carvings, and there was no way I would have missed this.

The images on the other side, where I'd been lying, were faded and ancient, but this little owl seemed new. The black patina had been carefully chipped away to expose the lighter sandstone below. More than anything, I was struck by its delicate beauty. The outline was stylized, yet very simple.

Then I did something I had never done before. I touched the image. I gently ran my fingertip over the owl's big eyes. These were dark circles of smooth varnish that had been left by a master.

For some reason I felt uneasy. I stood up and looked behind me. I expected to see someone, but I was alone.

I waited there for a long time. The silence had a loneliness to it, and this was somehow comforting. There was nothing to do. I walked around to where I'd been lying, picked up my backpack, gave the rock a gentle pat, and continued walking.

7

LATER THAT DAY, I walked through a long shady, stretch of the same canyon, and the route narrowed between smooth, overhanging walls. I passed around a corner and found myself in a beautiful amphitheater of sculpted sandstone. The sound of my footsteps crunching in the gravel echoed back at me, ringing clear in the still air. I stopped and waited for the noise to settle down to silence.

I faced the wall and said, "Hello." There was a lovely resonance as that one word bounced around me for the next few seconds.

I don't have much of a voice, but I'll often sing while hiking. There are a few songs I do okay with, and if I walk with someone, I'll sometimes sing the refrain from *The Lonesome Valley*. The Kingston Trio did a song called *The Reverend Mr. Black*, and so did Johnny Cash. I had both versions on a mix-tape of country music that I'd lost years ago. This was a corny cowboy ballad with a repeating chorus lifted from a traditional gospel hymn, and something about it always unnerved me.

I found out later this was a folk standard, and pretty much everybody did a version of it, including Woody Guthrie, who sang it with a bunch of his own lyrics.

My singing is sort of wavering and slow, especially if I'm walking. I sang that song enough with others around to know that it could create a spooky mood. I'd do my best to play up the drama, hoping to get a reaction. I took a deep breath and sang to the wall.

> You've gotta walk that lonesome valley
>
> You gotta walk it by yourself
>
> Lord nobody else can walk it for you
>
> You gotta go there by yourself

There are more lyrics, but I stopped there. Those shaky words echoed round and round and were slowly swallowed by the ever-present silence. Parts of this canyon felt like the eeriest place I'd ever been.

About a decade earlier, I walked into The Great Gallery. It was over four hours of highway driving from Moab, then thirty miles on a terrible road, and then about four miles of easy walking in a beautiful canyon. That day was miserably hot, and I sat in the shade of an overhang and ate pineapple chunks out of a can. I found a few tiny pictographs along the way. Then I turned a corner, and there it was. I wasn't prepared for the power of what I saw.

I stood before a wide wall protected by an overhanging roof. The images were enormous. There were a series of ghostly overlapping figures, tall with long robes and odd helmets. I had seen plenty of pictures of this site in books, but standing alone in their presence was haunting.

The rust colored figures loomed above the canyon floor, and I saw a small ledge below this wall of huge images. I scrambled up, and walked along the bottom of these amazing works. Up close, you could see there were layers upon layers of other images that had faded over the centuries. The soaring ghost figures were painted on top of a collage of smaller antelopes, lizards, spirals, and chiseled dot patterns.

Whoever painted these mammoth images had used this same narrow ledge. It was impossible for me to stand there and not feel a powerful kinship with the artists who had created something so rich in mood. This is hard to describe, but I went through a kind of vivid daydream, almost like *déjà vu*. I took off my shoes and walked barefoot along the ledge. It was as if I could remember building ladders and mixing the pigments for the paints used above me. I know what it means to create a piece of art and how it can take on a sort of obligation. But what I felt on that ledge was different, it was a kind of reverence. There was a need to honor something elusive, a mystical quality that could only be shared through art.

I paced back and forth along that ledge, and the echoes of the past rolled through me. It felt inspiring, at first anyway. There was something else, a sadness, and it made me uneasy. I wanted to stay longer but couldn't. This wasn't an easy place to be, so I climbed back down to the canyon floor and walked out.

I was now hundreds of miles and more than a decade away from that sacred canyon, yet it still whispered in my ear. I tried to listen, to understand, to feel what it wanted to tell me, but its voice was too quiet, even in this empty place.

There's always been a need in me, an urge to create, but it can be fleeting. When it's gone, I feel lost. At times in my life, the weight of being uninspired could crush me.

It can be so hard to trust my own creativity. It's impossible to point to, or define, or understand. But it's there, it's in me. Trying to be an artist means battling doubt, the indecision of my own ideas. Are they worthy? Why should I trust putting paint on a canvas? Who do I think I am?

As a child, drawing was a way to get some praise, to be the center of attention. A kid in elementary school has permission to show off. Some kids are funny, and some can hit a baseball over a fence. There's nothing wrong with being proud of these things.

I was always drawing, and I was good at it. I loved it and remember seeing my obsessive sketching pay off. I was getting better. I could see my skills improve. But now, I fight with what's a skill and what's inspiration. I'm skilled at looking at something and then drawing it with some flair. But is that skillful rendering inspired? Where's that magic spark? I've asked myself these question all my life, or maybe it's better to say all my adult life.

For me, right now, it's gone. I'm skilled, I know that, but I'm uninspired, and that emptiness is unbearable.

As a boy, drawing meant white paper and a pen with black ink. My dad would bring these pads of paper home from work. They were maybe five by eight inches and sacred to me. Each white page had infinite potential. I still feel that, and feel it deeply. Even now, a single sheet of white paper is something holy.

I remember sitting at Katie Kellie's kitchen table with one of those pads, a pencil, and a fine line black pen. She would say something, and I would draw it.

She'd say, "Lion." And I would do a quick swirling sketch with a pencil. Just a few lines and barely touching the paper. I would set down my pencil and use that light outline as a way to frame the ink of the pen. Katie didn't know it, but I had been drawing lions from pictures in National Geographic. I'd also been drawing eagles and whales and pine trees and mountains, so I was ready for almost anything she'd ask of me. This was a time when my skills were minimal, but my inspiration was on fire.

Katie's older sister would babysit for us. They lived across the street from me, so we spent a lot of time at each other's homes. Katie had bright red hair and freckles, and I could tease her. We were the same age, so we walked to school together, had classes together, rode bikes together, and looked at the stars together. Katie would sit close and watch me draw, and this was joyous.

I used that energy to keep me going through the low points of my life, and it worked. I would hit a wall, feel helpless and insecure about my work, and I could tap into that feeling—that my gift had a power to it. Yet, as the years went on, this got harder and harder, and finally, it was impossible.

When burdens overwhelmed me, I could think about the frog pond. This was a pressure valve. Some awful thing would well up in my life, and I'd think about climbing the oak tree and jumping off that huge arm of a branch. The water was green and cool, and every summer seemed to last a thousand lifetimes. All the kids from the neighborhood could swim and jump. We'd see who could stay underwater and hold their breath the longest, or someone would find a big, creepy spider and we'd dare each other to touch it.

And there were all kinds of frogs, from giant bullfrogs to tiny tree frogs, small as an M&M. In the spring and summer, the frogs were so loud we could hear them from our front porch.

The pond was visited by blue jays, red cardinals, and big woodpeckers. I remember seeing a fox. I was alone at the pond when I saw it, and nobody believed me—but I saw it.

This funny little pond was surrounded by cattails and mud, but there was one perfect section of sand where we could wade into the water. This corner had tall grass along the little beach and was shaded by huge, arching maple trees. There must have been a spring under this sandy corner because the water was always cold and clear, yet green and cloudy everywhere else.

There was a path from Katie Kellie's backyard to the frog pond. You'd go through a gate in a tall wooden fence and be at the water in a few minutes. Kids from the neighborhood would use that gate all the time. Katie's parents knew we were at the pond, and they were okay with that, but it always felt a little sneaky going through their backyard. I remember they would yell at us from the kitchen window if it was getting dark, telling us we should go home.

The last time I swam in the frog pond was the night before I left for college. That evening after dinner, my parents told me I was adopted. This was big news, and I was surprised, but not in any of the ways I should have been. They had been acting worried for the previous few days, and now I knew why. In a way, I ended up comforting them, reassuring them everything was all right. They cared for me, and did their best, but they never truly understood me.

That night I snuck out the back door and went behind Katie's old house. The new owners locked the gate, but I hopped over and walked that long path without a flashlight. It had been a hot, miserable summer, and the water was warm. I didn't swim very long, but it felt important to be there. I forgot a towel and lay in the grassy spot, looking up through the trees, waiting in the dark to dry. I wasn't sure what it all meant, but I knew I'd never be coming back.

The next morning I hugged my parents, got in that old truck and left for art school. I dropped out at the end of my first semester and started driving around out west.

I loved that spot so dearly, and I wish Katie would've gone there, too. I don't know why she never did. I mean, it was right out her back door, and I know she would have loved it.

The frog pond is part of my nightmare. Yet it's never the pond, it's the path behind Katie's house. This conflict has been difficult for me—my most cherished memories are tangled up with something harrowing. But I couldn't let the joys of that place get stained by the demons of my sleep.

Walking helped me escape my mind, and I needed that. I spent the rest of the daylight trying to focus on the beautiful memories and ignoring the nightmare. It took some effort, but in the end, joy and beauty won out. When it was too dark to walk, I found a flat spot and slept.

8

I WOKE FEELING RESTED. The sunrise was absolutely perfect. I found a pool of water close to where I'd slept, and it was clear and delicious. I drank, filled my bottle, and began walking.

I'd been out for a few days at this point, and at times it felt so normal, like I was supposed to be here. The morning travel seemed effortless. The smooth, hard sand in the dry river bottom was level. The canyon walls seemed storybook perfect. Right and left were wildflowers, and the air was ringing with canyon wrens.

It seemed serendipitous that I could've wandered into a place this spectacular. But being down in the narrow canyon didn't allow for any kind of open view. I thought it would be nice to find a spot where I could look around and see the overall landscape. A few steps later, I turned a corner in the canyon, and there in front of me was a gentle slope leading up to the edge of the cliffs.

I began a long, steady uphill, and I was up on the rim before I knew it. After being in the narrow confines of the canyon, the openness was exhilarating. The huge sky brought a magnificent sense of liberation. There was a freestanding pillar of sandstone nearby. It was the tallest thing around, maybe a hundred feet high, and from where I stood it seemed unclimbable. I walked around to the back side and found a sort of blocky section of steps. It seemed like this would lead right up to the top. This was too inviting to ignore, and I set about an easy scramble from block to block. It was fun, and I got lost in a playful mood, something I hadn't felt in ages.

Then I was on top, and it surprised me because getting there had been so quick and easy. The summit block wasn't much bigger than a kitchen table. I stood in the center and slowly turned around, making a full circle. The sense of endlessness in all directions was unbelievable.

When I was a boy, I watched *The Wonderful World of Disney* every Sunday night. I loved the outdoor stories on that show and how everything was bathed in a magical orange sheen. It felt like I'd stepped into one of those episodes, like I was living a perfect nostalgic memory.

From that high stance I could see another canyon stretching off to the north. I worried that getting down into it might be difficult, but it would be the best place to find water. I scrambled back down the beautiful pedestal and walked across the slickrock toward the other canyon.

The sun was warm but not hot. The desert can be oddly calm, but the air was hushed in a way I'd never experienced. There was a kind of otherworldly magic in the stillness. I could hear birds singing, yet there was a silence to the landscape. Even my footsteps seemed muffled. As I moved onward, the soft crunches in the sand were a steady metronome.

I got to the rim of the canyon, and before me were a series of stepped ledges that offered an easy route to the bottom. As I made my way down, I was overcome with an odd sensation. It felt like I was being watched. I stopped and looked around.

I saw a set of little eyes staring at me from atop a boulder, and it took a second to realize it was a ring-tailed cat. I had always wanted to see one. These are part of the raccoon family, but smaller with a skinnier body and a longer tail, and it was adorable. We stared at each other for a while, and then I took a few steps downhill and stopped. The little guy hopped across a few boulders, and he stopped, too.

I walked a little further and watched as he skipped across a few more boulders. The little guy was walking with me. I marched down to the canyon bottom, and he stayed right there with me the whole time, playfully bounding from rock to rock.

This canyon was narrow, and the river bottom was an easy path for walking. My little friend hopped and looped in the rocks beside me. I'd lose sight of him, and then he'd reappear a few rocks further along.

Then there were two little cats, one a bit smaller than the other. Both trotted with me, and they were obviously mates. It was so endearing. Then there was a third, but it was tiny—a baby! The little guy was waddling and jumping to keep up. I walked side by side with a family of ring-tailed cats.

They all pranced along on a sort of sandstone bench next to the dry river bed. The baby seemed to be working hard to keep up, so I stopped, and they all froze the moment I stood still. It was like three little statues lined up on the rocks. It was weird. I started walking, and they sprang back to life.

I did it again, and it was the same thing. They would freeze when I stopped and move again when I did. It was too weird and felt like I shouldn't stop. It was too much, so I kept walking, and they did, too.

The rocks were aligned like a little road for them. Then it dipped down, and they all went into a tiny tunnel and popped out a few steps later. Then it was like a little rollercoaster, and when I walked faster, they kept up. The rocks were a bright red playground, and they all raced along, making loopty loops next to me.

I felt ecstatic. I had three little friends, and I felt so happy. It was like being swallowed up in some crazy bliss. The colors, the views—everything, it was joyous, overwhelming. Then I opened my eyes, and there wasn't anything to see. It was all white, and I didn't understand what was happening. I was on my back looking up into a realm of perfect whiteness, and I couldn't move, and something passed just above my face. I thought it was an arm, but it was way too skinny. It was creepy. Someone touched my head and a voice said, "Everything will be all right."

And it all ended.

9

I WAS SUDDENLY AWAKE AND THRASHING. I was stuck, and it was so fucking hot I thought I was dying. The tarp was wrapped too tight, and it took all I had to kick myself free and crawl away. I was fighting, lashing out, but there was nothing there.

I thought I was having a seizure. I was shaking and dizzy and stayed on all fours, trying to calm down. The heat was brutal, and I pressed my forehead into the sand in hopes of getting my heart to stop racing. I don't know how long it took, but eventually my breathing slowed enough that I could think. I crawled to my pack, found my water bottle, and drank a little, but it stung my mouth.

I panicked. What happened? I'd slept until the sun was high in the sky, and that wasn't like me. And it didn't make sense how the tarp got wrapped so tight. I couldn't have done that by myself.

I drank more but stopped after one mouthful. It was bitter. I held the bottle up, and the water was pale and milky. Desert water might be a muddy brown or green, but not white, and this upset me. I was terribly thirsty and forced myself to drink. Yesterday seemed so perfect, and now I felt awful.

I didn't understand where I was. It must have been dark when I arrived last night, because I didn't recognize it in the daylight. I stood up and slowly turned around. I had no memory of how I got here.

I gathered up my stuff, put on my shoes, and started walking. A thousand thoughts raced through my head, and I fought to ignore all of it. It took a while, but the steady pounding of my footsteps began to quiet my spinning mind. I walked and walked and walked.

The days and nights were blurring together, and I slipped into a simple routine—walking, sleeping, and drinking when I could. I tried my best to keep heading north, but without a compass I was only guessing. The terrain would continually push me off course and loop me around. There was no way to know where I was going, and I was way past the point of turning around. Pressing onward was my only option.

Keep walking, keep moving forward, keep going—this was all I knew. That, and finding water.

I was alive because it was still springtime. A month later and pretty much all of the water I was finding would be gone, and the heat would kill me. It was plenty hot, but it wasn't summer hot. I had one water bottle, so I could only carry a liter. This meant drinking as much as I could at any source, filling my bottle and moving on.

Travel was easier up on the rim, but water was unlikely. I was finding seeps and trickles in the canyon bottoms, but I worried I'd get trapped down there. Some stretches had shade but never enough, and walking their snaking route ate up a lot of energy.

There was a day I got dead-ended in a canyon and needed to turn around. The route twisted to the point where I was walking south, and each step meant going the wrong way. But I kept walking, hoping it would eventually turn back north. I rounded a corner and saw the canyon stretching south for what seemed like miles.

I stood facing the sun. I'd already walked the wrong direction far too long, and couldn't keep moving south, so I turned around. I eventually climbed out of the canyon the way I'd entered it.

When I was finally back up on the rim, I got hit with a wave of fatigue. It felt like the whole day was lost. I had only found a small puddle in the canyon—I drank and filled my bottle both ways, but it wasn't enough.

I was still walking as the sun went down, and the stars were out when I finally found a spot to lie down. I emptied my pack in the fading light, then set out all my remaining food, and there wasn't much. I lined up the Pringles can, the cracker box, and the bag of gummy bugs. There was almost nothing in them. I sat on the sand and poured the Pringles dust in my mouth. The salt stung my tongue, and it hurt to swallow. The last of the crackers were broken and stale. I ate them all, then licked my palm for any crumbs. There were two gummy bugs left, one red and one green.

I put the green one in my mouth, and the lime flavor tasted was so fake, but the sugar was sublime. I had hoped to suck it slowly and enjoy the sweetness, but I chewed quickly and swallowed.

I tried again with the red one. I wanted the sensation of something in my mouth to last as long as I could, to stretch it out, to savor it, and let it melt. I couldn't. I chewed and swallowed, and it was gone. That was everything, I had no food. I drank the last of the water, and that was gone, too.

Then I put on all my clothes—my thin green sweater over my white shirt, then a pile vest, then my Marmot DriClime jacket over all of it. That was everything, and I longed for more.

I took off my shoes and kept my socks on. They were filthy, and I wanted to take them off, but I needed the tiny bit of warmth they offered.

I set my hat in the sand off to the side, with the brim up. I put a rock inside to keep it from blowing away. I scooped and pushed some sand into a pile for a pillow. I put my feet in my pack and pulled it a bit above my knees. Then I wrapped myself in the tarp and set my head on the pile of sand.

I aligned myself with the North Star, with feet pointed to geographic north. The Big Dipper, *Ursa Major*, was resting above the North Star, *Polaris*. If I were on the equator, the North Star would be right on the horizon. And if I were lying on the frozen ocean at the North Pole, it would be exactly centered in the sky. From where I lay in the sand, it was a little less than halfway between the horizon and straight up, and it would stay there in the same spot, night after night. It's been there forever and would always be there.

I woke a few times that night, and each time the Big Dipper was in a different position. The sky was turning like a giant wheel, with my toes aimed at that steady, shining point. The axle of heaven.

10

I WAS WALKING BEFORE THE SUN CAME UP. It was cold, and I needed to get moving. I love this fleeting time when there's barely enough light to see. I walked toward the North Star until it was gone. It led me to a canyon, and I found a way down as the sun broke above the horizon.

I was moving roughly north through a dry river bottom. I had almost no energy, and the walking felt slow. My bottle had been empty since last night's final sip. I was making my way along the canyon bed as the sun got higher and the shadows shrank. Hours had passed, and it was hot.

I stopped. I could smell damp sand and green plants. I was standing next to a small draw. It wasn't much, but it looked like it would run with water in a heavy rain. I turned and walked up the center of its curving path. The draw ended in a shady corner against the overhanging canyon wall.

I faced an alcove of green grass and wildflowers growing along the edge of the wall. The sand was darker here, and I got on my knees. I dug with my hands and after only a few inches, it felt wet. Moving more sand, the hole got deeper and slowly filled with tan water. There must have been some sort of seep in the canyon wall, but not enough to create a flowing spring.

I spent a few minutes digging the hole deeper and wider, then stepped away to let it fill up. I walked along the wall and found a few stalks of horsetail rush. This stiff, hollow plant grows in straight green stalks to about the height of my hip.

I pulled up one thin reed and snapped off the top and bottom, then blew through it. I now had a hollow straw a little over a foot long, and could suck up water from the hole. Despite the cloudy color, it was cool and delicious. I scooped out a few more holes, and the time it took to dig allowed the other holes to fill up, so I ended up drinking a lot. By the time I was full, there were four deep holes in the sand.

I filled my bottle by sucking water up into my mouth with the straw, then letting it drain into the bottle. I realize that's sort of gross, but I couldn't figure out what else to do. When I'd drunk as much as I could, I walked out of the draw and back to the center of the canyon. I had a full liter in my pack but no idea when, or if, I'd find any more.

Later that day, I was dizzy, and my head hurt. I'd been sipping as I walked and now had only about two inches in the bottom of my water bottle. I stopped and drank it all. Now it was off my back and in me. I found a smooth pebble and put it in my mouth. Sucking on it would keep my tongue from getting too dry. I'd done this before, but it never worked very well. About an hour later, I spit it out.

The sun and lack of food had weakened everything in me, my pace, my thoughts, and my faith. I know I can sermonize about my life, like all the choices I've made have been high and mighty. I tried to convince myself that being out here was some sort of noble quest, and things like washing my clothes in a bucket were a kind of moral act. I wanted to make myself into some brave rebel, but it was my own fucked up feelings of worthlessness—my insecurities parading around as morality.

This headstrong stance came with a price. It meant cutting myself off from people who cared about me. I ended up alone a lot, I drank too much, and all this fed some need to act out more, to play a superior role. But I knew it was just me pretending. I figured if my performance was good enough, it should carry me on, and it did for a while. But all that ended.

Later in the afternoon, at what must have been the hottest part of the day, I came to a fork in the canyon. I had been walking upstream along the dry river bed for hours, and now two narrow corridors stood before me. Two lean tracks in the sand defined the water course of gravity, and I stood at the point where they joined to create the barren river behind me.

I stared at the two routes and knew it was doubtful either would make it all the way up to the rim. There were a thousand things that could go wrong. One little steep section could force me to turn back, or the canyon might wind around in ways that lead nowhere. If I went too far or got dead-ended, I wouldn't have the strength to backtrack. And turning around to find water wasn't an option. My last water meant digging in the sand, and on a day like today, those holes would dry up completely. Even if I did make it to the rim, I might not find water. This was serious. The wrong choice could mean death.

I stood before two canyons, staring into the shadows of each.

A voice said, "This way."

It came from the left canyon, the darker of the two. I ran a few steps in and stopped. I tried to listen, but everything was silent.

I heard it. *I heard it.* Nothing about it felt like a dream or anything in my mind, it was real, and I heard it. And I knew who it was. It was Donnie's voice.

I marched into the shade of the narrow canyon and called out, "Donnie? Are you here?"

No one answered. He wasn't here. I knew my friend had died.

I spoke to the emptiness, "Donnie, I ran away from you. And I'm running away now."

"That's okay. You are doing good. Better than you think."

This sounded like it came from just around the next corner. It was spoken in that slow way he had, without emotion. And whatever I would say, no matter how heartfelt, he would say the opposite. He would stare at me blank-faced, and I knew he was laughing inside.

But he was wrong. I wasn't doing good at all. Death was somewhere behind me, following me. My mind was trying to find some hope, but so much had happened, things that should be impossible, and it was crushing me. I stood still and asked myself, "Is this really happening?"

"Yes."

It was his voice. It was clear, and it came from somewhere further up the canyon. I was angry and yelled into the darkness, "Donnie! I hated all your fucked up backward mind games when you were alive, and I hate it more now that you're dead!"

Shouting between those walls was awful. My own words pounded back at me in a mocking echo. I stood still for a long time after my voice faded away. When I started moving again, my first few steps were quick. I was desperate to get away from this haunted spot.

The darkness of the canyon felt so dismal after the brightness of the day. I would walk for a little bit then stop, waiting for his voice. I did this a few times and then gave up. I was too tired to care and needed to keep moving. I cautiously picked my way through a jumble of loose, sandy rocks, then up and over some big, awkward boulders. The canyon widened a little further on, and any shade was gone. I was funneled into a gully of loose rocks. The route was trending slightly east and getting a lot steeper, so the full force of the sun bore down on me like some punishment from God.

The uphill travel was slow, and everything was covered in a fine dust. The handholds were coated with it, and these were right at my face. The heat caused an updraft, and each footstep created a chalky cloud that rose in slow motion, and there was no escaping it. The powder got in my eyes and nose and mouth. I was trapped in a pall of dry filth. It clung to me and wouldn't let go.

When I finally reached the rim, it was like climbing out of a hole. Getting over the edge was difficult, and I grunted as I pulled myself up and onto level ground.

The fatigue was crippling. I had been without water since mid-morning, and that was miles ago in the bottom of the canyon. I walked a little bit and looked out at the terrain. It was flat and featureless. There would need to be a drainage or a pothole for any water, and nothing out there offered any hope.

I crumpled to the ground. The heat had been brutal, and I had nothing left. I sat on my knees and tried to swallow, but couldn't.

My mouth and throat were dry in a way that wouldn't allow it. Trying meant gagging, and it hurt.

I once told a friend that blinking in the desert can feel like running your windshield wipers when it's not raining—how they stick and grate across the dusty glass. We both thought it was funny, but it wasn't funny now.

My nostrils felt like they were coated with dried glue, and my tongue scraped coarsely across the roof of my mouth. My back and thighs ached.

And now the was sun setting, like some grand tide retreating, and there was a gentle chill in the air. This would soon be replaced by the brutal cold of the night.

I reached in my pack and got the water bottle. It was empty, but I opened it anyway and pretended to drink. I held it above my mouth and waited for even one drop. Nothing came. I put the lid back on and threw the bottle off into the sand.

I was drained of everything, including hope.

There was a clear knowing—I would die tonight. The cold and exposure and exhaustion would take me away. I was kneeling in an area of uneven rocks. I needed a patch of sand to sleep, but I was too tired to look around. I put on all my clothes and put my feet in my pack. I awkwardly laid down and tried to cover myself with the tarp. It was uncomfortable, but I was too far gone to do anything. I looked up and watched the gentle progression as the sky turned pink, then purple, and one by one the stars began to show themselves. This would be my last sunset.

It got darker, and the cold bore down on me. I succumbed to a kind of blankness, and I could no longer understand my thoughts. My breathing had almost ceased, but there was nothing I could do. There was an absolute stillness to my body that was so peaceful. I was looking up at the stars when I simply stepped aside. I had been lying on the sand between the rocks, and now I was next to myself. Whatever happened was as gentle as sliding a letter out of an envelope. I looked down at myself, and my face was gray in the starlight.

I should have been confused, but wasn't. There was no sense of being cold or tired. It felt familiar, like I was home again. I want to say I was looking at myself for hours, but it wasn't like that. Time was different, it meant nothing.

Then I was leaving. There was a smooth motion of rising above the rocks, but it wasn't like going up or down, it was more a feeling of being pulled. The landscape below was an ocean of rock and sand, and the stars were all around. It was dark, but I could see everything so clearly. All around me, everything, all at once.

Then I heard Donnie again. He said, "You can't run away from this."

I turned, and he was right here with me. We stood together, surrounded by stars. He looked young and strong and full of life. I asked, "Am I dead?"

"No, not quite."

I said, "But you're dead."

He smiled a big, genuine smile. This was something I'd never seen him do. That smile was like ten thousand symphonies rolling through my soul.

"John, you are fine. You are still alive."

His words hit me like a slap, centering me, focusing me. I asked, "Why is this happening?"

"Because it needs to happen."

I think I groaned. Even in this weird blissful state, Donnie was doing that thing, avoiding my question with a backward half-answer.

"John, you were my student, and I was your teacher, but I can no longer teach you."

I heard his words, but his mouth never moved. I waited for more, and he simply smiled with that same untroubled ease. Then we walked together across the dark landscape and came to where I was lying in the rocks.

I said, "I look like I'm dead."

"You aren't."

Then he calmly gestured to my body, and I knew what he meant. He was telling me to get back in that thing. But I didn't want the pain and emptiness again.

He heard my thoughts and laughed, "Too bad. You can't stay here."

I knew I was about to leave. I pleaded, "Donnie, please help me. What can you tell me?"

As soon as I asked, he was gone, and I was standing in front of an owl and a coyote. Both were sitting side by side, and above and between them was a glowing orb of blue light, and it was getting brighter. There was a rising sound, like an ancient god inhaling.

Then there was a violent slam, and I was back.

I opened my eyes and saw the sky. The stars were gone, and I cautiously turned my head to the east. My neck was so stiff it creaked. I caught the first thin sliver of the sun peeking above the horizon. I lay still and watched the dawn. At first, I could look right at the sun as it slowly rose into view. The warm orange soon changed to an oppressive white.

Below the sun was my water bottle. I stared at it from my bed of rocks. It was upright and all alone in a flat area of sand, about twenty feet away, backlit by the dawn. It sparkled.

My whole body hurt. Every motion was a challenge. Yesterday's heat and last night's cold had crushed me. I spent the next few minutes trying to sit upright, and even longer to finally stand, but I did it.

I looked at that water bottle. I remembered throwing it into the darkness the night before. It shouldn't have been standing upright. I walked out onto the sand and picked it up. It was full. I opened the bottle and took a drink. It was cold and delicious.

I looked at the sand and the only footprints leading in were my own. There was an indented ring where the bottle had been standing and no other marks.

I drank a little more, held the bottle high, and said, "Thank you." My voice was hoarse and weak. I took another sip and bowed my head, surrendering to the fatigue. I didn't understand what had happened. Yet, I got to see Donnie smile.

11

MY FOOD WAS GONE, and there was nothing I could do about it. I tried to ignore what this meant, but that was tough. Thinking about it was like facing a cloud of dread and watching it creep ever closer.

Yet, despite the weight of my present reality, some things seemed easier. There was a new simplicity. I could focus on the fierce beauty of my surroundings, and I recognized a power in that.

Without the calories, everything slowed down. I walked slower, and my thoughts were slower, too. The cold hit me harder, and I couldn't stay warm at night. I'd lie awake and cling to myself, trying to find answers in the stars. I worried my mood would plummet, and at times it did. Yet the landscape still amazed me, and my slower pace allowed me to better appreciate the world around me.

I lost track of the days. My thoughts were too slow to wander much, and for the most part, the focus was on what was right in front of me, and not what was beyond the next ridge or behind me. This was a curious blessing.

I'd get up at first light and start walking. This had become my sacred time, before the darkness faded and while the air was still cool. I could give myself over to the colors and quiet, but it wasn't long before the world got dusty and hot. The view ahead was nothing but more slickrock, all stepped and irregular. I needed to walk up a little and then down a little.

I was making my way through this lumpy terrain when I saw the canyon, or more sensed it. When you're moving through open country, there's no way to see a canyon from a distance. You won't know it's there until you're right on it. The first thing you'll see is the opposite wall, but only a long sliver across its top, and you'll never know how deep it is without getting right up close and looking down into it.

The stepped travel ended, and I moved across a smooth expanse of sandstone. I walked a little further, not more than a few steps, and stopped when I saw the edge out ahead. I was standing on a big, flat section of rock, and the point where it dropped off was only a few yards away. I sensed it was deep but didn't move any closer. I was flooded with the most intense feeling of *déjà-vu*. It was palpable in a way I didn't understand. This block of sandstone seemed to sing with a kind of haunted familiarity.

I'm usually pretty comfortable around steep drop-offs, but this spot really spooked me. I got down on my hands and knees and crawled toward the abyss. As I got closer, I dropped to my belly and eased my face out over the edge. I looked straight down at a curving river between soaring red walls. I've spent most of my life in the southwest, and I've seen a lot of amazing places, and this was the most beautiful spot I'd ever seen. I lay there in awe for what might have been an hour, trying to drink in its power.

The platform was an arrow-shaped block jutting out over the void, a stone pulpit, and I was staring down from its very tip.

It looked to be at least a thousand feet from where I was lying to the river below, but that was only a guess. It could've been a lot more. Most of the wall under me was hidden. The way it overhung meant all I could see was the last few hundred feet of sandstone along the river. Water in these parts is usually a muddy brown, yet even from this height I could see it running clear. There was an almond-shaped island in the sparkling river, with green grass and a tree.

This mighty view cast a spell on me, and I lay there enthralled. Then I turned to my left and said, "It's you. You're leaving."

I waited for a reply, but nothing came. Then I pushed myself back from the edge and sat cross-legged. I didn't understand why I said that, and it scared me. Nothing felt right out here—it was all too real. I wasn't sure how many days I'd been walking north. I tried to count them out on my fingers, but there was a more urgent issue.

I'd been stopped dead by a deep canyon. The opposite rim was close enough that I could talk to someone on the other side without raising my voice, and I needed to figure out how to get across.

I stood up, slapped the red dust off my white shirt, and looked around. These canyons can run for miles with dozens of side canyons that are just as deep. So trying to find a route around this monstrous obstacle might take days, or even weeks, and the thought of going on that kind of search without a map was pointless.

The other option would be finding a way down into it, crossing the river, and then finding a way back up and out the other side. The problem was, I'd been in this kind of terrain enough to know this was pretty much impossible. It would be better to find a way around. I tried to think, but something nagged at me. It took some time to understand what I was feeling, and it was deceptively simple. I wanted to walk in that beautiful canyon below me.

If there were any way down, which was doubtful, it would either be to the right or left. So I started walking right, or east. I don't know why I turned that way. It was early enough that I faced the sun, and it bothered my eyes. I should've turned west, so the sun would be at my back, but I didn't. I kept the big canyon to my left as I walked, peering over whenever a good spot presented itself. It was only a few minutes before I was dead-ended at a narrow canyon. This obviously drained into the main chasm to my left.

I turned right, so now I was walking south along this side canyon. I wanted to find a point where I could either cross or get down in it, and hopefully to the sparkling river below.

My route snaked along the canyon's edge. It was twisted and convoluted. The further I walked, the narrower it got, and it was eventually thin enough that I could step across to the other side, which I did. I followed the crack a long way, and this fissure lead me to an open spot in the slickrock, like a trapdoor in the floor out of some old haunted house movie. I looked down into the shadows, and realized the passage would be cramped, but easy to move through. It was inviting me in.

I sat on the edge with my feet dangling and eased my way down, like getting into a cold swimming pool. I shimmied lower and left the open realm of sky and heat. I was now in a different world, where everything was close and intimate. The swirling passage was glorious. The orange walls were sculpted in bold twists and ripples. It was like moving through music. The narrow slot stepped down and down again, and each section had less sunlight than the one before. There came a point where it was dark enough that I had to wait and let my eyes adjust.

As I squeezed my way further down, the vibrant orange gave way to dirty browns. What had been ecstatic near the surface now felt gloomy. There was a stench of stagnant water, and I was gripped by a menacing chill. The deeper I got, the wetter everything seemed.

I'd been touching sandstone for days now. Climbing over it or through it, and on the surface in the sun it felt chalky, like it might crumble to dust by merely scratching it with my fingernails. Yet way down here in the dark, the cold stone felt almost soggy, like it was wet enough to squeeze.

I walked through a few muddy pools, but this meant nothing more than wet feet. Then I got to a bigger pool, the first of many. Each was cold and brown, like wading through melted chocolate ice cream. The walls of the corridor were smooth and vertical so there wasn't any option but to slog through the thick muck. There was no way to see the bottom, and I ended up in water over my pack, so I balanced it on my head in the deepest sections.

The next pool was deep enough that I couldn't touch the bottom, so I pulled my pack along as I swam. The pack floated, but now everything was soaked, and it felt a lot heavier when I got out on the other side.

Then I came to a pour-off. It dropped about a dozen feet down to a big brown pool, and the corridor continued on the opposite side. This open area was brighter than the narrow slot behind me, and a thin shaft of sunlight hit the water and reflected eerily on the walls.

A "pour-off" is a point in the canyon where it drops vertically. In technical canyoneering, travelers would wear harnesses and carry ropes. They would rig an anchor using stainless steel bolts hammered into the wall and rappel down the steep sections.

All very adventurous for them, but I had nothing.

I leaned out as far as I could and tried to get a sense of what was below me, but the platform where I stood was overhanging, so there was nothing to see. I could easily jump from where I stood to the water below, but if the pool was shallow I would probably break both legs. If I jumped without injury, the wall below me might be too steep to climb back out, and that meant retreat would be impossible.

I was cold and miserable, and the thought of turning around and climbing back through the freezing muck seemed hellish. If I jumped, I'd be betting my life on finding a way out further on.

I sat down and hugged my knees. Everything had worn me down, and it wasn't just the sun and the emptiness of the desert, it was losing all the joy of creating, and letting that joy wither away. I loved making paintings, but not selling them, or selling myself, or pretending to be something I wasn't, and I hated myself for what I'd become.

I was fucked and I knew it, but too empty to feel scared.

I had jumped into the frog pond from the big arm of the oak tree, and that was every bit as high as what I was looking down at right then. The water in that part of the pond wasn't very deep, so jumping meant a sort of cannonball with arms outstretched to slap the water. I'd leaped off that big arm plenty of times, and it would be easy enough to do here.

I tossed my pack, and it hit the water with a dull plop. I spun my hat out, hoping it would make it to the dry spot on the other side of the pool, but it bounced off the walls and landed in the mud.

Then I jumped. The water was deep enough that I didn't hit bottom, so I was fine. I pushed my pack in front of me as I swam to the opposite side. I got out and looked up across the pool at where I had jumped from. The rock below was polished smooth and overhanging. One glance was all I needed. Getting back up that wall would never happen. I put on my pack and hat, turned away from the pool, and made my way onward. I would find a way out further down the slot, and if I didn't I would die.

Moving through the narrow passage felt different now. It had the burden of fate. Part of me was too tired and too cold to care, yet another part knew to keep moving. I needed to follow this passage to its end.

It got colder and darker as I moved on. The light from above was barely making it this deep. Some sections were so narrow I needed to pull my pack off, and sometimes my hat, too, and push them ahead of me. My shoes seemed too wide and kept getting stuck. I had to step with careful intention, shimmy forward, then yank hard to free them from the pinching crack behind me.

There were points when I really had to work to squeeze myself along. My face could barely turn, so there was no way to see what I was getting into, and all I could do was feel my way further. Both sides of my forehead rubbed along the gritty walls, and sometimes I'd get stuck, unable to move forward or back. This gave me a chance to rest, and those moments were peaceful. I know this must sound weird, but it wasn't claustrophobic, not at all. It felt more like an embrace, and I wasn't sure if I was stuck, if I'd given up, or if I was merely resting.

Each time it happened, I stopped and waited. I think I fell asleep a few times. After these long standstills, I'd wake, then grunt and wiggle, and somehow get through. Eventually, I emerged into a small, narrow chamber. There was a glint of light from the crack above, barely enough to make out what was around me.

This felt more like a cave than something in a canyon. The floor was tilted somewhat, and I couldn't quite stand, so I sat awkwardly in the corner near where I'd entered. I was cold and tired, and wrapped my arms around myself, trying to find any warmth. There was a long, skinny pool of murky water in front of me and nothing more. There was no place to go. I had reached the end.

I wasn't surprised. I knew this could happen. I knew what it meant to jump into that muddy pool, and here I was, with nothing left to feel.

The light from the crack in the ceiling was dimming. Somewhere far above, the sun had moved in the sky, and I watched the chamber slowly darken. Eventually, everything went black.

I faded in and out, but I don't think it was sleep, more that the silence and darkness had cast a spell, and I was free. It was easy to let go. It was a blessing.

I was trying to release myself, to float away in the emptiness. I tried but couldn't. Something was here, a companion—a soft golden glow. I thought my mind was playing tricks on me, so I opened and closed my eyes. I looked away and then back.

I could barely see it, but it was there. The glow was coming from the pool in front of me. There was light in the water. I still had a sense of the area around me. I could visualize the size and dimensions. That faint glow was coming from somewhere far away, and given how muddy the water was, it must be bright.

I moved a little, sliding to align myself with the pool. There was a glow. It wasn't some trick of my eyes, I was seeing it.

The slot I'd come through was the same crack that stretched across the ceiling. It dropped down the opposite wall and into the water. The muddy pool was maybe the width of a bathtub and twice as long. The golden glow was at the far end, lined up with the crack.

The corridor continued.

I focused on the glow at the end of the muddy pool. That light was coming from somewhere.

I could try to swim through and find a way further on. I had no idea if I could fit through whatever opening led to the pale light. I pictured myself getting stuck and dying, but I would die here if I sat and did nothing.

Touching the water meant disturbing the muddy silt, and the glow would disappear. I knew this. I put my legs in the pool and gasped. I was already cold, and the water was much colder than I expected. Instantly, the glow was gone, and everything was black again. I eased in and stood on the bottom with the water about at my chest. I jammed my hat in my pack, and let it float on the surface.

I felt the walls of the pool and reached down and found a hollow spot below me. I took a couple of deep breaths, then dropped underwater. All I could do was feel my way forward with my eyes closed. I wasn't truly swimming, more pulling myself along the rock. I kept reaching back to the pack, fighting to keep it with me. It floated and got stuck, pinned in the constrictions above. I yanked and pulled it with me, squirming further, bumping my head and creeping forward.

I'm a good swimmer, and can hold my breath for a long time, but there came a point when I crossed a line. I had gone too far, and I knew it. The slot was too narrow to turn myself around, and I didn't have enough in my lungs to make it back. I started to panic. I pulled and twisted, swimming lower and deeper. I was blind and forcing myself further. I tried to keep pulling the pack, but it was gone.

I needed to breathe, and it hurt. There was this sudden knowing —*it's happening now. It's all ending*. I don't know if I gave up, or fought harder, or blacked out.

Then I was out. I was standing. I was breathing. It was bright and beautiful. I stood in the river and it was sunny and open and I was out.

I was gasping deep and hard. I looked around. I had done it. I was alive and in the canyon, the beautiful canyon I'd seen from above. I was knee-deep in sparkling water, and I leaned over and splashed my face to clear the mud from my eyes.

Holy Mother of God, I was cold. I was in the middle of a wide stream between towering walls, standing in the shade. There was a sandy island a few yards away, and it was in the sun. My body had seized up and I staggered like an old man.

I walked slowly through the shallow water and up onto the sandy shore of the island. I lurched into the sunlight, and awkwardly unsnapped the buttons of my wet shirt. My hands were like claws, and peeling it off took forever. My arms and shoulders were stiff and ached.

I sat down in the sand and worked to get my shoes and socks off. I was about to lay back and let myself warm up in the sun when I saw a black shape gliding downstream. It wasn't much, and I wondered what I was seeing. Then I knew—*that's my pack!*

I jumped up and ran into the water. It was mostly submerged and moving slow. I grabbed it and carried it back to the island. It was waterlogged and heavy. I set it aside, pulled off my jeans and underwear, and lay naked in the sand.

The sun felt glorious, and I was asleep in seconds.

12

THE BLUE LIGHTS WERE ALL AROUND ME. I wasn't on the path. I wasn't running. I was behind the bushes, trying to hide with my back pressed against the fence. I was here again and didn't understand why. I was in her backyard, looking up at her window. It was Katie's room, and something terrible had happened.

The yard was heavy with some presence, and I could feel it. Something was so close, some menacing force, and if I moved it would find me, it would trap me—it would take me. I was flooded with dread. Oh God, the guilt hurt.

Then there was a black shadow in the yard. It was big, a lot bigger than me, moving slowly—searching. I stayed still, but it knew I was there. Then it faced me and rushed right up close. It loomed above me, and I was trapped.

I don't know why, but I whispered, "Is Katie all right?"

Then it was over. I wasn't in her yard anymore, everything was white, and it felt completely different. There was nothing to see, and nothing to feel. My physical self was gone, like I didn't exist. I heard a gentle voice say, "Everything will be fine. We did this, not you."

It was her voice, and I was instantly calm. It was the tiny girl from the limbo room. I didn't see her, but I knew she said it. I asked the black shadow a question, and she answered me, and I wasn't scared anymore.

I slowly opened my eyes. I was looking up at a narrow crescent of bright blue sky. Soaring sandstone walls, rusty orange with long black streaks, surrounded everything.

The sun was hot, and the brutal chill was gone. I sat up. I had the dream again, but the fear was gone. For the first time, when I woke, I wasn't crushed by the weight of shame. The dream had lost its power. I felt alive and content.

I stood up. I was dry and moved around easily. The aching stiffness was gone. I picked up my wet clothes and carefully hung them on the branches of a scrubby tree.

There was no wind down here, but the sun would dry everything soon enough. I emptied my pack, and hung the extra clothes. I unrolled the tarp and set it out on the sand with rocks in each corner. My hat was muddy and a bit flattened, so I tapped out the dents as best as I could and rinsed it in the river. It cleaned up pretty well. I put it on, and the cool wetness felt nice on my head. Then I hung the pack on the tree with everything else.

I walked around the island. It wasn't very big, maybe the size of the infield of a baseball diamond, but narrower. The edges were all sand, with a grassy mound and the tree in the middle.

I stood at the water's edge and looked at the crack running up the wall a little upstream from the island. This is where I'd emerged out of the darkness. It was just a thin seam at water level, and it widened further up. Following higher, it became its own large canyon, a cleave in the giant wall above me. Looking up at the skyline and a little bit right, I saw the outline of the rock pulpit where I had lain with my face out over the edge. From down here, it was only a tiny point jutting out from the vast silhouette of the rim.

The river appeared motionless, but it moved slowly around the island. Its calm surface was as flat as glass, a giant mirror without a ripple.

I walked back into the stream. It was cold, but the sun was hot and felt so good. I marveled at how clear the water was. It looked so still, but there were tight, swirling eddies downstream of my legs. I walked up to the thin crack and touched it. It was barely the width of a penny. I pushed my nose to the crack and inhaled, wondering if I could smell the cold, black corridor locked behind this wall. I couldn't. I had been inside this giant stone, alone in the darkness and all set to die.

I stepped away and walked back and forth on the sandy bottom, trying to find the passage that had brought me to this spot. I circled wider, feeling with my toes for any clue. I was barefoot, and except for a summer straw Stetson, I was naked. I must have been a sight, tromping and splashing, hoping to find a hidden gateway. But there was nothing.

The walls were enormously high, and no wider than the length of a school bus way up at the rim. Both walls were overhanging, so there was lots more room down here where I stood.

The canyon ran straight in this section, and turned upstream and downstream of the island. Both hallways curved, hiding anything beyond.

I walked past that little crack and followed the river upstream. I entered a curving corridor of stone, easing to my left. The mammoth red walls narrowed and came right down to the river, so there was no sand or grass on either side. I was astonished at the power and beauty of this spot. Its perfection left me in awe. Following this graceful curve was so seductive, and the passage eventually straightened out, and I could see down a long, narrow corridor.

I kept walking and was confronted by something I had never seen before. The giant canyon opened into a wide round room, and there was nothing more—it simply dead-ended. There was a beautiful, shiny green stripe running down the back wall. Plants and moss grew on the surface, feeding off seeping springs in the rock. Water was running, I could hear it, and it created a set of ripples on the surface of the river.

I walked closer, and at about the height of my face was a single crack. Water flowed in a steady stream no wider than my thumb. Orchids and lilies hung down in long wet vines, an elegant dripping garden in an empty canyon. I leaned into that open crack, put my mouth to the clear water, and drank. It was the most satisfying thing I had ever felt.

I drank until I couldn't anymore. I backed away and stood there like a patron at an art museum. I was overwhelmed with wonder and stayed until my feet began to cramp in the icy water. Then I turned around and followed the river back to the island. I stood in the sun and shook my legs until they warmed up.

There was a sandy area across the river from the island and a bit downstream. The canyon wall was set back, allowing for an open grassy meadow with willows along the overhanging sandstone. I had studied this spot from above, and it looked much more lush from down here.

When my feet were warm again, I stepped back into the cold water and started downstream. As I walked past the sandy beach, I saw wildflowers in the grass, and beyond that was an alcove hidden in shadows.

Continuing down the middle of the river meant following the magnificent curve of the huge walls. The giant hallway turned to the right, and like the upstream section, there were no banks on either side. The soaring walls rose vertically out of the water. I walked for a long stretch, and the corridor steadily tapered with each step. Eventually, it was narrow enough that I could spread my arms and touch both walls with my fingertips. I've been in similar places, but none had the perfection of this canyon.

The hallway gently bent around a smooth swirl of a corner. This graceful turn allowed the musical splashing of my feet to reflect back at me, singing with clarity. I studied the sculpted rock as I walked. A millennia of storms had raged through here and polished these twisting walls, and all that rushing water meant a powerful spinning vortex.

Turning the final corner presented me with another unexpected view. It ended ended with a wide, round pool surrounded by soaring walls. Canyons in the Southwest don't just end like this. I was standing in knee-deep water, and the ripples that began at my legs stretched out in front of me and swirled into a lazy spiral. The water was deceptively calm, but after watching for a bit, I could see a steady rotation on the surface. It was like watching a giant bathtub drain in slow motion.

I was about to walk out further but stayed where I was. The water was going somewhere—draining down to some netherworld below. The water was clear at my feet. I could see my toes and the glittering sand, but it got darker ahead of me. There wasn't much to see, just a shadow in the center of the round pool. I sensed more than saw, but I could perceive a cone-shaped hole easing down to blackness. I was on the edge of oblivion, and it was hauntingly beautiful.

I had looked at death as a friend during much of this trip. I had walked away from everything and marched toward my own darkness. I'd been willing to take each step forward, and I knew what that meant. The gentle revolving pool before me could swallow my body, and I would be done with all this pain. Minutes ago I drank from a flowing spring at the other end of this river, and that simple act felt so perfect. Cold, clear water is such a simple thing and right then, being alive felt good.

I turned around and walked back upstream.

I waded slowly until I got to the beach across from the island. The meadow was tucked in an overhanging cove beneath the soaring wall of rock. I got out of the cold water and stood in the sand. The area was about the size of the lot where I'd grown up back in Wisconsin. The lawn I mowed as a boy would just about fit here, with our little ranch house set in the middle.

Further in from the beach was an area of tall grass and desert flowers, without any of the Russian olive that choke most of the canyon bottoms in this country. Past that was a thick mess of sandbar willows against the back wall of the cove. I walked a few steps into the grass and saw a slot tucked into the rock. It looked narrow and dark. I hadn't seen it while standing in the river because of the deep folds of the sandstone wall.

The flowers and green grass smelled perfume sweet, and I was careful with my footsteps. Over the decades of walking outside, I'd achieved a gentleness underfoot. The tall, thin grass had a tough time down here, and I was mindful with each step, honoring the fragile life rising from the sand.

I would need to squeeze through the willows to get to the slot. From where I stood I felt cool air softly escaping the narrow opening, and that seemed promising. I'd walked the length of this canyon, from the river's source to where it fell away into the Earth.

I'd seen nothing else that looked like a way out, and all I could do was hope this would lead me up and out of here.

I turned around, walked back to the river and crossed to the island. I stepped out of the water and sat in the sun. There was a calm feeling of satisfaction. I had found something remarkable, and I wondered if I might be the first person ever to walk in this magical canyon. It seemed impossible, but I didn't see any signs that anyone else had been down here.

This place might have been deeper than it was long, and I guessed the river bottom would measure less than a quarter mile. It began with a flowing spring at the east end, and terminated in an ominous whirlpool at the west end. At points along the bottom, it was barely six feet wide. The area around the island and the grassy beach was the widest, maybe a hundred feet from wall to wall.

This morning I was on top and could have easily walked around this canyon, but at the point I found on the drop-off, there was no way to tell what I was seeing or how long it might have stretched. I was at the bottom of a single-slice toaster in the desert floor. Seen from above, the sparse opening might be nothing more than a wrinkle in the surface of the slickrock. Map makers scrutinizing satellite images could have simply overlooked this obscure feature. Somehow, I had managed to get down here, deep within the Earth itself.

The shade line was creeping close to where I sat. When that shadow crossed over me, it would get cold and wouldn't warm up until tomorrow. I stood up, found my bottle, and filled it from the stream. I took my shirt off the tree and put it on. It was stiff and dry. I stuffed everything in my pack except my shoes, socks, and pants—I carried these. When I was a few steps into the water, I turned around and thanked the tree. I told it I was grateful for its help in drying my clothes.

I crossed the river to the beach, rubbed the wet sand off my feet, and put on what I carried. I felt clean and alive. I cautiously walked across the meadow and pressed through the dense wall of willows. I stepped into the cool darkness of the slot and didn't look back.

13

THE NARROW CORRIDOR WAS EASY WALKING. Flash floods have raged down these canyons over the centuries. Gravel and sand got dragged through with the rushing water, and when it settled and dried, long stretches of the floor ended up perfectly level. This made for smooth travel.

The canyon walls undulated above me, so much so that barely any sunlight made it this far down, and I moved steadily through a warm orange glow. At times the passage widened a bit, and other times I needed to scramble up blocky boulders. There were a few points where the canyon branched, and I had to pick which fork to travel. There was no way to know which might lead out, so I didn't waste any time, I chose and kept walking. I got dead-ended a few times, and I'd turn around, retrace my steps and take the other fork. I snaked my way through this maze and little by little gained some elevation. After what felt like many hours, the occasional views of the sky above seemed closer, and I sensed I was nearing the surface.

The twist and turns of this dark hallway ended in a round, open area. I was standing at the bottom of a giant chimney in the sandstone. It went straight up in a tidy, smooth cylinder, with the corridor I'd traveled behind me, and a thin crack in front of me. Water and gravity had created something amazing. An eternity of pounding water events carved this hollow tube out of the sandstone. The sky above was blue and clear, and I sensed the rim was close, maybe a hundred feet above where I stood.

The crack in front of me looked like it might be climbable. I couldn't step back enough to get much of a view, but I could see a little platform above the steepest part of the crack, and all I could do was hope there would be a way to keep pressing forward. From where I stood, that platform looked about fifty feet up, and any fall after fifteen or so feet would probably kill me. But something as simple as a twisted ankle down here would be a death sentence, and not trying meant the same thing.

I got close and examined the crack. It was about six inches wide, and the sides were clean and straight, unwavering for about the first twenty feet. It looked hard but not impossible.

I put my hands in the crack and tried to shimmy my way up, but I barely got a foot off the ground, then slid down to the sand. I tried it a few more times and didn't do much better. If I couldn't get up this, I could walk back down to the river, drink spring water, and after a few weeks I'd die of starvation. I tried again and dropped back down. I felt something under my feet. I looked and saw something blue.

Kneeling down, I cleared some sand and saw a patch of pale blue fabric. I brushed more away and found what I thought was a smooth white rock, but that's something you'd never see here. Something about it didn't seem right. I dug deeper and realized it was a human skull. It was clean and white, and now I knew I wasn't the first person down here.

I moved more sand away and saw the skull wasn't attached to anything. Clearing more revealed his spine and ribs, all held in place by a faded jean jacket. The bones, for the most part, were free of any flesh, and what little was left had dried like hard lacquer. Whoever this was, he must have been here a long time, but I didn't know if that meant a few months or a few decades. He either fell trying to get down into the canyon, or trying to get out of it, like I was trying now. He stared at me with empty eyes, and they weren't very encouraging.

I pulled on the jacket, working it partially up out of the sand. I cleared away more and saw he had been wearing blue jeans. I searched the pockets to find anything that might identify who it had been. All I found were four quarters, a dime, and a penny. I looked in the chest pockets of the jacket and found a small key. I put the change in the left front pocket of my pants, and the key in the little fifth pocket on my right side.

I made a few more attempts and slipped each time. The brim of my hat scraped trying to move up—I needed to get my face closer to the rock. I tried again and failed. The sand made for a soft landing, but I wasn't getting anywhere. I stepped back and looked up. There was nothing to hold for a long stretch. The wall was smooth and featureless, yet I could see blocky handholds above my high point. I needed to get there.

I took my pack off, pushed my hat in, then put the pack on again. I tried one more time and got a bit higher, but felt only smooth stone at the full length of my arm. I needed something to hold onto. I slid my hand into the crack in hopes of finding any little bump or feature, but there was nothing.

I dropped back to the sand. I could see where my hand had gotten to, and everything seemed blank. The width of the crack changed slightly at my high point. Above that, it got slightly wider.

I looked up at the crack, and then down at the skull in the sand. I said, "I'm gonna need your help."

It didn't answer.

I tucked my shirt in my pants and took the skull and stuffed it down my shirt at my chest. I started up again and got to where I could touch the high point. Then I steadied myself, put my hand in my shirt, grabbed the skull, reached as high as I could, and pushed it in the crack. This was where it narrowed, and I tried to lock it in place. I hit it with my fist, pounding it tighter, then hit it again harder. I grabbed and tried to wiggle it. Nothing.

I dropped again. My hands ached and I shook them. The skull was solid, so I had something to grab and could use it to get higher. I hoped so anyway. I walked in circles and massaged my fingers. I needed to be rested to get past the steep part, but I didn't want to stand around long enough where I'd overthink everything and get scared.

I stepped back as far as I could to see if there was anything further up that might stop me, but it all looked difficult. I bent over and tightened my shoes, then stood up, stepped over the skeleton, and got up to the skull in a few quick moves.

I clung to it and grunted and muscled up higher. It held me, and I got to where it was at my chest, and put both hands on it, then worked to jam my feet in the crack below so I wouldn't topple over. I reached higher and found a hold that fit my hand perfectly. I pulled and got high enough to stand on the skull.

I did it. I was past the smooth section of rock. I could rest and tried to breathe. Looking up seemed hard, but looking down was a mistake. I was now higher than I was willing to fall. I wanted to stay here, but couldn't. I needed to move.

I pulled down on the one good handhold, and my foot left the security of the skull. I'm not sure what happened after that. My face was so close to the rock that I didn't see much, and each time I moved upward, I gasped, "A little more, a little more." I was fighting to get higher, but I also fought not to panic.

"A little more, just a little more."

Then I was at a big ledge. It was sandy and covered with pebbles. Without anything to grab, all I could do was shimmy forward using my palms and elbows. Then my belly and knees. I lay there with my face in the dust and waited til my breathing calmed down.

It wasn't until I crawled forward and stood up that I realized I'd made it. Looking down over the edge from this platform unnerved me. It seemed a lot higher and scarier than it did from the bottom.

I turned around and looked up. From here the climbing would be simple, just moving through some blocky steps. I could see more of the sky, and it was no longer blue. The color had deepened, and it would be dark soon.

The sun was down when I climbed out of the slot. I was back on the surface, and everything felt different. I had returned to the realm of infinite space. I followed the North Star until it was too dark to walk. I stopped and drank the last of the water from that glorious canyon, then lay down and slept.

14

THE MORNING WAS COLD. There was enough light in the steel gray sky to start moving, but it would be a while before the sun could offer any heat. I walked with the plastic tarp around me like a robe, desperately trying to stay warm. I was tired and moved slowly.

I found a tiny pool of water in the surface of the slickrock. It was no bigger than a cup, and I knelt down and tried to drink with my lips. My face didn't fit into the small depression, and I only managed to suck up a few drops. I used the plastic bag from the Gummy Bugs like a scoop, dipping it in and trying to lift out some water. It didn't work, and I spilled it all. I found four more little cup-sized pools, managed to drink from two of them, and spilled the others.

I cowered on my knees, holding the tarp tight around me. What I drank wouldn't be enough. I stood up and kept walking north. I was drained from yesterday and all the previous days. I shivered and prayed for the sun to rise faster.

Then I stopped. There was a barbed wire fence blocking my path. I looked right and left, and it stretched off to both horizons. The wire was old and rusted, and the upright posts were weathered. It was the typical fence you'd find in the backcountry, but something about it left me wondering. I had to think, and after a bit I realized I hadn't seen anything manmade for I don't know how long.

Stepping over barbed wire is never easy, and I was brutally tired. I walked alongside the rusty barrier until I found a sagging fence post. The bottom of this pine picket had worn away after decades in the sun, so it hung about an inch above the sand. I grabbed the top, pulled it and put my shoe on it. Now it was folded flat on the ground, and one long step was all it took to get to the other side. Once I was off, it sprang back up, and I kept walking.

My travel was slightly downhill with a grand open vista before me. The terrain tipped gently to the north, and the view expanded with each step. Something out there in that giant emptiness urged me on.

A few minutes later I stood at the edge of a cliff, and saw something I didn't expect. Below me sat a little town. From way up here, it looked like nothing more than a set of toys, a model on a boy's bedroom floor. Each tiny building was an ashen gray, all clustered along a thread of road. I should have been relieved, but I was too tired to feel anything.

The town was alone in a wide, crooked valley. There were rugged hills and buttes on the far side. The basin looked too dry to grow anything. If there was a river down there, this time of the year it would show up as a green stripe, but there was nothing to see. It seemed like a giant hand could reach down and brush the town away, as if it were nothing more than dust on a lonely floor.

I was at the top of a drop-off, and this is an awful way to try and find a route. The cliff in front of me seemed huge. I looked east and west, and both ways seemed impossible. I started walking west along the cliff, toward the town below. I followed the edge and passed a few gullies, and each was too steep to descend. The cliff changed as I moved west, and I ended up traversing along a thin shelf with vertical terrain above and below. The further I went, the worse it looked. I managed to get around an awkward corner, and there was a free-standing tower across from me. It wasn't that far away, but the hollow space between me and the tower dropped sharply.

There was something remarkable a little further west. A long block of sandstone had bridged the gap. It was pinned between the cliff where I stood and the tower wall. This thing must have once been a tall pillar along my side of the cliff, and at some point it fell over and got stuck.

Inching closer, it looked like one breath could knock it down. I felt stuck on this side, but it looked like I could get down on the other side. I could see a set of ramps and ledges across from me, and these led into easier terrain. I could get around the base of the tower and keep moving downhill.

Imagine two five-story buildings separated by a narrow street with a long plank between them. On one side, the plank rests right on the edge of the roof, and on the other side it's stuck on something you can't quite see. To make matters worse, the plank wasn't laying flat. It was canted at an awkward angle. This description is a whole lot more inviting than what I was looking at on the big cliff face.

I stepped closer and kicked the block. There wasn't anything to sense, and after kicking it a few more times, I stepped out onto its tilted surface. The first couple of steps were fine, but about halfway across it teetered a few inches sideways. It made a hollow *clunk* that echoed back up from the void. I retreated half a step, and it made the same noise as it tipped back in place. If this were a table in a restaurant, the tipping could be solved with a matchbook under one leg. Still, it was creepy to have this thing lurch underfoot while standing over fifty feet of emptiness.

My fatigue was a burden, and any patience was long gone. I said, "Fuck it," and walked on. It tipped and clunked, then settled back when I stepped off the other side.

Making my way down the ledges was slow going, and I eventually got to the bottom of the tower and kept working my way north. But now I no longer had a view of the town and worried I had dreamed it.

All I knew was I needed to keep moving down. I eventually found a narrow gully that looked passable—maybe. I started down a steep, miserable jumble of rocks, all stacked in an unstable mess. I was trudging through a house of cards made of boulders, and some were enormous. It felt like one misstep would release the whole gully on top of me. Plenty of rocks tumbled as I made my way down, but they were all too small to worry about.

I spent the rest of the day slowly picking my way down rounded ledges and loose rocks. I got dead ended again and again, and needed to backtrack through the same awful terrain. It felt like I never got more than three steps in a row on comfortable footing. I didn't know where I was going, but every step sapped what little energy I had left. I ended up in a big clutter of blocky boulders. I climbed over some, and squeezed under others. I was all turned around, and forced myself through the huge maze of rocks. All I knew was to keep moving.

I stopped. I could smell the town. It wasn't like any one thing, more that there was a smell of people. I worked around a few more boulders, and saw it again. It was downhill about a half mile away. At this point, there was nothing but an open slope between me and the buildings. I stood there, not sure what to do.

I saw the back of a row of buildings facing the main street. Everything was so still, like an abandoned Hollywood movie set. The area in front of me was all rocks, and steep enough to be careful. But my momentum was gone, and it took a lot of work to take the first shaky step.

It wasn't long before the zone of rocks ended, and I followed a gentle ridge of easy walking, and this led me to the sparse row of buildings. As the hill leveled out, the ground glittered from flecks of broken glass. There were plastic cup lids and sun-bleached candy wrappers. I was back among my fellow man.

My last obstacle was a barbed wire fence with tumbleweeds and old plastic bags stuck along its length. I walked to a gate and opened it. I stepped through and onto an asphalt alley that ran along the back of the buildings.

15

I STOOD ON THE PAVEMENT FOR A LONG TIME. I wasn't sure what to do, and I waited for some emotion to well up, but there was nothing. I could smell the asphalt. And I could smell the perfume from cleaning products, and creosote on the telephone poles.

The familiar sound of a door opening broke my daze, and I turned to see a tall young man step out of a building and toss a black plastic bag into a dumpster in the alley. He looked at me and said, "Hello."

The way he said it was more of a question than a greeting. I said hello back, and then he asked, "Are you all right?"

I thought for a moment, and answered honestly, "Yes, I'm all right."

I must have been a sight, standing like a statue in the middle of the alley. He asked, "Do you need anything?"

"Maybe some water."

The young man told me to come in, that he had water. I walked along a cracked cement sidewalk to the door, took off my hat, and followed him inside.

I was in a long hallway, and I could see the brightness at the other end of the building. It was confining, and my shoulders pinched inward, like I was about to get crushed. He led me past a few doors and a small kitchen to a bright, open room. The ceiling was high, and I stood upright and took a deep breath. I'd nearly panicked from being in a building again.

I was in a modest coffee shop. It had a wall of tall windows looking out onto the main street. He pointed to a water cooler with a big plastic bottle on top, "Here's water." There were cups next to it, and I thanked him as I filled one.

While I drank, he said, "I'm closing up, but you can stay until I need to lock the doors."

I thanked him again, and he stared at me with concern. I think he was worried I might topple over.

"Sit down. Do you need any food? We have coffee from this afternoon. It should still be warm." He had a beautiful, deep voice. I set my pack on the floor and sat at a small table next to the window.

He brought out a basket of muffins and explained they were a day old, and he would be throwing them out, and if I wanted any, I could have them.

He asked, "Would you like any coffee?" I nodded, and he walked back to the counter. I'd eaten most of the first muffin when he returned with the cup.

I was chewing and covered my mouth with my hand. I took the cup with my other hand, and our fingers briefly touched. I tried to thank him, but with my mouth full, all I could do was nod. Then he left me alone.

I ate all the muffins. There were probably about five of them. Some were tan and had apple slices in them, and some were darker brown with raisins. They were the most delicious things to ever touch my tongue. I drank the coffee, and it seemed to calm something in me. There was a little plastic honey bear on the table, and I stared at it until he left the kitchen and walked down the hall. When he was out of sight, I tilted my head back and squeezed some into my mouth. The sweetness was like electricity. I swallowed it and squeezed more, and kept at it until the bottle was empty.

I looked over at the counter, and there was a glass jar with a card taped to it with the word 'tips' written in magic marker. I got up and put the coins in my pocket in the jar. When I sat back down, my heart was pounding, and I gripped the edge of the table. I took some deep breaths and tried to figure out if I was reacting to seeing another person, or from eating again.

He came back, refilled my cup, and introduced himself, "My name is Tony, and I work here most days."

I needed to think for a second, and said, "My name is John." Then I added, "Thank you for your kindness."

He seemed a little uncomfortable and said I could clean up in the bathroom. He was nice about it, but I took that as a hint. He was telling me I looked terrible.

I walked back down the hall, and he handed me a small towel as I passed the kitchen. Opening the bathroom door meant the shock of my face in the mirror. I cautiously approached my reflection, like a cat meeting another cat. I looked into the haunted eyes of a stranger. My beard was now completely white, and I was gaunt in a way that unnerved me. My skin was dry and tan, and the sunblock was caked in the wrinkles around my eyes and nose. I looked like a crazed zealot who'd been struck by lightning.

I washed my face and hands, and the water in the sink turned muddy red. The little bar of soap smelled so fake I was almost afraid to touch it. I washed and rinsed again, and the water was still dirty, so I did it a third time until it ran almost clear. I wet my hands, did my best to press down my hair, then dried myself with the towel. I came out and told him the towel was dirty. He wasn't bothered, and tossed it in a bin across from the kitchen. He explained they had a lot of towels and not to worry.

I waited in the hall while he locked the front door and flipped the window sign from open to closed. Then he walked past me, held the back door and gestured for me to walk out first. He followed and locked it behind him. We walked across the alley to a small building, not much more than a shed, and he opened the padlock with a key. We stepped inside, and he reached up and pulled a string. A bare bulb lit the room, yet even with the light on, it seemed dark. He said I could sleep here.

There was an army cot with a wide sleeping pad. One wall was entirely shelves, with mostly cardboard boxes of paper cups and napkins for the coffee shop. Tony took a nylon duffel bag off a shelf, set it on the cot, and said it had some blankets. He apologized, saying it wasn't much. I told him not to worry, that I was grateful. He said he would be back at five-thirty the next morning to open the shop.

I said, "I don't have a watch."

"I'll be there a little bit before dawn."

We were both quiet, and I sensed he was embarrassed. I said I would be fine and thanked him again. After he left, the room was perfectly still. I set my backpack on the floor near the cot and looked around. It was dark and dusty, but it felt heavenly. The floor was dirt but level and packed down. There was a sink in the back corner, but no bathroom. Next to that was a workbench with hardly anything on it. There were two windows, one next to the door facing the coffee shop, the other on the wall facing west. I took a sip of water and realized I was about to collapse.

I was up at sunrise and walked across the alley to the shop. Tony had started the coffee and asked how I'd slept.

"Very, very good."

He poured coffee in a paper cup, handed it to me, and I thanked him. He was prepping for the day, and I offered to help. Right as I spoke those words, I realized how I must have looked. I wore the same clothes and was still unwashed after all those days alone in the desert. I mumbled, "I know I'm a mess right now, but I want to help. I'm sorry, I should clean up."

Tony didn't answer right away. He looked at the floor, and I could tell he was thinking. After a moment he said, "There's a secondhand store down the street a few doors past the church. They won't be open yet, but I'll call the lady who runs the place in a little bit. She'll have plenty for you. There isn't a shower here, but there's hot water. There's a fence behind the shed, and you could wash up there. It's not much, but no one will bother you."

I nodded.

He said, "Give me a few minutes, and I'll make you something. Would an egg and cheese burrito be okay?"

Again, I nodded.

"Okay, give me a few minutes. If you could sweep the sidewalk out front, that would be helpful."

I said, "Of course."

"And the patio on the west side of the shop."

I could tell he was unsure what to do or say, and I asked, "Where do I find a broom?"

He pointed down the back hall and said it was behind the door before the bathroom.

The morning was calm, and the sun was still low in the east, so it wasn't hot yet. I swept the dust off the sidewalk and into the street. It was a straw broom with one side curved to a point from years of use. I dragged this pointed end all along the front of the store where the building met the sidewalk, cleaning out gravel and sand. My motions were slow and deliberate. Then I moved around the corner to the patio. I hadn't seen this the night before, but there was a covered area with a few tables, chairs, and a picnic table. There was a low divider along the far edge. It was made with barn wood boards and stood about two feet high. There were parts you could sit on, and the rest was an open planter box with some cactus and dried grass. I swept the chairs and the tables, and then the patio tiles. All that dust ended up in the empty lot next door.

I walked back out front and took a few steps into the street to get a full view of the coffee shop. It was in an old white brick building, with a hand-painted sign above the door that read *Trail's End Café*. There was a silhouette of an Indian above those words. He was hunched over on a downcast horse and I remembered this image from a Beach Boys album. I could see the old record player in the dark corner of the basement in the house where I'd grown up, and I could smell the cardboard cover. That Indian and his horse hit me with the same sadness I'd felt as a kid.

Looking up and down the main street seemed familiar. From where I stood, I could see the wide open landscape out beyond the few blocks that made up this little town. There are places like this all across the West—dusty, empty, and beaten down. And all these places have a sad story, the mine closed, the timber got cut down, or the train stopped coming. Something happened here, too.

I heard the door open behind me and turned around. Tony was dragging a big plywood signboard out onto the sidewalk. I took a few steps toward him and helped him prop it open. The hand-painted sign read, "Open, c'mon in."

A car pulled up and parked. A tall lady got out and said, "Good morning, Tony."

He held the door and followed her inside. The car had Utah plates, and I stood in a daze, looking down at my long shadow on the sidewalk. A pickup truck made a U-turn in front of the store and parked behind the lady's car. It had Utah plates, too.

A man with a short gray beard got out and stepped up onto the sidewalk. I held the door for him and said good morning. He nodded and said, "You bet."

I followed him in, stood off to the side, and watched as Tony handed them both coffee. He knew what they wanted without anyone asking. After they stepped away from the counter, Tony motioned me forward. I walked up, and he handed me a plate with a burrito and a little cup of salsa. He poured me a second cup of coffee and pointed to a table with silverware.

I asked, "Are we in Utah?"

He smiled and said, "Yes, we are, in pretty much the emptiest part of the state."

I sat at the table next to the window, in the same chair I'd sat the afternoon before. Tony came over as I ate and stood looking out at the empty main street. Without facing me, he said, "I spoke with the lady who runs the secondhand store. I told her you'd be by after you ate. She knows you're coming, and she'll help you out."

He pointed left and said, "It's on the next block past the church in a yellow storefront. It's on this same side of the street. Her name is Betty."

I wasn't used to anyone doing so much for me. I expected some feeling of awkwardness or shame to surface, but all I felt was gratitude. I ate everything on my plate and finished the coffee. I got up, put the napkin in the trash, then set the plate, silverware, and mug in a gray plastic tub.

He hadn't moved, and I stood quietly by the dirty dishes. I hesitated before speaking, and after a bit, I said, "I don't have any money."

He kept his gaze on the town and said, "She knows that."

16

I LEFT THE COFFEE SHOP and walked west on the sidewalk, and with the sun at my back, my shadow stretched far in front of me, leading me on. I passed a red brick LDS church set back from the street, and what was once a lawn was now clots of yellow grass. Most every town in this part of the country has a church like this, but this was one of the smallest I'd seen. I came to a yellow building and stood in the front of the glass door. I'd only been there a few seconds when I saw a white-haired woman through the window eagerly gesturing for me to come inside.

I went in, and she hurried up to greet me, "Welcome. Come in, come in. You must be John. I'm Betty. It's very nice to meet you."

I told her it was nice to meet her, too, and she handed me a big canvas tote bag with a garish flower pattern. The store was mostly one big room with shelves on all the walls and various racks crowding the floor. There was a smaller room off the back wall with a set of chairs and more shelves. Everything had that cloying smell of perfumed laundry detergent.

She led me to a circular rack with men's shirts on hangers. These were crushed together in a way that seemed like there wouldn't have been room for even one more. She looked at me carefully, then pulled out a short sleeve madras cotton shirt and held it up to me. She was quiet for a moment, then said, "Yes."

She left it on the hanger and pushed it in the tote bag. Then she did it a few more times. I simply held the bag open like a kid at a door on Halloween. We got into a nice rhythm, and I spoke up a few times, saying, "Maybe not, I don't think I'd wear that." She would nod and put it back on the rack. I could tell she'd remember what I did and didn't like.

We went from shirts, to pants, to socks. I sat in a chair and tried on some shoes. She brought over a pair of sandals, the kind river guides would wear. I sensed this caring was normal for her. She asked simple questions like my shirt size and what colors I liked, but never anything about myself.

The tote bag was getting full, and she zipped away and came back with a bigger canvas bag, the kind of thing a carpenter would use at a job site. After about fifteen minutes, I had a new supply of clothes, towels, sheets and blankets.

She asked if I needed anything else. I thought for a little bit and said, "Do you have any soap or shampoo?"

She said, "I do. Let me show you what I've got."

She went through a door, and I stood alone in the middle of the store. For some reason, I felt incredibly calm. It was a kind of serenity that ran like tingles up and down my spine. I could tell she wanted to help me, and her kindness gave me shivers.

She returned carrying a cardboard box. "Maybe this will help."

She set it on the counter and explained, "I got all this when the motel closed about seven years ago. The couple that ran the place asked if I wanted any of this, but I haven't done much with it."

The box was filled with little bottles of shampoo and moisturizer. There were also those tiny bars of soap, and travel sized toothpaste and toothbrushes.

I asked, "It's okay if I take some of these?"

She smiled and said, "Yes, yes, of course. Whatever you need."

I said I couldn't pay, and she told me not to worry. I didn't know what to say and stayed quiet. I put a few of the bathroom things in the tote bag, and Betty reached in and pulled them out. She stepped away and found a little vinyl toiletries pouch, put it all in that, then set it in the tote bag and said, "There."

She seemed perfectly satisfied, and I took that to mean we were done.

I said, "There must be a story about this town."

She smiled and said, "Not much of one."

I nodded, urging her to tell me more.

"We used to get some traffic here before the bridge fell. Since then, it's an awfully long drive to get across the Colorado. I always hated that bridge. When I was a little girl, I'd start crying whenever we drove over it. My brothers made fun of me, but my mom and dad felt it, too. That thing collapsed in 1966. I was just a teenager. And there was lots of talk about building another one, but nothing ever happened."

She pointed to the west wall of the store and said, "You take the main street out that way, and it dead ends at a pretty view, and then you turn around. With the bridge gone, we aren't connected to anything west of here, so the only way to get out of the valley is east, and it's an awfully long way to Hanksville."

She talked about the hardship of neighbors trying to raise cattle, "We had a little river that would run through here in the spring, and it was enough so things would green up some, but that got diverted upstream by the Feds a few years after the dam went in."

She talked about all the people who couldn't survive here and how nearly everyone she grew up with was gone. It could have been a depressing story, but she laughed and said, "This little place has been hurtin' all my life, but it ain't dead yet, and neither am I."

I thanked her, and asked, "Why is there a coffee shop in a Mormon town like this?"

She said, "This valley has never been in good graces with the Church. The empty lot across the street from the Trail's End used to be a bar, and old Lonnie did a tidy business for a while. We used to get our share of upstanding folks who would do the long drive from their righteous towns, park behind the bar, and go back home with a paper bag full of bottles. Lonnie didn't have a license to sell packaged liquor, and the county seat threatened to shut him down, but that never happened. The story was that nobody wanted to drive all the way out here and lay down the law."

She smiled and added, "I think the real story was that some of the fine Church Elders who were in a position to lay down that law would once in a while take that long drive themselves and park behind Lonnie's."

I asked, "What happened?"

"Lonnie died. His two sons didn't want the bar. They moved to California and never came back."

She had a delightful presence, and I was captivated by her stories. Then I asked, "Why are you being so kind to me?"

She poked me in the arm and said, "You stop. Tony called and asked if I could help, and I told'm yes. He's been a sweet kid, and he's made this town a nicer place."

I got a few more things, including a pair of scissors, a disposable razor, and a small handheld mirror. I left Betty's store and walked through the alley to the shed behind the shop. I set the two bags on the porch, then went in the back door of the coffee shop, through the hallway and to the counter. Tony asked how it went, and I told him Betty was very helpful. There were two people seated together near the window, and Tony wasn't busy. He walked me back down the hall to the room past the bathroom, showed me some plastic five-gallon buckets, and said the big sink had hot water. Then he went back to the counter.

I filled two buckets a little over halfway with hot water and carried them out the back door of the coffee shop.

There was a wooden fence behind the shed. I went through the gate and set the buckets on a cement slab. I went back to the porch, grabbed a towel, washcloth, and the bag of toiletries, brought it all behind the shed and closed the gate. It was very private back here. I could look over the fence boards if I stood on my toes. The day had warmed, and there was no wind. I took off my clothes and dunked the washcloth in the hot water.

I spent the next hour or so washing, re-washing, and rinsing. One bucket was for washing only, and I repeatedly soaped up the washcloth and squeezed it out. The water in that bucket got progressively darker during the process. I used an old plastic yogurt container as a ladle, dipping it in the other bucket and pouring the clean water over me for the final rinse. I used my new towel some, but mostly air dried in the sun.

I trimmed my beard, shaved the edges of my neck, under my chin, and some around my cheeks. I put on a pair of olive denim work pants, sandals, and a plaid short sleeve shirt.

I walked back across the alley and into the coffee shop. It was still before noon when I told Tony I could help with anything. He showed me how he liked the dishes and cups washed and rinsed, and where to stack them to dry. There wasn't really a lunch crowd, but for a time there were a few more people coming in and out. When I finished, he explained a few more chores. All of this was easy, and I was happy to help.

During my time that day, and all the days after, there was always such wonderful music playing in the shop. I feel like I have a wide knowledge of music, but I knew none of it. He had a laptop in the back room, and it was plugged into an old stereo on a shelf. There was also a cassette player and a stack of tapes. There were four speakers, two in the main room, and two smaller ones in the kitchen. The volume was never high, and the mood was always even and calm. Some of it was jazz from the 40s, some was acoustic guitar, and some was electronic music from last month. I was amazed at the spell it cast over the little shop.

I asked him about the music, and let him know I was impressed. He dismissed it as nothing special, simply saying, "I just play things I like."

Then the sidewalk sign was in, the window sign got flipped around, and the front door was locked. I was setting out the cups for tomorrow, and Tony walked up to me with a serious look. I was concerned and asked, "What is it?"

He said, "You smell like Betty's store."

I rolled my eyes and said, "I know, it's pretty smelly."

He reached under the sink and handed me a clear bottle of dark blue soap and explained that this would get the smell out. He said he'd used it before on things from her store. I thanked him.

Then I pointed to the chalkboard menu and asked, "Is that your handwriting?"

He eyed me suspiciously and asked, "Yes, why?"

17

THE NEXT MORNING, I was prepping the kitchen for the day, and Tony was at the counter. We hadn't had a customer yet, but I had already set the sign out by the street and swept the sidewalk. My back was to the main room when I heard the front door open, and then a woman's voice saying, "The menu looks beautiful."

Tony's reply was muffled, and there was some small talk. I heard the steam from the espresso machine, and they laughed in the quiet way people do in the morning. I looked out from the kitchen, and it was the same tall woman I'd seen on the sidewalk yesterday while sweeping. She thanked Tony and left.

It wasn't long before I heard another customer saying, "Wow, nice menu." I leaned out to see the man with the gray beard, the one I'd held the door for yesterday.

All throughout the morning, pretty much everyone who came in said something about the chalkboard. I re-did it yesterday after the shop closed. Tony stayed, and we took it down from the wall, and it was a lot heavier than I expected. Then I copied everything from the old menu board down on a pad of paper. After that, I carefully washed the hard surface, first with a soapy rag, and then rinsed it twice. I watched it dry in what seemed like seconds.

I told him most chalkboards you find now are masonite painted a matte dark green. I said, "Those new ones are cheap and light, unlike this beauty. This is real slate."

Tony said, "Yeah, I know. I went into the elementary school up the block and took it."

I asked, "You just took it?"

"Yes. A woman who used to teach there let me in. Her key to the back door still worked. She was happy to help me get it out of there. The chairs are from the school, too."

He gestured to the straight-backed wooden chairs at each table. They looked sturdy and were stained pale orange. "We had to search a bit to find adult chairs. Most of them were tiny. The people who went to school there love them. An old guy flipped one over, and pointed to some gum stuck under the seat. He was insistent he'd put it there when he was a kid."

Tony pointed up at the wall, "We took that clock, too."

It was a standard wall clock with simple black numbers on a white background. I remembered almost the same one from my elementary school. Tony explained how a carpenter cut a hole in the wall and wired it up so there wouldn't be a cord showing. This guy grew up here and had gone to the school, too.

I made a rough sketch on the pad of how I wanted the sign to look, then started writing in chalk. As I worked, I'd ask Tony how to spell some words, like *espresso* and *cappuccino*. I had it written down next to me, but it was easier to ask him. That way I could keep my eyes focused on one thing. He wiped down the counter as I wrote, and when he did come around to where I sat and looked over my shoulder, he said, "Oh, *that's* why you wanted to do this."

There wasn't much to write, and it helped to get into a rhythm. I didn't want to labor over this because the quickness of my hand gave the words some life. The staccato taps of chalk on slate sounded so good. The upstrokes were different than the downstrokes, all of it ringing out like the high hat in a drum kit.

When I was done, we hung it back in place. I said, "If anyone asks who did this, please don't say it was me."

He agreed, and we left the shop through the back door.

Life was slow here, and the endless quiet was soothing. There was a pace to the town and the mornings. The locals were mostly older. It seemed anyone with the energy of youth would need to flee this place. Typical of this part of the west, there was a stoic quality to the people who remained here. If it was ever windy or hot or cold, and it could be all of these in the extreme, nobody said much about it.

We had a day when clouds of red dust raced down the main street. The gusts were violent and rattled the windows. I had to chase the signboard down the sidewalk and drag it back inside. A soft-spoken lady entered the shop and simply said, "Ooh, it's nice in here."

I would stay mostly in the kitchen or in the back, and let Tony deal with everything at the counter. But after a while, he showed me how to use the espresso machine. His mentoring was all about the subtleties and traditions of this craft. The coffee at the shop was wonderful, unusually so, and during one of Tony's teaching sessions, I asked, "Why is the coffee so good?"

He went to the sink and filled a small glass, then handed it to me and nodded. I drank some of it and waited, but he didn't say anything. I asked, "It's because of the water?"

He said, "I think so. The coffee is exceptionally good. You're right to ask. I've asked it, too. We use good beans, but they're not that good, so it must be something else. This end of town is on well water, and I love what comes out of our tap."

I drank the rest, and it tasted perfect. I thought about the canyon and that slow-motion whirlpool. Maybe that glorious water traveled down through the bedrock and found its way here, under this town.

It didn't take long before I knew what people drank, and I'd start their order as they walked in. We had a tall pump thermos in the back with hot chocolate. We made it with a powdered mix, then added warmed up half and half, ground ginger, and a tiny bit of vanilla extract. Quite a few folks here were addicted to it.

There was an air conditioner in the shop, but we only used it in the afternoons on the hottest days. The rest of the time we did fine with screen doors. The windows on the front of the building faced north, so we never got direct light. Both doors, the front and the one to the patio had old style transoms. These had screens, and we left them open at night.

I found some old wood in the alley, mostly scraps that had been lying around in the sun. The bleached surface was so nice to work with, and I made a few signs. I found black paint and a small brush in the back room, and wrote out things like, *dirty dishes here*, and *restroom down the hall* with an arrow.

I drew some afternoons after the shop closed. Other days I'd visit Betty at the store. She came in the shop and got hot chocolate, and sometimes I'd walk up the street and bring her a cup. I painted the front of her place with a new coat of yellow, and did the trim around the doors and windows with a warm ochre. The sun took its toll, and you could almost hear the fresh paint getting sucked into the desiccated surfaces. I painted over the folding signboard and cleaned up the lettering. A few days later, I put a new coat of paint on the sign over the coffee shop door. I picked new colors, but carefully traced the letters and the Indian and his horse.

I offered to do this for Tony and Betty, and they both said yes. I wasn't sure if either of them really cared about it, but they saw I wanted to help, and they let me. Tony introduced me to a man who came into the shop, and he had cans of acrylic paint in his barn and a collection of brushes. He gave me whatever he had and seemed happy to see it getting used.

I explored the town, what little there was of it. It was easiest to walk around in the evening when the sun was low. Most of the main street was boarded up and empty, and the same with the homes on the side streets. The heat and dryness had been merciless, like every building and fencepost was about to fade away. This might seem depressing, but it was so engrossing to look at—and I wanted to draw all of it.

I'd walk the dry river bed that snaked its way along the northern edge of town. I was told it filled after a heavy rain, but that was rare. I'd call this an *arroyo*, but that's more of a New Mexico thing.

There wasn't really any path, and the river rocks made for awkward walking, but the shade was nice. The cottonwoods along its banks were healthy, and their tangled branches hid most of the buildings. The leaves were out, so it felt more alive than the town itself. There were a few bridges and old corrals, but not much got built along its course. I found a few trails and tried to follow them. They might have been used by people at some point, but the only tracks in them now were antelope and deer, neither of which I saw.

The shop was never truly busy, but there was a morning when it seemed like a few more people than usual. Tony stood at the counter taking orders, and I was at the sink washing dishes with my back to the room when I heard a woman say, "Thank you."

I hadn't heard her ordering anything, but I caught her voice when she picked up her drink. I don't know why, but I spun around and saw her just as she turned away from the counter.

Without thinking, I grabbed a rag, wiped my hands, and ran to find her. She wasn't in the shop. When I got out to the sidewalk, I saw her down the block. She was on the street unlocking a car door. As I approached, I realized I had no idea why I was so intent on talking with her. I stepped into the street, and as I got closer, all I could get out was an awkward, "Ummm, excuse me."

She turned, and there were a few seconds of uncomfortable silence. She was blond and held herself in a very confident way. Then she said, "Yes?"

I didn't know what to say, and I blurted out, "Were you born in 1967?"

Her expression was perfect confusion, and she said, "Yes."

I asked her name, and without skipping a beat, she said, "Kelly Kadie."

"How do you spell your last name?"

She looked absolutely baffled and said, "K-A-D-I-E."

Then I asked, "What do you do, I mean for work?"

"I'm a psychic for the FBI."

All I could do was stand there and stare at her. She seemed annoyed, and I mumbled, "I'm sorry to bother you."

She got in her car and drove away.

Her name was the reverse of Katie Kellie, almost exactly, and she was born in the same year as both Katie and me. Something very strange had happened. I'd raced out of the coffee shop to find this woman, and I'd asked questions without thinking and didn't understand why.

18

I told Tony to go home, that I would finish up. Later that afternoon, about a half hour after closing, I stepped out the back door of the shop.

I tossed the day's trash bag in the dumpster, and was heading back in when something made me stop. It was an odd feeling, and I turned and looked around.

There was a car down the alley, across the street and facing me. It looked new, which was unusual here. I could see someone in the driver's seat, but with the sun on the windshield, I couldn't make out much. I stood there staring, and sensed the driver looking back at me. Then the car rolled slowly along the alley and stopped directly in line with the back door. The driver's window slid down and a man looked at me.

He asked, "Mr. Wilson?"

Nobody here knew my last name, and I didn't say anything. The driver had short hair and sunglasses. He gestured for me to come closer, and I stepped out onto the asphalt. After a long bit of silence, he said, "Your agent wants to talk with you."

This meant Ted had been looking for me, and now he'd found me. This guy must have been some sort of private investigator, and he obviously knew who I was, so there wasn't any point in pretending.

I said, "You can tell Ted I'm here."

He nodded and said, "I will."

We stared at each other, and I think he was waiting for me to say more. After a little bit, I said, "You can tell him I'm at peace here."

He nodded and waited, but I didn't say anything else. Eventually, he said, "Thank you," and rolled up the window. Then he drove down the alley, turned at the corner, and was gone.

The next afternoon, Ted walked into the coffee shop. We saw each other right away, and I nodded. He walked up to the counter, looked past Tony and right at me, then asked, "Can we talk?"

I poured two cups of coffee and said, "Let's sit outside."

The tables on the patio were empty. It was hot, but not too bad under the canvas awning. Ted said, "I recognized your hand on the sidewalk sign."

There wasn't much I could say, so I just sat there. Finally, he looked at me and said, "John, I've been worried. You really fucking scared me."

I said, "I know. I'm sorry."

With that out of the way, he told me what happened after I walked away. He talked about the sheriff, the search party, the helicopters, and the news coverage. He tried to contact my family back in Wisconsin, but my parents were dead, and no one was there anymore. I tried to listen, but I kind of shut it all out. I didn't want to hear it. It was clear nobody thought I might have simply walked away.

I interrupted and asked, "How did you find me?"

He said, "From a drawing you did. There was a comment on Facebook. Someone said it looked like Art Amiss drew it."

I had no idea what he meant, and asked, "What was the drawing?"

"It was a sketch of a desert scene with a coyote and a cactus."

I thought about that day and said, "Really? I did a little scribble with a Sharpie on a piece of cardboard and gave it to a kid."

It was a slow afternoon, and I remember sitting alone with some pens. A mom had coffee while her little son ate a cookie at the next table. I'd never seen them before, and drew a little cartoon and gave it to him. They both said thank you, and I didn't think much of it.

Ted said, "I hired a detective, and he did a search online and found that comment. He showed it to me, and it looked like something you would've done. He contacted the kid's mother, who had posted it on her page, and she explained where she got it."

"Okay. I didn't expect anyone to find me."

Ted looked at me and asked, "Do you know about Facebook?"

"I've heard of it, but I'm not sure what it is."

He told me it didn't matter, and that it ended up being pretty easy to find me. He asked if I had been following the news, and I said not really. He explained there had been a big collapse in the real estate market.

I said, "Yes, I know. I'd heard some before I—" I paused, not sure how to say it. "It was in the news before I left."

"Things have gotten worse in the time you've been gone."

I gestured around me, and said, "This isn't a place where anyone is much worried about real estate values."

He explained that I'd lost everything, and he'd lost nearly everything.

"You're my agent. Aren't you in a position to control my accounts and property?" I asked like I knew, but I really wasn't sure.

He said, "I tried and did what I could. But the bank took the house, and most everything has been auctioned off. There's nothing to go back to. It's all gone."

I asked, "What about my paintings?"

He said, "I'm holding some of your work, what I already had in the gallery. But everything was stolen from your studio. It's gone."

"Stolen?"

"Yeah. At first the police thought you might have done it, but that didn't make sense."

I asked, "What do you mean?"

"Whoever did it was too thorough. They took everything. I was there with the police. We spent a lot of time in your studio, and they asked a lot of questions. Your paints and brushes, all your files, all of it was gone. It must have involved a team and a moving truck. I told them you would've never been so determined."

I was mystified. In my heart I didn't really care, but I tried to make some sense of it.

He said, "Most of the big homes in the development where you lived are now either empty or for sale. The prices fell to a ridiculous low point, way below what they were valued at a few months ago, but nobody has the money to buy them. It's the whole country."

I asked, "How are you doing?"

He laughed and said, "Terrible."

He explained that his wife and kids had moved to a smaller place out of town. The gallery was still open, but nobody was buying, and without sales he couldn't pay the rent. He'd probably lose that, too.

We sat in silence for a long time. I thought I should do some paintings and give them to him. I knew exactly what would sell, and maybe this could help him out. I could easily paint a few oversized canvases with garish sunsets over hot pink mesas. But even as I had the thought, I knew I'd never do anything.

Ted changed the subject, "I found a little about the mysterious character who bought your painting."

"How did you find him?"

"He found me. I got a call from some guy, and he told me he represented an art buyer, and he wanted to know about you. I said you were missing, and it was a police matter. He knew that, and he said he was interested in investing in the art market. We talked for a few minutes, and it didn't add up. I could tell he was lying about something. I told him I'm not talking to a middle man, tell your boss to call me. He back-peddled like it was no big deal and kept pressing me. I said tell your boss to call me, and I hung up."

Ted leaned forward like we were in some kind of spy movie.

"About two minutes later, the phone rang, and I'm talking to the guy who bought your painting. He asked a lot of questions about you. He wanted to know where you were."

"What did you say?"

"I lied. I told him you went to a hospital. I hinted you were drying out after a binge. I didn't know what else to say."

I shrugged and said, "Okay, fair enough. Did he believe you?"

"I don't think so."

"What else did he say?"

"Not a lot. We didn't talk long. He gave me his name and phone number, and we said goodbye. I wrote it all down, and the detective looked into it. The phone number rang, but nobody answered. There's an art trader in New York with a very similar name, but it wasn't the same guy. I called him, and he had a different voice."

I could tell he was nervous about all this, and I didn't want anything from my life, my own strangeness, to impact him. I tried to dismiss it all by saying, "Well, whoever it is, I hope he got his money's worth."

Ted asked, "Have you been drinking?"

"Not a drop."

"Can I do anything for you?"

"I don't know. Just do what you can to make sure I'm left alone."

I asked about his wife and kids. He told me his wife was really upset when I went missing. He said, "John, she's heartbroken. She adores you. She thought something terrible had happened, and she cried a lot, and right now, I don't know what to tell her."

I looked down at the patio tiles. I said, "Tell her she was right to worry, but that I'm doing okay, and that I'm sorry."

He said, "I will."

I didn't know what to say. He put his elbows on the table and rubbed his forehead like he was in pain. I waited for him to say something.

"John, I feel like I know you pretty well, and I know you suffer. But you need to understand there are people who care about you. Please know, you are connected to so much."

I heard him. I heard every word. And I wanted to tell him, "You have no fucking idea what I'm connected to, and how messed up it's gotten." But I didn't say anything. I stared down at the tiles by my feet and thought about how I'd be sweeping them tomorrow morning.

He eventually said, "My wife will be relieved you're okay. She'll understand, and she won't say anything."

I asked if he needed any more coffee. He said he had a long drive to get back home, and that would help. We got up and went into the shop. He stood looking up at the chalkboard menu as I made him a double espresso. I didn't need to ask him anything. I knew what he wanted.

I slid it across the counter to him. He pointed to the chalkboard and said, "John, that's really beautiful."

I said, "Thank you," but I couldn't look at him.

19

I was in the alley and didn't know how I got there. I was barefoot and could feel pebbles under my feet. It was cold, and I was alone on the asphalt between my shed and the back door of the coffee shop. Everything was normal, but I didn't understand what had happened.

I looked over, and the lights were off in the shed. Had I walked in my sleep and woken up out here? It was quiet, but that was normal here. This was different, like every bit of sound had been sucked away to nothing.

I had this feeling I wasn't alone, and I turned around and she was there, right in the middle of the alley. She was facing me. She was closer than I had ever seen her, and something wasn't right. She looked so skinny, and I worried something was wrong with her. She almost seemed like an insect. I stared at her, and she tilted her head.

There was something huge above me, but I couldn't look up. I just knew it was there, some empty void. Then I was floating, I had that elevator-up feeling, and it happened fast. I guess I should've tried to scream, but I didn't do anything. All I could do was look at the ground as it raced away below me.

I opened my eyes. I was on the cot in my little shed. It didn't feel like I had slept. It was like I'd barely blinked, and now I was awake on my back and looking up at the window.

I sat up and looked out at the alley. She had been there, standing there, looking at me, just seconds ago. *She had been right there.*

I got up and walked outside, and it all seemed perfectly normal. It was still cold, and the pebbles under my feet felt exactly the same. The sky above me was endless and empty, and it seemed impossible anything could've been there.

What I'd seen and felt was impossible. The sun would be up soon, and I hoped the memories of the girl would fade away with the shadows.

I walked over to where she stood and looked down at the asphalt about where her feet would have been. I tried to find some footprint or disturbance, but there was nothing to see. The brightness of the day would soon hide all this. I needed to push away these fucked up thoughts and forget all of it.

I saw the lights come on in the coffee shop. Tony was there. He must have entered through the front door, something he rarely does. I was barefoot, wearing only shorts and a t-shirt. I went back in the shed and changed. Then I walked across the alley, got the key from above the electrical box, opened the back door, and went in.

Tony said good morning, but all I could do was nod. Our routine had been running smoothly, and we each set about our tasks. Yet, I was terribly shaken, and it was hard to hide. I didn't say much, and he didn't press me on anything. He made coffee, and I started the oven. Mixing everything and prepping for the baking felt good. I could get lost in the routine. Before long there were people at the counter and dishes to wash. I kept busy even when there wasn't much to do.

There was a point before lunch when the shop was empty, and I asked, "Could I leave early today?"

He said, "Sure, I can manage everything."

I told him I wouldn't be in tomorrow, and probably the day after, too. He said that was fine, then asked, "Is everything okay?"

I couldn't tell him I woke up in the alley and got sucked into a big black void. Instead, I asked if I could take some of the leftovers, and he said, "Sure, go ahead."

I asked, "There's some rope in the back room. Can I use it?"

His face changed, and he looked at me with deep concern. I put up my hands with my palms facing him, and almost laughed. "No. Tony, it's not that. I want to use it for a few days in the backcountry."

His expression softened, "Sure, of course."

I asked if I could take some of the unsold breakfast items, and he gave me a thumbs up. I filled a paper bag with muffins and cheese burritos. I took the rope from the wall of the back room and walked out the door to the alley. It was hot, and all I could think about was drinking the cold water from the spring in that canyon. I had been thinking about it for days. I needed to sleep under the tree on the little island.

It was a little after noon, and that meant about eight more hours of daylight. I figured I could get there even if it meant walking the last few hours in the dark.

I pulled three crinkly water bottles from the shop's recycle bin, filled these from the sink, and put them in my backpack. I added the bag of food, a blanket, and the black plastic tarp. I also put in some warmer clothes, sunblock, a toothbrush, a little headlamp, and the rope.

I put on my hat, walked to the main street, and headed east. I stumbled into this town after navigating a crumbly maze of cliffs. That was brutal, and I didn't want to repeat the route going back up.

I saw a better option the first time I looked east from the main street. From the edge of the town, you could see a gentle ramp of sandstone rising from close to the highway. It was like the tail of a giant alligator, and walking along its spine looked like a much easier way to get back up to the high country.

I figured I could thumb a ride at the east end of the main street. I've hitchhiked a lot, and it was nearly impossible back east or in California, but in this part of the country I almost always got picked up by the first car. It was normal enough that I expected it, and if it didn't happen I worried something was wrong. If nobody picked me up, it would have been easy enough to walk the highway for a few miles. I went past the edge of town and listened.

20

I HEARD A CAR BEHIND ME and put out my thumb. An old Subaru wagon slowed and stopped next to me. Two young women were in the car, one in the front seat and one behind her. I opened the passenger door and said, "Thank you," took off my hat and got in. I set my pack between my feet and my hat on top. I said I only needed to go a few miles.

The woman driving said, "No problem."

She told me her name, but she talked so fast I didn't catch it. I wanted to ask her to repeat it, but that would mean interrupting. When I finally got the chance to ask, she said, "I know, I know, everyone acts that way. My dad gave me a weird name. Just call me Ellie."

I turned to say hello to the woman in the back seat and was caught off guard—it was the same person. Ellie must've seen my expression and said, "Yeah, that's my sister Maia. We're twins."

They both had straight black hair cut a little above their shoulders, and pale skin, and each had the same little glasses. Ellie had this fiery way of talking, like she was incredibly excited about every word. She pointed to a row of photos taped to the dashboard and said, "We have five other sisters." She pointed to each picture and told me their names, but with the windows down and the road noise, I couldn't follow much. All the pictures looked similar, young women with straight black hair.

The windows were down, so she needed to talk loud over the noise of the wind. She sort of shouted, "Sorry, the air conditioning is broke, and I haven't gotten it fixed."

I said, "That's fine. No need to apologize."

I turned and looked at her sister in the back seat, and she wasn't paying any attention to our conversation. It looked like her hands were cupped around something in her lap. I tried to listen to Ellie in the driver's seat, but I was curious what her twin was holding.

Then I saw a tiny bird poke its head up from her cupped hands. I blurted out, "You have a little bird!"

Ellie said, "Yeah, Maia has a hummingbird," and kept talking.

I was astonished. All I could see was its little green head peeking out and looking around. It was cute and seemed perfectly content, even with the windows open and the hot, desert air rolling through the car. There was something so focused about Maia and the way she cupped her hands. Her gentle presence was absolutely saintly.

When I turned to look forward there was a strong *whump*, and Ellie flinched. Something slapped the back window hard. She jammed on the brakes and cried out, "Oh God, I hit something!"

I looked behind me, and Maia was cowering against the door with an expression of total shock. Her arms were wrapped close to her chest, trying to protect the hummingbird. As we slowed, I saw a set of huge wings awkwardly rise up behind the back seat. Something big was in the hatchback.

I shouted, "Stop the car! Stop the car!"

We pulled over, and I jumped out and ran around to the back. I was astonished to see a beautiful great-horned owl. It stared at me through the rear window with huge yellow eyes.

Maia was peering over the back seat at the owl, and I was trying to open the hatchback, but the latch above the license plate didn't work. By that point, Ellie was next to me and gasped, "Holy mother fuck! That's an owl!"

I said, "This won't open."

"Fuck! It's broken. I need the key."

She darted back to the driver's door while I stared at the owl. We locked eyes, and it was like electricity drilling into my soul. It was only a few seconds, but it felt like an hour before she returned and worked to get the key in the lock. Her hands were shaking, and she stammered, "Jesus. C'mon."

The key slid in, she turned it, and the hatchback popped up about an inch. We both stepped back. I grabbed the corner and asked, "Are you ready?"

She anxiously stammered, "Yes, yes, yes."

The old hatchback creaked as I eased it up. We both moved away as it opened. I'm not sure what I expected, but the owl stayed still. Unlike us, it seemed perfectly calm.

Ellie asked, "Maia, are you okay?"

Her sister nodded from the back seat. Then we all waited. The owl was a little over a foot tall and stood peacefully in the mess of luggage and duffles in the hatchback. Maia's eyes were wide with emotion, staring over the edge of the back seat.

Then, in one smooth motion, the owl turned its head around and looked back at Maia. I knew exactly what she was feeling. I could see her eyes, and I understood. She was connecting somehow, just as I had. The owl stood perfectly still with its head twisted backwards, and her face was barely a foot away. They were locked in a hypnotic trance.

Ellie broke the silence, "C'mon, Sis, it's okay."

Maia blinked and looked up at us. Then the owl slowly turned its head forward and shook itself like a cat waking up. It waddled to the opening, hopped up on the edge of the hatch, then dropped onto the pavement. The owl landed between us and we stepped aside, like some formal ritual when confronting royalty.

The owl looked up at us, leaned forward, and casually opened its wings. I was thunderstruck. They seemed impossibly large. It snapped them once, and that was enough to rise up and fly a few inches above the road. Then it flapped again, rose in a long graceful curve, and landed gently on top of a telephone pole.

Ellie said, "Holy shit, that was fucking intense."

Her statement was like a sigh of relief, and I asked, "What happened?"

She said, "I don't know. It flew in the car somehow. I think through the back window, behind you. I saw a blur and heard it."

I said, "I didn't see anything, but I could feel it before it hit. We were going like fifty miles an hour, and that seems insane."

Ellie went to Maia's window, leaned over and quietly asked, "Are you okay?" Her sister nodded.

"And your hummingbird? She's okay, too?" Again, she nodded.

I looked at the back window, and there was a ghostly impression on the inside of the glass. I said, "Look at this. You can see where the owl hit the glass."

Ellie came closer, and we tried to figure out what had happened. Both of us needed to bend forward and twist ourselves to look up at the glass. Then I eased the hatch lower so we could look at it from the outside. There was a faint imprint of what seemed like talcum powder. I reached under and touched the dust with my fingertip.

She said, "It's like it's staring at us."

She was right. You could clearly see the face of the owl, its eyes and beak, and on each side, its outstretched wings. The owl had slammed hard into the glass of the hatchback and somehow left its ghostly imprint. I realized that since we stopped, not a single car had driven by in either direction. Ellie and I looked up at the owl on the telephone pole, and it looked down at us.

Ellie pointed and said, "That pole isn't connected to anything, it's just there alone. The other poles are across the road, and those all have wires on them."

Again, she was right. It was the only one on this side of the highway. I said, "Maybe it's an old pole that nobody took down."

This lone pole had a single, short cross post a foot or so below where the owl was perched, and nothing else. We talked about how strange this was, and I realized the car was aligned with the tail of the alligator, the giant feature I'd seen from the main street. It rose out of the sand a few yards away from the highway. The exposed rock eased upward in a long, gentle grade. We were parked right where I needed to be.

I took my pack out from the front seat and explained that this was as far as I needed to go. I would walk from here. We talked a little longer. It was like the power of what happened was still ringing like a gong, and neither of us wanted to let go of the moment.

Ellie was about to close the hatch and said, "There's blood back here."

I saw a few drops of bright red blood on one of the duffels. We looked around and found more. There wasn't much, but the owl was obviously bleeding. We turned and looked up to the top of the post, and it sat in perfect majesty.

I thanked Ellie and walked around to the back seat, and said, "Goodbye, Maia. You take care of your little hummingbird, okay?"

She nodded. There was something so gentle about her.

I put on my hat and made my way across the sand and weeds to the open rock. I could hear Ellie talking to her sister, and she was obviously still amped up from everything with the owl. I heard the car doors slam and the engine start. I was walking slowly when the horn honked.

I stopped and turned. Maia got out of the back seat and passed something through the driver's window. She handed the hummingbird to her sister, then came around the car and started running towards me. I hadn't walked very far, and I stood there and watched. She ran in this awkward way, like her legs were too long and she wasn't used to them yet. She got to where I stood and stopped. She looked at me, her eyes heavy with concern. Then she stepped forward and hugged me. I put my arms around her. I'm not sure how long it lasted, but her anguish was palpable.

She eventually let go and took a half step back. I waited for her to say something, and she turned and ran in that same funny way back to the car. She stood for a little while by the driver's window, took her hummingbird, and got in the back seat. Her sister put her hand out the window and waved above the roof. Then they drove up the highway. It was a long, straight road that seemed to stretch on forever. I watched as their little car slowly disappeared in the distance. Then I looked at the owl, still perched atop the pole.

I said, "I'm sorry, my friend. I hope you'll be all right."

I turned and continued up the hill. I looked back only once, and the owl was gone.

21

I WAS WALKING AGAIN. The steady motion of one foot in front of the other seemed to shut something down in me. I wanted to disengage the chugging cogs in my brain.

Walking up the ramp was straightforward and pretty much matched what I had imagined from the edge of town, which almost never happens. This gentle spine of rock would lead me back to the high country, and I felt prepared. I still didn't have much, but the few extras on my back eliminated so many worries. I was glad to have the extra water and rope. I don't understand my need for this kind of extreme escape, but it's in me and I have to feed it.

I wore the same shoes and hat as the lonesome odyssey that brought me to this town. Instead of jeans, I wore a pair of baggy chinos from Betty's store, and these, together with a nylon belt, set me back a dollar. I had a similar snap button shirt, but it was pale blue plaid. I also had a pocket knife, a lighter, chapstick, extra socks, and thin wool gloves—all from her store.

After a few hours, the uphill travel eased off, and I walked onto a grand plateau. Every direction felt like infinity—the sky, the horizon, and even the rock beneath my feet. It all seemed endless. I didn't know how long it would take to find the entrance to my canyon, but I wasn't worried. If it didn't happen tonight, I could sleep up here and keep looking when the sun came up.

The terrain was open but not level. It was the weird rolling sandstone that makes up a lot of this country. It's like walking on a frozen ocean. A low point is like being between the waves, and a higher spot might offer a view, but all the waves end up blending together. I could pick a feature off in the distance, a high bluff or something, and this allowed a way to keep a line of travel. But there was no way to truly know where I was or where I was going. I was alone at sea.

I moved across this stark terrain and stopped at a high point. I was looking for the slot canyon I'd emerged from, and that would be west of where I stood. I had a vague idea of where I was in relation to the highway and town below me. The sun was lower, and this gave me a fix on west, but that wasn't enough. Hopefully, I'd see something I remembered and could use it to find the slot, but I didn't recognize anything.

By most anyone's definition, I was lost. Yet that's what I wanted. I needed to be adrift. The day had been tough. Seeing the girl again and then trying to do something normal like wash dishes was so hard. There was a grave disconnect. Nothing fit or made sense. I needed to walk and be lost, to shut down my thoughts and give myself over to the land. I wanted to abandon myself to the silence, but so much had happened I couldn't turn off my mind. It was screaming at me.

I tried to shut it all out and just walk, but it wasn't working. One of my socks kept slipping down in my shoe, and I've always hated that feeling. I had another pair in my pack, but didn't have it in me to stop and find them.

This used to happen while walking to elementary school in the rain, and I remember how annoying it felt when they slid under my heels. Something about my wet cotton sneakers made it impossible to keep those cheap tube socks pulled up. A neighbor down the block had this low brick wall along the sidewalk that held a little flower garden, and Katie Kellie would sit with me as I worked to get my socks back up again.

I can still feel how sticky they were, and how angry I got. But she didn't seem bothered at all—I got emotional while she stayed calm. I remember she talked about the color of the flowers in the rain, and how they seemed so bright on such a gray morning. The raindrops would sit like perfect little glass beads on the violet pedals, and Katie would point them out like they were the most beautiful thing she had ever seen.

We both wore long yellow raincoats. They were rubber and clammy. We'd walk, and I'd need to stop to pull my socks up, and five steps later they were down in my shoes again. I'd get so frustrated, and she would punch me in the arm. It wasn't much, just her way of saying, "Hey, this moment now."

I stepped across a thin crack in the sandstone and stopped. I smelled something. I got down on all fours and put my nose to the crack. It was barely half an inch wide, and I could sense cold moisture. I'd found it.

I stood up and started south. I knew this crack. As I followed, it got wider and pitched off to almost nothing, then opened up again. At points, I could peer down into the slot, but there was nothing to see, only darkness. Eventually, I came to the spot that had worried me, the deep round hole in the slickrock. This was where I had jammed the skull into the crack.

Looking across this huge hollow shaft, I could see the crack I had climbed up, and the platform near the top where I had laid on my stomach. I got as close as I dared to the edge, but couldn't see the bottom. This big shaft into the earth was creepy, and I backed away.

I walked around the huge opening and continued along the thin fissure in the surface of the slickrock. It wasn't very far along the surface before I recognized the spot where I'd climbed out.

I didn't pause. I scrambled down into the crack. The sky was gone, and I was back in the confine of deep red rock. It was only a short stretch of easy travel through the narrow slot, and I was back on the small platform, the spot I had seen from above just a few minutes ago.

I peered over the edge and looked down into that hollow chimney of stone. I was scared.

I took off my pack, got out the rope, and uncoiled it at my feet. I turned my back to the open shaft and saw what I remembered. There was a block of stone pinched in a crack. It was about eye level and an arm's length deep. I reached in and felt the rock. It was about the size of a shoebox and wedged tight in the back of the crack. I took one of the ends of the rope and fed it around the block and tied it off.

I picked up the coils of rope and tossed them off the edge. I peered over but couldn't see if the tail made it all the way down. I shook the rope and saw the end swing out. I only saw it for a second, and it wasn't touching the sand. I'd been worried the whole walk up here that the rope would be too short. I sensed it was close, but didn't know if it would get me all the way to the bottom.

It was about fifty feet down, maybe more, and the steepest part was at the bottom. I held the rope tight and leaned out over the edge, but it felt thin in my hands, and I realized that trying to shimmy down that far would never work.

I pulled it back up and stacked it at my feet. Then starting at the tail, I tied a knot about every three feet, and when I was done, I threw the rope off again. I looked over the edge again, but the end was hidden under the overhang near the bottom. The knots had used up some length, and I hoped there would still be enough to make it all the way down.

I drank some water, put on my pack and eased my way off the edge. I grabbed each knot, one after another, and tried to walk down backwards. I wish I could say I performed with the grace of a seasoned alpinist, but I floundered the whole way down.

The angle got steeper the lower I got, and my shoes started skidding on the rock. I needed my arms more, and gripping the rope hurt. I knew the skull was somewhere below me. I had to stop and rest my hands, but I kept going and held tight, moving from knot to knot.

When I got to the skull, I put my foot on it and steadied myself. I needed it. Leaning in, I put all my weight on that foot, and took a few deep breaths. My face was pressed up against the rock, and my arm and shoulder were wedged in the crack. I shook the rope and saw the tail swinging in the air, still a long ways up from the bottom. There were only a few knots left under the one I was holding.

The pack made standing there awkward, and I needed to keep moving. I leaned out, took my foot off the skull, and slid my hands down to the next knot. Then the next. My feet skated down the face, and I fought to keep steady. Then the last knot. I had jumped from around here before, so I kicked myself away from the wall and let go.

I landed in the sand. I looked up and the last knot on the rope's tail was about the level of the skull, so I knew I could get back out. A longer rope would have been better, but I was grateful it hadn't been shorter.

I realized I was standing on the bones, and stepped back. It looked like a little bit of new sand had blown in from above and covered part of him, but his ribs were plainly visible. I couldn't leave him here like this. I reached in and pulled up on the jacket, working to get him out of the sand. The spine was still attached to the hips, and I cleared the sand away from his pants and pulled those out, too. After a little work I had the entire body on the surface—well, except for his head.

I dragged him to the side, away from the bottom of the crack. There wasn't much to him, and his clean white skeleton was mostly held together by the clothes. I scooped out a shallow trench, slid him in, then covered the body in sand one handful at a time. It wasn't much of a burial, but it was the best I could do without a shovel. Before leaving, I looked up at the skull, bowed, and said a quiet thank you.

I started down the slot. Without the rope, my pack was lighter, and the sand on the floor was damp and flat. I'd get an occasional glimpse of the sky as I moved, and I knew the light wouldn't last much longer. Burying the body had taken up a lot of time, and I quickened my pace. I wanted some distance behind me before pulling out the headlamp. There's an anxiety that comes with the setting sun and walking, yet it all goes away once it's dark. I've been through this many times.

It wasn't long before I came to a short drop through some blocky boulders. I stopped, put on my headlamp, and kept moving. Climbing down was pretty easy, but I needed the light. I came up this way before and knew the travel would be fine. It was musty and stale, and for the next bunch of hours, my world was nothing but two cold walls and the floor, all of it framed in a haunting pool of light from my headlamp. Everything else was nothingness.

At times, I could see my footprints from when I came up from the bottom, and it was reassuring to have something familiar in the dark. I walked and walked, further and deeper. Then I felt the temperature drop, and a few steps later I was out of the slot and pushing through willows. Then I walked in tall grass.

I was back. Even in the dark, the air was sweet with life.

I walked to the river and stepped in without pausing. The water was cold enough that it had a jolt. I made my way up the middle of the stream, and the sounds of the water seemed rich and alive. It had been a bright hot day when I was here before, but I felt the same sense of magic, even by headlamp. I waded upstream past the island, around the corner, and up to the spring. I put my mouth to it and drank. Dear God, it was good to be here again.

22

I DRANK AS MUCH AS I COULD, then filled the three water bottles from the pouring spring. I walked slowly back out to the open part of the canyon and then to the island. I stepped up onto the sand and sat near the tree. I took off my wet shoes and socks and set them under the branches. These wouldn't fully dry this close to the water, but I could carry them in the morning and cross the river barefoot.

I opened my pack, tipped it over, and dumped everything onto the sand. This is the easiest way to deal with finding stuff. I put on my wool sweater and then my wind shirt. I took off the pants and hung them in the tree. I brought a thin pair of long underwear and put them on. These would be a lot more comfortable to sleep in than wet pants. I set my hat on the grass, found the wool ski cap, and put it on.

I sat and ate two cold burritos and two cranberry muffins. I wiggled my toes in the cool sand as I chewed. The only noise was the faint trickle of the spring whispering from around the corner. I was completely at peace.

I walked around the island looking for a flat spot to sleep. I would see an area that seemed okay, kneel down and inspect it. If it wasn't level, I moved on. Everything sloped gently down from the tree to the water, and I wasn't going to spend the night tipped on an angle. I probably circled the island three times until I found the perfect spot. It was close to the tree, along the widest part of the river.

I carefully laid out the tarp and the blanket. I took everything out of my pack, and put it in a plastic grocery bag. There wasn't much. I was wearing most of it. Then I partially filled the pack with sand, scooping it in with my hands, then set it in place as my pillow. I spun around. I thought I saw something in the tree, a glint of light. It might have been some kind of a reflection from my headlamp. I stared at the tree for a long time, but there was nothing.

The rectangle where I would sleep was as wide as my shoulders, and as long as I was tall. It was hardly anything, but for tonight, this would be the most sacred place on Earth. I aligned myself in the center of the blanket and pulled both sides over me, and then the tarp over that. I turned off my headlamp and laid it in the sand near my shoulder. Then I took my time and tucked the edges of the tarp under each side, carefully wrapping myself in a cocoon. Finally, I set my head on my pack.

With the light off, I was hit with the magnitude of where I lay. I was looking straight up, and the only thing to see was a glorious arching strip of stars. Everything else was perfect blackness. My body aligned with the long, narrow crescent of open sky, a bright blue-violet flooded with stars. There was no way to comprehend the scale, yet the enormity was mind-bending.

My day had been difficult, and lying here was something beautiful, a sort of ritual of solace. I needed to honor this moment and surrender to the sand and sky. I took a deep breath and spoke aloud, "Okay, Universe, I need to ask something of you." My words echoed softly off the walls.

"I don't understand what's been happening or what it means, but I know it's real. I want to declare that I am open and receptive to whatever you have to offer me."

Right as I finished saying those words, a bright orange dot slowly slid across the sky. The open stripe of the canyon was so narrow that it passed out of view before I could make sense of what I saw.

I was baffled. My first thought was some sort of satellite. I've seen plenty of tiny dots traverse the night sky, and those all have a similar look, but what I saw was entirely different. The dot was much bigger, and its color was unusually rich and vibrant.

All it did was move across the sliver of visible sky, but the movement wasn't normal. It was like one of those little water bugs that skim across the surface of a pond, slipping sideways in an odd liquid motion.

I wanted to keep looking at the sky, but the gentle sound of the river was hypnotizing. I inhaled, long and slow, and before I could finish exhaling, I dropped into a deep, hard sleep.

I was still facing straight up when I woke. I hadn't moved since lying down, and I stayed still, looking up and drinking in the view. There were just as many stars within the opening above, but the sky beyond was no longer the same deep violet. It was now nearly black, almost the same tone as the hidden walls. I was warm in the blanket, and felt completely rested. I had become a part of this magnificent place.

Then I sensed something. The stillness was changing. I felt something inside me, an awareness. The feeling was subtle and slowly expanding. Then it was all around me, throbbing in a low vibration. I lay motionless as it slowly got louder. It was a steady thumping. At some point, I realized it was a helicopter, and it was getting closer. I stayed still and listened.

Then it passed across the open sky, exactly as the orange dot had done, and I was shocked at how small it looked.

It was much louder for the brief moment it was in view, and then the noise dropped off. I could feel it circling above, its pitch changing and distorting around the canyon walls.

Then it got louder, and the helicopter slowly eased back into view. It floated in the center of the void, and a set of bright lights came on, shining in several directions. I lay there, my head on my pillow of sand, and watched it slowly descend between the giant walls.

I sat up, mystified by what was happening. I was scared the canyon was too narrow for a helicopter, yet it continued lower. The huge walls above me were lit up in bright moving pools. It got lower and louder. The helicopter had a bunch of lights, but one was white hot and scanning the walls. Then that beam pointed down and locked in on the grassy beach across from me.

The light hurt my eyes, and the roaring pounded off the walls to the point of pain. It moved in and hovered above the beach. The rotors blasted the river, and I was hit with a spray of cold water.

The helicopter hovered a few inches above the shaking grass, then set itself down with a gentleness that seemed impossible. The wet mist gave way to a brilliant twinkling reflection on the river between me and the helicopter.

Eventually, the booming power of the rotors began to calm down, and the descending drone was like a grand sigh from the canyon itself. I was sitting upright, still wrapped in my black plastic cocoon, as the noise and wind eased away. The lights stayed on, and I stared at the dazzling sight as everything slowed. I sat still for a long time, the thunder still echoing inside me.

Then the door opened, and Katie Kellie stepped out and onto the sand.

PART TWO

23

THE DOCTOR STARED AT ME. He blinked a few times, then pulled a handkerchief out of his jacket pocket and took off his glasses. He cleaned both lenses and exhaled a few times on each. When he finally put them back on, he set them in place with exceptional care.

Then he leaned forward and asked, "Let me get this straight. Katie Kellie, your friend from across the street, got out of the helicopter?"

I nodded and said, "Yes."

His eyes narrowed, "And what did you do?"

"I sat there and watched."

He asked, "What were you thinking?"

"Well, that's not easy to say. I should have been shocked. But right then, as it was happening, it all felt normal. Like, perfectly ordinary."

He waited for more, but I didn't say anything else. Finally, he asked, "What happened next?"

"After a little bit, other doors opened, and two men got out and walked around on the beach. They seemed busy, but I wasn't paying much attention to them. Katie just stood there. I got up, and this was all in a sort of slow motion, or more like, I don't know, a weird clarity. I took off my wool hat, pulled my long underwear up over my knees, and walked into the water. She didn't see me until I was almost to her side of the river. When she saw me, she smiled. She recognized me right away."

The doctor raised his eyebrows in an expression of doubt.

I said, "I know. Believe me, I know."

He sat up, struck a more wistful pose, and said, "Please, go on."

"I was still in the water, but close enough to say, 'Hello, Katie,' without raising my voice. I walked onto the beach, and we hugged. It was a quick sort of polite hug. I felt uneasy. I was dirty and barefoot and standing there in wet long underwear. And she looked so beautiful."

He leaned forward and said, "Go on."

"She introduced me to the other people from the helicopter."

The doctor asked, "Did anyone think it was weird that you just walked out of the river and that Katie knew you?"

"Nope."

I could see him thinking, and he asked, "What else happened?"

I smiled and said, "I got a helicopter ride back to town."

I don't think the doctor believed me. Maybe he did, but the look on his face wasn't very assuring. He looked at his little recorder and said, "Please give me a moment."

He reached down alongside his chair and brought his briefcase onto the table. He opened it and searched around. He took out a little cassette and switched it out with the one in the recorder.

He put the briefcase back on the floor, set the recorder between us, and started it. He looked at me for a long time, staring into my eyes. I waited, thinking he would say something profound, but after an awkward silence, he simply said, "Please, go on."

I took a deep breath and tried to explain how strange it all felt. Watching that helicopter land across from me was like reliving a dream. The power and noise in that narrow canyon was almost too much to bear. After it landed, it took forever for the sound to fade, and the door didn't open until everything was silent. The helicopter had lights all over it, and from my side of the river, it was like a brightly lit stage in a dark theater.

When Katie stepped out, I recognized her immediately. I hadn't seen her since we were twelve, but she stood the same way—tall and strong. Her thick red hair was tied back, but some of it fell across her forehead and onto her shoulders. She wore a short khaki jacket, black jeans, and low leather boots.

I was worried I'd scare her, so I moved slowly across the river. Her back was to me when I stepped into the water, but she turned and faced me when I was about halfway across. When she saw me, I stopped. She squinted and tipped her head, as if she wasn't sure what she was seeing, but that was only a second. Then she smiled and marched to the water's edge. She was backlit by the helicopter lights, a silhouette facing me, with both hands on her heart.

I was still in the water when she opened her arms and said, "Oh, John."

I stepped out of the river and hugged her. My mouth was near her ear and I whispered, "Hello, Katie."

I know I said it was a polite hug, but that's not quite true. We held each other for a while, and it was emotional. When we eased apart, she smiled and grabbed my hands. She called over the two men from the helicopter and told them, "This is John. We grew up together."

I nodded, but I'm not sure if I smiled. I was still adrift in that overwhelming feeling of peace. It hadn't left me since I first lay down on the island. I said, "Katie and I are good friends."

She laughed and looked at her comrades, "And don't call me Katie, only John gets that honor. It's Katherine for everyone else on earth, especially you two."

She stood close to me, and I held out my hand as one man came right up to me and said, "Wow, John, great to meet you. I'm Tim. Wow, this is awesome."

He seemed really happy and vigorously shook my hand, pumping it up and down, patting my shoulder with his other hand. He wore a light blue button-down dress shirt, and pressed slacks. His shirt was tucked in, and he had a black leather belt. He wore high-top nylon hiking shoes, which seemed out of place with the rest of his attire.

The pilot approached me, and he was much less enthusiastic. He also shook my hand, but with a firm, measured grip. He said, "Hello," and not much more.

He wore a one-piece flight suit. It was olive green without any insignia or markings, and he had what looked like military-issue desert boots. He seemed preoccupied and, after shaking hands, walked around to the other side of the helicopter and opened one of the doors. A second later, most of the lights went off. The ones still on weren't nearly as bright, and now the area felt somber.

Tim asked, "Where were you? We didn't see anyone."

I turned and pointed into the darkness and said, "I was sleeping on that little island out there."

He smiled and looked out at the river, "Wow, really? You were camping there?"

I said, "Yes." From where we stood and the way the lights were shining, you could see the tree and the grass, but you couldn't tell it was an island. It looked like a little peninsula up against the canyon wall.

All this was terribly strange. We were making small talk like we'd met in the parking lot of a grocery store. I was sort of dazed and don't think I said much.

Katie turned away from Tim and the pilot and faced me. She asked, "Are you still drawing?"

I nodded, "Yes, I still draw a lot."

"Oh, that's wonderful. I'm so glad to hear that. You were so talented, and I've always hoped you kept at it."

I said, "Thank you," and she asked where I lived. I said, "In a very small town a little bit north of here."

The two men were gone, and I hadn't noticed them walking away. I tried to ask Katie things, like what she'd been doing and how her life was. She smiled and didn't answer much, deflecting my questions in an agreeable way. I saw the pilot and Tim walking around past the helicopter in the tall grass, but I was focused on Katie.

I asked if she ever got married or had any children, and she said, "No." This was the one point when I noticed her smile fade, and I didn't press her on it.

At some point, the pilot interrupted us and said, "We should get going."

Katie held my arm and asked, "Do you want a ride out of here? We're going to a little town near here." She said the name of it and asked if that's where I was living.

I said, "Sure," and she smiled in an easy way. This was exactly how I remembered her, steady and confident.

She said, "Good. We can take you there. Is that okay?"

I told her I needed a minute to get my things.

"Sure, do you need help?"

"No, I'm fine. Keep your feet dry."

"Do you need light? We can give you a flashlight, or point one of the lights out across the water for you."

I said, "There's no need. I'll be fine."

I walked back across the river and packed up my stuff, and it didn't take long. The last thing I put in the pack were the three full water bottles. I stood and looked back across the river, and saw them talking together. I couldn't hear anything, but I had to wonder. I was suddenly hit with a sinking feeling. Something didn't seem right, and it scared me.

I hung my backpack off one shoulder, carried my shoes in one hand, and my hat in the other. I walked back to them, and when I saw Katie's smile, all my fears melted away.

I put on my chinos over my long underwear, then sat on the ground and put on my socks and shoes. This took some time because my feet were wet and sandy. Katie knelt next to me as I tied my laces. She didn't say anything. She just looked at me and smiled. This wasn't at all awkward. It felt entirely sincere.

We had been facing the river, and when I stood up, Tim and the pilot were both waiting alongside the helicopter. We joined them and all climbed aboard. They were in the front seats, and Katie and I sat behind them. The pilot turned around and handed me a headset. Once it was on, he told me how to use it. Katie helped me buckle the seat belts.

The pilot sat directly in front of me, so I couldn't see much of what he was doing. The rotors started spinning, and all the lights outside got switched back on. Tim leaned around, looked back at us with raised eyebrows, and gave an exaggerated thumbs-up. I looked at Katie, who was hidden behind his seat, and she sort of rolled her eyes.

The lights in the cabin went off, and everything outside seemed brighter. The pilot's voice buzzed through the headset, "Okay, here goes."

I blurted out, "Please, be careful."

I couldn't help myself. His voice cracked back, "I'm not gonna hit anything."

He sounded annoyed. Then the rotors spun faster, everything got a lot louder, and we floated up off the sand.

Katie grabbed my hand. My first thought was that she was scared. But when I looked at her, she was clearly trying to comfort me. She was composed and grinning, tipping her head as if trying to see me better.

Outside, the grass whipped around, and the river was a mess of ripples and spray. Then the red walls slowly rolled by, lit by pools of hot white light. I had never been on a helicopter before, and it was much smoother than I would have guessed.

Looking forward, I saw a series of colorful screens for the pilot. From what I could tell, these displayed the distance between us and the canyon walls. Our upward progress was steady. The sandstone walls out the windows looked like vertical conveyor belts, rolling downward in slow motion.

It was impossible to comprehend the size of everything around us. It felt like we were riding a little toy inside some stretched out diorama. The bright lights on the walls created a weird sensation. The enormous sculpted surface seemed to ease away and pull towards us as we floated up along the undulations. It didn't make sense. The only frame of reference I had was the helicopter, and even that was tough to hold in my mind.

Then we were out. We were above the rim, and the pilot shut off all the outside lights. We made a big smooth turn, and everything sped up. The pilot opened up the throttle, and this thing got going a lot faster than I expected.

We raced above an ocean of slickrock, and it looked so familiar. This was exactly what I'd seen before Donnie appeared. I had soared above this landscape, beyond the confines of my physical self. Now I was in a screaming metal machine, and it was just as beautiful.

I turned from the window and looked at Katie, and she was focused on me. I don't know why, but I thought she'd be looking out the window. She was still smiling and reached up and touched my heart with her finger. It took everything in me to keep from crying.

Our time in the air went quickly, and we landed on the north side of the old motel. There were people on the ground with flashlights when we all got out, and they huddled around the pilot.

There were two semi-trucks parked nearby, and a row of neatly parked cars and pickups. I had walked around this motel a few weeks ago, and none of this was here.

Katie and Tim led me away from the helicopter, past a row of trucks and cars, and then around the corner to the other side of the motel. I carried my backpack in one hand and my hat in the other. We stopped in an open field, and stood together in the dark. Tim asked, "Can we drive you anywhere?"

I said, "There's no need. I can walk."

Tim said, "Okay, we're all staying here, and we'll probably be here for a while."

I put on my hat and Katie burst out laughing, then said, "Oh my God. I'm sorry, but that looks so good on you. I didn't expect that, you being from Wisconsin and all."

I touched the brim and said, "Don't worry, I'm not a real cowboy. But it helps in the sun."

Tim said, "Look, John, it's late and the sun will be up soon, and I really want to talk with you, and I will, but I can't say much now. All this here—" He gestured to the motel and the cars. "We're doing geology work, and this project is still in its early stages. There's all kinds of legal stuff, with permits and federal requirements, and all kinds of red tape. For now, a lot of our work involves proprietary techniques, and I hope you understand, but we need to keep everything on the down low."

He said all that with a cheery optimism, and I said, "This is a very small town. And you have a helicopter and a fleet of shiny new trucks, and in a place like this, everyone is going to want to know about it. You won't be able to keep much on the down low."

He laughed and said, "Yes. Yes, we know that, for sure. But, for now at least, please help us out. If anyone asks, you can tell them what I told you. Just in the short term. Okay?"

His politeness seemed out of sync with what he was asking. I looked at Katie, and then at Tim. I said, "Of course. You have nothing to worry about."

He hugged me and slapped my back, "Great. That's great, thanks!"

Then he said goodbye and walked away, but he only went to the corner of the motel and stopped.

Katie watched Tim, and it looked like she was waiting for him to walk out of view, but he stood there watching us. He was far enough away that he couldn't hear us. She turned back to me and spoke in a very serious tone, "Are you okay?"

That was a good question, and I needed to give her an honest answer, "Yes, right now I'm fine. My life has been a mess at times, and I've searched a lot for some kind of—"

I stalled out, trying to find the right word. I said, "Hopefulness. Something that gives me some peace."

She took my hand and squeezed it, and said, "You deserve that."

It looked like she wanted to say more, but somebody in the distance called her name and she said she needed to go. We both said goodnight, and she hurried back around to the other side of the motel.

I left the field and followed a narrow path across the dry river bed, then past the elementary school and back to the main street. There was a hint of pink in the east when I arrived at the shed.

I lay on the cot, fighting to make sense of all this.

Something happened tonight that went far beyond what I could hold in my mind.

After what might have been only a half hour, I sat up and looked out the window. The lights were on in the shop, and that meant Tony had started the coffee.

24

TONY LOOKED SURPRISED when I walked in the back door. He said, "Good morning. I didn't think you'd be in today."

I muttered, "Yeah, neither did I."

That's all I said, and he didn't ask anything. I was back a day earlier than what I'd told him yesterday afternoon. It felt like I'd lived an entire lifetime since then. I hadn't slept but wasn't tired. Whatever peace I felt in the bottom of that canyon had been overridden by an unbearable confusion.

I washed my hands and put away yesterday's dishes. Then I started the muffins, swept the sidewalk and patio, and carried the signboard out front. The duties at the shop were easy enough, and I did it all on autopilot. Tony didn't seem to notice anything, and that was a relief.

My head was churning with all the weirdness of last night—I knew it happened, but it was impossible, and I was stuck in a mess of fear and doubt.

Later in the morning, Tony sold a black coffee to a guy I'd never seen before. He sat at a table in the corner and read a paperback. He was out of place in this town. People here all seemed sort of weather-beaten, like they'd spent their lives leaning into the wind, and he had none of that.

I knew he was part of whatever was going on at the motel, and I doubted he came in for coffee. It felt like he was here to watch me. I wasn't intimidated, at least not much. It was more a feeling of curiosity. I walked around the room and wiped down the tables. I did this on purpose. I wanted to get a closer look at him, but there was nothing to pick up on. He was around my age with short hair, and he sat quietly and read. After a while, he finished his coffee and left.

Later, in the quiet part of the afternoon, all the emotions of the last twenty-four hours caught up with me. I stacked the last of the clean dishes, and then ground to a standstill. I was in the back corner of the kitchen, a spot hidden from anyone in the main room. I stood motionless, staring at nothing.

Then I heard the screen door out front. The hinges make a distinct squeak when it opens, and a dry clack when it slams shut. There's a slight difference in the sounds when someone comes in, or leaves. I was in the back corner of the kitchen, and couldn't see into the main room. Hearing that door slam was normal, but I jumped like I'd heard a gunshot. My instant reaction was to dart out of the kitchen toward the counter.

Three steps later, I saw Katie standing alone in the middle of the main room. She turned to look at me, smiled and said, "John, you did that."

She was pointing to the chalkboard, and I said, "Yes, I did."

"I knew it. I saw it right away. And the sign out front, too."

"Yes."

Her hair was beautiful. I couldn't really see it last night in the dark, but seeing it now, I was struck by the power of its color. It was the same magic shade of red, exactly as I remembered from our childhood. She wore it down, parted a little off-center. It was wavy and came to her shoulders, with sunglasses resting on her head.

She wore a simple yellow ochre short sleeve summer shirt with buttons down the front. Her skirt was pastel green with a pattern of tiny leaves, and came to just above her knees. She had leather sandals and a rectangular canvas purse hanging from one shoulder.

She walked up to the counter and said, "There's nobody here. When do you close?"

"There's never anyone here this time of day, but we're still open, so don't worry."

Tony came out from the hall, saw us, and paused for a beat. He was carrying two boxes of paper cups, and set them on a table near the counter. Neither of us said anything. He nodded a silent hello, then turned around and disappeared in the hall.

I whispered, "I'm sorry. I wanted to introduce you, but I wasn't sure. I mean, after what your friend said this morning about keeping quiet."

She said, "I understand, but it's okay, you can introduce me."

"Good. What can I get you?"

She smiled and said, "A latte in a big mug."

I held up a wide sixteen-ounce ceramic cup, "Big like this?"

"Oh, yes."

I asked, "Two shots of espresso?"

"Absolutely."

I started the process and asked, "Can I join you?"

She smiled, "Yes, of course. I'd love that."

We talked as I worked. I had gotten good at this. Each step had its own sound, and it took on a nice rhythm—from tapping, to grinding, to a few different kinds of hisses and a whoosh.

Katie asked, "Do you have wifi?"

"Nope, there's no service anywhere in the valley. Some folks use their phone lines to access the net, but I'm not sure. And, for the most part, there's no cell reception either."

Her eyes lit up, "Wow, that's awesome. It's a relief to be cut off from all that, at least for a little bit."

"Yeah, it's pretty nice."

I tilted her mug and poured the last of the foamed milk on the surface of her coffee, wavering a bit to create a pattern. Then I put the mug on a saucer and slid it to her side of the counter.

She said, "Hey, you made a little tree."

I said, "No, it didn't turn out. I tried to make the goddess Durga, and those were supposed to be all her arms."

I made my own latte and poured it into an eight-ounce mug. When I set it on the counter Katie leaned forward and teased, "Is that the goddess Kali with her many arms?"

I said, "Nope, it's just a scrubby tree."

"The Bodhi Tree?"

"I wish." Then I asked, "Anything else?"

She looked at a tall glass jar on the counter and asked, "How are the oatmeal raisin cookies?"

"They're very good. I made 'em."

She smiled and said, "Then I'll have one."

I put a cookie on a plate and said, "We can sit in or out, whatever you want. There's shade on the patio."

She said it was too hot outside, so we set everything on the small table next to the window. I sat on the bench with my back to the street and she sat across from me. She said, "I was so happy when you said you were still drawing. It felt great to hear that."

I wanted to tell her that I paint, too, or used to, but I didn't have the heart to bring it up. There was so much I wanted to avoid. I said, "I have a thousand questions for you, and I'm not sure where to start."

She lifted her mug and said, "Let's start with cheers."

I tapped her mug with mine and said, "Cheers." Then we both took sips, and she gave me a serious look and said, "Wow, this is really good."

I nodded and said, "You bet. The coffee drinkers in this town are spoiled."

She took another sip, and I asked, "How old were you when you moved from the neighborhood?"

"I was twelve. It was the summer between seventh and eighth grade."

"Where did you move to?"

"We moved to Oklahoma, but we were only there for two years, then we moved to California. It was hard to show up at new schools. It felt like I never fit in. I was a lot happier once I got to college."

"Where did you go?"

"I did my undergrad at Stanford, and then went to the University of Chicago. I started with a religion major, but switched to psychology." She said this in a sort of dismissive way, and I sensed her evading something.

I asked, "What did you graduate with?"

"A PhD in behavioral psychology."

She said it very casually, then asked, "Did you go to art school?"

I said, "Yes, but I dropped out halfway through my freshman year." I explained I needed to because of money issues, and I figured I could get the same experience working. That was true, but what I didn't say was that I was a lousy student and was having a hard time with my mood. She could see my hesitance to talk about myself, and she gracefully guided our conversation away from the things I wanted to avoid.

Tony came back in the room, and I waved him over. I said, "Tony, this is my friend Katherine. We grew up together. She lived across the street from me."

His eyebrows raised, and he said, "Really? It's nice to meet you."

They shook hands, and Katie asked, "So what brought you to this little town?"

He replied, "Well, I sort of needed a place like this. I had been trying to work on some book ideas and wasn't getting anything done, and I needed somewhere to write. My life was quiet, but not quiet enough. My lease ran out, and I packed up my car and came out west. I drove through a lot of small towns, but none were small enough, until I found this place."

She asked, "Has it been working out for you here?"

He lit up, "Yes, it's been good. Managing this place is easy, and I can spend my afternoons writing. It's cheap here, and there aren't many distractions, so I'm freed up from of a lot of worries."

Katie said, "That's wonderful!" There was joy in her voice, and she almost clapped her hands.

I didn't know any of this. I had never asked Tony those simple questions, and that was on purpose. If I'd asked him why he came to this town, he'd have permission to ask me the same thing, and I didn't want to deal with the answers.

Katie asked Tony, "What are you writing about?"

"Well, I'm working on a set of short stories and a nonfiction book. I've been trying to work on both at the same time, and it's been slow going."

She said, "I'm excited for you, and I'm certain both will be marvelous."

She asked a few more questions, and he was quick with his answers. Watching them talk was intriguing. Neither said anything remarkable, but their tenor was curious. I had never seen Tony so open. His presence was completely different. He was totally shining.

Katie has this magic way about her, and it matches all my memories. She's always been so easy to be near, and it's completely disarming. And she sits beautifully. I know that must sound funny, but it's true. She has a kind of grace in the way she holds herself, and how she looks at you, and how she listens when you talked—as if every word is the most important thing in the world.

There came a point when Tony took a half step back, and I could tell he realized he'd taken all her attention. He smiled and said, "I should let you two catch up."

He said it was nice to meet her, and he was heading home. I told him I'd finish closing up and see him in the morning. When he left, Katie and I were alone in the building. I sat across from her in a faded dark blue t-shirt and stained Carhartt's that wouldn't stay up without a belt. These were from the secondhand store down the street, and I paid for all of it with quarters and dimes from the tip jar.

I could've felt worthless in her presence, yet her manner was so genuine that I was truly at peace with myself. I had lived with talent and money and even a little bit of fame, but I'd so rarely felt this degree of gentle peace.

Most of my life has been weighed down under a kind of haunted shadow. It's an ever-present feeling of insecurity, like I'm unworthy of even the simplest things in life. I don't understand it, but that's how it's been. Yet now, I could wash some dishes and see them clean and dry on a shelf, and I could find comfort in such an ordinary accomplishment. And now, a woman I knew as a girl, someone who walked to school with me, could so easily smile while sipping the coffee I'd made for her.

I said, "I want to get something."

I got up, went to the back room, and returned with a cardboard box. I sat across from Katie and said, "The paper cups come in these boxes, and each box has three sheets of cardboard that separate the stacked cups so they don't get dented during shipping. These have a texture and a color that I love, and I've been drawing on them."

I opened the box, pulled out one sheet and set it upright on the bench below the window. It was a simple still life of the chrome pitchers we use to steam the milk. I did it using a fine-line Sharpie from a drawer behind the counter. I used coffee to add a slightly darker tone, painting it with a rolled-up scrap of paper towel. And I used white chalk for the highlights.

She didn't say anything, but she leaned in closer with a curiosity that surprised me.

I set another image on the bench, and said, "I did this one on the patio." It showed the empty lot and alley. The upper part of the image was crisscrossed phone lines, and there were fences and buildings, and lonely buttes and clouds in the background. Like the other, this was done with a Sharpie, coffee, and chalk.

She looked for a long time, then slowly sat upright and said, "Oh, John."

After that, she reached out and cautiously touched the edge of the cardboard on the drawing of the patio. She turned to me and said, "John, these are beautiful." Her words were slow and poignant.

I know when something is special. For years I had painted enormous canvases with bold colors and sweeping vistas. They were skillful and stylized, but they lacked some vital spark. These sketches on cardboard were modest compared to the garish bigness of my previous work, but they had that spark, and Katie saw it.

She asked, "Are there more in that box?"

"Yes, lots."

I set them all out and lined them up on the bench along the window. Katie pulled the tables and chairs back to see them better. I explained that after the shop closed, I would use the big table in the middle of the room to draw. The windows on the street faced north, and the light could be nice in the afternoon. Sometimes I would sit out on the patio, but usually the wind and heat were too much.

She looked and looked, walking back and forth along the row of sketches. She wasn't saying anything, and if it were anyone else, I'd be nervous. But this was my oldest friend, and her silence soothed me. She studied every image, sometimes kneeling to get a little closer. I stood behind her, very aware she was focused on my work.

After a long time of careful examination, she stood up straight and faced me squarely. She said, "John, these are all very simple, yet there is something in them—a joy." She put her hand gently on my arm, and added, "You have a gift."

This wasn't a compliment. She said it in a way that was free of any constraints. For her, it was a bright, cloudless fact. People have complimented my work all my life, but Katie's sincerity felt so different. I smiled and asked, "How was the cookie?"

She punched me in the arm and said, "It was divine."

We talked for a while, and much of it was me pointing out things in the sketches. Things that I had struggled with, or things that turned out well. How the chalk worked to accentuate the light reflecting on a surface, or where I'd cheated and scribbled rather than truly drawing something in the background. Nobody had seen these, not even Tony, and it felt good to show her what I'd been doing.

She said, "John, this has been so wonderful. And I hate saying this, but I should get going."

I stood up and thanked her, then put the drawings back in the box. She helped me slide the tables and chairs back in place.

I walked her out to what she called "the staff car." It was a new Subaru Outback, shiny and deep gray. We hugged. She said she had such a nice time, and I said I did, too. I stood on the street and watched her drive away. I waited until she made the left turn that would take her to the motel, and I stood there long after I lost sight of her.

It felt so good to see her again. In many ways, she was exactly as I remembered, smiling and easy to be with. We sat and talked well past closing time, and everything felt comfortable and perfect. But I had no idea why she was in that helicopter or what she was doing in that canyon, and I was too scared to ask.

25

THE NEXT MORNING, I arrived at the shop a few minutes before Tony. I'd already started the coffee when he walked in the back door—and his head was shaved bald. It surprised me, and I said, "Whoa, that's new."

He rubbed his head and said, "Yeah, I've been thinking about doing this for a while."

Obviously, he looked different, but any trace of the boy in him was gone. As trite as it sounds, he was now a man. I said, "That's a good look for you."

He grunted a low "Hmm," and that was his reticent way of saying thank you.

I added, "Be careful in the sun."

He said, "I will."

I poured black coffee in two small mugs and handed him one. We took our first sips together, and he said, "You know what's weird? I can feel the temperature differences as I move from room to room. I sense it with my head."

I told him I'd had that same experience after shaving a beard. I could feel it with my chin. I took another sip, set my mug behind the counter, and went out to sweep the sidewalk and patio. The morning air felt cool and clean. I needed something normal, and this simple routine helped quiet my turbulent mind. When I got back in, Tony asked, "Why is your friend Katherine here?"

His question caught me off guard, and I needed to answer him in a way that would avoid all the strangeness. I said, "She's here as part of a research team of geologists. She didn't tell me much, but I think they're doing some kind of land survey and looking at the mineral rights around here."

He asked, "Is she with the crew at the motel across the river?"

"Yeah, that's where she's staying."

"People have been wondering what's been going on out there."

I said, "Who has? I haven't heard anything."

"Some of the regulars have been asking about it. Nobody knows who's there or why."

I didn't say anything. Then he asked, "Did she really live across the street from you?"

"Yeah, she really did. We walked to kindergarten together."

"How did she know you were here?"

I said, "She didn't. She walked in the front door and we recognized each other right away." I was lying, but didn't know what else to say.

He furrowed his brow and said, "Wow, that's odd."

"I know, it surprised both of us."

"When was the last time you saw her?"

It took me a few seconds to do the math, then I said, "Thirty years ago."

I could see he was mystified, and I understood why. He asked, "And you knew it was her?"

"Instantly."

He looked down, and I waited. Then he said, "She's so beautiful it hurts."

I understood how he felt. I was juggling a thousand thoughts, and had no idea what any of it might mean. I took a deep breath and said, "Yes, she's always had that same shining way about her. It was there as a little kid."

Trying to talk about Katie was emotional. It was too strong, and I changed the subject, "I didn't know you were working on books. Forgive me, I never asked."

"That's okay. I haven't told anyone here. It's been a personal thing. I came here so I wouldn't have to talk about it, so don't worry."

Yesterday afternoon, Tony was so eager to tell Katie about his writing. He seemed proud and beamed with energy. I tried asking a few questions about it, and he was guarded in a way he hadn't been with Katie, so I didn't ask anything more.

Tony's attention turned to the front window. Then he walked quickly around to the back of the counter and faced the espresso machine. A car had pulled up and the tall woman got out. I could hear the taps, clicks, and whooshing sounds as he pulled the espresso and steamed the milk.

She came in the front door, made a funny squeal and cried out, "Oh my God, Tony, I love it!"

She's always talkative, but a lot more this morning because of Tony's head. They had been chatting for only a bit when the man with the gray beard walked through the door. These two were usually our first customers in the shop. Tony knew their orders and started them when he saw their cars pull up out front. Sometimes one or the other would stay, but mostly they'd leave after getting their coffee. Every once in a while they would sit together at the table furthest from the front window. I never asked Tony, but I gathered they were a couple and trying to keep it secret.

Tony's bald head was the big news for anyone walking through the front door. They all had something to say about it.

The day progressed in its lazy way. The early morning crowd gave way to the breakfast crowd, and by crowd I don't mean it was actually busy, it's not that kind of place. At times there was no one in the shop but me and Tony, and other times most of the tables were filled, but that was rare. There was a gentle flow as morning eased into afternoon, and a slow dissolve as closing time drew near. I had come to love these quiet days and their peaceful rhythm.

It was well before noon, and I was cleaning the counter, and Tony was somewhere in the kitchen behind me. There was a constant need to clear away the coffee grounds from in front of the espresso machine, and we kept a dedicated bucket on the shelf below this working area. I'd hold the bucket under the edge of the counter and wipe the grounds into it, then slip it back on its shelf.

When I looked up, the helicopter pilot was standing across the counter. I hadn't heard him walk in, and he had the same stern expression as the other morning. I asked, "What is it?"

No reply. He stood still and stared at me. He was dressed in khaki pants and a black polo shirt.

I asked, "Do you want anything?"

"No. I came here to see you."

"Okay. I'm right here."

"Have you talked with anyone?"

I thought for a second, then asked, "You mean about the other night?"

"Yes."

I spoke steady and clear, "Katherine was here yesterday, and I introduced her to the one person I work with here."

"Go on."

"This morning he asked about her. I told him that she was staying at the motel, and the people there are looking into mineral rights in the area. That guy Tim told me I could say as much, and it's all I said."

He said, "Alright, good."

His expression didn't change. There wasn't anything more I could say, and he asked, "Have people been talking?"

"I haven't heard anyone say anything, but there's been some talk here. It's a very small town, and people are curious about what's going on at the motel, but to what degree I don't know."

"Okay. I had to ask."

That was an odd thing to say. It sounded like he was following orders. I asked, "Did you come here to intimidate me?"

"No."

"Well, if you don't want coffee, there isn't much I can do."

He turned and left the shop without saying goodbye. Part of me wanted to holler 'have a nice day,' but I didn't think he'd appreciate my sarcasm.

This guy unnerved me. I didn't know if he was putting on an act to see how I would react, or if this was really how he was. Before I could think too much, three people came in with an involved set of orders, and the momentary busy work kept me from descending into paranoia.

There was usually a point in the early afternoon when things quieted down. The regulars had had their fix, and the shop took on a mood of serenity. This was when I felt the urge to sit and draw, and often did. There were still a few people here, but it all felt peaceful.

Any tranquillity was broken when that guy Tim put his face to the glass and waved at me. He hurried into the shop and stood in line behind an older man who wanted coffee in his thermos, but said it needed rinsing first. I filled it with hot water, shook it, and poured it out. I needed to do this a few times before topping it off with coffee. This was easy enough, but Tim was obviously impatient. The man paid, took his thermos, and left.

Tim stepped up to the counter and said, "John, I wanted to stop by and say hello."

I replied, "Okay. Hello."

He said, "This is nice. It really is. I didn't expect anything like this here."

"What can I get you?"

He looked up at the chalkboard and said, "Hmm, um, wow, there's a lot."

I said, "Take your time."

"Okay, I will have a cappuccino. Do you make that with whipped cream?"

"I can, yes."

"And chocolate?"

"That would be a cafe mocha."

"Oops, sorry. That's what I'll have."

"Okay, a mocha with whipped cream. We use Hershey's syrup. Sorry, this isn't Milan. Is that okay?"

"Oh, yes. That's great, yes."

I started his order and said, "Your pilot buddy was here earlier."

He rolled his eyes and asked, "Oh, jeez, how did *that* go?"

"Fine I guess, but that guy is kinda grim."

"Oh, my, that's an understatement."

I finished his order and slid it toward him. Then he asked, "Would it be okay to sit and talk for a little bit?"

I said, "Gimme a second." I went to the back room and asked Tony if he could cover for me if a customer came in. He said sure.

Tim and I sat at the table furthest from the only other people in the shop, two women talking in the opposite corner by the window. Tim had started his mocha, and I had a small mug that I'd refilled with decaf after talking with Tony. Tim said, "Thank you for this. I didn't mean to take you away from your work."

I said, "It's fine. It's quiet now."

He leaned forward and said, "I just wanted to make sure you're doing okay. The other night was a whirlwind for all of us. I didn't get any sleep, and I'm still out of sorts." He waited, watching me, then raised his mug and took a sip. He said, "Oh, wow, this is marvelous, exactly what I needed."

I asked, "Have you talked with Katherine since yesterday afternoon?"

"Yes, we work together, and she told me she visited with you here. She was so happy to hear about you and your life."

I said, "I told her very little about my life."

He took another sip and said, "But you showed her some of your artwork, and she was very impressed. She absolutely raved about it."

"She knew me as a boy and had seen plenty of my drawings back then, so it felt nice to share a little bit of what I'm doing lately."

"Yes, yes. She said you've always been very talented."

I took a long, slow drink. His compliments felt hollow, and I needed to think. This guy was trying to get something out of me, and I didn't know what he was after. I set down my mug and said, "Your pilot friend asked if I had talked to anyone. And he seemed very concerned about it."

Tim looked around the room, then leaned closer and whispered, "What did you tell him?"

"The guy that works here with me met Katie yesterday afternoon, and this morning he asked why she was here in town. I told him she's here with a small team doing a land survey, and researching the local mineral rights. I said it in a way that made it clear that I didn't know much, which I don't."

"Oh, that's just fine. Just fine."

"And he asked if she was staying at the motel where we landed, and I said she was. He met Katie here, and it would've sounded a lot more odd if I said I didn't know. So I only told him what you told me, what you said was okay to tell."

"Oh, that's all fine. And thank you so much for saying that."

"That's what I told the pilot this morning, the same thing I told you now."

"I haven't seen him yet today, so I didn't know any of that." He leaned forward again and asked, "How did he react?"

I thought about how I should answer, and then said, "He acted like he'd kill me if I said the wrong thing."

With that, Tim let out a high, squeaky laugh—it startled me. He tried to hold it in, and managed a few seconds with one hand over his mouth and the other slapping the table. Then he started again, laughing loud in pulsing little shrieks.

I looked across the room and the two women were staring at us and laughing, too. When he finally calmed down, he took a deep breath and said, "Oh, good gracious, I am *so* sorry. Oh, my, I just made a complete ass of myself."

He turned around and waved to the women in the opposite corner, calling out, "Sorry, ladies!"

He turned back and said, "Oh my God. You don't realize it, but that was funny."

After that, he took another sip from his mug, and started asking me about the weather here, and the surrounding mesas and high country. He was asking questions, but didn't give me a chance to reply. He even used the term "stark beauty" to describe the landscape. That was a fair thing to say, but the way he said it sounded absolutely sinister.

He drank the last sip from his mug, and said, "This was so great, really."

I explained that the guy I work with had a lot of experience with the espresso machine, and he'd been teaching me. He didn't want to be stuck at the front counter, and I could give him a break if I got up to speed and shared the duties. Tim acted like he was listening, but I could tell he didn't care.

After he left, Tony came out from the back and asked me what had happened. He'd obviously heard the laughing. I told him I said something funny and left it at that.

I said goodbye to the two ladies as they left, then cleared their table and carried the tub of dirty dishes back to the kitchen. This had been a really messed up day. First the pilot, then Tim. They were trying to get something from me, and I had no idea what they wanted or why. I stewed over all of it while washing the dishes. I was setting them neatly in the drying rack when it hit me—*they don't know why I'm here*. It seemed neither of us knew why the other was here, and this realization made my heart sink.

26

IT WAS GETTING NEAR CLOSING TIME, and I saw a car make a U-turn on the main street. It came around and parked in front of the store. It was the gray Subaru staff car from the motel. Katie got out, and I immediately felt better.

She walked in, took off her sunglasses and set them on her head. She stood still for a few seconds, staring forward. Almost everyone did this after the midpoint of the day. They needed to let their eyes adjust after the brightness outside. The walls were white, and there were plenty of windows, so it wasn't really dark in here, but it was a sharp contrast to the desert sun.

In that moment, I could look at her. She wore the same sandals as yesterday, faded blue jeans, and a black t-shirt with the single word "dream" centered on her chest.

She blinked and said, "I did it again. It's close to closing, isn't it?"

I said, "Soon."

She walked up to the counter and said, "I wanted to get here earlier but couldn't get away."

I said, "Don't worry at all. It's not a problem. What can I get you? Same as yesterday?"

"Yes, and with a cookie. Please."

I started her order by tapping the wet grounds out of the metal filter, then rinsed it with hot water. Katie watched as I worked. I lined up two shot glasses on the tray of the machine and said, "I like your shirt."

She smiled and said, "I love this shirt. Thank you."

She gently touched the fabric just below her neck. I wanted to say more, but I worried she'd think I was lying. I said, "It's not as hot today. If you want to sit out on the patio, we can."

"I'd love that."

I finished making her latte and started mine. She stared at hers on the counter, and I knew what she was thinking. I said, "Don't worry about waiting for me. Go ahead, enjoy it while it's hot."

She lifted the mug with both hands and took a sip. As she set it back down, Tony walked into the main room, and Katie shrieked, "Look at you!"

He froze, and I watched his face turn red. Katie ran up, and eagerly praised his freshly shaved head. She asked him to turn around, and he did. I could see he was embarrassed, but at the same time, he was absolutely smitten by her attention.

Tony had come out front to ask me if I could close up. I said it would be no problem at all. He thanked Katie and left out the back door.

Katie picked up her cup, and I carried mine and grabbed a plate with two cookies. We went out the side door next to the counter, and I held it for her with my elbow as she stepped onto the patio.

She sat across from me at a bleached wooden table under the canvas awning. We tapped our cups, and I took my first sip. The sun was still high in the sky, and the air was unusually still. It was hot, but comfortable. She looked at the shop, then turned in her chair and looked past the alley to the foothills south beyond the fence line. She faced me again and said, "There is something nice about all this."

I said, "Yes, I know."

She said, "Thank you again for yesterday, for showing me your drawings. That was wonderful for me. I remember all the times we would sit at our kitchen table, and you would draw for me. I loved that. It's a really vivid memory."

"I remember it, too. And at your kitchen table, I was showing off."

She pointed her finger at me and said, "No. You were very talented, and I was totally in awe of what you could do."

I've never done well with praise, and when this kind of thing happens I'll do anything to change the subject, or figure out a way to reject it. But Katie had an entirely different effect on me, and it was a relief.

I said, "I'll be right back."

I got up and walked inside. I grabbed a sheet of cardboard from a small stack behind the counter. I had been saving them from the cup boxes, and these sheets were stored upright on a shelf under the cash register. I opened the top drawer and found a fine point Sharpie, a yellow number two pencil, and a piece of white chalk.

When I got back outside, Katie saw what I was carrying, and her eyes lit up. She smiled and said, "Oh my God, John. Really?"

I sat down and set the cardboard in front of me. She got up and dragged her chair around to my side of the table and sat to my left. This was how we'd sit together as kids.

In the center of the table was a cheap terra cotta pot with a stubby little cactus. I moved it slightly closer, and turned it a bit. I took the pencil and made some loose lines to define the shape of the pot and the cactus. She put her elbows on the table and leaned in to see better. I didn't press hard with the pencil, and the faint lines looped around and around in ovals and circles.

I took the cap off the pen and said, "You need to stay still. I don't want the table to shake."

She said, "Okay." That one word was spoken so softly, and it triggered something in me. I was overwhelmed with a shimmering calm.

I said, "The pencil lines are helpful, but I'm not going to follow them. The shapes on the paper don't match the shapes in front of me, and they never will."

I was about to touch the pen to the cardboard, but I stopped. "I need to say something. I love the page, this cardboard. And I love the black ink in the pen. I really mean that. I've tried to explain this to people before, but I could tell they didn't understand."

I drew the first line, the outside edge of the pot, then the shape of the dish below it. I was using the pencil lines, but only as a rough guide. I defined the outside edges of the cactus in lumpy scratches of ink. Then I made short little black marks, and spoke as I drew,

"Right now, I'm playing the banjo on the front porch. I have to be careful not to worry too much or overthink. I need to let go and let the music happen, to trust there's something nice emerging. Does this make sense?"

"I think so." Again, that disarming whisper.

I rotated the cardboard on the table to do the shading on the pot. I said, "My hand wants to move in a certain arc, so I turn the page to fit how the curve wants to happen."

After the initial shapes were set in place, I started with a bunch of speedy little scratch marks, enough to bring out the three-dimensional quality. The pen zipped along, and this part happened quickly.

She said, "Wow, you're really fast."

I said, "I'm showing off. Drawing a little plant on a table is pretty easy for me, and I'm not worried. I know there's a nice image waiting to emerge."

I filled in some of the darker shadows and scribbled a little to capture the dirt. Then I started the shadow on the table. I said, "I don't want to put too much in here, but I want to make it look like old weathered wood."

I scribbled and scratched for a little bit and then put the cap back on the pen. I leaned over and looked in her mug. There were a few drops left at the bottom.

I asked, "Can I use this?"

She said yes, and I picked up her mug. I ran my finger around the bottom and rubbed the coffee along a few spots in the drawing with my fingertip. All I wanted was some tone to define the shadowed edges of the pot and cactus. The coffee adds a darker brown to the speckled surface of the cardboard. I said, "That'll be dry in a minute."

I took the stubby bit of chalk and made a sparse line on the rim of the pot, and then on the rim of the dish. It wasn't much, just enough to show where the sunlight was reflecting. Then I laid the chalk sideways and dragged it down the edge of the pot, and smeared it with my finger to soften it some. I put a few small white highlights on the cactus and set the chalk on the table. It turned out well, and I knew it.

I said, “There,” then slid the sheet of cardboard over to Katie.

She said, “This is amazing.”

“Thank you. But it’s easy for me. Sort of a trick, like an annoying magician who pretends to pull a quarter out of your ear.”

She asked, “Could you draw me?”

I didn’t say anything. I looked down at the table and tried to think. I said, “I feel like I know what I can and can’t do. A lot is very easy for me, but some things are daunting. I can capture a shadow, or certain details, yet capturing beauty is—”

I trailed off to an awkward silence, fighting for what to say. She was waiting for me to finish, and after what felt like too long, I said, “I don’t think I should try to draw you. It would be impossible for me to capture what I see. It’s too delicate, and I know I would fail.”

I looked at her, and her eyes seemed too radiant. I thought she might cry, or that I might.

I reached up and set the pencil, pen, and chalk side by side on the table. I carefully lined them up so they were all parallel and the same distance apart. Then I said, “Both the helicopter pilot and your friend Tim were here today.”

She looked down and said, “I know.”

“They both came to talk to me. I answered their questions, but they didn’t really ask much.”

She kept her head bowed and didn’t say anything. There was something weighing on her. I waited for a while, then said, “You know I have to ask you about the night with the helicopter.”

She replied quietly, “I know.”

I waited for her to say something more, but everything about her was suddenly hopeless. She seemed resigned to something, and her silence mimicked the still desert air.

I asked, “What’s going on? Because I don’t know.”

She turned her head and looked out at the red foothills, then tipped her gaze down to the table. She said, “It’s complicated. The work that brought me here—there are a lot of issues—and some things I really can't talk about."

I asked, "Can you tell me anything?"

She said, "I can't say much. But we don't know much. We're struggling, too."

"Is that all you can say?"

She didn't answer. She lifted her head and looked at me with those magical green eyes, but there was no spark. She seemed ashamed.

We both sat in silence for a long time. Finally, I said, "I drew that word on your shirt."

She said, "What?"

She didn't understand, and I quietly explained, "I drew the word 'dream' for that shirt. It's my hand lettering. I did it."

She looked down at her shirt and then at me, "What are you saying?"

"I drew that. I got hired by a place that makes t-shirts in Sedona. They were connected with a crystal shop called Dream, and they wanted a simple image for a shirt, so I drew it for them. I'd forgotten all about it until you walked in today."

"This is my favorite shirt." Her voice was almost fearful.

I asked, "Where did you get it?"

"I don't know. I had it when I lived in Chicago. I have no idea how I got it. I thought maybe a roommate had left it in our apartment, but I'm not sure. That was like twenty years ago."

"I was living out of my truck near Sedona when I did it. I remember the people at the store were happy with how it turned out, and so was I."

The letters were all lowercase and very simple. The sketch they used probably took me less than ten minutes. The image on her shirt was screened with silver ink on black cotton, and it had aged perfectly. Earlier in the shop, she said she loved it, and it fit her beautifully. She had that rare grace to wear a simple t-shirt and have it come across as glorious.

She turned in her chair and faced forward. There was nothing to see but the weeds in the lot beyond the patio, but she didn't seem to be looking at anything.

She spoke softly, "I don't want to lie to you, so I can't say much. I'm not able to talk about the work I'm involved with here. Please try to understand, there's no easy way to make sense of all this."

Then she turned and looked at me. She smiled weakly and shrugged her shoulders with regret. I was astonished at her beauty. There was nothing I could say. I tried to smile, but couldn't manage much. I sat upright and took a deep breath. I needed to quiet some dark unease in me, but didn't know how.

I tapped the drawing of the little cactus, and said, "You can have this if you want."

Her smile got wider, and she said, "Good. I was going to ask, so thank you."

"It's not much, but it felt great to draw for you again."

Our moment was over. I stood up and went into the shop, got a big manila envelope, and came back out to the patio. I said, "This is a quirk of mine. I try to treat my work well, even the simple things." The drawing barely fit in the envelope, and she held it open as I gently slid it inside. She offered to help me close up the shop, and I told her not to worry, there was very little to do.

Like yesterday, I walked her out to the car and said goodbye. I stood in the street and watched her drive off. I had never felt so alone.

27

EVERYTHING WAS ELECTRIC BLUE. I sat up. There was a bright light on the other side of my truck, and I knew exactly where I was. This was where I slept when I worked in Sedona.

My first thought was that it was somebody's car, and they were doing the same thing I'd done, looking for a place to sleep for the night. But it was weirder than headlights. Those point somewhere, and this was entirely different. It didn't feel like a normal light. It was more of a boundless glow.

I sat up in my sleeping bag and tried to make sense of what was happening. The desert at night can be very still, but this was beyond quiet. It was eerie. I thought I should get up and find out what it was, but I didn't do anything. There was no moon, and everything seemed so strange, like it was all too vivid. The light had this urgency, this clear sense that I'd seen it before, or more that I'd felt it before—many times. I was spellbound by its sharpness on the bushes, and how all the details on every branch seemed so vibrant.

Then I opened my eyes, and I was looking at the ceiling of the shed. It was still dark out, and I felt rested. Normally, I'll gently ease out of sleep, it's something slow and murky. Yet I was fully awake without any kind of transition, and it didn't have any of the mixed-up feelings of a normal dream. It felt like a memory.

I used to sleep in that spot when I was doing odd jobs in Sedona. It was a few miles south of town on a dead-end Jeep track off Highway 89. I found an open, flat area in the weeds about a dozen yards from the little turn out where I'd park my old short-bed Toyota pickup.

The dream exactly matched my sleeping spot. I have a foggy memory of waking up to the light, but the feeling that I'd seen it before, that familiarity seemed new. Yet there was something about the dream that felt empty. I want to say it was meaningless, but that's not quite right.

I remember that night because a cop pulled up the next morning. He got out of his car while I was stuffing my sleeping bag into a duffle, and asked me what I was doing. I told him that I'd slept there. Then he asked if I'd had a fire during the night, and I told him no. He said there had been a report of a fire in this area. Again, I said I hadn't had a fire but didn't mention the weird blue light.

We talked for a while. He said it was all right to sleep here, then he asked what I was doing in town. I said I'd painted some signs and was looking for work. He asked about the signs, and I said they were for a store on the main street. One was wide and mounted on the awning above the door, and the other was smaller and hung under the awning on hooks. He lit up, telling me he'd noticed them the day before. He said, "That isn't the kind of store I'd ever go in, but they looked good."

The signs were for *Dream*, the store I did the t-shirts for, and it was normal for a silk-screen shop to give the illustrator a few shirts for free, so there would have been a handful with me in my truck.

After the cop left, I walked into the sagebrush where the blue light would've been. There was nothing unusual, just a tangle of thorny bushes. There were no footprints in the dust, and it was obvious nobody had been there the night before, and certainly not a car.

I remember standing there alone, and I was ashamed. It didn't make any sense, but I felt it. I was guilty about something, and talking to a cop wasn't the issue. It went way beyond that. The sun was warm, and it was a beautiful morning, yet I had done something wrong. I knew this, but there was nothing. That feeling weighed heavy on me, and I don't think I've ever gotten rid of it, not entirely. It's always been in me.

I sat up slowly and looked out the window. The lights were on in the shop. I got dressed and crossed the alley. Tony pointed to the coffee when I walked in, and that meant it was ready. Then he asked, "Did you check the tip jar last night?"

I said, "No, I put it behind the counter. I figured you'd count it in the morning. What's up?"

He said, "There was a hundred-dollar bill in it."

He showed it to me, and something didn't seem right. It made me nervous, and I said, "Really?"

"Yeah. It's odd."

He counted out yesterday's tips, which wasn't much. Then he made two equal piles, set the hundred on one, then moved two twenties and a ten to the other. He slid this stack of bills towards me, and said, "Here you go."

Before heading out to sweep the sidewalk, I asked, "Did we have many strangers in here yesterday?" The pilot, Tim, and Katie had been here, and I wondered if there was anyone else from that crew.

He said, "A few. I know because they didn't say anything about my head."

I asked if they might be from the motel, and he said maybe, but didn't know. Then I went out the front door with the broom. I loved this quiet time alone in the morning. There wasn't much to do, but the steady sweeping motions and the act of cleaning a set area felt so satisfying. I stopped and looked to the east. After a bit, I saw a gray car turn onto the highway from the north, and I knew it was Katie. I stopped sweeping and waited. I waved as she got closer, and she waved back. She turned around on the empty street and parked in front of the shop.

She was smiling when she got out, and said, "Hi there."

I said, "Hello."

She stood near me and said, "It's really beautiful here in the morning."

I nodded, "Yes it is."

"I came to get coffee for some of the people I work with."

I held the screen door for her and said, "Tony's in there. He'll be happy to help."

I swept for a little bit, or pretended to, but mostly looked at Katie and Tony through the big window. Her back was to me, and she was reading off a piece of note paper. I couldn't hear them, but

I could see Tony's face, and he was clearly delighted to have her in the shop. Watching them should've seemed like something normal, but it wasn't, not at all. She was a radiant light in this bleak little town, but something felt all wrong.

I finished sweeping along the front of the shop, but stayed by the window, dragging the broom, over and over, across the same spot in the cement. I didn't want to be around the corner sweeping the patio when Katie came out. She had a large order, and it took a while. I could see Tony putting cups in a cardboard box, and I watched as she paid.

I held the door again as she came back out. She said, "Thank you," then raised the box slightly and added, "This should brighten some spirits."

I said, "Katie, let's do something this afternoon. If you can."

I could tell I caught her off guard, and she said, "Okay, what are you thinking?"

"I'm not sure. We could take a walk or something."

She looked serious, then smiled and said, "I would love that. I'm pretty sure I can get off from work a little earlier, if that's okay."

"Sounds good. I don't need to close up, Tony can do that easy enough, and I'll figure something out. What time?"

She thought about it, and then said, "Maybe three o'clock. How's that?"

"Easy. Can I pick you up at the motel?"

I could tell she was thinking. Then she nodded and said, "Sure, that sounds fine."

"Then I'll be there at three, and I'll bring you a coffee."

She smiled and said, "Good. I should go. I don't want these to get cold."

"Go."

She stepped out onto the street and got in her car. I watched her drive away and waited until she made the left turn toward the motel. Then I went inside and asked Tony if I could borrow his truck.

"What for?"

"Well, I think I just asked Katie out on a date."

He stood up taller and said, "Okay, sure. No problem."

I thanked him, and asked, "Have you ever been out to the old bridge site?"

"Oh, yes, it's worth visiting."

"Okay, good. She asked me to pick her up at three o'clock. So I'll have to leave before closing."

Tony told me not to worry, whatever I needed was okay. He said his bike was in the back of his truck, and he could ride it home. He told me to leave the truck in the alley for the night and he'd ride back tomorrow morning.

I said, "Thank you, really."

"It's no problem at all." He said that right as the tall woman's car pulled up outside. He stepped behind the counter and started her order.

The rest of the morning wasn't all that busy, but I noticed some new faces, and they had that same look—short hair, their clothes were a little too new, and they seemed serious. I let Tony work the counter, so he was dealing with them, and I spent most of my time in the kitchen.

This morning's dream kept replaying itself as I worked. There was an intense clarity to it that made it hard to shake. Yesterday Katie and I sat on the patio, and I told her a bit about my time in Sedona, and that's where I did the lettering for her shirt. I wasn't sure when it happened, but thinking about it now, I'm certain it was 1989. I say that because the main street of Sedona is US Highway 89, and I remember the same number on the road signs. So that would've been exactly twenty years ago.

I was stacking dishes in the drying rack when Tony stood in the kitchen door and told me, "I pulled my bike out of the truck. You should get out of here."

I nodded, thanked him, and crossed the alley to the shed. I washed my face and trimmed my beard, then put on my Wranglers and the long sleeve white shirt with the snap buttons. I realized I hadn't worn either of these since the morning I'd shown up here.

They'd been washed twice, and the shirt had been bleached in a bucket. I put two water bottles in the cotton tote bag Betty had given me, and walked back across the alley to the shop.

I started two lattes, one big and one small, both in paper cups. Tony walked by the counter and I said, "I'll need the keys."

He said, "They're in the cup holder between the seats. That's where I keep 'em."

I asked, "Anything I should know about your truck?"

He thought for a bit, then said, "The ride can be pretty rough, and the road is in bad shape for the last few miles before the old bridge site. You'll wanna slow down."

I said, "I don't have a driver's license."

He rolled his eyes like I'd said something dumb, "Don't worry about that. There won't be any other cars after leaving town, and we never see cops out here at this end of the highway."

I thanked him, put some cookies in a paper bag, then put them in the canvas tote, and slung it over my shoulder. I held both coffees and said I was on my way. He looked at me like he was going to say something more, but he just nodded and got back to work. I walked out the back door and got in his truck. I found the keys and started it. Before pulling out, I saw Tony standing at the back door. I rolled down the window and waved. He waved back in a way that felt serious. I tried to read his body language, and I wasn't sure, but it seemed like he was telling me, *don't fuck this up.*

I drove east down the alley, turned left, and then made a right onto the main street. I hadn't driven in a long time, and it felt so good. I turned left on the road that led to the motel and crossed the bridge over the dry river bed. I turned left again, this time onto a dirt road that passed through a stretch of cottonwoods. The road curved, and I saw the motel. Whoever built this back here had a good vision. The trees along the dry creek hid it from the rest of the town, and the view to the north was big and empty.

The asphalt driveway made a loop around the lot, and any paint showing the parking spaces had faded long ago. I stopped out front. The place looked abandoned, but I knew it wasn't. The windows were all taped over with brown paper from the inside, stained and faded like they'd been covered for years.

I got out and looked around. I thought about knocking on the door of what would have been the front desk. It was papered over from the inside, and I doubted anyone would be in there. I leaned against the truck and figured someone would see me.

It wasn't long before I heard a door open and turned to see Katie stepping out from one of the rooms. She closed the door and waved hello. She wore a mustard yellow sundress, nylon running shoes with short socks, a floppy cotton hat with a pattern of stars on the band, and she carried the same canvas purse from her first time in the coffee shop. She looked amazing.

I opened the passenger door and said, "There's a latte in the cup between the seats. It should still be hot."

She gasped, "Oh, yes, thank you."

She had taken the first sip by the time I walked around to the driver's side. When I got in, she said, "I'm really happy we're doing this."

I said, "I am, too. This isn't the kind of town with tourist attractions, but it can be nice here. I asked Tony about the old bridge site west of town, and he said it was worth the drive. Have you been there?"

"No, I haven't."

"Neither have I, but it's a nice afternoon for a drive."

She asked, "Is this Tony's truck?"

"Yep, he let me borrow it."

She pointed to a box by her feet and asked, "Are those cassette tapes?"

"I guess so. I haven't been in his truck until now."

Katie reached down, pulled up a shoe box, and set it on her lap. It held two tidy rows of tapes. I said, "Pick something."

After shuffling through the box, she said, "These are all labeled with dates and not much else."

"Pick one."

She opened a case, took out a cassette and pushed it into the slot above the radio on the dash. We had only been driving a short time, but were already well past the west edge of town. I said, "I haven't been out this way. It's all new for me."

She said, "Me, too."

She turned up the volume and asked, "Who is this?"

I said, "I have no idea."

She leaned forward, listening intently. It was an instrumental with acoustic guitar and what seemed like a synthesizer. She smiled and said, "I really like this."

I said, "I know. Tony does that. All his music is like that. I've never heard any of it, and it's all pretty great. It makes working in the shop really nice."

Katie sat back in her seat and looked out at the huge, open landscape. The valley floor seemed perfectly flat, and there wasn't much out there but worn down fences and abandoned homes. Both sides of the road were barren in a way that felt grim.

Katie said, "Wow, it really feels empty. It's eerie."

"I was about to say it's peaceful, but yeah, it is. It makes for easy driving."

I glanced at her, and could tell she was overwhelmed by the starkness. I asked, "Have you spent much time in this area?"

"You mean around this town?"

"No, I mean this part of the west. The desert."

"Not really, it's all new for me. It's amazing."

We talked and laughed for about a half hour, and I slowed as we crossed a cattle guard. There was a sign on the fence that said the road was unmaintained beyond this point. Katie exclaimed, "I hope there's a sign that says *Danger, bridge out.*"

I asked, "Like in a Road Runner cartoon?"

"Exactly." She said it with obvious delight.

The asphalt ahead was bleached a few shades lighter than the highway behind us. The chalky gray surface was lumpy, rutted, and without a center line. The wide open part of the valley narrowed ahead of us, and the highway led to a point on the horizon between the red cliffs. Eventually we drove through that gap and dropped into a completely different realm.

The road tipped, and we began a long, gentle curve downhill through tall free-standing rocks. We got a glimpse ahead, and the world felt endless.

Katie said, "Wow, this is beautiful."

We snaked our way down a series of staggered benches. Then the road turned, and we found ourselves back on flat terrain. I saw a barrier ahead and slowed down. As we got closer, I saw it was nothing more than a metal bar across the road with a small sign that read *No vehicles beyond this point.* I parked on the gravel along the road and got out. It was weird to have driven again. The speed and smoothness were familiar, but it felt better to stand on the ground.

28

KATIE GOT OUT ON HER SIDE, and I reached behind the driver's seat and grabbed the tote bag. I said, "Looks like we walk from here."

We stepped through a narrow gate in a fence that lined up with the barrier, and continued down the road. It was hot but not too bad, and we walked a lazy pace. The asphalt beyond the barrier hadn't been maintained in decades, and long stretches had blown over with sand. There was nothing to see ahead, no bridge and no canyon, just a wide-open vista.

We walked for a ways in silence, then Katie said, "I had a weird dream last night."

I asked, "What happened?"

She said, "I was in Chicago, in the apartment I had during grad school, and there was a bright light in my room."

I waited for her to say more, but she didn't, and I asked, "Did anything else happen?"

"No, that's all I remember, but it felt like I was really there."

I was cautious about saying anything, but I had to ask, "Was this the apartment where you ended up with that shirt?"

"I'm pretty sure, yes."

"You said you thought your roommate might have left it behind when she moved out?"

"Yeah, that's what I thought at the time."

"Why did she leave?"

Katie paused before answering, "I don't know. One morning she said she was leaving, and she was gone when I got back from class that afternoon."

"And you think she might've left that shirt in your apartment?"

"I don't know. Maybe. I didn't get to know her that well. She seemed normal enough, but she was really freaked out that morning. I remember that."

That her roommate left like she did was an odd detail, and we both had dreams with bright lights. All this worried me.

The route turned at a big rock feature. We walked around the curve and finally saw the bridge, or what was left of it. The road led straight to a short empty platform, and out beyond was a majestic red canyon.

Our pace slowed as we approached. There were posts on each side of the road, and a chain stretched between, with a metal sign at the low point that read DANGER in all capital letters.

Past the sign was about twenty yards of pavement jutting out over nothing. A four-foot-tall hurricane fence was fixed across the pavement, and this was the final barrier before the drop-off.

I walked up to the chain and stepped over. Katie stopped, stood still, and looked down at it. I waited. After a while, she stepped across, too. I started toward the edge, and she stayed a bit behind me. She was trying to act calm, but I could tell she was nervous.

She said, "Something feels wrong. I don't like this spot."

I turned around and stepped back across the chain, then put my foot on it, holding it low and steady. I held out my hand and said, "It's okay. We don't need to go out there."

She took my hand and stepped over, and I watched her calm down the instant she was back on the other side of the chain. I said, "Let's get away from here."

Looking around, I saw a footpath leading north. I walked to it, and she followed. It ran alongside the canyon, but far enough away from the edge to be safe.

I led the way for a few minutes, and we arrived at a low wall of exposed rock. It was about as high as I am tall, and it looked flat on top. The path ended at a cleave in the steep sandstone face, and someone had chiseled a few small steps in its surface. I used these and my hands to get up onto it.

I turned around and offered Katie my hand, but she didn't need it. She stepped up confidently, unlike her shaky emotions back on the bridge. The top was huge and open, like the deck of an abandoned aircraft carrier. The western edge hung out over the river like the prow of a giant ship. I walked out closer to the drop-off, and she followed cautiously. From this spot, it was obvious we were way above the water, and I said, "I'm comfortable in this kind of terrain, but I realize not everyone is."

She didn't say anything. We were far enough away from the edge of the prow not to worry, but from this point we could look back at the remains of the bridge on this side of the river.

It was weird to see from this angle. The scale of everything made it difficult to take in. The profile of the broken bridge was insignificant against the immensity of the canyon. The stubby section poked out from the rim like some tiny prop on a toy train set.

From where we stood, you could see the stanchions below the platform, and where they'd been cemented into a chopped-out shelf in the bedrock of the cliff face. You could also see part of the curved arch of the load-bearing steel that once spanned the canyon.

The other end of the bridge was across the river, a nearly identical stub jutting out from the rim. It was a mirrored reflection, more than a football field away. You could see how they'd once been connected, and it looked like God had snipped out the middle with a giant pair of scissors.

I moved a little closer to the edge, and she cautiously joined me. I wanted a better view without getting too close to the void. Sometimes the terrain along a cliff is too sandy, too rounded, or too broken up—making it difficult to see down to the bottom. We walked out a little closer to the prow, and stood in a safe spot where we could see the brown water below.

I said, "That's the Colorado."

From where we stood, we had a powerful vantage point of the endless terrain around us. I pointed to the right, and said, "The Green River joins upstream, and further north is Moab." Then I turned around and pointed left. I explained that Lake Powell was further downstream, and beyond that was Arizona and the dam, and then the Grand Canyon.

Katie was quiet, and I could see she felt uneasy, so I led us away from the edge. We walked to a spot in the middle of the expanse. I sat down and set the canvas bag to my side.

She sat across from me, and I asked, "Has this been okay?"

She smiled and said, "Oh, this is amazing, yes. Thank you."

I opened the bag and set out two bottles of water, and the bag of cookies. I slid a bottle closer to her. She thanked me and took a long drink.

She gasped, "Wow, that's so good."

I opened the paper bag with the cookies, and gently rolled down the edges to make a sort of open display. After she took another sip, I said, "That's from the canyon. I filled it from a spring down there."

She looked at the bottle, and then at me, and asked, "*That* canyon?"

I nodded, "Yes, that's why I went down there, to drink the water."

She looked at the bottle again, and said, "You saved this for me?"

"Oh, yes."

We sat in silence for a long time, and she took a few more sips. I set the open bag of cookies between us, and we both ate one. Neither of us said anything. We just looked around at the enormous landscape. The quiet was easy, and I felt peaceful, but I wasn't sure what she was feeling.

I watched her hand, the one nearest me. She was absently passing it back and forth over the surface of the sandstone where we sat. Her fingertips ran slowly along two shallow cups in the rock, gently rubbing the chalky sand.

She lifted her hand and looked at the dust on her fingers. I could see her expression. She looked like she was trying to solve something.

She rubbed the hem of her dress to clean her fingertips. She looked at the dull red color on the yellow fabric, then tried to brush it off with her hand. Then she hit the area hard. She stood up quickly and slapped at the edge of her dress. Her motions were fearful and frantic.

Then she stopped. She stood upright and straightened her dress. She took off her hat, held it in her teeth, combed her thick hair back with the fingers of both hands, and calmly put her hat back on.

She took a few steps toward the edge, and I sat still, watching her. She turned slowly, taking in the view, and then stopped. Something about her was different, she was looking out at the huge, open space in a way that concerned me. Maybe she was worried, maybe about me. I didn't know what it was, but something was weighing on her.

She stood there for a long time, facing away from me. There was no wind, but the heat of the day had eased off some. She was as still as a photograph, and I thought about drawing the curves and the shadows of her dress in the bright sunlight. She eventually turned around and walked back to where I sat.

"The bigness of all this is messing with me." She said it plainly, like a simple observation. I wasn't sure what she meant, if it was the bigness of the desert, or the bigness of what had been happening.

"I understand." I said it as calmly as I could.

She looked down at the water bottle, and I knew what she was thinking. I said, "Go ahead, don't try to save it."

She picked up the bottle, drank, and set it back down. She said, "Thank you. It's wonderful."

I put her bottle and mine back in the bag, and then the few remaining cookies. I stood up and shook my legs, first one and then the other. They were a little numb from sitting so long.

I said, "Let's head back to the truck."

She nodded, and we walked back to the chiseled steps. I carried the tote bag, so I sat and slid down to the sand. I offered my hand, but she didn't need it. She moved deftly with both her palms flat on the rock. Once down, we made our way along the footpath. I let her walk ahead to set the pace, and she moved a little quicker than I expected.

She was facing away from me and said, "That red dust bothered me. I don't know why."

I didn't say anything. That dust was everywhere, and there was no escaping it, so better to be silent.

As we got closer to the bridge, I said, "There's a woman who comes in the coffee shop, and she told me how the town used to be a lot busier. But after the bridge collapsed, nobody came through anymore. She said a funny thing to me. When she was a kid, she hated driving over it, and her parents felt the same way. It collapsed when she was a teenager."

Katie said, "I'm surprised there isn't a plaque or something out here, like a historical marker."

"She told me it fell in 1966."

The trail ended at the old road, and we stopped at the chain. Beyond was the broken bridge, and then empty space.

She pointed and asked, "What's that thing on the guard rail?"

There was a small metal box attached to a post above the railing on the right side. It was about halfway between where we stood and the drop-off beyond. I said, "I have no idea."

I stepped over the chain and walked out to it. It was about the size of a shoe box and looked like cast iron, with the raised words "Utah Department of Highways" on its front. The face was a door with a keyhole and fat hinges. It was something from another era, with its old lettering and sculpted surfaces.

I spoke loudly, and said, "I don't know what it is."

"It looks like a phone box." I spun around. Katie was standing right behind me. She startled me, and I could tell she thought it was funny.

I said, "Sorry, I didn't mean to yell. I thought you were still on the other side of the chain."

She said, "Police would use phone boxes before radios. They'd have a key."

I tried the little door, but it was locked. I said, "Maybe the road crew had a phone out here to monitor the bridge."

I leaned out over the guard rail, and there was a pipe coming out of the back of the box that led down under the bridge. I looked at its front again, and tapped the door with my knuckles. I don't know why I did that.

There wasn't much we could do. We walked back towards the chain, and I stopped. I touched the right front pocket of my jeans, then put my fingertips in that little pocket and pulled out a key.

Katie saw my expression and asked, "What is that?"

"Something I found."

Then I turned around and walked back to the metal box. The key slid in easily, but it wouldn't turn. I wiggled it, twisted hard, and the door opened.

Katie was next to me, watching with a serious expression.

There was an old black phone in the box and nothing else. I lifted it up and put it to my ear. I expected to hear a dial tone, but there was nothing. We both inspected the box and the phone. There was no dial, and she thought lifting it off the hook meant it would have rung in an office somewhere.

We both commented that the phone still looked new, like it hadn't aged in that box. Then I did a weird thing. I smelled the receiver. Memories of the old dial-up phone in my boyhood home came rushing back. Then Katie said, "Gimme that thing," and she smelled it, too. "Oh, Jesus, I miss phones like this."

Then she asked, "Why do you have that key?"

I said, "I found it."

"Where?" Her question was quick and intense.

"Out in the canyons."

"You found it? What does that mean?"

"Well, I found it on a body."

"Where did you find the body?"

"In the desert. He'd been dead a long time."

"Did you find anything else?"

"Some coins."

"Did you look at the dates on them?"

"No, I didn't think to check."

"Do you still have them?"

"No."

"Why did you have the key with you in your pocket?"

She asked the questions like a cop, and I didn't have a chance to think. I looked at her and said, "I'll tell you why I have this key if you tell me why you were in that canyon with a helicopter."

Her face changed, and she looked away. She seemed ashamed, but that quickly changed to a sort of sadness. She spoke slowly, "I can't tell you now, but I will when I can."

I studied her face and tried to figure out what she was thinking. Then I said, "When I opened that box and saw that phone, for maybe a second, I thought I could pick it up and someone would be on the other end, like God, or someone like that. Maybe a voice would tell me what's been going on, and they'd explain everything to me."

She stood still and said, "I wish it could be that easy, but it's not."

I said, "I know that. I know it's not easy. But I'm tired of—I don't know—of living at the whim of all this."

She looked down at the road, and I could swear I heard her say, "Me, too." But I knew she didn't.

I closed the door on the box, locked it, and put the key back in my pocket. Without saying anything we walked back to the chain, stepped across, and started toward Tony's truck.

We took our time and walked side by side on the sandy road. I said, "I forgot all about the key. I washed these pants twice, and I'm surprised it never fell out."

She didn't say anything, but I'm certain there were a thousand things she wanted to ask. I said, "We used to walk to school together, pretty much every morning."

Katie didn't respond. After a while she asked, "Do you think anyone jumped from the bridge?"

"I don't know. I could talk to Betty, she might know. She's the woman who told me what the town was like before the bridge collapsed."

She shrugged her shoulders, "Okay. I was just wondering."

I asked, "You said something felt wrong when you crossed the chain and walked out onto what was left of the bridge. Is that what you were feeling?"

She looked down and said, "I'm not sure, maybe."

I didn't know what might have happened on that bridge, but Katie felt something. I could see she'd taken on the weight of some dark event.

I said, "The bridge fell a long time ago. Don't let the ghosts of the past follow you on such a beautiful day."

I spoke those words like I was some kind of spiritual master, and I wish I hadn't said it. I was fully aware of my hypocrisy, and I was about to say as much when she said, "You're right. It is a beautiful day."

Then she punched me in the arm, just like walking to school in the morning.

29

THE DRIVE BACK TO TOWN WAS WONDERFUL. Katie was thrilled to dig through Tony's tapes and play his music. We joked and laughed in ways that felt so easy. I told her I could make dinner at the coffee shop, and warned her it wouldn't be much. She said, "I would love that."

We got back to town after the shop had closed. I parked in the alley, and we went in the back door. The sun was low, and without the brightness of the day, the main room had a completely different mood.

Katie said, "It's nice here now."

I filled a pitcher with water and ice, poured some in two glasses, and handed her one. We went into the kitchen, and she hopped up and sat on the stainless steel counter.

I said I could make burritos, and she said that would be great. The kitchen was small, and we talked as I gathered up everything and set it out. She asked if she could do anything, and I said she could put on some music.

I explained the stereo was in Tony's office. She asked if it was okay if she went in there, and I said he wouldn't mind at all. She stepped out, and a minute later there was music. She came back and hopped up on the same spot on the counter.

I said, "We mostly serve food in the morning, so sorry if this seems like breakfast."

She laughed, "Don't worry, I'm hungry."

I made four burritos with scrambled eggs, peppers, green chilies, brown rice, black beans, and a little bit of cheese. I fried them in a pan with butter and turned them repeatedly. They were done when the tortillas were crisp, and Katie helped carry everything out to the main room. She brought out the water and glasses, and I put out a bowl of green salsa and a few different hot sauces. I told her to sit, and I went back into the kitchen to get the pan.

When I came back out, there was a lit candle on the table. It was tiny and set in a shot glass. I asked, "Where did you find that?"

"It was on the window sill in Tony's office. I hope he won't mind."

"He'll be fine, no need to worry. It's nice."

I put a small folded towel in the middle of the table and set the pan on it. As I sat down, she asked, "Can I eat these with my hands?"

"Yes, absolutely."

They were hot but easy enough to hold. We said cheers and tapped our burritos. We ate and talked, but it was mostly about nothing.

As we started in on our second burrito, I said, "Can I ask about your dream?"

Her tone changed, and I worried I shouldn't have asked. But after a pause, she said, "Sure."

"If you don't want to talk about it, I understand."

"It's fine, you can ask." From her voice, it didn't sound fine.

I asked, "You said the dream felt like the apartment you were in during grad school. When was that?"

She lowered her eyes in thought, then said, "It would have been '89 and '90. I was in that apartment both years."

"You said your roommate moved out, and you didn't know why. Is that right?"

"I had two roommates, and one left. She never said why."

I asked, "How did she seem the morning she left?"

Katie sat motionless. I could see she was thinking, and after a long time she quietly said, "Horrified."

That wasn't the word I expected, and I saw the emotional effort it took for her to say it.

I asked, "Did she leave the same morning as your dream?"

"It's not like that. I had the dream last night, and she moved out twenty years ago."

I had to think. I had somehow treated the bright light in her room as a real event. I said, "Sorry. I mean, the way you explained it out by the bridge, it got mixed up in my mind. I'm really sorry, I didn't mean anything."

I was back-peddling and must have sounded flustered. Katie reached across the table, patted my hand, and said, "John, don't worry. It's okay."

She saw I was embarrassed, and her gentle touch melted that away. Part of me wanted to tell her about my dream from last night, but I needed to ask more, "The bright light in your dream, can you describe it?"

She shrugged like it was nothing, "I don't know. There isn't much to say."

"Please, anything you remember."

She was quiet before speaking, "It was really still in the room, like weirdly still. I know that's not how it looked, but more how it felt."

"Okay. Anything else?"

"It was different than normal light. You know how the flash on an old camera has that kind of slow burst of light? It was like the flash stopped time, and I was there, stuck in that frozen moment." She tilted her head and asked, "Does this make sense?"

I nodded yes. She was describing the same strange quality of the light I'd seen in my dream from this morning. I saw her struggling and waited for her to say more. I asked, "What is it, is there something else?"

She said, "Sorry, no. It was just a weird dream."

I wanted to ask more, but she seemed upset. We had been done eating for a while, and I asked if she wanted any coffee or tea.

She smiled and asked, "Do you have decaf?"

I gave her a haughty look and said, "Well, this *is* a coffee shop."

I got up and started gathering our plates. She stood up, too, and I said, "Please, let me. Just sit."

She ignored me and helped carry the few things back to the kitchen. We put the dishes in a tub, and I got a little stovetop espresso maker from a shelf. I said, "The machine on the counter takes a while to warm up, but this will be very good."

She sat on the counter in the same spot. I filled the little pot with water and coffee, screwed it closed, and set it on the stove.

I asked, "Do you want steamed milk?"

"How do you drink it?"

"Sometimes I take it black and use those." I pointed to a set of tiny cups on a shelf.

She said, "That sounds great."

I took two cups and two saucers and set them on the counter. Katie looked at me with this funny expression, like she was trying to make up her mind about saying something. I gave her an impatient look and said, "Katie, what are you thinking?"

"Do you remember those tests they made us take?"

The seriousness of her tone caught me off guard, and I asked. "What do you mean?"

She seemed uneasy, "I remember we took these weird tests."

I thought for a moment and said, "You mean in elementary school?"

"Yes, there was some testing thing, and we ended up staying after school."

I said, "You mean just you and me? When was this?"

"I'm not sure. Maybe fifth grade."

I was quiet for a while and then said, "They put us in the cafeteria and said they'd called our parents to tell them we would be staying after school. Is that right?"

"Yes."

"I haven't thought about that in forever. Do you remember what they were asking?"

She looked down and scrunched her eyebrows in concentration, then said, "No, I don't remember."

"I don't either." That wasn't true. I remembered some of what they were asking, but not much. I said, "There were two people in the cafeteria with us, and they seemed really serious."

She said, "I thought they were both substitute teachers."

"I don't know who they were, but they weren't anyone from our school, I remember that."

"It was two men."

The espresso maker started hissing. I said, "Yeah, I think so," and bent a little to see the flame and turned the heat down.

I turned back to face Katie, and something changed. She looked terrified. She said, "I'm sorry, we shouldn't talk about this. It's wrong."

I asked, "Katie, what are you saying?"

Now her voice was stern, "We should *not* talk about this. We should forget this."

Her face seemed heavy with dread, and I was about to say something when she was suddenly back to normal. She was bright-eyed and beautiful again, like she'd been moments before, like she's always been.

I asked, "Katie?"

She smiled that radiant smile and said, "I still think about elementary school. It was such a beautiful time."

Her words were heartfelt and real, and I believed them. Yet, the panic I saw was real. Something had taken control of her, and then it vanished.

The metal pot was hissing louder, and I took it off the stove. I was shaken by what I saw, but I filled both cups and slid one to her. She took a sip and said, "Wow, this is strong." Then she asked, "This is decaf, right?"

I told her yes, and not to worry. We talked a bit, and whatever happened was gone. She was calm and gracious, without a trace of fear. Everything felt nice in a way that I had to wonder if it had happened at all. But I know it did. I saw it, and something about her swept me along, and all I could do was get lost in her presence.

I got the glass jar of cookies, and we each had one. We finished the coffee, and I said I could drive her back to the motel, or we could walk.

She said, "Let's walk. It's a nice night."

Katie got her bag, and I opened the front door. We stepped out onto the sidewalk, and the air was cool and calm. I told her I knew a shortcut back to the motel. She smiled and said, "It's nice to be in good graces with the locals."

30

I KNEW A FOOTPATH that led from the main street to the motel, so there was no need to walk all the way out to the edge of town and double back. I found it while walking around the town. It cut around the playground behind the old elementary school, through a gate, then into the cottonwoods and across the empty river. This led to an open field, and from there you could see the motel.

I locked the front door, and we crossed the empty street. We stepped onto the sidewalk, and walked east. The storefronts were mostly vacant and all dark. I said, "This town isn't much for window shopping."

She laughed. I tried to downplay the dreariness of this place, but wasn't very convincing. There were a few street lights along the main street, and most didn't work, so there were some stretches of darkness. We approached one of the street lights that was on, and right as we walked under, it went off.

Katie looked up, and looked at me, then said, "Is that light trying to tell us something?"

I replied, "Maybe."

When we got to the old elementary school, I pointed to a dusty path in the dry grass and said, "This is it."

She looked down at it and said, "Okay, I'll follow you."

Her voice was game, but I could tell she was surprised the route was so meager. We stepped off the sidewalk, and I led the way. The path went between the school and an abandoned garage, then to the playground in back. There was a lone security light on the edge of the roof, and we passed under it and around the corner. We stopped and looked in one of the school windows. It was an empty classroom that hadn't been used in years. It was too dark to see much, and Katie said, "Oh, my goodness. This is kind of spooky. Aren't you scared?"

I said, "No."

She didn't seem scared, so her question seemed odd. It would've never occurred to me to feel scared in a quiet place like this. It was the opposite, I felt a profound sense of peace.

We walked around to the back of the school and saw the old playground. There wasn't much, a swing set, a slide, a jungle gym, and a broken merry-go-round. I had tried to spin it a few weeks earlier when exploring the town, and it wouldn't budge. Everything was overgrown with thorny weeds. The security light was around the edge of the building behind us, so there was no direct light back here, only a soft glow fading off in the darkness.

Katie said, "Wow. This is funny back here. It's cute."

I agreed. I had only ever been back here in the heat of the day, and it all felt harsh and barren. Now, in the cool of the night, it all seemed quaint, like we'd stepped into a shadowbox of some hazy memory. The swing set seemed huge in the dim light. It once had four swings, but now there were only two, side by side in the middle of the wide bar.

I said, "I don't think they can make these things this tall anymore. There are probably all kinds of liability issues. I haven't seen any like this since I was a kid."

She said, "Was ours this tall?"

By "ours" she meant the swing set at our elementary school. I said, "Maybe. We were shorter then, so it's hard to tell, but it was pretty tall."

She looked up and said, "I remember ours were giant, like this."

She sat in one of the seats, and the old chain made a quiet creak. She looked at me with a funny smile and said, "I don't know the last time I sat in a swing like this."

I stood still and looked at the empty swing next to her. I wasn't sure what to do. I was aware of what I had become. I was essentially a broken hobo, while Katie lit up everything around her with such dazzling grace. She was exactly like she'd always been, self-assured and calm.

My life had been a mess of twists and turns, and so much has been a struggle. I'd faltered and failed along this uneven path, and it all led me here, to this lonely spot. Yet, somehow it felt perfect, and the magic of this moment eclipsed my worries. I sat in the swing next to her. I could have felt awkward, but it was the easiest thing in the world.

Except for the creaking chains, everything was quiet. I tried to swing a little bit, but my feet were scraping the dust. I said, "It's not working. My legs are too long."

I tried again with my feet tucked under the seat on each backswing. I built up some speed, arcing higher with each pass, but the old framework of iron pipes groaned with each motion. I dragged my feet on the ground, skidded to a halt, and said, "Yikes, I could break this old thing."

Katie laughed and thanked me for stopping, "It felt like it was about to come apart on top of us."

We sat for a few minutes, and I pointed behind us into the darkness and told her, "That's the gate, and the path to the motel." Then I said, "I used to sneak through your backyard, through the gate in the fence to get to the frog pond. You remember there was a path there, right?"

She looked at me like I had said the dumbest thing imaginable. "John, of course I remember. I spent every day of every summer swimming there. Summer after summer, all the years I lived in that house."

I sat motionless and looked at the ground between us. I was suddenly confused and wasn't sure what to say. I thought about it and then cautiously explained, "I did, too. I was there, swimming all the time. Every summer day. I mean that, *every* day."

Katie described the narrow wooden dock that stretched out over the deepest part of the pond, and how everyone would run and see who could dive furthest. I added that there was a small area of sand to the right of the dock, and she described the big patch of beautiful grass further around the pond hidden in the trees. I agreed, and explained about the cattails across from the dock, and the lush smell of it all on those hot, humid days.

She was talking fast, "There was that huge tree at the edge of the pond, and we could get out on that big branch. It hung way out over the water and we'd jump from there."

I laughed and said, "I nailed some of those two-by-fours into the tree, so we could get up to that branch."

"Like a ladder, yes!"

I said, "Remember the nails on the dock? They were awful with bare feet, and we kept a hammer there to pound them flat. The hammer was hidden—"

"—in the crook of that knobby tree by the path." She finished my sentence.

We laughed and listed off all our friends who were there. I remembered the faces of all the kids from the neighborhood, and the songs on the radio. She described walking in the slimy mud, and how it felt between her toes. We remembered everything, except for one detail.

I asked, "You were there? It's funny, I can't remember you ever being there."

She looked puzzled and said, "I can't remember you either."

"I was there every day." My voice was slow and serious.

She looked at me for a long time, then whispered, "So was I."

The nostalgic mood was gone, and I could see the concern on her face. This didn't make sense, and we both knew it. I was about to say something when we both flinched. There was a quick blur above us, and we looked up to see an owl landing on the top bar of the swing set.

It was a big handsome barred owl. It sat calmly on the outside edge of Katie's side, and stared down at us. We looked at each other in astonishment.

Her eyes were wide with awe, and she mouthed the word, *Wow!*

The owl had landed in total silence, and it was both menacing and magical. I've seen plenty of owls, and they all have a weird kind of majesty. Neither of us dared say anything, knowing it might fly off and end the power of this moment. We looked up at the owl, then at each other, and then back up at the owl.

Her eyes sparkled with excitement. Then something white passed through the beam of the security lamp. She knew I saw something behind her and spun her head around. We both watched another owl fly toward us and spread its giant wings. With an impossible slowness, it landed on the same top bar of the swing set at the corner above me.

It was another barred owl, identical to the one on her side. Both of us were wide-eyed with wonder. Seeing one was amazing, but seeing two was absolutely mystical. Then the owl on her side let out a booming call, and Katie jumped. Barred owls are loud. I've heard them off in the distance a handful of times and marveled at the power of their voice. Hearing one so close was thunderous, and the other hooted just as strong. They began a forceful chorus, and all we could do was sit in our swings and take in the crazy power of it all. Her smile was huge and genuine, and I felt her pure amazement running through me.

I'm not sure how long it went on, but I saw Katie flinch. Her expression changed, she looked startled, and before I could ask what was wrong, I shuddered. My spine was zapped with a tiny electric jolt. It didn't hurt, but I'd never felt anything like it.

She whispered, "What's happening?"

I held up my arm, and even in the dim light, I could see the hairs standing straight up. I tried to show it to her, but she was looking up at the owls and gripping the chains with tight fists. Then I felt something. I was vibrating. It was subtle, like some buzzing music welling up along my back to the top of my head. I should have been scared, but I was delighted.

Katie giggled, "Do you feel it?"

And I nodded yes.

The owls continued their loud call and response. Each ringing squeal was more focused in its intensity. All at once the chains felt icy cold, and I don't know why, but we both pulled our feet up off the dusty ground.

I looked over at her beautiful face, stared into her bright green eyes, and without knowing why, I let go of one chain and held my index finger out, aiming it at her.

She smiled and did the same, pointing her finger at me. Neither of us said anything, we eased our fingers closer. It felt so weird, like pushing through jello. It reminded me of shuffling across the carpet with wool socks when I was a kid, trying to generate a spark on the doorknob.

Our fingertips got to about an inch apart, and she nervously asked, "What's happening?"

I didn't know what to say. All I could do was look at her and try to convey the sense of awe that had overwhelmed me. It was like she could read my expression, and she slowly moved her finger closer.

Both owls shrieked as we touched, and what happened next might be impossible to describe. I blacked out, and I guess I fell off the swing. I don't remember, but that's not important. It was like the power went out in a movie theater, and everything was dark, but another movie was now playing in my mind—a more important movie. I was struck with an immediate, perfect awareness, like some lightning bolt of knowing had ripped through me.

I said I blacked out, but that's not right. Part of me thought I had died, but I knew I hadn't. It was like entering a dream where time didn't exist. I saw Katie as a girl again, and I saw her now, all at once. It felt like her entire life slammed into me with a sudden, total knowing. And the girl was there, the skinny girl from the limbo room. I could see her clearly, and for one brief instant, I understood everything.

And there was more, a lot more.

31

I WAS LYING IN THE DUST when I came to. I looked up at the swing set, and the owls were gone. I sat up quickly, bumped the seat, and pushed it aside. Katie was lying next to me, and I touched her shoulder.

She didn't respond. I shook her gently and said, "Katie—Katie, come back."

She opened her eyes and stared blankly up at the sky. Her face was empty as a mannequin. I whispered, "Katie, I'm here. I know."

Her eyes widened, and she flinched. She turned and looked at me with such a haunted expression, and before I could say anything, she got up and started toward the gate. I jumped up and followed her, calling out, "Katie, wait."

By the time she passed through the gate, she was running. I followed her on the path through the cottonwoods, then across the dry river bed and up the other side. It was dark, and she moved fast. It was hard to keep up, and I pleaded, "Katie, please wait, please, it's okay."

She didn't slow down. I was a few steps behind her when we left the trees and ran into the big open field across from the motel. I cried out, "I saw her, too!"

I said it loud, and Katie stopped. She turned and faced me, eyes wide with anguish.

We stared at each other, and I said, "Katie, I've seen her, the little girl."

She looked like she might crumple to the ground. I said, "I don't understand it, but I've seen her."

She whimpered, "No, no, no, no, no—"

I stepped forward to hug her, and two men rushed towards us, they'd come from the motel. Katie had her back to them, and she saw me looking past her. By the time she turned, they were at her side, and they took hold of her. One was the helicopter pilot, and I didn't recognize the other. They held her arms like she was helpless.

The pilot asked her, "Are you all right?"

She replied, "I'm fine."

Her voice was shaky, and she clearly wasn't fine. I wanted to push them both away. I desperately needed to talk with her.

The pilot stood close and faced her. He said, "Look at me, Katherine, look right at me. Stand up straight. Breathe deep for me."

She stood a little taller and inhaled loudly. He didn't say anything else, but looked at her with grave intensity. I watched her face change. She went from helpless to something more neutral.

Then there was a third man, and then a fourth. All of them focused their attention on her. The pilot told one man to take her inside, and this guy started to lead her away, and I said, "Wait."

My voice was firm. I stepped toward Katie, and the other men lined up between me and her. I snapped, "What the fuck? Let me talk to her."

Katie turned and looked back at me, but I was blocked. They were trying to intimidate me.

The pilot said, "Stand down. It's okay."

They all eased off. He turned to me and said, "Go ahead, you can talk."

I said, "Tell your goons to back off and give us some room."

The pilot spoke to them quietly, and all but one stepped away, the one holding Katie's arm. I walked up and told him, "Give me a minute, please."

This was the guy who sat alone with a book at the coffee shop. He ignored me and looked at the pilot. He must have gotten some nod or something because he stepped away. I reached out and held Katie's hands, and said, "I'm here, I'm not going anywhere."

She looked at the circle of men around us, and then at me. She whispered, "I'm sorry about all this."

"Katie, I don't understand it, but we share something. Please know, I care. I do."

She managed a faint smile, but I could tell she was shaken. I leaned in close and whispered, "You aren't alone. I've seen her, too."

She shuddered, and I thought she might collapse. I grabbed her shoulders and steadied her. Then I said, "I'm glad we found each other again."

She nodded and said, "Me, too."

The men around us seemed on edge, and I knew I didn't have time to say much more. I said, "Please know, I'll be here. I'm close by."

I stepped back, and the crew moved in quickly and walked her back to the motel, all of them except the pilot. We stood in that empty field and watched as they all entered one of the rooms.

After they closed the door behind them, everything was quiet, and he asked, "What happened?"

How was I supposed to answer that? I looked at him for a long time, and his expression and manner told me a lot. I could tell he was aware that something strange had happened, and it was something he was used to.

I pointed to the motel and said, "I don't like what's going on here. All this."

"Yeah, I can't imagine you do." He looked around us, then up to the stars. He asked, "Was she hurt in any way?"

"I don't think so."

"I've worked with Katherine enough to know some of what she does. She's very determined."

He waited for me to say something, but I wasn't sure what he meant or how to respond. I stood still and stayed silent. He went on, "She's tough. You shouldn't worry."

"But I am worried."

I looked at him, wondering what he knew and what he wanted. I said, "Those men deferred to you. You were nice enough about it, but you gave them orders. And I'm curious, who gives you your orders?"

He didn't reply. It felt like both of us wanted the other to talk, but it was clear neither would say much. I said, "Tell your boss I want to talk with him."

He bobbed his head in a thoughtful way, but his expression didn't waver. He said, "We'll take good care of her. I'll tell her you're very concerned."

He eventually said goodnight, and it was clear that the conversation had ended. He wasn't going to say anything else. I walked back the way I came. Once I was in the shadows of the cottonwoods, I turned around. The pilot hadn't moved. He was watching me, and for all I knew, he would spend the whole night standing there. I walked back across the dry river in the dark, then through the cottonwoods, through the gate, and across the playground. Everything seemed perfectly ordinary, but I knew it wasn't.

I made my way to the main street and cut through the empty lot next to the coffee shop. It felt like I was being followed, and I turned around a few times, but no one was there. It would be pointless for anyone from that motel to feel the need to shadow me. Where could I possibly go?

I entered the shed and drank from a jug of water I kept near the door. It was a calm night, and I carried blankets, my pillow, and the pad out to the juniper bushes behind the shed. I needed to sleep on the ground.

32

My mind was racing. All I could do was lie there and stare at the cold, lonesome stars. Something happened in that playground, and I was desperate to understand what it was, and what it meant. And Katie's panicked reaction told me it happened to her, too.

I'm not sure how long we were lying in the dirt under the swing set, maybe only a minute. But that didn't match what took place, what I saw and felt.

I went somewhere, and it was utterly incompatible with this day-to-day physical realm. Wherever I was, it was more real than anything I'd ever felt.

It was like a dream within a dream, but saying that isn't enough, it's too simple. It would be like every moment in my life was a domino, with dominos lined up on both sides, and one of them was now, this moment, and the one next to it captured the moment before, and the one on the other side expressed the moment after. And each was a dream within the dream of the next. Going further down the line meant going deeper into a dream within a dream within a dream.

And all the dominos were falling, racing off in both directions, forward and backward in time—all of it happening at once.

Yet every domino is now, this moment, *all of them are now,* and there's nothing else. And each tipping tile is its own grand novel, full of joys and sorrows, insights and discoveries, all of it overflowing in mythic power. Yet each tile, each novel, is connected to the one next to it, and each is oblivious to the other's narrative, and all these infinite tipping moments are unaware there is something more, a grand consciousness fully absorbing all of it, looking down from above and drinking in every glorious story spilling forward and backward. And the author is heedless that anyone is reading their beautiful unending masterpiece. But it's more than being read, it's being experienced and lived.

I knew every word of every novel. I could feel the power of my unending line of stories, and Katie's, too. Not just the words, but the sea of roiling emotions, all of it alive and vital. All of it rushing off in both directions for eternity.

I could see my own life, and I could see Katie's, too, and I could see something was going to happen. It had a force to it, and I want to say it was bad. Maybe not bad, but important, and approaching fast, and it was important in ways I understood while I was there, but it was all fading. I couldn't remember what I knew so clearly, but I knew it was coming.

I must have fallen asleep at some point, or at least drifted in and out a few times. I hadn't moved at all. I'd been flat on my back facing up the whole night. And each time I woke, the Big Dipper had turned a little further around the North Star. And each time I woke, the memories from that timeless realm were further away. I wanted to hold onto it, but that was impossible. I know I saw the skinny girl, and there was no fear. I understood why she was there, and why it was important. And I could see into Katie's life, and how it was tangled up with so much, but this was all drifting away.

While I was in that place, I understood why she was here. I saw everything unfold and felt it from her perspective. Yet this was nearly gone. All I could sense was the terrible weight of it, and how trapped she seemed.

It was like she'd been playing some role, and she was good at it, and she was fully immersed in that surface reality, fully living it. But something else was happening on another level, at a deeper level, and she was unaware of it, as was I. But this hidden life was welling up, invading her waking life, yearning to make itself known.

This wasn't like forgetting snippets of a movie, because it hadn't happened that way. It was like the film was a million years long and I knew the entire thing, every frame, all at once. But it was impossible to remain tethered to so much.

When I sat up, I realized it was gone. It was like my ability to hold that knowing, the totality of it, was incompatible with being here, stuck here, in *this* realm. And now, sitting alone in the cold, I didn't understand how I could've held onto even a tiny fragment of it, let alone all of it.

The churning chaos had subsided, and I was no longer connected to that infinite well of knowledge. But something very real had happened to me—I was no longer in doubt. I fully knew. I fully understood.

I am a part of something, and I can't go back.

I put on my shoes and stood up. Now my head was above the bushes, and I could see across the alley. The lights were on at the shop. I gathered up my sleeping gear and carried it back to the shed. I set it all on my bed and changed my shirt. Then I crossed the alley and walked in the back door to the shop.

Tony saw me, and right away he could tell something was wrong. He asked, "What is it?"

I hadn't thought of what to tell him. After a long stretch of silence, I said, "Katie passed out last night. It happened when I walked her back to the motel. I'm not sure if she is okay or what might be wrong."

He asked a few questions, and there wasn't much I could say. I told him I needed to walk over to the motel to find out how she was doing.

Tony said, "Of course. Don't worry, I'm fine here alone."

I thanked him and poured coffee in a paper cup. I walked out the front door, crossed the street, and followed the same path around the empty school and through the playground. Everything seemed different in the daylight. There was no longer any charm. It felt dreary and abandoned. I walked past the swing set without slowing, and then through the gate. When I saw the motel I stopped and waited. I stood in the same spot on the grass where I'd spoken with Katie last night.

I waited, and after about five minutes, the pilot came out from one of the rooms. He wore the same green jump-suit he had on the night I first saw him in the canyon. He walked fast and stopped in front of me.

He said, "Katherine is doing okay. We've been monitoring her. Physically she is fine."

"What does that mean? Is she okay or not?"

"Her vitals are all normal, but she seems upset. She didn't sleep last night, she paced around a lot, and that's unlike her. She's usually very composed."

"Can I see her?"

"No. Not yet."

"When?"

He bobbed his head in this slow, brooding way. I could see he was trying to sort out his thoughts. When he answered, all he said was, "I don't know. Hopefully soon."

"How soon?"

He said, "It would help us if we knew what happened last night."

"I don't know. I truly don't."

"Is there anything you can tell me, anything at all?"

I thought for a long time, then said, "We both passed out, and we both woke up at the same time."

He asked, "How long were you unconscious?"

"I don't know. Maybe a few minutes."

"Where did it happen?"

I turned and pointed behind me, "Across the river bed, in the playground behind the old elementary school."

"Did she fall, or hit her head? Anything that might have caused an injury?"

"No. We were on the swing set talking. Sitting in the swings. There was something that seemed like static build-up. We both felt it."

He asked, "Were you near a power line or anything?"

"No, it didn't feel like that."

"What did it feel like?"

I stood there and looked at him. I could tell he cared about Katie and wanted to help. I wanted to tell him about the owls, but something in me told me not to. I said, "Right before it happened, the chains felt cold. The chains on the swings."

He heard me, and I could tell he was turning it over in his mind. Then he asked, "Do you have a phone number where I can call you?"

"No. You can find me at the coffee shop during the day." I was going to tell him I lived across the alley behind the shop, but I had a feeling he already knew that.

He said, "If you think of anything, please tell us. No matter how insignificant it seems. It might help."

I wanted to help, but I didn't trust him. It all seemed too weird, and his team, and Katie, they were all here because of that weirdness. And so was I.

I said, "Tell your boss I want to talk with him."

He looked at me but didn't say anything. I'd said that last night, and I got the sense he didn't like being told the same thing twice.

He said, "Everybody working here knows Katherine and cares about her. She'll be fine, and I'll come find you when she's able."

"I'm worried."

"I know you are, and so are we." I sensed he meant that, and I thanked him.

33

I WALKED BACK ALONG THE TRAIL through the cottonwoods and then to the playground. When I got to the main street, I passed the coffee shop and walked another two blocks to Betty's store.

The door was locked. It was still early, and I knocked on the window. I waited and saw Betty coming out from the back room. She walked across the store and opened the door.

Her eyes were bright and clear, but I'd obviously surprised her. She said, "John, what is it?"

"Could we talk?"

She said of course and let me in, then closed the door. We stood in the front of the store, and she asked, "Are you all right?"

"I'm okay." There was a lot I wanted to know, but I wasn't sure where to begin. I said, "I went to the site of the old bridge yesterday. It was the first time I'd been there."

She looked at me, waiting for me to say more, and then asked, "Did anything happen?"

I tried to collect my thoughts before speaking, then asked, "Do you know if anyone ever jumped from the bridge?"

"I don't think so. I don't remember anyone ever saying anything about that. Why do you ask?"

"I'm not sure. The site had a weird feeling to it."

She gave me a look that told me she understood. I asked, "How did the bridge actually collapse? There's no sign there, or any kind of historical marker."

She said, "Nobody really knows. I know it fell at night. The story was that a car started across and didn't realize the middle had fallen out. This guy jammed on the brakes and had to drive in reverse to get off the bridge. Thinking about that terrifies me."

"Was anyone hurt when it fell?"

She looked away, her eyes focused on nothing, then said, "Nobody knows, but I remember everyone in town was worried at the time."

"You told me the bridge scared you, and your parents, too."

"It scared a lot of people. After it fell, I remember people saying they'd always had a bad feeling about it."

She was quiet, and I could tell she wanted to say more. I asked, "What is it? What are you thinking?"

"People said stuff. There was some talk before the bridge fell."

"What kind of talk?"

"There were some weird stories. People were seeing big birds. Kids in my school talked about it. Even my dad saw something, but his story wasn't much compared to other things I'd heard."

"What happened with your father?"

"He was driving home and said he saw a giant bird standing on the side of the road. This was at night, and he was heading east, and it happened right after they crossed the bridge. My mom was in the car with him, but she was asleep and didn't see anything. I know that doesn't sound like much."

Her story ended awkwardly, and I waited for more. Then I asked, "Was there something else?"

"This is gonna sound weird, but he said he was hit by a wave of dread right before he saw it—the bird."

Betty usually spoke in a quick easy manner, but her cadence had slowed. What she said next was steady and solemn. "My mother felt it, too. She was asleep when they drove past it, so she never saw anything, but she felt that same dread. She felt it when she woke up, and for weeks after. I was in high school when it all happened, and I remember how she was. She never talked about that night, but I asked her before she died, about the feeling. She said it was like getting tar on her hands, it wouldn't go away. Something was sticking to her."

I asked, "When did it end?"

"When the bridge fell."

"You said there were other stories. What were those like?"

"Some were just stories. There was a place to park out near the bridge, and kids from high school would drive out there at night. For this little town, it was sort of our Lover's Lane. Kids would say they'd seen glowing eyes off in the dark, or some big thing would stand at the window of their cars. Spooky stories. I had friends that said they'd seen things out there, but I wasn't sure what to believe."

"You said you'd heard other things, other stories. What did you mean?"

She looked at me in a way I hadn't seen in her before. Her eyes were just as bright, but her bearing had changed. When she spoke, her words were uneasy, "Why are you asking this?"

"When I was out there yesterday, at the bridge, I was with a friend. She seemed frightened in a way that didn't make sense, and it bothered me."

"Frightened how?"

"I'm not sure. It was like the site was haunted, and she was somehow picking up on that."

Betty looked at me with concern. I didn't know what to say, and waited in silence.

She asked, "Was this the pretty lady with red hair?"

I straightened up, trying to think of some lie, or a way to change the subject, but I said, "Yes."

"You said she was frightened. Is she doing okay?"

I didn't want to answer that, and I asked, "How do you know about her?"

She smiled softly and said, "Oh, John, it's a small town. I saw you with her on the patio of the coffee shop after it was closed. It was something very nice for an old lady like me to see."

I didn't want to talk about Katie, and I asked, "What other stories have you heard about the bridge?"

She nodded toward two chairs in the back corner, and said, "Let's sit. I don't want to stand anymore."

I walked with her, letting her sit first, and I sat in the chair facing her. She patted the armrest and said, "I priced this one a little too high. I sit here and read a lot, and I would miss it if it left the store."

I couldn't relax, and leaned forward with my elbows on my knees.

She said, "A man worked here back then, but he wasn't from here. He worked for the state. The story I heard was that he—" She stopped, and I waited as she looked out at the room. Eventually, she took a long deep, breath and went on, "He had been working out at the bridge, and it was dark by the time he left. He said something felt wrong, and he'd been feeling it the whole day. He was parked on the west side of the bridge, and he had to cross it to get back to this side, where he lived."

She stopped again. Betty had told me plenty of stories, but this was somehow different. She was very deliberate with her words.

I said, "Please, go on."

"He said he saw something on the bridge, and it followed him. He said it was some kind of bird, and it was big."

She held out her hand, and it was trembling. She said, "Oh, dear me, I haven't talked about this in a long, long time."

"Betty, I would like to hear it, if that's okay."

"It was night and he was driving across the bridge, but he couldn't see much. It was flying right at the edge of his headlights. People said it was a big bird, but he didn't know what it was. He said it seemed black, and it stayed right alongside him as he drove. When he got off the bridge, he started driving faster, but that road winds around, so he needed to slow down, and it slowed down, too. And it would speed up when he did, and he said it wasn't flying like a bird. It wasn't flapping its wings. It wasn't like that. It was more like a fish swimming through water."

She was anxiously gripping the arm of her chair. I reached out and set my hand on hers, and said, "It's okay, please, go on."

"He said it would dart forward. It was slow, but at the same time it stayed near his car. And other times, it was right up close to his window as he drove, and it scared him terribly."

She looked at me, waiting for some approval to say more. I kept my hand on hers and squeezed gently.

"He said he had to stop, and this doesn't make sense, but there was a tree, or some kind of bush, growing in the middle of the road. He had to drive out on the sand to get around it, and when he got back on the highway, the black thing was gone."

She looked at me and said, "There wasn't any tree growing out of that road, and he knew it."

I asked, "Did you hear this story from someone else, or did he tell it to you?"

Her eyes were glassy, and she whispered, "He told me."

I could tell there was something more, and I asked, "What happened?"

"He disappeared. Nobody saw him after the bridge fell. People thought maybe he was on it when it happened, and they looked for a body in the river and in the wreckage, but never found anything."

She stopped and turned away. I stayed still with my hand on hers. She looked up at the ceiling, then down at the floor, and when she spoke it was hushed and distant.

"I was sixteen, and he was thirty-two. He was this kind soul, and for me, at that time in my life, to know someone so caring, I was—"

She trembled, and then she was crying. She wiped the tears with her hand and turned in her chair. She reached down to a shelf behind her, and then set a box of tissues between her knees. She said, "Oh, look at me. I can hardly talk. Things just rush back."

I said, "You are doing fine, don't worry."

She wiped her cheeks with a tissue, and I sat quietly. After a while she said, "You don't want to live in a small place like this and get pregnant, not when you're so young."

I asked, "What was his name?"

"Zachary. Everyone called him Zack, but I always called him Zachary. He never knew."

She slumped in her chair, and said, "That was an agonizing time, and he was gone before I realized I was pregnant. The church had a place for me to go, and I had the baby, and they made all the arrangements. I only ever held him once, and then he was gone."

"Oh, Betty, I'm so sorry."

"It was a long time ago. But these things never really leave you."

She was quiet, and I didn't move or say anything.

She took a slow, deep breath and said, "I was gone for all those months, and it was very difficult when I came back. Everybody knew. Some people were so harsh. The most pious were the worst, and that was a lot of people in this town. Some folks were gentle and understanding, but not many. Zachary had a few friends here, and they were heartbroken, and they looked after me some. Giving up a child is a wound. There is such a burden, a burden of loneliness."

I shifted in my chair, reached in the little pocket of my pants and pulled out the key. I showed it to her. Then I said, "This opens a metal box on the bridge."

She took it and looked at it, then set it in her palm and squeezed. She held it to her heart and said, "He used to call me from that phone. He worked for the state highways, and there were always problems out there. The lights wouldn't work, and he had to check on things. He'd call the county switchboard from that box, and they'd connect the call to our phone. I remember my mom would answer sometimes. She didn't approve, but I knew she liked him. They would always talk some before she handed the phone over to me. This wasn't too long after the black thing had followed him across the bridge, and the tree in the road. But he still needed to go to work, and it really bothered him being out there alone."

She took a deep breath and said, "He called me from that box the night the bridge fell. The police had the phone log, and they came to the house and talked with me. They were concerned with his emotional state, and wanted to know what he said, if he was all right. I told them he seemed fine. They'd found out from people in town that he had the experience with the bird thing, and they knew that others had seen something, too. I guess there would have been reports with the sheriff's office."

She carefully turned the key in her hand, examining the back and the front. She asked, "Where did you get this?"

"I found it out in the desert, in the high country out south of town."

She looked at me and narrowed her eyes, "What do you mean you found it?"

I waited before speaking, and after a slow, deep breath, I said, "I found it on a body. It was in his pocket."

I could see she was thinking, and it was unclear if she was upset or relieved. She asked, "Was it a nice place for him?" Her voice quavered with emotion.

"Yes. It's a beautiful place, more so than any place I have ever been, or could ever imagine."

She stared off at nothing, and said, "Oh, my sweet Zachary."

She touched the key to her lips and kissed it softly. Then she asked, "Did you—do you know how he died?"

I knew what she meant, she was asking if he had killed himself. I replied, "It looked like he had fallen. I found him at the base of a steep section of rock. It was an accident."

She said, "He was my first love. My true love."

She looked around the room like she wasn't sure where she was. My heart ached for her, and I asked, "This all sounds so hard. Why didn't you move away from here?"

"I thought about it, but this was my home. I stayed. I sort of gave up. I could never say this to anyone, but part of me always hoped that one day, maybe, there would be a knock at the door, and I'd open it, and I would see his beautiful blue eyes again."

There was nothing to say, and we sat quietly for a long time. Her eyes were searching for something that wasn't there. I kept my hand on hers, and was still leaning forward in my chair. She eventually took her other hand and set it on top of mine, as if to reassure me. She smiled and said, "It's nice that you are part of our funny little town. It's been very nice for me."

"This town has been nice for me, too. It feels good to be a part of something."

She stood up, and so did I. We hugged in a way almost no one ever does. These memories and emotions had taken a toll on Betty. I could feel it as I held her. I wanted to say more, but couldn't. I kissed her forehead and stepped back.

I said, "I'm grateful we talked."

All she could do was nod. I glanced over at the door. She understood and walked me out to the sidewalk.

I looked up and down the main street. It was silent and empty. I said, "I found something in this town."

She smiled and said, "Most people leave this town to find something, that's why there's no one here anymore."

"You're here, and so is Tony."

She smiled and said, "And the pretty lady with the red hair, she's here, too."

I didn't know what to say. I had no answer to why I was here, or why Katie was here.

I looked at Betty, "This town, this beautiful valley. I just sort of ended up here. That journey, and why it happened, I don't understand it. I've been here all this time, and no one, not one person, has asked me where I'm from or why I'm here."

She said, "John, nobody would ask that. This is the end of the road, and everyone here knows that."

Walking back to the coffee shop was like swimming through anguish. So much had unfolded so fast, and I struggled to keep up with it. I should have told Betty that I was adopted, and that my parents did their very best for me. She gave up a child, and I could feel her grief. I stopped on the sidewalk and almost turned around. I wanted to tell her, but couldn't. I was afraid telling her would add to her suffering, so I kept walking.

When I got to the shop, Tony asked about Katherine, and how she was doing. I said I had talked with someone she works with, and she was okay, but I didn't know much. I could tell he was concerned, and that meant the world to me.

34

THE REST OF THE DAY WAS A BLUR. Tony left the shop a little early, and I did everything to close up. When I was done, I sat at the table in the middle of the room with a few pens and a sheet of cardboard. The page was blank and stayed that way. All I did was stare out at the street.

As the afternoon turned to evening, a big gray pickup truck made a U-turn and parked out front. I watched the pilot get out and walk up to the screen door. He saw me sitting alone and tried to come in, but the door was latched shut from the inside.

He leaned close to the screen and said, "The boss wants to talk with you."

I asked, "Now?"

"Right now."

I came out and locked up, and when I turned around he was waiting on the street, standing next to the open driver's door of the truck. He looked annoyed, like I was dragging my feet. He pointed with his chin and said, "Get in."

I opened the passenger door and froze. I had this ominous thought, like I was a bit player in a crime movie. He saw how I stalled out, got behind the wheel, and slammed his door. He looked at me through the cab and said, "Just get in. I'm not gonna kill you."

I climbed in. The drive meant going a few blocks east, then turning north. I asked, "Does this guy talk to many people?"

He replied, "What do you mean? Like, does the boss normally ring the dishwasher at the coffee shop to come and have a nice chat?"

That was deliberately spiteful, and I felt tempted to snap back, but he was right. I don't think he was used to being the boss's errand boy, and he wasn't who I wanted to talk with anyway, so I stayed quiet.

After about a quarter mile, he said, "I saw Katherine earlier this afternoon for a little bit."

His tone surprised me. There was concern in his voice, and he stared ahead as he spoke, "She's doing better, but she isn't able to see you, not yet. It seems she needs some time to recover, and everyone thinks it will be soon."

I said, "Thank you."

He never turned his head to look at me. We crossed the bridge over the dry river and turned onto the road that led to the motel.

As we approached, he left the asphalt driveway out front and followed a gravel path around to the back of the building. He parked the truck and we got out. There were two 18-wheelers blocking part of the dirt lot. These were 53-foot trailers, and that's as big as they get. I know this because I spent a season painting these things when I lived near Vegas. I used to paint logos on them, but that was a long time ago. Now it's all done with computer-printed vinyl panels, so I might be the last man on earth to have actually painted one with a brush.

We walked around the back of the trucks to the other half of the lot, and the pilot stopped. He pointed to a covered wooden deck out at the far end of the motel and said, "He's there. He's waiting for you."

He was looking right at me as he spoke, and there was a quiet humanity in his voice. Then he turned around and left me alone. I stood and watched him walk away. When he was gone, I walked toward a free-standing deck set away from the back of the motel. It was built recently. I know that because it wasn't here the morning I'd arrived on the helicopter.

This thing was like something you'd see behind a home in Palm Springs, a place to sip white wine in the shade. Everything was raw lodgepole and beautifully crafted. It had a canvas-covered trellis and a low wall around its perimeter topped with plants. The plants were tall, and the fabric hung down low enough that the interior was mostly hidden. It looked dark inside.

As I approached, I saw a man standing in the shadows. He walked to the entrance, parted a thin mesh, and held it aside. He smiled and said, "Welcome. Come in."

I went up three steps, ducked under the mesh fabric and stepped inside. The shade felt cool and pleasant. It seemed like I was no longer in this beaten down little town. The north end was open and faced out onto the emptiness of the valley floor, and the barren cliffs in the distance were beautiful in the evening light.

He stood tall and said, "Hello, John, it's good to meet you."

I was surprised by his presence. He had an ageless face, and was affable in a way that seemed disarming. He wore khakis and a short sleeve shirt. He was dressed ordinary, but didn't seem ordinary at all. He reached out his hand, and I shook it.

Now that I was inside, I could see the plants were fake. Some looked plastic, but most were some kind of paper, like a stage prop. He asked me if I wanted anything to drink or eat, and I said no. He asked if I was sure, and I said I was. He sat down in a chair at a round wooden table, and gestured to another chair across from him. He said, "Please."

I sat, and the chair was surprisingly comfortable. There was a pitcher of water on the table and two glasses, and a thin aluminum laptop. I didn't notice it as I approached, but the sheer black mesh ran around the entire deck. This is what he held open for me when I stepped up into the shade. Thin cords were connected to the mesh at a few points along the inside of the trellis frame, as if the whole thing was electrified. At first, I thought it was for mosquitos, but it's too dry for them here.

He looked at me and said, "How can I help you?"

This was a simple thing to ask, but his directness caught me off guard. I had been desperate for some understanding, yet I wasn't sure what to say.

I had to think for a bit, then said, "Things around here—things have happened—and it's been difficult for me. There's so much I don't understand. I've met a few people that seem to be working for you, and I've asked why they are here. Because of—" I was struggling and stalled out, I needed to think. This wasn't easy to express. I took a deep breath and went on, "Because of what's been happening to me. I've tried to ask, but they sort of brushed off my questions. And, I'm hopeful you can answer some things."

He smiled and said, "I'll do my best."

I asked, "Why is Katie here?"

He said, "You mean Katherine, right?"

"Yes."

He leaned back in his chair, and turned slightly to face the open view to the north. He said, "I've known about Katherine for a long time, yet we've only been working together a short while. She's very good at what she does, and she's been a very strong member of our team."

He stopped there, and I waited for more. Then I said, "Okay. That's all fine, but why is she here?"

"Yes—why." He spoke those words deliberately, then looked out at the land and seemed to study something off in the distance. After some time, he said, "To answer why Katherine is here, I'll need to try to explain why my team is here. We are trying to understand something. And that something has evaded us. It defies our attempts to study it, or to understand it, or even to define it. We've made some headway, but this work has been very difficult. Does this make sense to you?"

"More than you can know." There was a bit of anger in my voice.

"Yes, I imagine you understand."

I asked again, "Why is Katie here?"

He nodded thoughtfully, and then said, "This is something very subtle, very difficult to pin down, and it might be hard to explain."

"Try me. I'm very patient."

His head tipped down in thought before speaking, and I could see a resolve in him. Eventually, he said, "Let me ask you a question, why are *you* here?"

I spoke slow and clear. "I have no fucking idea why I'm here."

He said, "And neither do I. I have some ideas, but I truly don't know."

"What are your ideas?"

"My foremost idea is that reality is not what we perceive it to be. And that's a very open-ended way to frame an idea."

I asked again, "Why is Katie here?"

He answered in a restrained cadence, "She brought us here. She brought my team here."

"How?"

"Katherine was the first to, well—to find this site. She was working with Timothy. I believe you've met him."

"Yes, we rode together in your helicopter."

He smiled and said, "It's not actually mine."

I thought he might laugh, and I cut him off, "Please, I need to understand what's happening here."

He sat up. Until then he'd been sitting back in his chair. Now he was leaning forward and looking straight at me.

"Katherine and Tim have been partnered on a series of projects, and much of the work they've been doing is very advanced. They had been working together in an office. We call it 'the lab,' and they were getting good results in a series of projects. Very good results. These have been new avenues of research."

His voice was serious, and he waited, as if he needed my assurance before saying more. I said, "Go on."

"Something happened almost a year ago. Tim sat with Katherine in the lab. He held a sealed envelope, and inside was a single piece of paper. The paper had nothing on it but a randomly generated set of numbers. I had those same numbers locked in a file in my office, and this was over two thousand miles from Tim and Katherine. These numbers were created on a computer by one person, typed on the paper by another, and put in the envelope by someone else. It was then put in the mail by another person. This package went to three sites around the country until it arrived at the lab. None of these people knew what the other had done. So before Tim ever touched the envelope, it went through at least seven people, each passing it on to the next, and nobody knew what was inside. Are you following this?"

"Yes."

"Good. We did this in an attempt to ensure there would be no external influence. We needed it to be an overly redundant blind test, and we adhere to a set of strict protocols to safeguard the process. Tim worked with Katherine in a designated room, and Katherine never touched the envelope. Tim held it, but never opened it. He simply asked her to describe what was in it."

I interrupted, "Wait, is Katherine some sort of intuitive, or psychic—is she doing remote viewing or remote sensing?"

He narrowed his eyes and said, "Essentially, yes. How do you know about this?"

"I used to do my work at night, and I listened to a lot of AM radio talk shows."

"I see," he replied with a smile. Then he opened the laptop, and said, "I want to play you a recording of what happened." He clicked something on the keyboard and slid the laptop to the center of the table, so it was closer to me.

The first sound was some shuffling, as if people were shifting in chairs. Then I heard Tim's voice saying, "Katherine, describe the contents of this envelope."

The audio was very clear, and after a long pause, Katie said, "There is water. I'm looking down at it. I'm on my stomach, lying down, and looking down."

Tim asked, "What do you see?"

"There's water. There's sand. And, it smells nice."

Tim said, "Describe what you see."

"I'm looking down at water, and it's—it's way down there. I'm way up above the water, above the river. It seems so small from where I am, so far above it, and there's a little island."

She spoke slowly, and you could hear the uncertainty in her voice. After a pause, she said, "There's sand. And orange rock, and red rock. It's big and grand. And—and, it's beautiful."

Then she gasped. Her emotion startled me, and I flinched. You could hear her breathing, it was quick and anxious. There was some noise, like someone was moving, and Tim asked, "What is it? Katherine, what do you see?"

"I've—I've been here before—it's—it's—oh God, I'm back—."

Katie was crying, I could hear it, and Tim asked, "What's happening? Tell me."

She sounded scared and started sobbing, "I'm here again—that was him— he's leaving—he's gone." Then she cried out, "Oh God, he's gone!"

There was noise in the room. Something was happening. Tim said, "Katherine?" He was away from the mic, and his voice echoed differently. He was panicky, "Katherine—wake up. Wake up!"

There were more sounds, like someone moving quickly. The man across from me clicked the keyboard, and the computer went silent.

He looked at me and said, "That got the attention of my team."

I asked, "Was she all right?"

"Yes. She passed out, and we don't know why. It didn't last but a few minutes. She came to, and she was fine. This surprised Tim, and everyone on the team."

I stared hard at the man across the table from me. Katie had described the canyon, and we both knew it.

I asked, "The numbers on the paper, where did those come from?"

"From me. I asked something aloud before going to sleep. I've done this before when I've been stuck in this work. I needed a way to access the issue our team had been trying to solve. I keep a pad of paper by my bed, and the next morning there were two words on the page, and I have no memory of writing anything. It wasn't there when I went to sleep, and it was in my handwriting."

I asked, "What was it?"

He said, "I can't tell you. But I can tell you that I was in the room as a team member generated the numbers. I was thinking about those two words, but I didn't tell him anything."

I said, "Then the numbers weren't random. There was an intention to them."

He gave me an odd look, like he was enjoying our little talk. I asked again, "What were the words?"

He smiled but didn't say anything. I was about to ask again, but his face told me not to. Then I asked, "What was the question you asked before going to sleep?"

"I asked to be shown a way to cross over into another realm."

"What do you mean by another realm?"

He looked straight at me and said, "If you found that canyon, I think you know what I mean."

I didn't say anything. We just stared at each other.

Eventually, he said, "After that first session, everyone was worried about Katherine, especially Tim. So it wasn't until the next day that he opened the envelope, but it was only numbers. The protocol was that he would contact someone in my office and read the numbers over the phone. Normally we'd send a photo, or an explanation, as a way to verify the accuracy of the session. But not this time."

He paused and thought for a bit, as if wondering how much to share. When he spoke again, it was slow and deliberate, "I sent Tim another envelope. It went through the same string of measures. At this point I hadn't met Tim or Katherine, so neither knew the source of these requests. Nobody knew. It took over a week for it to arrive at the lab, and in that time they had been working on a long list of other assignments. She had been trying to view other targets, so this was simply another envelope among plenty of others. Inside that envelope were the same set of numbers, and this second reading was very different."

He searched the laptop for a little bit, then said, "Okay, here's what happened."

He clicked something, and I heard Tim's voice saying, "Katherine, describe the contents of this envelope."

Within seconds she said, "White walls. It's well lit. There are lines, things lined up, like vertical lines. It's quiet. There are people there, not many. It seems tidy, the room, it's clean and there are straight lines. It's not a big room, but it's tall, like the ceiling is high. There are windows. It's bright."

Her voice was calm and quick, as if this was effortless. She said, "This place, this room, it has a nice feel to it."

Then we heard Tim's voice asking her if she could draw what she was seeing, and she said yes. Then the man across from me stopped the recording, opened a folder, leafed through a few pages, and handed me a single sheet of paper. He said, "Katherine drew this."

It was a simple sketch, and I recognized it immediately. I said, "This is the back room of the Shiprock Gallery in Taos."

He nodded, "Yes, we know that."

I'd been in this room many times. The vertical lines were big paintings set upright in narrow floor-to-ceiling stalls. The windows on the back wall looked out to the alley behind the gallery. The sketch captured it accurately.

I asked, "How did you figure that out?"

He said, "During the session, Tim had Katherine move her awareness from this back room out to the street. She read the sign and the address."

I set Katie's drawing on the table between us and said, "You bought my painting."

He nodded and said, "Yes, I did."

"The painting with the tree, *The Dream*."

He nodded again, this time much slower, and said, "Yes."

I wasn't surprised. At this point, even the weirdest stuff seemed normal. I tapped the image Katie drew, and said, "For a time, this place had that painting in its collection. It would have been in this room, in among those canvases."

I don't know why I bothered to say that, because he'd obviously figured out it had been there. He gave me this untroubled smile, like this was nothing more than a normal conversation.

I slid the picture across the table, and he put it back in the folder. Then I said, "I don't understand what's happening. Why are you here?"

He took a deep breath, looked past me and stared out at the emptiness. I wasn't sure if he was posturing for drama or was genuinely trying to compose his thoughts.

He said, "We had a lot of pieces to a puzzle, a very complicated puzzle, but nothing was fitting in a way that led us anywhere. We needed a map."

I thought for a moment, and then asked, "And my painting was a map?"

"Oh, yes. It was a very good map. It was a vital part of what led us here."

"And what is here?"

"We don't quite know that. We have a lot of ideas, but we are struggling to understand something beyond *this*." He gestured with his hand, sweeping it in a slow wide arc as if saying *everything*.

He went on, "There are places that hold a special power. There are energies, and these points are very difficult to understand."

I asked, "What are you saying, that these places are some kind of magical doorways?"

"I wish it were that simple. I understand a door. What it means, how it works. I am trying to understand something much more elusive." I could see him formulating his thoughts, and then he asked, "If a door is locked, what do you need?"

"A key."

"Yes, precisely."

He looked at me and waited. I said, "And Katie is that key."

"None of what is happening here, right now, could have happened without Katherine."

"Yeah, well, I don't know what that means. What *is* happening here?"

"John, I can only imagine some of the things you've seen and experienced. But I know you've experienced them. These are a part of something that is terribly difficult to comprehend. We get a little glimpse now and again, but our hope, our goal, is to truly understand these things."

"Is that possible?"

"I believe it is, but maybe only up to a point."

"Why Katherine?"

"She has a unique gift. Yet, to fully achieve her potential, she needed something."

"And what would that be?"

He smiled and said, "That—would be you."

I was suddenly very cold. That wasn't what I thought he would say.

Part of me wanted to run, and part of me wanted to lash out, to jump across the table and hit him hard. But I did nothing. All I could do was sit perfectly still and stare at him.

35

We looked at each other in silence. I was fighting back a feeling of dread, and there was no hiding it. He read my face, and I saw concern in his eyes. He stood up and said, "Come with me."

I pushed my chair away from the table and got up. He went to the edge of the deck, parted the mesh, and we stepped back down to the hard ground. The sun had set, but it wasn't yet dark. We walked together across the gravel toward the big trucks, and he said, "For a while we had quite a crew here. There was a lot of work to get things set up. Mostly they're gone, and it's only the core team now."

He pointed out to the open landscape and said, "The helicopter is out there." I looked but saw nothing. He smiled and said, "You don't see it, but it's out there."

He sounded so proud of himself, like he had invented some advanced technological camouflage. It seemed absurd, and I figured he was lying.

We approached the rear of the closest truck, and there was a black metal platform with stairs lined up with the back door of the trailer. We climbed up, undid the latch, and opened one of the tall doors. There were boxes on pallets along both sides of the interior, and a narrow aisle between them. This passage was one pallet deep and ended at a wall of wooden boxes stacked to the ceiling.

He stepped in, moving between the pallets to the wall of boxes. Then he pulled a card from his shirt pocket, touched it to something, and a door swung inward. There was nothing to see before it opened. It was obviously built to be hidden. He took a single step into the darkness, then turned to me and said, "Come in. You'll want to see this."

He moved in further and held the door for me. When I was inside, he turned on the lights. The interior was maybe forty feet long, with a narrow table in the middle. Beyond that, centered on the back wall, was my painting—*The Dream*.

He closed the door and turned on a few more lights, and now my painting was lit with the elegance of a museum. I walked the length of the room and stood before it. The canvas was eight feet wide and nearly five feet tall. It was mounted with only a few inches of empty space on each side, any wider and it wouldn't have fit.

The colors were much brighter than I remembered. My only reference for over a decade had been the black and white photo in the three-ring binder in my studio, so its boldness surprised me. It was painted with a rawness that didn't match my other work. I got up close and saw the lumpy thickness of the paint. Usually, I work hard to create a smooth surface on the canvas, brushing everything flat.

I took a step back to take in the whole image. A lonely tree was centered on the canvas with a blue ball of light floating in its gaunt branches. Psychedelic lines, little dot patterns, and swirling colors flowed out from the glowing focal point of the tree.

A horizon line divided the image, the trunk and branches rose up from that line, and below, gnarled roots reached down into the earth. All this was painted with an eerie radiance, as if every part of the tree were glowing.

I could hear him walking behind me alongside the table, and I heard him stop.

I've gotten stuck in my ways, producing the same big paintings with the same themes for too many years. When I look at the things I've done, there's an internal flip-flopping that never goes away. Part of me recognizes there was skill involved in creating it, and a voice in my head can rationalize that it could be called good or pleasing. But there's another voice that says it's lifeless, there's no heart. These clashing thoughts have always been in me, and the uncertainty can be brutal.

Yet standing there, I felt none of that tension. This painting has a heart.

I stepped back further, and gave up trying to examine all the colors and details. I let it all in. I felt a calm familiarity with that scrubby tree, and I suddenly realized something—I'd slept under it. This was the tree on the island in that clear river at the bottom of the canyon. I knew it with a clarity that scared me.

I turned around and looked at this odd man. He'd been standing next to the table, watching me as I looked at my own painting. Did he know that this was the tree on the sandy island? I don't think he did, and there was no way I was going to tell him.

I took a deep breath and said, "I haven't seen this for almost twenty years."

He said, "I've spent some time looking at your other work, and this is an outlier of sorts. It's nothing like your other paintings."

"Yes, I know."

I was standing with my back to the painting, and he pulled a chair back and sat down. He leaned forward, put his elbows on the table, and asked, "Could you tell me about creating it?"

"What do you want to know?"

"Given its title, I'm assuming it is based on a dream."

"Yeah, the dream was vivid, but I don't remember much. This was a long time ago, but I remember the power of it, even now. I saw a bush with a glowing ball of light in its branches, and that's pretty much it. But there was this mood to it, and that would be hard to describe. Something about it felt important. I made a sketch when I woke up, but that's how it looked, not how it felt."

"Why does it look so different than your other work?"

I paused before answering, "Well, I was tripping on peyote when I painted it."

He smiled and nodded, "We suspected something like that."

"What do you mean?"

"The many small dots are similar to ancient aboriginal cave art from Australia, and the use of ceremonial psychedelics is thought to be part of how these works were created."

I said, "Well, this wasn't exactly ceremonial. I was in my twenties and wanted the rush of it."

"What happened?"

"I'd found a peyote cactus. I broke it up and left it on my porch for a while. The sun dried it out, and I chopped up two of the buttons, and boiled them into a tea. It tasted awful, and there was a lot of vomiting, but after that I went to the studio and started painting. I worked all night and don't remember much. I do remember mixing the paint felt intense. I mean, squeezing the tubes, and seeing those little shiny wet blobs on the pallet. Jesus, it was so weird. And adding other colors, and the wet noises of mixing them with linseed oil, and the smells. It felt like some grand, eternal myth was unfolding."

By the way he looked at me, I could tell he was paying very close attention.

I said, "At some point, I left the studio and walked around in the sagebrush. I watched the sunrise, and that was amazing. I remember I tried to sleep after that. All I did was lie down in the sand next to my truck, and the sun was pounding when I woke. It was so hot. I went back to the studio and when I saw what I'd painted, I was shocked."

"Shocked?"

"I didn't remember doing it. I have weird visions of the brushes and paints and the colors, but I don't have much memory of actually painting it."

"Did it match what you remember from your dream?"

"Somewhat. It's hard to say. The dream was lifelike and clear, but the painting isn't in any way realistic. The painting sort of captures my dream in the way it felt, but not so much the way it looked."

He said, "Sit down. I should explain some things."

I sat on one side of the long table, and he got up and walked to a row of file cabinets next to the door we'd entered. He opened one of the drawers and searched, and as he did, I looked around.

The interior of this trailer had been paneled with finished plywood, and the roof had been painted black and mounted with an array of lights. The long table was yellow pine, with the planks sanded smooth and sealed with hardwax. And the floor was a rust colored industrial carpeting. All this gave the room a warm, sheltered feeling. There was a whiteboard, wiped clean, on the long wall across from me, and a bulletin board behind me. He closed the file drawer and walked back. He sat down, set a folder on the table, and opened it.

He said, "We didn't understand why we were brought to your painting. And we put in a lot of work to figure out why. We tried to analyze the details of the images. We measured the shapes and created overlays, hoping to see some pattern. We were trying anything to come up with a way to decipher any hidden clues. It wasn't until we counted the colored dots you had painted, that things began to take shape."

He set a few printed pages in front of me. One was a color image of the painting with each of the little dots numbered, and this was almost impossible to read because there were so many tiny dots, and the numbers were so small. The next page was a similar image, but with dot clusters circled and labeled. He slid another page in front of me. This was a spreadsheet showing the totals of the dots, with a set of columns listing the groupings. He explained what they'd done, but it was difficult to follow.

I asked, "Did you try looking for any numbers that matched latitude and longitude?"

He smiled, "Yes, we did, and UTM marks, and even ley lines and magnetic anomalies. But nothing was matching."

I asked, "How was Katie helping in all this?"

He said, "Well, she was putting in a lot of energy, but she wasn't counting dots."

"When did she realize it was my painting?"

He laughed, "Not at first. Your paintings are all signed Art Amiss, and it took us a little time to figure out who you were. Katherine found a photo of you in an art magazine. I was in the room when she saw it. She screamed, and I nearly jumped out of my skin."

I thought about her and her reaction. I might have laughed if this all wasn't so strange. I pointed to the painting with my thumb and said, "That was the first time I signed something as Art Amiss, and I don't know why. I made it up that night and thought it was funny."

He raised his eyebrows and said, "It is funny."

"You talked to my agent." Right as I spoke those words, I realized he'd know I had talked with him, so there was no use in lying.

"Yes, I spoke with him. We suspected he knew where you were."

I thought about Ted, and our friendship, and that he found me without needing a team of psychics.

I didn't trust the guy across the table from me, but I needed to understand what was happening. I said, "He didn't know where I was for a long time. He hired a detective and found me. He drove here, and we talked. We were close, and he was really upset when I left. I told him I wasn't coming back and asked him to let me alone. I said this was a good place for me."

He nodded but didn't say anything. Then I said, "You took everything from my studio."

He answered in his calm, charismatic way, "Yes, we have it all. The foreclosure on the property was imminent, and we needed to gather it all up before the bank seized it. You can have it back. We didn't find much in it."

I didn't respond to that. What I wanted to say was that my life had been more peaceful since leaving all that behind. For a time anyway, because it wasn't peaceful now.

I changed the subject and asked, "If Katie has psychic abilities, did you try to use them to find me?"

"We tried for a while. And Katie was—" He caught himself, and raised his eyebrows, "I just called her Katie, and if she heard me say that, she'd lash out with a fury I don't want to think about."

He smiled and started over, "We tried for a while, yet Katherine got very little. And this was unlike her, she's normally quite reliable.

She didn't attain any tangible data, and that's something she's usually very good at. Instead, her mood was influenced."

"What do you mean, her mood?"

"She got very withdrawn. We all saw it, and she asked not to search for you anymore."

"When you say search, you mean searching by using her psychic skill."

"Yes, she said she couldn't keep looking. She was suffering."

Hearing that, I needed to look away. I know how I can be, and if she was able to tap into anything about me, maybe she could feel what I was feeling. That she would be able to feel my pain was heartbreaking.

Without realizing it, I was crying. I stood up quickly, walked to the corner by the door, and held my face in my hands. I kept my back to him and sobbed quietly. It didn't last long, maybe a minute. When it passed, I dried my eyes with my sleeve and took a few deep breaths. Then I slowly walked back and sat down in the same chair.

He looked at me with an untroubled gaze. His hands were on the table, one over the other. There was enough emotion in his eyes that he didn't seem cold, but not so much to come across as mawkish. He was very measured.

I said, "If Katie was looking for me, and reached out for me, and she was suffering, then she found me."

He nodded and said, "We didn't push her."

He gave me a moment, then handed me another sheet of paper. This one had a set of loops and spirals, all graphed out with angles and technical notations.

He spoke as I looked at this image, "Those shapes come from the patterns and totals of the dots you painted. We ran that data through an advanced computer program that looks for visual geometry within number patterns. It came up with these images. It didn't mean anything to us, for a while at least."

I set down the paper and asked, "What is this? And I don't mean these shapes, I mean all of this. Your team. Are you part of the government?"

He said, "Not quite. We can reach out to certain agencies, and some can reach out to us, but we are each on the other side of a line, and that has been working well for both of us."

I asked, "Who pays for all this?"

He raised his eyebrows and said, "That's a very good question, and I have to say, I don't know. I truly don't. I submit a request for funds, and the money arrives. And I have no idea where it comes from."

He spoke with a breezy composure that I didn't know how to gauge. If he was lying, what could I do about it, and how would I know? He had enough money for a helicopter and seemingly a lot more. What I truly wanted to know was something impossible to ask. I wanted to know if he was evil.

He picked up the page with the swirling lines, the last one I'd looked at. He said, "There are three distinct points where the lines converge in this image."

He made a dot with a red Sharpie on each of the three points, and passed it across the table to me. He said, "We overlaid this image onto a set of maps, and it took some time, but we found something."

Then he handed me another piece of paper with a map of the lower forty-eight states. This map had been marked with three circles, one in the midwest, and the other two were somewhere in the Four Corners area of the desert southwest.

He said, "One of the younger guys on the team organized all this with a computer. He made a little video, and it's easier to see on that, but I'm unsure how to find it. But I can explain it with the paper."

He set two of the printed pages on top of each other and said, "Pinch these together, and focus on the center of the swirls. Now hold it up to the light."

I sandwiched both pages and held them up to the ceiling light above me, and asked, "What am I looking for?"

He said, "You might need to slide the pages some."

I did. I manipulated the two pieces of paper, slowly rotating them around. And then it happened, the three red dots aligned perfectly with the three circles on the map.

I said, "Okay, they line up. What does it mean?"

He leaned across the table with the map of the forty-eight states between us. He pointed with a pencil and said, "This circle is in Wisconsin. The convergence was very tight, and it lines up close to the street where you and Katie grew up." He moved his pencil to the west, "This one here is your studio in New Mexico. It's very precise. It pinpoints your studio exactly." He moved his pencil again and said, "Now this convergence has the most lines, but it's much less exact, it creates more of a zone. This defines where we are. We're sitting in that zone right now. It's bigger than this town, but it has a fuzzy boundary."

I didn't say anything.

I looked at the page with the swirling lines and the three red dots. I said, "There's another convergence here, but you didn't mark it." I put the pages together and held them up to the light again.

He spoke as I looked, "That point is a bit east of Seattle. There are fewer lines crossing at that point than the other three, and we don't know if it's of lesser importance, or if it means anything at all."

"What's at that spot?"

"We checked. It's an asylum for the criminally insane."

I set the pages down and said, "Jesus. This is really fucked up."

He shrugged and said, "Yes, I know."

I tried to look at the pages he'd shown me, but I didn't have the energy. I slid them across the table, and he put them back in the folder.

I asked, "That covered deck, where I met you, what's that mesh for?"

He said, "I'm not sure what you mean."

"The entire deck is covered in some kind of a thin black mesh, like mosquito netting."

"It's a composite fabric, and it surrounds the entire structure. The base is fiberglass with a bonded silver as a conductant. It's there to protect from electronic eavesdropping."

I thought about where we were and asked, "Is that really necessary here?"

He shrugged his shoulders and said, "Probably not. But it's a simple bit of insurance."

"Is this trailer shielded in the same way?"

"Yes, with something very similar. And parts of the motel, too."

I asked, "Is Katie here now, in the motel?"

"Yes."

I turned my head to face the building, as if looking that way could somehow allow me to connect with her. He saw what I did, and he understood why I did it.

I asked, "How is she doing?"

He looked at me without blinking, "Whatever happened scared her. It's not like her to get so upset, and it's worried us."

"It upset me, too."

"We understand that."

"Do you have doctors here, working here?"

He narrowed his eyes enough to make me think he didn't want to answer, "The team here is small, and they are all very good at what they do. We have two doctors on site, and Katherine is one of them, but I'm sure you mean medical doctors. We've been in close communication with physicians. She is aware and lucid, and she's also trying to understand what happened."

"So am I."

"I know you're concerned. She has been anxious and agitated, and hasn't slept, but there is nothing medically wrong."

That was more than the pilot told me, and I felt some relief.

I put my elbows on the table and rubbed my temples, then asked, "How much does she know about this, what we've talked about?"

"All of it."

"How much have you shared with me?"

"A lot."

I asked, "But not everything?"

"No, not everything, but a lot."

He paused, then asked, "And how much have you shared with me?"

I said, "Almost nothing."

He nodded and smiled in a way that I'd gotten used to. He didn't seem concerned or worried, but it was crystal clear he'd been paying very close attention to everything I'd said, and my every nuance of body language. I assume I'd been recorded during all this, and probably videotaped, too. And I didn't like the way this guy looked at me.

He said, "My team doesn't have a deadline. All of this, what's been happening, seems to want to unfold on its own terms, not ours. Yet, there's something here, something I feel, an awareness, a sense of urgency. There is nothing I can point to as the source of my feelings, but I sense it."

I didn't say anything. I'd said enough to make it crystal clear that I'd been flooded with strangeness.

He asked, "What happened last night on the playground?"

He was as casual as if he wanted to know my favorite color. I thought for a bit and said, "I truly don't know."

That was an honest answer. The pilot would have shared what I told him this morning, so he knew that much. But I had no idea what Katie might have said. It was up to her to say what she wanted them to hear, and I wasn't going to tell him anything without talking to her first.

He said, "Katherine is a very strong woman, and I care about her. We all do. She was very upset last night, and she's doing better, but clearly something happened."

I said, "I care about her, too."

I didn't say anything else. All I could do was try to guess what he was thinking. I waited for him to ask more, but he didn't press it.

He said he should lock up, and this meant our meeting was over. We got up, and went to the door. After walking through it, I turned around and studied how the door fit in place so it would be hidden from anyone looking in the back of the truck.

He saw me looking. "It's good, isn't it?"

It was. He spoke about the craftsmen who'd built it, and how grateful he was for their skills. Then we walked out of the back of the trailer and onto the metal platform. He closed the big doors, latched them shut, and we went down the stairs. It was dark now, and there was a single light on the wall of the motel across from us. He asked if I needed a ride back to my home.

I said, "No thanks, I'll be fine."

Then I said, "A woman came into the shop for a single cup of coffee. This would have been before you and your crew showed up here. She told me she was a psychic for the FBI."

Even though it was dark, I could see the look on his face. He was surprised. It lasted only an instant, but I saw it. He faltered, and then slipped right back into his untroubled self.

He nodded and said, "How did you find that out, about her job?"

"I chased her down the street and asked."

He narrowed his eyes and said, "Why would you do that?"

I narrowed my eyes right back at him and said, "You seem to know me, at least a little bit, so you probably have a pretty good idea why I would've asked her that."

That shut him up, at least for a little bit. I could see he was thinking, and it was the same thing I was thinking—someone else had taken an interest in this dusty little town.

We stood for a while in silence. He knew I wanted to ask something else, and waited for me to say more.

I said, "You never told me your name."

He said, "I know. I don't use my name here. The team calls me The Foreman."

I said, "I've met a few people on this team of yours, and seen some others around town, and now after talking with you—this all feels so serious."

"Yes, it is serious." He spoke slowly, emphasizing every word.

"Whatever you're doing here, it scares me. Your team seems very dedicated, and they all seem to take orders from you, and I'm trying to understand what's been happening." I paused, then asked, "Is there anyone above you here?"

"No, not here at this site."

"Who do you answer to?"

He seemed amused. I don't think anyone had ever asked him that question so plainly, especially not the dishwasher at the coffee shop. He said, "Why do you want to know?"

"Because I got to the bottom of that canyon without a fucking helicopter."

He looked at me, and there was a guise of geniality on his face, but it was hiding something. He didn't change his expression, and he didn't blink. After a long stretch of silence, he said, "I answer to one man, and he gives me a lot of freedom, but he wants results. He's referred to as the Gavel."

He paused and I waited. Then he said, "I answer to the Gavel, and the Gavel answers to God."

He spoke those words for maximum drama, then let it sit in the air. It felt like I was being played, but given the strangeness of everything that's been happening, I didn't know what to trust or what to believe.

We shook hands and said good night. He stood there as I walked away. I went around the corner to the front of the motel and then into the trees. I wasn't in any hurry walking home, I needed this time to try and make sense of what happened. I saw my painting again, but that didn't mean much to me. I was worried about Katie and couldn't think about anything else.

36

IT WAS STILL DARK WHEN I WOKE, and all my fears came rushing back. I slept through the night without stirring or waking, and I stayed still for a while and stared up at the stars. There was some comfort in the smell of the sage and sand, but not enough. When I sat up, my head was above the bushes, and I saw a warm pink, glow along the eastern horizon.

I got to the shop before Tony. I started the coffee and prepped all the baked goods. He came in the back door as I poured the initial pot of coffee into one of the big insulated carafes.

His first words were, "Have you heard anything about Katherine?"

I told him no, and said I wanted to head over to the motel and find out how she was doing. He pointed to the front door and said, "Go on, get out of here."

I walked with coffee in a paper cup, and when I got to the motel, I stood in the grass and waited. It wasn't a minute before the pilot came out and met me. He spoke first, "She's still asleep, and she ate last night. This all seems good."

"Can I see her?"

"Not yet."

I said, "If she's doing good, like you say, why can't I see her?"

"All I can say is not yet. The team seem relieved she's sleeping."

I pointed to the motel and asked, "What if I ran over there right now, barged in and tried to find her?"

He said, "Oh, you don't want to do that."

Those words were spoken without emotion, and I didn't want to test him. I asked, "When can I see her?"

He didn't answer, and I don't think he knew. He looked me right in the eye and said, "If you want to help, you could tell us what happened."

He waited for me to say something. They knew enough to want to know more, and I wasn't going to feed them anything I didn't understand. I was certain that whatever happened to me happened to Katie, too, and it was powerful. All I could think was they wanted that power.

I said, "I don't know what happened, I really don't. We both blacked out, and I don't know how long it was before I came to. I sat up, and it was only a few seconds before I woke her. All I did was say her name and touch her shoulder. When she came to, she was scared. I asked if she was okay, but she didn't say anything. She got up and ran back to the motel. I ran after her, and that's when you saw us, here on the grass. I was trying to ask her what happened."

He said, "This is distressing. Katherine doesn't get scared and run away from things. I saw how she was, and we don't have an answer."

I waited, and he said, "How'd your little talk go last night?"

I wasn't sure if he was patronizing me or if it was a real question. I said, "My little talk went just fine."

"It was late when you left."

That was an odd thing to say, and I wasn't sure what he was getting at. I asked, "Did you follow me last night, when I left?"

"No." He said that plainly, like my question was something ordinary.

"What about the night before when you took her into the motel? Did you follow me home then? Or did anyone else?

"I didn't, and I don't think anyone did."

"When you picked me up yesterday, you were really an asshole."

He shrugged his shoulders. I waited for more, but that was his response.

I asked, "Is the helicopter out behind the motel?"

"Yeah, it's there."

"Is it hidden somehow? I didn't see it last night."

"It's there. There's an old gravel pit in the flats a few hundred yards from where I landed the night you flew with me. It's a big, open pit with a flat bottom, and it's easy to land there. It's deep enough that you can't see it from the motel. That and the sagebrush keep it hidden."

I rolled my eyes, and he asked, "What is it?"

"It's your boss. Last night, we were behind the motel, and he pointed out at nothing. He said the helicopter was out there. He said it in this ominous way, like it was hidden by holograms or something."

He half smiled and said, "Well, that's the kind of thing he'd say."

"Good, because I didn't believe him."

He looked at me like I was a real person. Until that point, every interaction felt like he was a cop and I was a criminal. He told me again that everyone was worried about Katherine, and he'd come find me if there were any updates.

I drank the last sip of coffee, turned the cup over and let the few drops fall in the grass. I asked, "Could you throw this out?"

He said sure, and I handed him the cup, which he crushed the instant he took it. I turned and walked away. I could tell he was concerned about Katie, but I had no idea what to think.

I walked through the cottonwoods and across the unstable round stones of the dry river bed. When I got to the gate of the playground, I saw someone standing near the swing set. I stopped and watched. It was Tim, and he hadn't been there on my way to the motel, only a few minutes earlier.

I walked through the gate, and he turned and said, "Well, good morning. Very nice to see you."

I said hello and walked up to him. He had what looked to be a small canvas tool kit, and was inspecting the bars of the swing set. He said, "It's a nice morning, and I wanted to do this early before it got too hot."

Then he added, "How are you feeling, I mean after everything the other night?"

"I'm fine."

He said, "That's good to know. Boy, did things get crazy when Katherine came in, the whole place was buzzing."

He leaned over, opened the duffel, dug around, and pulled out a little wooden box. He slid the top open and removed a gray block of metal about the size of a Zippo lighter. He moved it toward one of the poles of the swing set, and it jumped out of his fingertips and snapped against the pole with a sharp ring. He nodded confidently and said, "Well, it's iron, or partly so."

He tried to get it off, then asked me if I could try. I stepped closer and pried it off. He laughed, "It's a strong little thing, isn't it?"

He had a notebook, and he wrote in it. I went to hand the magnet back, and he said, "No, no, we need to do the chains, too."

I moved it toward one of the chains, and it leapt out of my hand and stuck to two links, twisting them crooked. He said, "We should do all four."

I stepped back and said, "Maybe I should let you do your job."

He said, "Yes. Yes, of course."

He hummed as he touched the magnet to the other chains, and slid it back into the wooden box when he was done. He wrote something in his notebook, then pointed to one of the two swings with his pen and asked, "You were in this one, right?"

"Yes."

He raised his eyebrows and pointed to the other one, "And Katherine sat there, right?"

I didn't answer. I asked, "What are you doing?"

"I'm writing up a report. I have a little checklist of things to do here."

"What's in the bag?"

"Oh, lots of things, like the little magnet."

He opened the bag, and spoke as he dug around, "There's a gauss meter, a black light, an EMF meter, I even have a Geiger counter, and a few things I'm not sure of."

He pulled out a little yellow plastic box, and said, "Like this thing, I have no idea what it does. They give me instructions on what to do, and I write down the readings."

He smiled and said, "If you'd like to stick around, you can."

He took out a roll of duct tape and a rectangle of what looked like black foam rubber. He said, "I'm supposed to attach this thing to the frame somewhere."

He struggled a little bit, and I helped. Together we wrapped a section of pipe in rubber and taped it in place. Then we taped the yellow box to the rubber, and he explained it needed to be insulated from any metal. After that, he plugged some wires to the box and taped them to the pole.

He said, "This sends a signal to a receiver at the motel, and it keeps track of something, I'm not sure what."

I let him talk and explain what he was doing. He walked around the area with a few different handheld monitors, and each time said nothing was showing up. Then he wrote in his notebook.

Then he pointed to the dirt under one of the swings and asked, "So you ended up here, right?"

I said yes, and he asked, "And Katherine was on the ground there, next to you, right?"

Again, I said yes.

He sat in the swing that Katie had been in, and looked up at the bar above him, and then at me. Then he used his feet to turn himself so he was pointed at the other seat, and asked, "Were you facing each other like this?"

"No, we were facing forward."

"Did you fall over backwards?"

I said I didn't know. And he said, "Well, falling back, you could have hit your head."

He held the chains and leaned back, "Oh, it would hurt to fall like this. I don't think I want to try that, not without something soft under me."

I said, "If we had fallen backwards, our legs would probably have gotten caught in the seat. It would've stayed hooked under our knees."

He said, "Okay. Okay, let me try. Can you help me so I don't hit my head?"

I got behind him as he leaned back and lowered himself. I held his shoulders as he slid off the seat, and set him gently on the ground. His legs stayed on the seat at his knees.

He said, "So you must have slumped and fallen forward."

He kicked the seat away and set his legs down. He was lying flat on the ground with the seat swinging gently above him. He asked, "And you woke like this? On your back, with your feet pointing that way?"

I said yes, and then he asked, "Did you bump into the seat when you sat up?"

"Yes, I pushed it away, so it was behind me."

He lay there on his back with his hands on his stomach and fingers interlocked, then asked a lot of questions. Who woke first? Did Katie say anything? Did I feel groggy? How long were we unconscious?

I answered everything honestly, but only said yes, no, and I don't know.

Eventually, he got up and said, "Oh, my goodness, I'm all dusty, I should head back and change." He gave me a quick thumbs up and said, "Thanks so much for all your help."

Then he turned and walked out the gate. I stood and watched him disappear into the cottonwoods. He had asked me a long list of questions, but never mentioned the owls. I have to think this meant that Katie hadn't mentioned them either.

37

I WALKED PAST THE SCHOOL and back to the coffee shop. Tony was behind the counter when I came in, and he motioned me to follow him back to the kitchen. He asked how Katie was doing, and there was almost nothing to say. All I could tell him was the people she works with said she seemed to be doing better.

He told me to take over at the counter while he made me breakfast. I thanked him and tried to keep busy. Nobody came in, and I moved around the shop and cleaned up a little. I was trying to understand what had been happening, but nothing made sense. I had cleared some dishes and wiped down the counters when he came out and handed me a plate. He pointed to a seat and said, "Go ahead and eat."

I sat and ate two burritos. I chewed and swallowed, but I wasn't thinking about food. There was some reason they weren't letting me see Katie. I knew what I went through in that time under the swing set, and the way Katie reacted when she woke meant she went through something similar. I didn't know what she told them, but if she hid the owls, I suspected she hid other things, too. Yet I didn't know what those might be.

They were avoiding something. Their refrain of "it's not like her to act frightened" and telling me "she seems upset and isn't sleeping" didn't cut it. They were giving me excuses, and I needed to know what was really going on.

I was staring blankly at my empty plate when Tony sat down across from me. He spoke, but I was too numb to listen. He said he wanted to help, I caught that much. I straightened up in my seat and thanked him. There was nothing I could say. Everything was tied together so tightly, and trying to focus on any one detail seemed impossible, let alone the whole knotted mess. Attempting to explain even a single thread would sound like madness.

I was tangled up in that knot.

Tony stood up without saying anything more and got back to work. Eventually, I left the table and helped with the chores, but there hadn't been many customers, so there wasn't much to do. About a half hour before closing, I told Tony I would finish up for the day and he could go home. Then I added that I could use the alone time, and he nodded and thanked me. A minute later, he was gone.

There were a few people still in the shop and on the patio. I walked across the main room and picked up the gray tub of dirty dishes, and was about to take them to the kitchen.

I glanced out the window and saw an SUV pull up and park across the street. I saw three men get out, and I wasn't in the mood for any more customers. They hadn't moved, and it looked like they were talking among themselves. I thought, "Please don't come in here." I carried the dishes to the sink, came back out, and set the tub in its spot on the table along the wall. The SUV was gone.

The people in the main room saw me cleaning up, got the hint, and left. The last two customers were out on the patio. I asked if they needed anything, and they said no, so I bussed their table and told them I'd be locking up soon.

I carried the big sign in from the sidewalk and flipped the little sign around in the window. I counted out the bills in the drawer, put them in an envelope, and hid it in Tony's office. All I did was slip it under the cushion of his desk chair. This wasn't much of a hiding place, but there was never much cash in the envelope.

I returned to the main room and put the tip jar on the lowest shelf behind the counter. Tony could count it in the morning. The couple sitting outside had left, and I locked the door to the patio.

When I went to lock the front door, there he was. It was The Foreman, as dapper as a movie star, standing alone on the sidewalk. He smiled at me through the screen door, and I opened it and let him in.

He asked, "Would this be a good time to talk for a bit?"

I said, "It'll be fine."

He said, "I don't want to keep you from anything."

"You don't need to worry about that. There's nothing I need to do." Then I asked, "Can I get you anything?"

"Oh, I don't want to be a bother."

"Look, I'm tired, so if you came here to talk, I'm going to make myself a coffee."

He said, "Then I'll have whatever you're having."

I walked behind the counter and turned the espresso machine back on. I said, "I just shut this off a few minutes ago, so it'll be ready soon."

He stood at the counter with an elegance that unnerved me. His white shirt was clean and pressed in a way that seemed impossible in this beaten-down corner of the world.

I got out two small mugs and two saucers, and pulled the milk from the fridge behind me. I lined it all up on the counter and checked the water temperature.

I faced him and asked, "Why are you here?"

"I've been wanting to talk with you for a while, long before last night. I'd been planning to introduce myself, so when I heard you'd asked to talk to me, I had you brought over. I let it play out like it was your idea, which it was. But I thought you should know I was about to reach out to you."

I waited for more, then said, "Okay. Thanks for that."

He didn't say anything, and I went on, "Look, I needed to talk to you for what must be some pretty obvious reasons. I was impatient. I needed to understand, at least a little bit, what your team is doing here."

"Yes, and I did my best to answer what I could."

I checked the gauge, and the water was hot enough. I started two-eight-ounce double lattes. He watched, and I could tell he was paying attention to my every move. I saw his focus as a challenge, and did each step with a heightened exactness. Tony had a grace about his role behind this counter, and I took that on as his apprentice. I was a performer on a stage, and this strange man was my audience. I was showing off.

The last step was pouring the steamed milk, and when I was done, I slid it across to him. I had made a perfect design on the surface of the foam, a tidy bush with smooth symmetrical branches reaching upwards. He didn't waste time, he lifted the cup and took a sip while it was still hot.

I started mine, and let him watch again. I shook the steel pitcher while pouring the milk in the final step. I tried to make the same bush image, but it wasn't smooth, it was jagged. I had a bit of foam left, and dropped a dot in the branches. From his side of the counter it was upside down, like roots, but for me they were reaching up to the sky.

I carried it to the round table in the middle of the room, where I would draw. We both sat down, and he took another sip and said, "I spent some time in Rome, and before then I didn't drink coffee. I never had, but there is something remarkable about that culture and coffee. Being back here has been difficult, and now, because of Rome, I have very high standards."

"How'd I do?"

He raised his mug and said, *"Il sapore di quel caffè mi ha fatto volare in cielo."*

I wasn't sure what he said, but it seemed like praise, and I replied, *"Grazie."*

We both sipped our coffee, and neither of us said anything. I asked, "How is Katie?"

He set down his cup and said, "Better."

I waited for more, then asked, "Anything else?"

He shrugged and said nothing. I was trying to figure him out. I think he wanted to trade, hoping I would share something worthwhile, and only then would I get anything in return. I was fine telling him things about myself, up to a point, but I wasn't going to say anything about Katie. I simply couldn't.

I said, "I was there when it happened, right next to her, and as far as I can tell, I'm fine. I have to trust that she'll be fine, too. She was upset when she came to, and that scared me. I told this to the pilot, and I hope he told you."

He thanked me, drank the rest of his coffee, and set the empty cup back in its saucer.

I said, "Katie was here two nights ago, right before the event on the playground. I made her dinner, and we talked. She asked me about something that happened when we were in elementary school. I had forgotten all about it until she asked."

He sat very still as I spoke. He had this thoughtful gaze that should have put me at ease, but it did the opposite. It worried me. I went on, "She asked if I remembered certain tests we used to take. She called them 'weird tests.' She said it was only her and me, and they happened after school."

He leaned back in his chair but didn't say anything.

"I had totally forgotten them, but it came rushing back right when she asked."

He said, "Go on."

"It felt like we had been singled out, I remember that. We were taken to the cafeteria, and two men were there, and they gave us these tests. We were probably only ten or eleven, but I remember something about it didn't feel right."

"What were the tests about?"

"I want to say they were about psychic things, or intuition, but I don't remember."

He nodded calmly.

"She asked me, and I told her I remembered, and we hardly said anything, and all of a sudden she seemed scared, and said we shouldn't talk about this. She was really upset, like almost panicking, but it only lasted a few seconds. Then she was back to normal, all smiling and cheery. It was strange, and I didn't know what to think."

"Why are you telling me this?"

I picked up my cup and took a sip. It had cooled down, so I drank the rest in one gulp. I should've finished it while it was still hot.

"She told me we should not talk about this. We should forget it. She said it. Her voice was harsh in a way that worried me, like it wasn't her own voice. Then she switched back, and was talking about normal things. I heard her say it, and at the same time, I wasn't sure it even happened, and I didn't trust myself. But she said it."

I started poking at the table, tapping with my fingertips. I was hit with a flood of emotions, and he saw it in me.

I said, "Look, I need to say this. It was like her question made that memory emerge, it was right there in my mind, instantly. And when she said we should forget this, I could feel it fading away. Like the memory was getting yanked out of me, and I needed to fight to keep it in me—that memory of us and those tests. I know—I know it happened, but—but I—"

I was stammering and struggling, and he asked, "John, what's going on?"

"I don't know, but something's not right—I feel all fucked up."

"Is it the coffee?"

"No. Listen. It happened. She brought it up—and I remembered those tests—I remembered it. And she said I couldn't think about it—and then I couldn't. I felt it in me. And her voice—scared me, when it changed. I needed to really think—I had to really fight to keep it in my mind."

"But, John, you did keep it in your mind."

"I did, but it was fucking hard."

What he said next was in a measured clarity, slow and steady, "John, if she told someone they should forget something, there aren't many people who could keep it in their mind. Until now, I would've said no one could."

I heard what he said, but didn't want to accept it. "What are you saying, that she's some sort of sorceress?"

He said, "I might not use that word, but I'm very impressed that you were able to hold onto that memory."

I didn't say anything. I took a few deep breaths and set both hands flat on the table. I looked at him and asked, "What just happened? It felt like I was gonna climb out of my skin."

He said, "You were fighting."

I lifted my hands off the table and shook them.

I said, "I had completely forgotten about those tests with Katie, but it all rushed back when she asked. We were taken to meet those men. It happened several times, it was always after school in the cafeteria, and it was never anyone else but her and me, and those men."

He nodded to let me know he was listening. He stared at me across the table, and I stared back at him. I asked, "That was you, wasn't it?"

His expression was unwavering, but I could tell something changed. He tilted his head, and replied peacefully, "Yes, it was me."

"Do you remember meeting us?"

"Oh, yes."

I needed this to slow down, and put up both my hands. He saw me pushing back and gave me some time to think. After a few deep breaths, I asked, "Did you go to other schools and meet with other kids?"

"A fair amount, yes."

I thought for a moment, then asked, "Tim, and the pilot, and the other people at the motel, did you find them like you found us?"

He narrowed his eyes, and I could tell I had asked a good question. "Some of them."

I was overwhelmed and had no idea what to say or what to think. He asked, "Did you recognize me?"

"No. It's not like that. I just knew."

"When did you know?"

"Maybe five seconds before I asked."

He smiled and rubbed the back of his neck. He said, "That was over thirty years ago. I was still in grad school, my hair was long, and I had a beard. So I didn't expect you would have remembered me."

I said, "I tried to fail those tests. I tried to give the wrong answers, or what I thought would be the wrong answers, the opposite of what you were hoping for. I remember that."

He said, "How interesting. I think Katherine tried to do her very best. And she's still like that."

I was going to say I'm still like that, too, doing my best to fail, but I stayed quiet. I looked at him hard and said, "You never told her it was you who gave us those tests."

He said nothing, but I could tell what he was thinking. He knew I would tell her. I followed up with my next thought, "Are you able to put some block on her psychic skills, or hide things from her powers?"

He didn't answer that either. He could have made something up, telling me what he thought I wanted to hear, but he didn't say anything. I had no idea what to trust, what were lies, and what were mind games to mess with me. I said, "There was another man with you. He was older."

"Yes, he was a mentor of sorts."

I heard his voice, and understood the words, but there was a veneer of deception over all of it. I stared at him, trying to read his stoic face, but that was impossible. I narrowed my eyes and told him, "Then I've met The Gavel, haven't I?"

He smiled and slowly raised his eyebrows, "John, you have surprised me, over and over. I am dazzled by your capacity within all of this."

I didn't want his praise, and the look I gave told him so.

He went on, "Failing those tests worked, we ignored you, but we were very intrigued by Katherine. We came back around from time to time and checked on her. We got her into colleges, we managed to test her again, and guided her into this work."

"Does she know about your hidden hand in her life?"

"Yes, mostly."

"And she's okay with that?"

"John, Katherine is at the forefront of some of the most remarkable work imaginable—very few have engaged in anything of this magnitude."

I didn't want to give in to his aggrandizing, and said, "Beyond our time in the cafeteria, has she met your mentor, this guy you call The Gavel?"

"No."

"Last night, you showed me those patterns, and one page marked the spot where the points converged, and you said one of those points was close to the street where I grew up."

"Yes, that's right."

"What's at that spot?"

"It's the parking lot of a Walmart."

"That wasn't there when we were kids. Where is it in relation to our street?"

"It was behind Katie's home about a quarter mile."

My heart sank. I tipped my head back and looked at the ceiling. The most sacred spot from my childhood had been covered in asphalt. I wanted to mourn the loss of that magical pond, but not now. I straightened up and faced him. I asked, "Did you share those maps and those points with Katie?

He didn't answer, and I could see he was thinking. Eventually he said, "We shared some things, but not everything. We've found that if some details align too closely with someone's life, or their personal experiences, it can corrupt the data."

"If she's psychic, wouldn't she figure it out?"

"That's a possibility, but we try to keep certain things separated. Objectivity in this work can be very difficult."

"So she never saw those maps you showed me?"

"No, we chose not to tell her about the point near her childhood home. We did tell her the information from your painting pointed to an area around this town. And to your studio. We told her that much."

I asked, "Did Katie ever mention the frog pond?"

He flinched, and I saw it. It was only an instant, and his composure returned.

I told him, "Whatever I said touched a nerve."

He sat perfectly still with the slightest smirk. I leaned in and said, "Look, I saw that. I saw you react. What is it?"

He sat up in his chair and repositioned himself. Then he picked up his mug, and looked in it. He knew it was empty, but he looked anyway. His gestures were smooth and composed, but he was squirming. He tipped the mug a little, as if studying the last drop in the bottom. Then he tipped it the other way. He did this for a while, tipping it back and forth, before quietly setting it back on the saucer.

He said, "Last night I told you I keep a pad of paper next to my bed, and sometimes I would make an intention before sleeping. I told you I wanted to solve this, this big mystery."

"Yeah, you told me."

He went on, "I was asking for help. I needed a clue. When I woke in the morning, two words were on that pad, and I didn't remember writing them."

I said, "And that was what you put in the envelope, that you wanted Katie to look at with her abilities."

"Yes, it was."

"And when she looked, she started crying and passed out."

"Yes, she did."

"And that session led to another session, and to my painting, and then to the canyon."

He didn't answer. I was telling him what we both already knew. Then I said, "And the words on your little pad were 'frog pond.'"

Long pause. "Yes, they were."

I asked, "Okay, I'll ask again, has Katie ever mentioned the frog pond?"

"No. Never."

Fuck. Whatever what going on, I was in it deep.

The Foreman's carefree smile was gone. He looked at me gravely, and asked, "John, what do I need to know?"

"I don't have an answer for that."

"What is the frog pond?"

"The kids in the neighborhood would swim and hang out there in the summer. It was a nice spot we all loved, and now it's under a parking lot."

"Please, what else?"

I held my hands out above the table. They were shaking, and I wanted him to see.

"John, please."

I shook my hands, and made fists, and shook them again. I set one over the other on the table, and gripped it tight.

I said, "The frog pond was down a path in the woods behind Katie's house. I've had nightmares all my life, and it's always the same thing. I'm on that path, and those dreams have scared the shit out of me."

"What happened in those dreams?"

"Not much. I'm always on the path, and it's always at night. I'm running away from the frog pond, and there's a blue light, and it always feels the same. I feel terribly fucking guilty."

"Why do you feel guilty?"

"Because I can't find Katie."

"Do your dreams ever take place at the frog pond?"

"No, it's always on the path between there and her backyard."

"Do you ever make it to her house?"

In these dreams, I run through the gate and look up at her bedroom window. But this wasn't for him, it was too intimate, too inward. I lied and said, "No, it's only on the path."

"What about the blue light?"

"It's a strong blue color, and it pulses."

"What do you think it means?"

"I have no idea."

I could see he was about to ask more, and I put up both hands with my palms facing him. I said, "Stop. Please, I can't."

My hands were still shaking. I got up, went behind the counter, filled a glass with tap water, and drank it. Then I took a clean rag from the bin next to the sink, ran it under the water and squeezed it out. He watched me as I wiped my face and the back of my neck. It was only a few steps from the counter to where he sat in the middle of the room, but he seemed miles away.

I put the rag in the dirty bin and walked slowly back to the table. I didn't sit. I stood behind my chair and asked, "Is this a job interview?"

He raised his eyebrows and said, "Perhaps."

"The thing about the frog pond, and getting so emotional, is that working for me, or against me?"

He smiled and said, "John, I would do anything to have you on my team."

My chest tightened when I heard those words. My entire body reacted with revulsion. I was angry and didn't try to hide it. I asked, "What's all this mean?"

"I truly don't know."

I spat back, "Take your best guess."

"It's about the fate of the world."

That wasn't the answer I expected, but given everything that had been happening, it seemed the only thing that made sense.

Neither of us said anything for a long time. I looked out the big windows. The sun had set and the harsh shadows of the day were gone. The twilight had softened everything. I said, "I'm wrung out. I don't know what more I can help you with."

He said, "I understand. This was a lot, and I didn't mean to set things on fire. That was never my intention."

He stood, picked up his dishes and mine, and paused. Before he could ask, I pointed to a gray plastic tub on a table along the wall. "You can put 'em in that. I'll wash them in the morning."

He walked over and set them in the tub, placing them gently with barely a noise, and I thanked him. He walked to the front door, and I followed him to the sidewalk. I said, "I need to get out of the building."

I saw the shiny gray Subaru, the one Katie had driven, parked a little to the east of the shop. He moved with an effortless grace, but I could tell he was shaken up, too.

He faced me, and before he could say goodnight, I asked, "What do the owls mean?"

His eyebrows raised in a way that meant I surprised him again. He asked, "Why are you asking that?"

I said, "I'm not sure. It's like they show up sometimes."

He seemed wary, gauging me in a way he hadn't up until now. He said, "I've asked that, too, about the owls."

"Then they've shown up in your life?"

"Occasionally, and when they do, it seems to be in the context of this work."

I said, "It must mean something, or trace back to something, or connect out forward to something. I say that because of how it feels."

"I've felt it, too, and you might be right. It must connect to something." His voice was tired. He looked up, and then side to side, as if examining the rooftops and power lines around us.

I got the sense he didn't know any more about the owls than I did, and I said, "Tell Katie I'm wishing her good health, and I hope to see her soon."

He bowed like a gentleman and said, "Of course."

Then he got in the car and drove away. I asked about the owls for a reason. It was a test, and his meager response told me with certainty that Katie hadn't said anything about the owls on the swing set.

The evening air felt cool and clean. The stars would be out soon, and I could surrender to the comforting silence of the night.

38

I DREAMT OF KATIE'S HOME AGAIN, and the path beyond the gate. Yet it was different, it felt so much more real. It was night, and I was walking alone through the forest toward the frog pond, and that never happens. I'm always running away from it. And there was no emotion—I was hollow. Like the spark that made me real was gone.

When I turned the final corner on the path, Katie was there. She was standing alone in the grassy spot along the pond. She wore a long white nightgown, and her hands were low with her palms up. Seeing her there felt perfectly ordinary, and I thought, "Oh, yes, of course. This."

She turned to look at me, and the forest started glowing, like the meadow was lit from above by movie lights and somebody was slowly turning a dial. The pond glittered behind her, and the air was so still.

All my emotions came screaming back, and I needed to talk to Katie, but before I could say anything, this part of the dream ended. It sort of jumped, like it started over, and now I was alone on the grass, and Katie was gone. She had disappeared, but it was different than that, and I didn't understand why.

The soft glow from above had been shut off, and it was dark again. I couldn't see much, but I knew she was gone—and all the dread hit me. I started running. I had to find her. I raced away from the pond, and the blue lights were out ahead on the path, and they terrified me. I should have turned around, but I ran toward them. Something happened to Katie, and it was my fault, and I needed to find her.

I went through the gate and saw her window, and everything felt worse. Her backyard was heavy with shame, and its power crushed me.

I wasn't alone—there was a shadow in the yard. It was big and moved slowly, lumbering around, looking for something. Searching.

It wanted me, and I needed to hide, but all I could do was back up and press myself against the fence. The shadow stopped. It knew I was here. I tried to stay still, but it rushed right up close to me, like a blanket of death—my own death. We faced each other, and I refused to give in, I wouldn't die. I was resolute. I faced it and demanded, "Tell me where Katie is."

A deep voice answered, "She's back, and she's fine." Those words weren't what I expected. They were sincere and kind, and they released me, like I finally understood something.

I was calm, and then I was awake.

The sky was beautiful. Most of the stars were gone, and there was a gentle glow along the eastern horizon.

I had been to the pond again. And all the fears from a lifetime of nightmares—the path, her yard, and the shadow—I felt them melt away. The burden had lost its power. The night would soon give way to dawn, and then the full brightness of day.

I got up and stood still in the cool sand. Everything was quiet, and I tried to drink in the stillness, but it was too cold to appreciate. So I put on my sandals, picked up all my sleeping stuff, and carried it back to the shed. I tossed it on the cot and changed my shirt. I walked across the alley to the shop. Tony hadn't arrived yet, and I made a single cup of coffee using the stovetop espresso maker. I wrote Tony a note, telling him I was heading to the motel and would be back when I could. I set the note in the center of the counter and left out the back door. I locked it behind me and hid the key.

I carried a paper cup, and sipped strong espresso as I walked. I crossed through the playground and saw a second yellow box taped to the swing set. I had no interest in why it was there. I went through the gate and down across the *arroyo.*

When I came out from the cottonwoods, the pilot was right there, waiting on the path. I was surprised and stopped.

He spoke first, "I heard Katherine may be able to get out soon. I'm not sure if that means today, but that was my sense."

I said, "That's good news."

"Yes, I hope it's true."

We spoke at the edge of the open area along the trees, further away from the motel than any of the mornings so far.

He faced me and said, "Yesterday, I was flying. I made a trip out of the valley, and was alone in the helicopter for the return."

I had no idea why he was telling me this. He added, "Something happened." Then he reached in his pocket, pulled out a phone, and handed it to me. There was an image filling the screen—it was an owl on the front seat of the helicopter.

I asked, "What happened?"

He said, "This was early evening, but it was still hot, and the starboard window was open a little, not much, I was eyes forward and there was a flicker of movement, and when I looked, this thing was sitting next to me."

I asked, "You mean it flew in the window while you were in flight?"

"Yeah."

"Is that possible?"

"I'd say no, but it happened." Then he pointed to the picture and said, "You can zoom in on it."

"Sorry, I don't know how."

He took it from me, did something with his fingers and handed it back. The close-up picture was remarkably clear. The owl seemed perfectly calm, and I felt like it was looking right at me.

I asked, "How big was it?"

"It was small, maybe ten inches or less."

I studied the picture, and told him it was a western screech owl. He said, "I was flying at around two thousand feet, and traveling about a hundred-and-ten knots. I don't know how it got in. Given the power of the rotor wash, it should have been impossible."

I asked, "Have you shown this to Katie?"

"No."

"Why not?"

"I don't want to scare her."

"Why would it scare her?"

"Because it scared me."

"Have you shown it to your boss?"

"No. Besides me, you're the only person who's seen this."

I handed him back his phone. He clicked something on it, and put it in his pocket. I studied him, and said, "You want some answer from me, and I don't have it."

He gave me an odd look, like he felt uneasy. I asked, "Why did you think that picture would scare Katie?"

I could see him clenching his jaw, and his head was tipped in an uneven way, like he was in pain. He answered me very quietly, "The night you and Katherine were here, after you left, I was in the motel with her, and there was a lot going on. She was really upset, and everyone was trying to help. It was too much, and I sent them all out of the room. We were alone, and I asked a few questions, not like an investigation, I was worried she might have been hurt. She was hard to reach and wasn't saying much."

Then his voice got quieter, "She said, 'We saw owls,' and then nothing. I don't know if she said anything else until the next morning."

I asked, "Did she tell that to anyone else, about seeing owls?"

"I don't know. I wasn't part of her debrief, and there were a lot of people involved in that."

I asked, "Do you *think* she told anyone else?"

"No." He said that firmly.

"How can you be sure?"

He turned around and looked at the motel, then back at me. He said, "I can't talk here. I'll come by the coffee shop. Gimme a couple of hours."

"Okay, I'll be there."

Then he turned around and walked to the motel. He moved fast, entered one of the doors and was gone.

I had been holding the paper cup the whole time we talked. I drank what was left, and it was cold and bitter. Then I walked directly to Betty's store.

I could see her inside when I got there, and tapped on the glass. She hurried to the door and let me in.

She simply said, "John."

I didn't know what to say, and just stood there. She asked, "What's wrong?"

I said, "I'm worried."

We stood near the door in the main room, and she waited for me to say more. She tilted her head and looked up at me, then patted my arm and said, "Please, it's okay."

"I'm scared something is terribly wrong."

"I know you are. I can tell. This is about the girl with the red hair, isn't it?"

"I abandoned her, it was my fault. I couldn't help her." My words came from some hollow place inside.

"John, it's not like that. I'm sure it's not."

"Betty, something happened. I don't understand it, but—I saw her. I saw it in her, and—she was so scared."

I couldn't shake the sight of Katie waking under the swings and the suffering in her eyes.

Betty whispered, "It's okay, it's okay."

I took a deep breath and tried to steady myself, and she stood solid in front of me. I said, "We were friends as little kids. She just showed up here, and I don't understand it. I haven't seen her in—like—thirty years, but I'm so worried. I see her alone on some stormy ocean, some dangerous place. I need to save her."

Betty spoke with perfect clarity, "John, you did nothing wrong. I'm sure of that. Please don't think that you did."

I whispered, "She is so steady and graceful. And I can see what I am, I'm this broken person, and I feel like—I'm one breath away from some—oblivion."

"Oh, John, I know about people. And you have a beautiful heart. I see it so plainly. I do. Don't doubt that."

Then she hugged me, and I could hear her crying. It wasn't like she herself was upset, more that she was absorbing my worries and fears. It wasn't long before she stepped back and held my arms, gripping them in her hands.

She said, "You go find her, and if she needs to be saved, you save her."

She smiled, but didn't say anything. We stood like that for a while, and after a little bit, I said, "I should get back. I told Tony I would be there to help him."

She walked me out, and we stood together on the sidewalk. I stared out at this lonely town, unsure of why I was here. Then I looked at her and said, "Thank you, thank you."

I was about to turn to leave, but couldn't. Her expression told a painful story, and I felt it in my heart. She spoke softly, "Oh, John, your eyes."

Her voice was hushed and far away. I tipped my head down in a sort of anguished reflex. Her kind words bothered me, and I ached to be free of this dark burden. But I couldn't succumb to it, not now. Then I stood tall and looked back at her.

39

I GOT TO THE SHOP, and Tony asked if there was any news about Katie. I told him she was doing better, but didn't say she might be able to leave the motel today. I'm not sure why I hid that from him, because he deserved to know. There were only a few customers, and I needed to be busy, so I went outside to sweep the sidewalk.

I ran the point of the broom along the edge where the storefront met the cement. I was trying to clean out any little pebbles when I saw a reflection in the window and turned around.

The pilot was standing there, and I said, "You're early."

He didn't reply, and slowly looked around the street. I opened the door, and he followed me in. I leaned the broom in the corner and asked, "Can I get you anything?"

"A small coffee, black."

I went behind the counter, filled a paper cup, and set it on the counter. He reached around and took out his wallet. I told him not to worry about it. He picked up the cup and asked, "Can we talk outside?"

I went into the kitchen and told Tony I needed to step away for a little while, and he said he would watch the counter. I filled a glass of water and went out onto the patio with the pilot. There was no one else there. He walked to the furthest point from the door and sat near the corner of the low wall around the patio. I sat on the other edge and faced him.

Again, he looked around, and I waited for him to say what he couldn't tell me earlier. He asked, "Why is it so empty?"

I said, "It's like this on Sundays."

I sat still and watched him take his first sip. Then he set the cup on the corner between us and methodically rotated it with his fingertips.

He wasn't looking at me when he finally spoke, "There were people here who weren't part of our team. They'd been called the night Katherine passed out. I flew out in the dark to pick them up, and it was barely sunrise when I returned."

"I saw you that morning. So you'd already flown and come back when we talked?"

"Yeah, I hadn't been back long."

I asked, "Who were they?"

"I'm not sure, but I didn't like them."

"What does that mean? Is she in danger?"

"I don't think so, but they spent a lot of time with her."

"Are they still here?"

"No, I flew them out last night, and I was alone on the return flight when the owl got in the cockpit."

I asked, "How did the owl leave?"

"It left after I landed. This was in the gravel pit. I opened all the doors, and it flew off after the rotors stopped."

"Why were those people here?"

"No one told me. I'm assuming they were a team of interrogators, but I wasn't part of any of that. They were very interested in her and what had happened."

"Were they military?"

"I don't know. They wore civvies and didn't say much to me."

"What's your guess?"

"They were ex-military. There were three of them, and they were serious. They wanted something."

"You said you didn't like them. What are you telling me?"

"I'm not sure, but them being here bothered me. I wasn't involved with anything they were doing, and most of the team was kept separated. We were told not to talk about anything among ourselves, and we didn't."

I asked, "Was that guy Tim involved?"

He narrowed his eyes and said, "Yes."

"What about your boss? The Foreman, was he involved?"

"Yes."

I said, "You're telling me more than you should."

He held his mouth tight, breathing loudly through his nose. After a few sharp breaths, he said, "It might have been rough for Katherine. I think they used hypnosis, and there might have been drugs."

He seemed worried, almost helpless. Why was he telling me these things? I thought for a moment, and asked, "Do you think they tortured her?"

He sat upright, "Why would you ask that?"

I snapped back, "Because I'm on the inside, right in the middle of all this, and I need to ask."

He stared at me, and continued breathing in that loud anxious way. Then he said, "I don't know. I wasn't directly involved, but I've been around during harsh interrogations, and it had that feel."

He gave me a look that told me he was baffled. Then he said, "I'm not on the inside, not part of the inner circle of all this here, but I've seen enough to be worried."

I asked, "Is Katie in this inner circle?"

He answered slowly, "At its very center."

We sat in silence and stared at each other. Both of us knew that we had every right to be worried. I was about to ask if he had talked with Katie today, when he said, "I met your friend Donnie."

This surprised me, and I asked, "When?"

"It was after they found the location of your painting. I was sent there, to the gallery in Taos."

I said, "He's dead."

"Yes, I know that."

He was quiet for a bit, I think out of politeness. I leaned forward and asked, "What happened?"

He said, "I went to the gallery and saw your painting, and made some inquiries. I spent a few days there, and was sending messages back to the team. This was a pretty easy assignment, and it surprised me when I realized I was being followed."

"What do you mean followed?"

"Your friend, Donnie. He was following me. I confronted him, and we talked."

"What did he say?"

"He didn't say much."

"Yeah, that sounds like him."

He took a long slow breath, then said, "I saw him a few times. He was parking in places that were pretty obvious. He even walked around one of the galleries while I was in there. He wanted me to know he was watching me."

"I don't understand. How did he know why you were there?"

"I have no idea. I ran the plates on his truck and got his name, and I talked with the staff at the gallery where your painting was, and asked around at the other galleries that had shown your work. I asked if anyone knew him. A few people said he would come in sometimes and look at your paintings, and one woman told me you and him were friends. At that point, all I knew was that your painting was of interest to the team in our office, and I acted like a potential buyer. People were fine to talk about you and your work. But I don't think anyone at any of the galleries had told Donnie about me.

"There was a day when I saw him parked on the street, so I walked up to his truck and talked to him. I told him I was working for an art dealer and was making inquiries into your paintings."

I interrupted, "I know the kind of people who buy my paintings, and so does he, and you don't fit the type. He would've seen that."

"Well, maybe. But I pretty much told him the truth. I was working for someone who wanted to know about you and your work. He seemed wary of me. My sense is he wanted to protect you."

I said, "Why would he want to protect me? I abandoned him."

That hurt to say, but it was true. I went on, "I'd had paintings in galleries before, but this was my first real opening, just me. It felt important, and I was nervous. I was drinking a lot then, and I knew I'd need to fight that at the opening, to stay sober. Part of me wanted Donnie there, but he was still drinking, and I was worried that I would be—I don't know—embarrassed by him. I didn't invite him. He knew it was happening and that it was a big thing for me.

And I hated myself. And I never reached out to him after that. I wanted to, but I never did. And almost twenty years went by."

Then I asked, "How was he?"

The pilot said, "It's hard to say, but that guy cared about you. And he didn't like me or how I'd taken an interest in your painting."

"How did he know anything about you or your intentions?"

"I don't know, but he knew."

I asked, "And what were your intentions?"

He didn't answer my question, but said, "In this work, I've met plenty of people who talk big and shrink when the hard stuff happens. I've met the real thing, too. They are rare, and it gives me some hope knowing they're out there."

He looked past me at the lonely foothills beyond the alley, and I could tell he understood that some big part of this mystery lay waiting out there. Then he said, "Your friend, he was the real thing."

Yes, Donnie was my friend, but in many ways he stayed a stranger. I knew one thing, there was an innate bravery in him. I saw it clearly, and the pilot did, too.

"You said he wanted to protect me. What do you mean, protect me from what?"

"I don't know. I had no agenda, not then. But after all that's happened, this work has gotten very strange."

He looked at me. His intensity told me everything. I was immersed in this strangeness, and so was Katie.

He said, "Something was going on, and your friend knew it."

I looked up at the sky and tried to think. It was a perfect, cloudless day, and I thought about his mocking voice in that dark canyon. I said, "He was powerful in his own ways. He must have had some knowing about that painting, and about me."

He said, "I found out later that he died. I made some calls about it. His truck was found upside down on a state highway. It had rolled down a hill and ended up in a draw. He died from a head injury. The patrolmen found open liquor in the car, and they determined it was an accident."

I asked, "What do you think?"

"They might be right, but it's possible someone killed him."

"I don't understand why."

"Neither do I, and I don't know why he was following me."

I asked, "Could he have found something?"

He said, "I'm not sure. I didn't find anything."

"What was important enough that someone would kill him?"

He didn't answer. He'd obviously been asking himself the same questions, and I could tell he was frustrated. We were both lost in the same maze.

I said, "I hadn't seen him in years, but he was my friend."

I was worn down with regrets. He died trying to protect me from something, and I needed to understand what it was.

I said, "That night, Katie told you she saw owls. I was with her, and I saw them, too. They were perched on the swing set above us, right before we passed out."

This guy was scared and confused, and I could tell he was struggling to make sense of all this. I said, "Your boss came here last night, and I asked what he thought about owls. He didn't react in any way that I could tell. So I'm pretty certain Katie never told anybody but you about the owls. And I don't think you should tell anyone either."

"Why did she tell me?"

I thought for a moment and then said, "So you would come to me, and tell me all this, what you've shared now."

He didn't seem fazed by what I'd said. It was obvious he knew what I meant, and that told me he was aware of Katie's abilities.

He asked, "Why was The Foreman here last night?

"I think he offered me a job."

"What do you mean, you think?"

"It was a little unclear, but that's what it felt like."

"That guy is never unclear."

"Maybe he wanted to see my reaction if he dangled that in front of me."

He said, "I don't think it's that. He wants to control all the pieces on the chessboard."

There was nothing I could say. I felt like a pawn on that board, and I wanted to convince myself that's all I was. But I knew that I was something more, and so was Katie.

He said, "Tim was at the auction in Santa Fe. He was the one who bought the painting. I'd been called back to the office when it happened."

What was he saying? I looked at him and asked, "Was this the same day Donnie died?"

"They found his truck the morning after the auction."

I didn't say anything. A wave of horror rushed through me. What had been a tangled knot was now a wire stretched tight—shivering at its breaking point.

He looked at me with stone cold eyes, and said, "You need to be careful."

"Is that a threat?"

"Not from me."

"Then what is it?"

"Just be careful, and if you need to run, then run."

"I can't run away from here."

He studied me and asked, "Because she's here?"

I didn't answer. I didn't know what he wanted, or what his role was in all this.

The pilot stood up and said, "I need to go."

He looked troubled in a way that didn't make sense. I got up, too, and said, "Don't tell anyone on your team about the owls. That's for Katie to tell, not for us."

He nodded, and we shook hands. I held his arm with my left hand. We were both scared of everything we didn't know. Then he turned around, walked out to the main street, and was gone.

I picked up his empty cup, and stood there trying to figure out what had happened. He told me a lot he shouldn't have, and I didn't want to admit it, but I knew why—it was Katie, she sent him here and made him tell me all those things.

40

I LEFT THE BRIGHTNESS and stepped back into the shop. My eyes needed to adjust, and I waited inside the door for the details to appear. It only took a few seconds, but in that moment I saw the room as a tiny diorama, a miniature scene in a shoe box. The tables and counter and walls all took on a kind of storybook magic, like a puppet show was about to begin.

Reality snapped back, and Tony came out to the main room and saw me standing by the patio door. He said, "I need to run home. I'll be back."

Then he was gone, and I was alone in the shop. It wasn't much past noon, and nobody had been here for a while. I carried the gray tub of dirty dishes to the kitchen and set it by the sink. This simple act was drawn out in a way that seemed futile. I was wrung dry from everything over the last few days, and wasn't in the mood for making small talk across the counter. I walked out to the sidewalk, carried in the signboard, then flipped the sign in the window. I went to lock the front door, but didn't. The air through the screen door felt nice, so I left it open for the final chores.

There wasn't much to do, but instead of starting anything I pulled out a chair and sat alone at the round table in the middle of the room. I faced the street. There was a gentle simplicity to this little town, and I found some peace here.

I looked out at the empty stores across the main street. The afternoon light was hot and white, and all the big windows reflected my side of the street. It was a giant mirror, and I could see myself, or my silhouette at least, centered within the coffee shop window. The window in front of me was also reflecting, like a mirror facing a mirror, like an echo chamber—stretching on and on forever.

I knew what was about to happen. I stood up and waited.

Katie entered the scene from the right, gliding like an actress on a stage. She was on the sidewalk across the street, and I watched her step off the curb, moving quickly toward the shop. She wore a white summer sundress and a flat straw hat, and her canvas purse hung low off one shoulder.

I took the few steps to the screen door and held it open. She paused for barely a heartbeat, then walked inside.

She smiled and blinked, but said nothing. We faced each other for a long time, and I watched her smile get bigger and her eyes get wider. I wanted to hug her, but the relief I felt kept me rooted to the floor.

She radiated the same confidence she'd always had, but there was something under that. There was nothing to see, but I sensed something fragile, and this seemed at odds with how she'd always been.

Finally, I said, "Can I make you coffee?"

"Oh God, yes."

She followed me behind the counter and set her purse on the floor. I faced the espresso machine and began by tapping out the old grounds from the metal filter, and she was close enough that my elbow touched her a few times as I worked.

She was paying attention, and I asked her to get closer for the final step. I wanted her to watch as I poured the hot milk from the steel pitcher into her mug. I moved smoothly and made a delicate little tree with the foam. It was symmetrical and perfect. The soft tan filled the circle, rising a bit above the rim.

I set it in front of her and said, "There. Drink it while it's hot."

She said, "It's too beautiful."

"No, no. Drink. Please."

She blew on the corner of the cup, and took a cautious sip. When I finished making mine, we lifted our cups and drank.

She looked past me toward the side door, and asked if we could sit outside. I said of course, and held the door for her as she stepped out to the patio. We sat at the table under the awning, and faced each other. We sipped our coffee but said nothing. The air was hot and still, and for that brief moment everything felt perfect.

I said, "I've been worried about you."

"I know you have. I wanted to get a message to you, but I couldn't. It was too—"

She trailed off to nothing. I saw her straining, and my heart sank. I asked, "How's the coffee?"

She smiled softly and said, "So wonderful."

She took off her hat and set it on the table. Her hair was tied back with an elastic band, and she tucked some loose strands behind each ear. We smiled and sipped our coffee. This was all so pleasant, but we both knew it would end.

I waited as long as I could, then set down my cup and said, "The night on the swings, we need to talk about that."

She didn't reply. Her smile was gone, and she was on guard, at least that's how it looked. It was hard to see her so serious. I said, "That night, while you were next to me, something happened. What I felt—truly felt—would be impossible to try to explain."

I looked at her with an unblinking focus that must have made her uncomfortable. I waited and tried to read her expression, then said, "I can't describe it, but whatever happened, I think you felt it, too."

She looked at me with such understanding, yet there was something helpless in her eyes. She spoke softly, "It happened."

I said, "I know it did. And it's been hard for me, returning here, being here, after what I saw, and what I knew there."

Her expression didn't change, but I knew she had experienced the same thing. I said, "It's all gone now. It started fading right away, right after we were running. I couldn't hold onto it."

She whispered, "I know."

"Katie, I saw into you. I saw things that happened to you, and felt them. It's been hard for you, your life. I know that."

I reached across the table and touched her hand. She flinched. I pulled away and said, "I'm sorry."

She straightened up in her chair and asked, "Can I see where you live?"

Her question caught me off guard, and I said, "You mean right now?"

"If it's okay, yes."

She smiled and grabbed my hand, squeezing it to comfort me. I stood up and said, "It's right behind the shop. You can almost see it from here."

I was about to step away from the table and added, "Tony's not here, and I should lock up."

She nodded and put on her hat. We carried our cups back into the shop, and I locked the patio and front doors. We left out the back, and I locked up behind us.

We crossed the alley and stepped up onto my sagging porch. I said, "It's not much."

She gave me a funny look, like I had said something meaningless. I opened the door, and we walked in. It was dark and cool. I pulled the string, and a single bulb lit the room.

She looked around, and I tried to read her thoughts. My little home smelled of sand and dry wood. The floor was dirt, and my blankets and pillow were rolled in a lump on the cot. There wasn't much to see, and I was aware how dismal it must seem.

She pointed to the wall and said, "Your hat."

She was delighted. My white straw Stetson was hanging on a nail. I had it with me the night we met in the canyon, and she laughed when I put it on, and in a very real way, she was right to laugh at me.

She turned around slowly, as if carefully examining everything she saw. When she had made a full circle, she faced me and said, "Let's go outside."

Her voice was calm and pleasant, but her face was deadly serious. I turned off the light and held the door for her. We stood on the porch in the shade of the awning, and she stared out at nothing. I asked, "What's going on?"

She didn't answer. She turned and stepped into the sunlight, and I followed her to the middle of the alley. She faced me and asked, "Where do you go at night?"

"What do you mean?"

"There are people I work with, and they drive by here at night, or walk by, I'm not sure. And they know you're not in there." She pointed to the shed.

I asked, "Is my place bugged?"

"I don't know, maybe. If it is, nobody has told me. But they come by, and they have some sort of unit, a device, and they can tell if you're in there and if you're asleep. I'm not sure how it works, if it hears your breathing, or it senses your body temperature, or maybe it detects your brain waves, but they know you aren't in there at night, and they don't know where you go."

I shrugged and said, "I don't wanna disappoint anyone, but sometimes I sleep in the sagebrush out back past the fence line." I pointed with my chin and added, "It's not very far."

"Can you show me the spot?"

I opened a narrow gate next to the shed, held it for her, and closed it after we both passed through. I led, and she followed, and we walked through the bushes with our backs to the town. I could see my footprints from the last few nights as I snaked around Mormon tea and blackbrush. I stopped at a little open area and pointed to a rectangular impression in the sand where my pad had been. We weren't all that far from the alley, maybe fifty yards.

She said, "I don't know if your room is bugged, or if the shop is, but I think it's better to talk out here."

I said, "Tell me what's going on."

"I was in a meeting where they talked about this. They thought you might be disappearing at night, like physically vanishing."

I almost laughed, but given what had been happening, their concerns seemed valid. I said, "No. I don't disappear. I've been sleeping out here since we saw the owls on the swing set."

She stepped into the rectangle where my sleeping pad had been, and shifted her weight like she was trying on shoes.

I said, "You didn't tell anyone about the owls, did you?"

"No, I didn't."

"Why not?"

"I'm not sure. I guess it felt like they shouldn't know."

"You mean the people at the motel, your team, they shouldn't know?"

"Yes. I tried not to tell them much." She said that in an offhand way, yet there was a tremor in her voice.

"The pilot told me you said there were owls."

She looked surprised, and I could see her thinking, she said, "When did he tell you that?"

"This morning. I talked to him at the motel."

She looked down at the sand, and even with her eyes hidden by her hat, I could tell she was upset.

I said, "You whispered about seeing owls the night it happened, not long after your team separated us and took you into the motel. The way he said it, it sounded like you confided in him. He told me he didn't tell anyone what you said."

She nodded slowly, like she was trying to sort everything out. I asked, "Should I trust him, the pilot?"

She looked up at me, and her eyes were troubled. She said, "He's tough to read, but I trust him."

I asked, "Your boss, the guy they call The Foreman, how well do you know him?"

She said, "He's not the kind of person you get to know, not in a way that would mean anything."

"We spoke, him and I."

"I know. He told me."

"How much did he tell you about our meetings?"

"Enough that I'm worried."

I waited for her to say more, but she just stood there, and I said, "I found that canyon before you and your team did, didn't I?"

She said, "Yes."

"I don't think you would have ever gotten there if it wasn't for me getting there first, like you needed me to find it for you."

She was quiet for a long time, then spoke slow and clear, "We'd been at the motel for three days, and we weren't allowed to leave. The team was waiting, and it was all on me. That's a lot to put on someone."

"What happened?"

"I woke up on the third night and said, 'It's time to go.' I woke everyone up, and we got in the helicopter."

"How did you know where to go?"

"I didn't. I was in the co-pilot seat and pointed and told him where to fly."

"Did you know I would be there?"

"No, that was a surprise."

I said, "You didn't seem surprised."

She leaned forward and said, "Neither did you."

Her eyes narrowed like she was angry. She'd lost her patience, but it wasn't with me, it was with everything that had been pounding down on us.

I said, "I'm in the middle of this, and I don't know what it is, but I know enough that I don't like it. So if you know something—tell me."

"I don't know everything, but—"

"But what?"

I could see she wanted to answer, but everything about her was conflicted. I said, "Katie, tell me."

Her voice was grave, "There is something in that canyon, and they want it."

"I know. Your boss said as much."

"He might have told you, but you don't understand—*they want to control it.*"

"What are you saying?"

"John, they want to weaponize it."

"How?"

She looked me in the eye, and said, "Through us."

I inhaled sharply. My head was a flood of thoughts, too many to think clearly. I waited for my breathing to settle down, and then said, "When we were behind the school, with the owls, we blacked out, and while we were out, I was in some timeless place where I knew and felt everything. *Everything.* I was left with almost nothing, but I know there's something bad connected to all this. I know it, and felt it—and I know you felt it, too, and it scares me."

She didn't say anything, but I knew she understood.

I said, "That *knowing*, it came from something beyond us."

She said, "I've tried to understand this, but I don't know what it is or what it might mean."

I asked, "Did you know when we were under the swing set, in that timeless place?"

She said, "Yes, I knew with certainty."

I snapped back, "Is that why they kept you locked in the motel, to find out what you knew?"

Oh God, she gave me this look. I don't know if it was fury or terror, but I had touched the third rail. She took a deep breath before speaking, "I don't remember anything."

I asked, "Then what do you think it might mean, all of this? What's your impression?"

She said, "I don't know what it is, but I know it's important."

Those words came out with a force and conviction that I understood. All I could say was, "I know it, too."

She asked, "What's at stake?"

I said, "The fate of our world."

She backed up like she'd been slapped in the face. She gasped, "John, why are you saying that?"

"Because your boss said it. He said it last night. I thought he was trying to rattle me, or to see my reaction, but I think he meant it."

"He's never said anything like that to me."

I asked, "Do you talk about this with your team, what it all might mean?"

"Not like this. We talk around it, about little parts of it."

I pressed her, "What is it, what does it all mean?"

"I don't know, but I know what I feel." She spoke with so much emotion I thought she might start crying.

"What do you know that I don't?"

"I'm not sure, but I can say this, my team is lost, and they have no idea what to make of me, or of you. And I don't wanna hear any of your *'I don't know'* shit, because you know a lot more than they do."

That shut me up. She looked indignant and said, "Nobody here has asked you, but I'm asking you now. How did you get to the bottom of that canyon?"

She stood steady and waited for an answer, and I could tell she didn't want some play by play of me turning left at a big landmark or squirming down some narrow drainage. She was asking something else. I studied her beautiful green eyes and said, "I let go. I let go of caring, I let go of my old life. I didn't care if I died. I let go of everything."

"And how do you feel now?"

"*Alive.*"

I spat that word out. I was angry. I was mad at everything that stood between me and a deeper truth. Katie and I were connected to something—we were swimming in it. There was a powerful knowing all around us, yet I couldn't tap into it. Neither of us could, not fully. But it was there, leading us on. Guiding us.

She said, "They want it, but they don't understand it."

"You mean what's in the canyon."

"Yes. They want to possess it, but they need us."

I asked, "Can we stop them?"

She said, "We have to try."

I asked, "What do you know about the bottom of the canyon?"

"I know what I feel. I know the door can be closed, but I need something."

"What do you need?"

"You. I need you."

She said what I already knew, but didn't dare admit. She went on, "It's us, both of us. I see it so clearly. Everything has been pointing to this—the whole time. I know it."

I asked, "Is this why we're here? Is this what it all means?"

"It must be. We need to keep them from accessing it—from having it."

I heard something behind me. I turned and saw Tony's truck come up the alley and park behind the shop. He got out and walked toward the back door.

I turned around and told Katie, "I can get to the bottom of the canyon. I found a way down."

She said, "We need to do this. We need to be there, in the canyon. I know that much."

"If we get there, what can we do?"

"I'll know when we're there. I hope I will."

I said, "If we leave now we could be there, maybe, before the sun comes up tomorrow morning."

She didn't say anything, but everything about her, from her eyes to how she stood, conveyed an unwavering purpose.

I said, "We're gonna need Tony's truck."

41

NEITHER OF US SAID ANYTHING as we made our way through the bushes toward the shop. I opened the gate, and after stepping through she said, "I can't go back to the motel. We need to leave right away."

I said, "I understand."

She went on, "When we get inside, don't say anything about leaving or needing a ride until I nod at you."

I said I wouldn't. We crossed the alley, and I led her through the back door. Tony was in the main room, and he lit up when he saw Katie. He said, "Hey, it's good to see you. How are you feeling?"

"I'm feeling a lot better, thank you."

"I'm so glad. That's great."

I told Tony, "After you left, I closed up the shop. Nobody was here, and I didn't know what else to do."

He said, "That's fine. Don't worry."

Katie went behind the counter, picked up her purse from the floor, and said, "I think I left something on the patio."

Tony walked and undid the bolt, and he opened the side door. She thanked him and stepped outside, into the sunshine.

Tony spoke to me, "I was thinking about closing up right before I left. I didn't mean to run off like I did, but I felt like I needed to get something at home."

I told him it wasn't a problem, and he opened the cash register to count the day's take. I was trying to run a checklist of what we'd need, from water to food to warm clothes. There was more, but I was too overloaded to think.

Katie came back in and nodded at me. I walked up to the counter and faced Tony. He looked up, and I said, "Could you drive us a few miles out of town? Katie and I want to camp out. There's a spot I know along the highway where we can get into the high country."

I sounded shaky, and could tell he noticed. He looked at Katie, and she said, "I'm having some problems with the people I work with, and it would be good for me to get away for a little bit."

Her voice softened the air in the room, and Tony said, "Of course, no problem."

Katie said, "That'll help us, thank you."

He said, "I was thinking about making a run to the grocery store in Hanksville. They're holding an order for the shop. They're closed today, but I've picked up things before on a Sunday. Let me make a call."

He left the room, and Katie led me behind the counter and started running water in the sink. She stood on her toes, put her mouth to my ear, and whispered, "I'm going to need a towel, some aluminum foil, and that clingy plastic wrap if you have it, and tape, any kind you might have."

I leaned close and quietly asked how big of a towel, and she said, "Not that big." I waited for her to say something more, and she pressed her lips to my ear and said, "I need those things now."

I shut off the water, took her into the kitchen, and without saying anything showed her the bin of rags, and pointed to the foil and plastic wrap on a shelf above the prep table. I walked into Tony's office, and he was on the phone. I gestured to a roll of masking tape on his desk, and he handed it to me. I went back to the kitchen, and Katie wasn't there. A second later, she came in with her phone and put her finger to her lips, warning me to keep quiet.

She set the phone on the steel table and wrapped it in Saran wrap, then in foil. Then she wrapped it in the towel and taped it tight. She moved quickly and efficiently. Then another layer of foil, more Saran wrap, and another towel. She was starting to tape the bundle again when I stepped out to the front counter and found a scrap of paper. I wrote, "I'm going to get the things we need."

I went back to Katie, set the note on the counter and pointed back to the shed. She nodded once, and I left the shop and raced across the alley. The first thing I did was change into my Wranglers, running shoes, and my white pearl snap button shirt, the same as the day we drove out to the bridge, and the same as the morning I walked away from my house.

I set my backpack on the cot, then searched around the shed and found two pile jackets, two warm hats, two long underwear tops, a long underwear bottom, and a nylon wind shirt with a hood. I put it all in a pile next to the backpack. I had a gallon-sized Ziploc bag that held a few things, like a small tube of sunblock, chapstick, a pen knife, and a Bic lighter. I tossed this on the pile with everything else.

I got this stuff at Betty's. She would show me things she thought I might want. I didn't need all of it, but nothing was more than a dollar, and I could tell it made her happy if I bought them. I admit I was eager to get warm clothes after all those nights with my arms wrapped around myself trying to stay warm. This pile included a second backpack, which was a little smaller than the one I carried getting here. I set that on the cot, too.

I stuffed most of it in the bigger pack, which I'd carry. The rest went in the smaller one for Katie. I wasn't worried about who got what. I was more concerned about getting out of here quickly. I put two headlamps in the outside pocket of my pack. I bought one at Betty's, and about a week later she showed me another that was a little brighter, so I bought that one, too.

It unsettled me to see Katie wrapping her phone. It was obvious she'd done it before, or trained to do it. I folded a blanket, then rolled it up and tied it with string. I did the same with another blanket. I added some socks, my Marmot DriClime jacket, a thin acrylic vest, and figured that would be enough. I took my white Stetson off the wall and put it on. I carried both packs out with me and put them in the back of Tony's truck.

When I walked in the shop, Tony and Katie were talking at the round table in the middle of the room. They were facing each other with an intensity that made it feel like I shouldn't interrupt.

I left them alone and went to the kitchen. I grabbed a bunch of cookies, a couple of muffins, and a block of cheese from the fridge. Then I filled four bottles from the sink.

I set the food next to the water bottles on the steel table. I stared at the pile, and had no idea what to think. I didn't know how long we'd be gone, or what we would do. But I never questioned the necessity of it—not for a second.

I added another block of cheese and put it all in a plastic grocery bag and carried it out to the main room. I faced them and said, "I'm ready."

They both looked at me, and I said, "I put both packs in the back of the truck. We should probably get going. It would be good to get some miles in before the sun goes down."

Tony got up, and said, "Great, let's go."

Then Katie eased her chair back, stood tall, and picked up her hat. Her movements were as graceful as a cat. She seemed perfectly calm, but I was on edge, and I'm certain Tony saw it in me. They walked down the hall to the back door, leaving me alone in the main room. I stood there for a few seconds trying to drink in the spirit of this place, then followed them out. I stepped into the bright sunshine, and Tony locked the door behind us.

42

TONY LOOKED AT OUR PACKS in the back of his truck, and I could tell he was skeptical of their size. He asked if we had everything, and I said, "Yes." Katie reached over and pushed her purse between the two packs. Then she opened the passenger door, climbed in, and slid to the middle. I got in next to her while Tony got in the driver's seat.

Katie asked, "Can I play one of your tapes?"

He said, "Sure," and she reached to the floor, grabbed a cassette out of the box, and pushed it in the dash. The music came on loud in the middle of the song, and she turned the volume down.

She said, "Thank you for driving us."

We left the alley and made our way to the main street. From there we could look down the highway. It ran arrow straight past the buildings on the east side of town and all the way out to the vanishing point on the horizon line.

I said, "I'm not sure how far it is, maybe six miles or so." I pointed and added, "You can see it out there, on the right side where the rock comes close to the highway. You can drop us off there."

Katie said, "I need to ask a favor. My phone is in my purse, in the back. I don't want to take it with me. I want to leave it with you."

He said okay in a good-natured way, but I could tell he was unsure what she was getting at. She spoke without emotion, "I'm going to need you to take it with you to Hanksville. I left my phone on, and the people I work with have a way to check it, so they'll see that I left town. I want them to think that."

He turned his head and looked at Katie, then back to the road. He said, "I understand. It's not a problem."

"When you get to Hanksville, find someone that will be traveling away from here, and I need you to hide my phone in their vehicle.

If you can drop it in the back of a pickup, that would be the easiest."

He nodded calmly and said, "I will. Don't worry."

She said, "Thank you."

I just watched Katie do the thing she does. She spoke to Tony with an ease that left me weak. I could tell he was thinking, trying to figure out the why of it, but I knew he would do exactly what she asked. She had cast a spell, and he was powerless.

Katie added, "When you get back, if anyone I work with asks where you took us, tell them we had a ride waiting for us at Hanksville, but you never saw us meet anyone or get in a car. I don't think they will, but if they press you on this, don't lie anymore. You can tell them where you dropped us off, and you can tell them everything I said now. They'll understand. It won't be a problem."

Tony nodded thoughtfully, but said nothing. We were all silent, and that meant hearing the music. And like always, it was beautiful. Katie said, "We listened to your tapes when we went to see the bridge. It was all really wonderful."

I added, "I second that. Your tapes make the time at the shop something especially nice."

He shrugged his shoulders and said, "Well, I try to create a mood there."

Katie said, "Well, it's working, the coffee shop feels magical, and being in your truck does, too."

It was like she rang a little bell. Her kind words had clearly embarrassed him. He kept his eyes on the road and tapped the steering wheel with his thumb. He asked, "How long will you be out there?"

I didn't know but had to answer. I said, "Two nights." I tried to sound confident, but there was doubt in my voice. I added, "We'll hitchhike back to town when we come out."

He kept tapping the wheel, and I could tell he was trying to figure out what was really going on. I pointed ahead and said, "It's coming up, the spot where you can let us off."

He took his foot off the gas, and everything slowed down. The whirring sound of the tires on the road waned as if the whole world was changing. We eased off the blacktop and stopped on the gravel. Tony put the truck in park and shut the engine off. The music stopped, and none of us moved. This was exactly where I had said goodbye to the twins and watched them drive away in their old Subaru. It wasn't that long ago, but it felt like a different lifetime.

Katie asked, "Could you keep the music on? I was enjoying it."

Tony turned the key half a click, and the song started again. She thanked him, and elbowed me in the ribs. I opened my door and got out. I pulled the two packs out from the back and set them on the sand a few steps away from the gravel shoulder. Katie shimmied out and took her purse from the bed.

Tony walked slowly around to our side. I pointed to an orange extension cord stuffed behind the passenger seat and asked, "Can I take this with me?"

He came closer to see what I was pointing at. He gave me a puzzled look, which faded quickly, and then said, "Go ahead. Take it."

I pulled it out and set it by our packs. Katie opened her purse and took out her taped-up phone. The bundle was about the size of a cigar box, and she held it up for Tony to see. She raised her eyebrows as if saying, *here it is*. He nodded once, and she stepped to the open passenger side, put it under the seat, then shut the door.

She looked at the two packs, and then at me. She turned to face Tony, opened her arms and hugged him. She said, "I'm so glad we met. Good luck with your books." Tony gave her a strong squeeze and stepped back.

I looked at Katie and gestured with a sort of small push with my hands. I was asking her to give me and Tony some time alone. She understood and knelt down to busy herself with one of the packs.

I walked out to front of his truck and waited. Tony followed, and we both leaned against the grill. We were side by side, looking down the empty highway.

I said, "I love it out here. This emptiness."

He slowly scanned the landscape, but didn't say anything. I said, "I showed up here at a tough point in my life. I walked away from a lot. Things had gotten pretty bad." I glanced at him, enough to see him staring at something in the distance.

I took off my hat and tapped it gently against my knee. I added, "I healed here, and you've been a big part of that."

After a long pause he said, "I found your drawings, the ones you've been doing on cardboard. I figured if you wanted me to see them you would have shown me, so I never said anything. I studied them. There's a grace to them, and I saw how you did things around the shop, and how you are with people. There's an artist in you, and I hope you know that. I'm not one to give advice, but you need to let that out. You have something important in you, so don't keep it hidden in a box on some bottom shelf."

He ran his hand over his head, like he needed to remind himself that he'd shaved it. He said, "If you need to do something, then do it."

I said, "That's advice for you, too."

He turned and looked at me. I sensed what he was thinking, but didn't want to admit what we both already knew. I got up from his hood and faced him. We hugged, and I slapped his back.

Tony walked around to the driver's door and called to Katie over the truck bed, "I'm honored to have met you."

She stood up and said, "The honor is all mine."

He looked at me, and I said, "*Adios amigo.*"

He saluted and said, "Godspeed."

After he drove off, the world was silent. I stood alongside Katie and the two packs, but I was looking back toward town, and the lone telephone pole on our side of the highway.

I said to Katie, "I need to check on something."

I only took a few steps before I saw it at the base of the pole. I didn't want it to be true, and my pace slowed. The owl was lying in the weeds. It was on its back facing the sky, wings open and crooked. Both eyes were gone, and its face was desiccated from the sun. Those feathers had been so regal when it hopped down from the hatchback, and now they were bleached nearly white.

I heard footsteps behind me, and then Katie said, "Oh, no."

She was at my side, and I told her, "I need to bury it."

There was an open spot on the ground a little further from the road. I got on my knees and tried scooping the sand with my hands. The surface was baked stiff, so I found a pointed rock to break it apart. Katie got on her knees facing me and helped pull gravel and rocks out of the little hole. When it was big enough, I walked back to the owl and picked it up by one foot. It was much lighter than I expected, and I set it in the hole. I tried to fold its wings into a more gentle pose, but they weren't going to move. I put a handful of sand on it, and Katie did the same.

After it was covered, we both patted the earth smooth, and stood up. I said, "You're finally free."

I looked at Katie and said, "We should get going."

We got to the packs and put them on. I quickly coiled the extension cord and tied it off. I had Katie set it over the top of my pack. We walked across the sand and onto the exposed rock. I said, "We're going to follow this ramp up into the high country. The travel is pretty easy, but I'm worried about being seen."

She said, "Okay, let's go." And we started walking. I led the way, and she was right behind me. She asked, "How did you know there would be an owl there?"

I said, "I've been here once before. I hitchhiked from town. A car picked me up, and as we were driving, an owl somehow flew in the window. It hit the back, and the noise was awful."

I thought about the power and emotions of that day. I said, "We pulled over and opened the hatchback, and the owl hopped out. It was something so beautiful."

I stopped and pointed to the telephone pole, which was now a little bit below us. I said, "It flew up and landed on the top of that pole. We found blood in the back of the car, and realized it must have been hurt."

She asked, "What were you doing out here?"

I looked at her and said, "I was on my way to meet you."

She was well beyond being surprised by any of this, at least that's what I thought. But I saw concern in her eyes, and felt it, too. I didn't want to think about any of this, so I turned and kept walking uphill.

Katie said, "That owl is buried under a cross, like a fallen soldier."

43

FOR THE FIRST HALF MILE OR SO, moving up the spine was concerning. The travel was easy enough, but we were in full view of the road. We only saw one car below us. It was heading west toward town. I saw it approaching when it was still a few miles away. We were both wearing white, and we'd be easy to see. There was a slight depression in the sandstone, and we hurried to its lowest point, hunching down until the car had passed.

We continued uphill, and it wasn't long before the angle of the ridge changed, easing off to a vast plateau. After that, the road was hidden below us, and if we couldn't see it, no one from down there could see us. My worries lessened, and we continued on at a steady pace.

I said, "When I brought you into my little shed, that was tough for me. I hadn't thought much about it til you were in there. Up until that point, I'd been grateful to have a home. I know I shouldn't, but I felt embarrassed."

She said, "Please, John, you don't need to worry. It's not like that."

We walked a ways before she spoke again, "There was a man at the church I used to go to with my mom. After Mass, if the weather was nice, we would sit outside with the congregation. This man, my mom called him Old Joe, he would sit with us sometimes. One Sunday, he told me a story. I'm not sure how old I was, but I was little, and I still remember it so clearly.

"He was in the army in the war, and he was in Paris after the Nazis left. He grew up in a small town in Maine, up near the border with Canada, so he spoke French. He was Catholic, and he went to Notre Dame to take Communion. While he was there, he talked to a monk. Joe was in his American fatigues, and the monk was surprised he spoke French. They talked, and the monk asked if he would like to ring the bells.

"Joe said, 'Oh, boy, would I!' It was almost noon, and they climbed up these spooky dark stairs, up and up, way up the tower. And when they came out into the sunshine, he saw a magnificent bronze bell.

"Joe said, 'There was a thick rope, and the monk explained how we needed to start slow to get the bell to swing, so we held the rope together and pulled.' At first the huge bell hardly moved, but they kept on pulling, and soon it was swinging, and when it rang it was a lot louder than he expected.

"When the bell was booming, the monk yelled, 'Hang on!' Then he let go and stepped back. Joe said, 'The bell was so big, the rope lifted me off the floor. And I started going up and down, up and down. We were way up in the tower, and the bell was ringing, and the wind was blowing, and the city was shining below us.'

"I can still see Old Joe's face. He was so excited to tell this story. He said, 'It was so loud and so beautiful. It was the most thrilling thing in my life!'

"And when it was over, they went back down the stairs and Joe asked the monk where he lived, and he said, 'I live here, in the cathedral.' And he took Joe through a little door behind the stairs where the choir would sing, and this narrow hallway led to the monk's room. It was very small, with only his tiny bed, and a little table with a lamp. There was only one small window in the room, but it wasn't to the outside, it faced inward, looking into the church. The stone walls were thick, so it was like looking out through a little tunnel, and it faced a beautiful statue of Mary holding the body of Christ, surrounded by angels. Old Joe looked at me and whispered, 'This man lived within a prayer.'"

A little bit later Katie asked for some water. We stopped, and I gave her a bottle. She drank and handed it back, then said, "That story has always stayed with me. I know Old Joe was excited to tell me about ringing the bell, but what struck me so much more was the beauty of the monk's little room."

We walked a long ways before she spoke again. She said, "I thought about that story when you showed me your home."

I wasn't sure what to say, and I asked, "So you see the coffee shop as my gothic cathedral?"

"No, I see this here, all of this, as your cathedral."

The sun had gotten lower in the sky, and the sandstone was quiet and beautiful. I said, "I'm not the caretaker of this big empty place."

She said, "Well, you should be." She sounded happy and forthright, and I didn't know how to respond.

Not long after, I stopped and surveyed the terrain ahead of us. I said, "At some point we'll need to trend west. We need to find the slot in the rock. The sun will be down soon, and I don't want to look for it in the dark."

I had walked this route once before, and it felt familiar, but it was impossible to know exactly where we were, or where we were going. The setting sun ahead kept us heading west, and that was all we could do.

I looked behind me, and Katie was wide-eyed in amazement. I said, "This is new for you, where we are."

She said, "I've never seen anything like it. It's like being on Mars."

We were on a rolling plateau of infinite slickrock. There wasn't much beyond the singular rock below us, and the wind and time had sculpted it into weird swirling waves and ripples. I said, "Yes, it's remarkable."

Over the years, I've met plenty of people who were new to this country. Most appreciated the eerie beauty of the terrain, but some were frightened. Its harshness unnerved them. I didn't know what Katie felt, but there was so much more going on than just seeing a lonesome landscape for the first time.

I said, "I don't want to stop. Once it gets dark, we'll have a hard time finding the route down. So forgive me if I seem impatient."

She understood, and I quickened my pace. We would rise up and dip down, over and through troughs and ridges. We could see the sun touching the horizon from the high points, and we'd lose sight of it in the low points. At the next high point, the sun was about halfway down, and the next it was gone.

I stopped and scanned the horizon, and Katie stood next to me. I was looking ahead, trying to guess where the entrance might be. I remember the area was mostly flat, but I wasn't seeing anything like that.

Katie said, "Dear God. The colors."

Yes, the colors. We were in that magic moment when the oranges and reds and pinks confused your eyes. Her hair was part of it, too, and the change in the light compounded the intensity. It rested on her shoulders, rich and shiny, a color I had never seen. I wanted to say something but didn't. I turned away and faced the violet sky before us, and simply said, "Yes, it's beautiful."

She said, "It looks like your paintings."

The last thing I wanted to think about was my paintings. I started walking, and she followed. We dropped down into a hollow and crested the next ridge. Then we did it again, and the colors along the horizon lessened each time we got a view.

Then we crossed the next ridge, and the world ahead was level. It was getting dark, and I didn't pause, I walked faster. There was an urgency, and I gave myself over to it. I thought about asking if I was walking too fast, but I could hear her behind me, and she was keeping up.

Then I stopped, and she asked, "What is it?"

I said, "We're here."

"I don't see anything."

"We're here, or close at least. I can smell it."

I took off my pack and handed her a water bottle. She drank as I got out the headlamps. I took off my hat and put one of them on my head, but didn't turn it on.

I asked if she'd ever worn one of these, and she said, "No." I told her to take off her hat, and handed her the other headlamp, the brighter one. I explained that the on-off button should be on top.

She clicked it on, and the world changed. What was once an infinite expanse was now reduced down to a confined little pool of light. I turned mine on and said, "I didn't want to pull these out until we really needed them."

We drank more and stuffed our hats in our packs. She asked, "Could you really smell something?"

"Oh, yes, there is water near us, or wet sand at least."

The urgency was gone, and a quiet peace settled over everything. I said, "If you get cold, we have enough to put on to stay warm. And if you're hungry, tell me. I know we're close, and I'm not worried."

I continued west, and she followed. We walked with our headlamps pointed down at the rock, and we hadn't gone more than a dozen steps when I saw the crack. I said, "This is it."

The opening was narrow enough that we could have easily jumped across. I turned to the right, and we walked parallel to it. After a few minutes, there was a wide black hole. We approached it slowly, and the glow of our lights only lit the upper edge. The surface where we stood rolled in like a funnel, and neither of us dared to get any closer. Below us was a defined tube, dropping straight down into the Earth.

This is where I had tied the rope when I descended alone. The sight was ominous, and Katie asked, "What are we looking at?"

I said, "This is the route down, part of it anyway, but we get in it further on, not here."

I stepped away and kept walking. That hole looked awful in the dark, and I wanted to move beyond its hellish presence. I knew where I was going, and led her to the spot where I had come out and later re-entered the canyon. The opening in the crack was narrow, but the interior was stepped and featured in a way that made for easy scrambling. In daylight, it was orange and inviting, but it sure didn't feel like that now.

I said, "We're here."

I took off my pack, and she did the same. I got out the bag of food and held it open for her. I said, "It'll feel cold down there. We should eat. It'll help."

She pulled out a cookie and took a bite. I handed her a jacket and told her to put it on. It was too big, and she rolled up the sleeves. I told her to zip it up, and she did. We sat down, and I took out one of this morning's muffins and started eating. I opened a block of cheese and cut four slices with my knife. She took out the other muffin and we chewed in our little pool of light.

I said, "Earlier, you made Tony leave the coffee shop. To give us time alone to talk."

She shrugged and said, "If I did, I didn't do it consciously."

I said, "You were plenty conscious when you told him to hide your phone in some stranger's truck."

"I know."

Her words were hushed and resigned in a way that broke my heart. She kept her head tipped down and ate. With the glare of her headlamp, I couldn't see her eyes.

I finished the muffin and licked the crumbs off my palm. Then I asked, "Why did you say that about me being the caretaker of this big open space? You don't know enough about me to say that."

"But, John, I do. I studied your beautiful paintings, and they capture something. And I know you walked away from your home and into the desert. We had helicopters and dogs looking for you."

She stopped, like she was struggling to catch her breath. Then she said, "And I was looking for you, too. So I know about you. I do. I didn't know where you were, but I could feel the force of your emotions out here."

I knew what she was telling me, and I said, "I'm so sorry."

"Don't be. Yes, I felt your turmoil, but I felt your appreciation, too, and your connection, and those emotions were so strong. I felt the enormity of it—of being out here."

It bothered me to hear her say all that. She had tapped into my withdrawal, and what I felt, alone for all those days. I said, "That morning, I left my house and figured I'd be back by nightfall. I don't understand what happened, I really don't. I know where I started, and I know where I ended up. And I know what it looks like on a map, or what it should look like. I didn't keep track of the days, but in all that time, I never crossed a road."

I said it. Until that moment, I hadn't allowed myself to even think it, but I said it out loud. I hadn't crossed a road, and there should have been a lot of them. Then I said, "I never saw a plane overhead, I never saw a speck of trash, or a fence, or any sign of another human."

This was impossible, and I knew it, and she knew it, too. But *all of this* was impossible.

I quietly ate some cheese and then a cookie. I lay down and put my pack under my head like a pillow. My back and shoulders were cradled beautifully in the gentle folds and dips of the rock. I turned off my headlamp. I said, "Katie, you should do this. Take a little bit and appreciate the openness we have now, because the route down is gonna feel cramped."

She set her pack on its side and lay down next to me. I said, "Turn off your headlamp." After it was off, I waited for her eyes to adjust, and it wasn't long before she whispered, "Oh God. The stars."

I said, "Yeah, you need the lights off to really see them."

"I didn't know. This is mind blowing."

"Well, you've been here a while. It's like this every night."

"I know, but they keep the lights on around the motel."

It was a beautiful night without any moon. There was no wind, and the air was still warm. I said, "Before electric lights, everyone saw this every night. These same stars. The natives say they are the campfires of our ancestors. So much is gone, but the stars are still here, shining down on us."

I didn't say anything more. I wanted to let her drink in the sky. It was sad to realize she'd never seen this. Lying on my back under the stars is something normal for me. I depend on their majesty.

44

I GASPED. The stars were all I could see, and it took me a bit to remember where I was. I turned and saw an inky black silhouette floating on a luminous infinity. It was Katie. She was lying next to me. The slickrock shone softly under the starlight, and she was suspended in its milky glow.

I asked, "Was I asleep?"

She replied, "For a few minutes, yes."

Her voice was much closer than I thought, emerging from the dark void. I asked, "Did you sleep?"

"Oh, no, not with all this. These stars. I'm too astonished to close my eyes."

The profile of her face was outlined sharply against the pale radiant background. She was motionless and looking up.

I asked, "When we get there, to the bottom of the canyon, and if we open that door, what does that mean?"

I waited, but she didn't answer. The night was perfectly still in a way that seemed otherworldly. I wanted to stay here, in this silent heaven, but that was impossible.

I spoke softly, "We should get moving."

"I know." Her voice was barely a whisper, but it rang out true and clear in this tranquil realm.

I got up, and she did, too. We drank water, and each ate half a cookie, then put on our packs. When we turned our headlamps on, the infinity around us vanished. We were trapped again in our little bubble of light.

It was only a few yards from where we had been lying to the point where we could enter the crack. I said, "Say goodbye to this big, open world." I led, and she followed. We squeezed down between the walls, and everything changed. We moved deeper into the crack, back in the direction we came, toward the deep tube.

The passage was straightforward, and our headlamps lit up everything in front of us, making it easy to see where to put our hands and feet. But looking further down the slot was different. The distance and shadows distorted things in ways that felt menacing.

I had been through here twice before, so I led the way. As we moved along, I tried to be helpful, pointing out where Katie could put her hands, or where the best spot to step might be. I quickly realized she didn't need my help. She was very composed and agile in this environment.

It wasn't long before the passage opened up, and I saw the rope. We carefully climbed down onto the flat platform of rock, and I said, "This is the drop-off, and it's the only real obstacle we'll have to deal with."

We could only see about eight feet of the rope. The rest was over the edge. There was a single knot, and she grabbed it, approached the precipice and looked down. Then she stepped back and stood next to me.

I asked, "Are you okay?"

She said, "I'm fine." She sounded fine, and I didn't ask again.

Above was the big round opening to the night sky, and our headlamps barely lit the opposite wall of the tube. I aimed my light up and said, "That's where we stood, up there, and we looked down into this."

She said, "Okay." I sensed her mind working, visualizing where we were and how we got here.

The platform where we stood wasn't very big, so there was no way to stay away from the edge. I backed into the corner, took off my pack, and set it at my feet. Then grabbed the orange extension cord from Tony's truck, uncoiled it, and tied overhand knots about every three feet.

I shone my headlamp up into the crack where I had secured the rope to a chockstone. I said, "I tied this rope here, and it doesn't quite reach the bottom. The last bit was kind of tricky."

I pulled up the rope, and let it pile up at our feet. When I got to the end, I tied it to the extension cord. I double-checked the knot that joined the two, then dropped all of it over the edge. I explained the extension cord should be enough to get all the way down, and the knots would give us something to hold on to.

She nodded, and I said, "I should go first. That way I can see you and talk to you when you come down, if you need any help."

She let me finish and said, "I'll be fine."

She said it so plainly, and I realized how nervous I must seem. I envied her serenity. I gripped the rope and looked down over the edge. Then I looked at Katie and said, "Just so you know, there's a human skull jammed in the crack on the way down. It's at the steepest part, and you'll probably want to stand on it."

She said, "Okay," and nothing else.

Going down in the dark was oddly easy. I couldn't see the bottom. All I could do was focus on what was lit up right in front of me. Some of it was featured and low angle, but I grunted and muttered in the steeper spots.

I got to the skull, put my foot on it, and leaned into the wall. Finally, I could rest my hands.

The extension cord was tied to the rope at about the level of my hips. I looked down, and the end was on the sand. The section below was the part that had worried me. When my hands felt rested enough, I continued down. Switching over from the rope to the extension cord was much harder than I expected. The thin width of the cord hurt to hold, and it forced me to move quickly from knot to knot. And then I was down and standing in the sand.

I backed away from the wall and called out, "I'm down."

There was a bright point of light from Katie's headlamp far above me. I watched the beam turn around toward the wall. When she started down there was a circular glow on the face of the rock. She moved slow and steady, and as she got lower, I could see the outline of her body. Her white dress was lit up, yet she somehow seemed hidden.

I could hear her shoes tapping and scraping on the rock, but beyond that, she didn't make a noise. When she got lower, I said, "You're getting close to the skull. You can stand on it."

I said it louder than I needed to. The sound in this stone tube carried too well, weirdly so.

She stepped on the white skull, and I said, "You can kind of jam yourself in the crack and rest if you need to."

I watched her wedge in, and with one hand on the rope, she shook out the other. She switched hands and shook the other one.

I moved to the base of the wall, almost directly under her. I spoke calmly, "The steepest part is below you, and the face is smooth. When you get to the extension cord, it'll be harder to hold."

Her face was tucked away from me inside the crack. She said, "Thank you."

Her tone was calm and polite. I wanted to say something encouraging like *you got this*, but I stayed quiet. She shook her hands a few more times, then wriggled out of the crack, and quickly made her way down to the sand.

She stepped away from the wall and looked up, aiming her headlamp at the skull. It was stark white within the red shadows of the crack. I pointed my lamp at it, too, and it glowed brighter.

I said, "That key I had the other day that opened the phone box on the bridge, I found it in his pocket."

Katie asked, "Where's the rest of him?"

I turned and pointed my light to the sand a few yards off to the side of the crack. There wasn't much to see, only a slightly raised area. "He's there. I buried him."

She looked at the grave in the sand, then up at the skull, and then back to the grave. She said, "He's been here for—" She paused to think.

I said, "Forty-three years."

She asked, "Why did he have the key?"

"He worked for the highway department and was assigned to the bridge. The police thought he died when it fell. He disappeared that night."

"How did you find out about this?"

"I asked my friend Betty. She runs the secondhand shop down the street from the coffee shop. I told you about her before."

She looked at me, and the beam of her headlamp was right in my eyes. I squinted, and she turned her gaze back to the grave and said, "Sorry."

Neither of us said anything. She was staring at the lump in the sand where the body was. She broke the silence and said, "You aren't telling me something."

"I went and talked with Betty the morning after we were at the bridge. It was emotional. She knew him."

The beam of her headlamp stayed focused on his grave. She asked, "What was he doing here?"

"I don't know. She thought he had probably died at the bridge site, and when I told her I found the body, and the key, it confirmed he was dead. She was upset. She had been holding out hope that he was still alive."

"What else is there?"

She asked the right question, and answering it meant telling a sad story. I said, "She had a child from him. He went missing before she knew she was pregnant. She was young and gave the child up for adoption."

Katie didn't say anything. She stood frozen, and I could see where she was looking. The circle of light from her headlamp was unwavering on the grave.

She asked, "When did the bridge collapse?"

"I don't know exactly, sometime before Christmas in 1966."

She said, "Your birthday is August 15th."

I said, "How did you remember that?"

She spat back, "I remember stuff. You were born August 15th, 1967."

Her voice was sharp, and it startled me. She was close in the dark, and I could hear her restless breathing. I didn't respond, waiting for her to calm down. When she spoke again, it was hushed.

"John, you were adopted."

"How did you know that? I didn't know that until I was eighteen, and you moved away when we were twelve."

"I did research on your painting, and on you, too." She took a deep breath and said, "John, that's your father."

I didn't want to believe her and demanded, "Katie, why are you saying that?"

Now her voice was steady and resigned, "John, you know what I do."

I replied in anger, "I have an idea of what you do, but I really don't know, and I'm too scared to ask."

"I do psychic work, and I'm good at it."

"So you think that's my father?"

"John, there are things I know. I feel them. I know what it feels like when something is true. That man under the sand is your father."

I reached up and turned off my headlamp. I couldn't see Katie's face, only a bright dot of light above her body. The walls and the red sand created a soft orange glow around us. She hadn't moved at all since she turned her attention to the grave, and her frozen pose left me unsettled.

I said, "That means Betty is my mother."

She didn't move and didn't say anything. I looked at her outline in front of me. There wasn't much to see. Part of her dress was lit by the light from her forehead, but not much else. It was like gazing at a specter.

I said, "My adopted parents loved me, and I never doubted that. So when I learned I was adopted, I didn't feel like I was lacking anything. Yet, in some way, I felt abandoned. It wasn't overt, but it was always there, that my real parents had forsaken me."

Katie waited, but I didn't say anything more. She asked, "How did it feel when Betty told you about giving up her child?"

I said, "It was heartbreaking."

She asked, "Do you forgive her?"

"I don't have to because she didn't do anything wrong."

I stepped over to the grave and got on my knees. I set my hand on the cool sand and stayed still. I tried to feel something, but couldn't. The events and strangeness that led us here were too big, and I needed to keep moving. I stood up and said, "We should get going."

With that, Katie turned her head and pointed her light down the slot. It was the first time she moved since we saw the grave.

I told her to go ahead. The travel from here wasn't complicated. We left the tall, open tube and entered the slot. I walked behind her on flat gravel between narrow walls.

I said, "If that man under the sand is my father, then he saved my life."

"You mean because you used his skull to help you get out of here?"

I replied with a quiet, "Yes." My voice was hushed, but she heard me fine.

She said, "You came up this way. You didn't need to use his skull. You could have gone back and found a rock and jammed it in the crack."

I said, "I don't know. A rock that big would've been too heavy to climb with, and I wouldn't have been able to lift it above my head."

She walked and I followed, snaking our way through the slender canyon, twisting one way and then the other.

I added, "And I wasn't really in a state of mind where I could have turned back."

45

KATIE WALKED BEAUTIFULLY. I was a few steps behind her, in awe of the rhythm of her stride. It was the walk I remembered.

I asked, "Are you doing this? I mean, are you making me do this, like with your powers?"

"Making you do what?"

"Doing this, what we're doing now, heading down this canyon."

She replied, "I was thinking the same of you, that you're making *me* do this."

I said, "Really? You think I'm capable of controlling you?"

She said, "Yes, I do."

She sounded very sure of herself, but it seemed absurd. I said, "I doubt it. Maybe some other part of me is—some buried part that I don't know about."

"If it's not you, it's something else, because I feel pulled to do this."

She was right, because I felt it, too, and it was strong.

Katie stopped. The route dropped in front of her. She looked over the edge, then back at me, and asked me how I got down this before. I said I wasn't sure. I came up next to her and saw the floor below was about as far down as I am tall, but it was steep. The corridor was narrow enough that she could press her palms low against both walls. She stooped low and steadied herself, stepped down to a small ledge, and then to the sand on the floor. She made it look easy, and I got down the same way.

I said, "Last night, when I was with your boss, I said something, and it scared him."

She asked, "What did you say?"

"When we talked the first time, he told me you did a reading where you tried to describe something in a sealed envelope, and you passed out."

She stopped and turned around to face me, "He told you that?"

"Yes, and he played a recording of the session."

She said, "Jesus, I didn't realize he told you so much."

She turned and continued walking, a little slower now. I said, "And later, you did another session, the one where you got the address of the gallery where my painting was. It was the same words in the envelope for both sessions."

She was processing, and I waited. After a bit she said, "Okay. No one ever told us what was in the envelopes for those sessions, and I didn't know it was the same thing."

"That's what he told me."

"That's odd. I wondered about it at the time. Usually, at some point after a session, we'd open it, or we'd be told, as a way to confirm the accuracy of the reading. How did you scare him? What did you say?"

"I asked him if you ever mentioned the frog pond, and he flinched. I saw it, and I called him on it."

She was quiet as she walked, then she asked, "Was that it, *frog pond*, the words in the envelope?"

"Yes, for both sessions. He said he found it written on a pad next to his bed when he woke up. It was in his handwriting, but he didn't remember writing it."

"Why did you ask him about the frog pond?"

"I'm not really sure."

"Was that the only thing in the envelope for those sessions, just frog pond?"

"I don't know what to trust, but that's what he told me."

She walked a ways in silence, then said, "I've had dreams about the frog pond."

That nearly stopped my heart. I'm glad she was ahead of me because I staggered for a few steps. When I got my wits back, I asked, "Did you ever tell The Foreman about your dreams?"

"No."

I asked, "What are the dreams like?"

"It's always the same. I'm there at night, and I'm alone on that grassy spot near the pond, with my hands like this." I was walking behind her, but I could see her arms were up with her palms facing forward, and this was her pose in the dream I had this morning.

I asked, "Anything else?"

She said, "There's a voice. It says, 'bond us,' and I wake up."

I asked, "Who says that? Whose voice?"

"I don't know. I've always felt it was my guardian angel."

"What do you think 'bond us' means?"

"I have no idea."

"And what do you mean, your guardian angel?"

She didn't answer, not right away. We walked for a while and she eventually said, "The day after your painting sold at the auction, that morning, I got into my car and instead of driving to work, I started driving west. I just drove and drove."

Her voice was low and resigned, and I asked, "Why did you do that?"

"I'm not sure. I wasn't thinking. When the team realized I was missing, they started keeping track of my credit cards and saw where I was getting gas, and somewhere in Missouri, a trooper pulled me over. They had been alerted by the team, and a plane was waiting and they brought me back. Someone drove my car back. I didn't understand what I'd done, and the team was very concerned."

I asked, "Where did you start?"

"Virginia."

"Why did you start driving?"

"I don't know. I truly don't."

"What was it like, being brought back to the team?"

"It was terrible."

Her voice was shaky, and she sounded uneasy. I asked, "Are you okay?"

She muttered, "I hate what I've become."

"Katie, what do you mean?"

"I'm sorry. You asked if I was okay, and I'm not. I don't like what I've become. So much is messed up, and I don't know why I started driving like I did."

I thought about what I'd become, how I hated losing that spark, and how empty my work felt. She left in her car the same day I walked beyond my driveway and into the desert. The same morning after my painting was sold in Santa Fe. The morning they found Donnie dead.

This collision of events should have crushed me, but it urged me onward, pulling me to the river at the bottom of the canyon.

Katie said, "I saw my guardian angel."

"Wait, what do you mean?"

I wanted her to stop and turn around, to face me, but she kept walking. She said, "I saw her in my yard the night before I started driving."

I asked, "What did she look like?"

"Tiny, like some skinny fairy, or like an elf."

This was the girl, from down the street that night, and from the limbo room, and from the alley behind the coffee shop—and Katie saw her, too. I felt something, it was clear and simple, and I knew I needed to say it.

"Katie, that night, when I made you dinner at the shop, we talked about your dream with the bright light, and how your roommate left."

"What about it?"

"You didn't want to talk about it. Why?"

"What are you getting at?"

"You seemed upset, like you were afraid to say something."

We got to a short section where it dropped down. There were a few loose rocks, and it was steep enough that we needed to be careful. When we got to the bottom the floor was level again. She continued walking, and I followed.

I asked again, "Katie, what were you afraid to say?"

She walked in silence for a while, and when she finally spoke her voice was heavy with dread, "It was a long time ago, but I remember, when I woke up, I was sore."

"What do you mean by sore?"

"I felt like I had been with a man. That kind of sore."

"What are you saying?"

"I hadn't done anything the night before. I didn't go out, I didn't go to a party or anything like that. I stayed at home and nothing happened that should've made me feel that way."

"This was the morning your roommate left?"

"Yes."

She was walking faster, and I had to work a little to keep up. I asked, "Do you remember what I said the night we blacked out under the swing set?"

"When?"

"You got up from the dust and ran away from the playground. I begged you to stop, but you didn't. I chased you back to the motel and I yelled, 'I saw her, too,' and that's when you stopped."

She sped up, darting around corners. The light from her headlamp bounced out ahead on the walls, and I stayed right behind her. There was a smooth boulder in our path, pinched in the narrow corridor, and she started to climb it.

I was close behind her and said, "Katie, I saw her, too."

She dropped to the sand and ended up on her knees. She pressed her forehead against the rock, and her lamp lit her face with a garish intensity.

I knelt down and put my hand on her shoulder, "Katie, I saw her. We were in that place, that timeless realm, we were there together. She was there, I saw her, and you saw her, too. I know you did. It was real, that place, it happened."

She kept her head against the rock, and I spoke softly, "I saw her the night before I left my home, and the night before I climbed down that rope to sleep in the canyon below us."

She gasped, "Oh God—Oh God."

"Katie, that girl you call the guardian angel, I think that's our daughter."

She spun around and blinded me with the light from her forehead. "What the fuck! How dare you!"

Then she hit me—and with the light in my eyes, I didn't see it coming. She hit me again and again. I leaned back and let her. It wasn't like she wanted to hurt me. She was lashing out in frustration.

It didn't last long, and when she was done, I leaned back and sat against the wall. I took off my headlamp and set it in the sand, pointing up at the wall with the beam away from us. The rusty orange was beautiful, and it changed the mood of the corridor.

I said, "The dream I told you about with the bright light, when I was sleeping outside near Sedona, I had some of those t-shirts with me, the ones with the word 'Dream' on them. They were in my truck. Your roommate didn't leave one in your apartment. I think I gave it to you."

She took off her headlamp and set it in the sand next to mine, pointing up at the wall and widening the glow. She sat next to me and stretched out her legs, and said, "This is really pretty, right now, where we are."

My eyes adjusted, and I looked at her. I thought she might have been crying, but she wasn't. Her face was hard with a kind of resolve.

I said, "I think your roommate left that morning because she saw something, or sensed something from that night. Something in your apartment. Something that horrified her."

She faced the glowing wall, staring with determination. She asked, "That morning, what did you feel? Do you remember?"

"I felt shame. I felt like I had done something wrong."

Her expression softened. She said, "I missed my period that month, and the next month, too. I made an appointment at a clinic, and I knew what they were going to tell me. I was pregnant. I knew this with certainty, and I knew it was a girl. I woke up the morning of the appointment, and I felt different. Something had happened, and my baby was gone."

She leaned back and asked, "What's that?"

She looked straight up, and said, "There's something purple up there."

I looked up. It took a moment for my eyes to adjust, and I said, "That's the sky."

"Oh God, I'm sorry, I thought we were in a cave, I mean, it feels like that." She was almost laughing, but not quite.

Far above us, there was a thin sliver of neon violet in the blackness. I said, "The canyon is open to the sky, but the walls curve and overhang, so it's mostly hidden. So, yeah, it feels like a cave."

I took off my pack and got out a water bottle and the bag of cookies. I set them between us and our headlamps. Then I opened the bag and held it for her. She took out a cookie, and I did, too.

She said, "I didn't have a boyfriend, and there wasn't anyone else in that time. I knew I was pregnant, and I knew it was impossible."

I said, "Well, there's been a lot of impossible stuff with us."

She said, "My mom was very Catholic, and she had two framed pictures above that fake fireplace in our living room. One was me as a little girl, and the other was the Blessed Virgin. When it all happened, I was really upset. I mean, the idea of a miraculous pregnancy was kind of a big deal in our house."

She took a sip from the bottle, then asked, "What did she look like, the girl you saw?"

"It's not easy to say. She never seemed real. She was very skinny, and she wore a big hat, or it seemed like she did."

She asked, "How tall?"

"Short. Less than five feet."

"Did she ever say anything?"

"She said, 'Now is the time' but she didn't say it out loud. I heard it in my head, or that's how it felt."

Katie said, "I worked late, and that's pretty normal for me. I had an apartment near the office, and I saw her when I got home. I was walking from my car to the door of the building. There were trees along the parking lot. It was dark, and she was standing there, and when I saw her, I knew right away."

"Knew what?"

"That it was her, the voice from my dream."

She finished her cookie and asked, "Did you make these, too?" and I said, "No, this batch was Tony's."

We drank most of the water in the bottle, and she asked if we should save what we had left. I pointed into the darkness and said, "Don't worry, drink it all. There'll be plenty down there."

We got up and put on our headlamps, but I told her to leave her pack off. I remembered this boulder from the other times down here, and it was easiest to squeeze around it without packs. I went through first, and she handed me the packs one at a time, and then she followed.

We put on our packs, and I gestured with my hand, asking her to lead the way. She punched me in the arm and said, "I've always loved that shirt."

Then she turned and strode into the darkness.

46

THERE WAS ANOTHER DROP. It was only a few easy steps lower, and we were on level ground again. The passage was wider and straighter than we'd been through so far. I remembered this section was easy travel, and I knew we were getting close to that glorious canyon.

It was wide enough to walk alongside Katie, and I did. I said, "I still think about the years we walked to school together, and I treasure those memories."

She said, "Dear God, life was so simple."

I said, "So much for me has always traced back to that time."

"Yeah, for me, too, so much." Her words didn't ring true. There was something unnatural in her tone. Maybe it was fatigue, or I was misreading her.

I thought for a bit, then said, "You talked about the tests we took in elementary school. You mentioned them the night we were in the kitchen."

She said, "I remember."

"When I talked with your boss, I asked if it was him. I asked if he was the one who gave us those tests."

She said, "Did you recognize him, or did he give any hints?"

I said, "Not at all, I just knew."

She didn't seem surprised, and I asked, "Did he tell you, or did you figure it out?"

She said, "I knew right from the start. He met with me again in high school a few times, so I always knew."

I said, "He never bothered me again after those tests in the cafeteria, and I'm glad he didn't. Well, I guess not until now."

She said, "He's asked a lot of me."

I wasn't sure what she meant. She might have been griping about her boss, but given all the strangeness, her comment could mean anything.

I said, "You told me in the kitchen, about that testing, as kids. I had forgotten all about it, but I remembered right when you asked me. And then you tried to remove it from me, erase it from my mind."

She said, "I know, but if you brought it up to my boss, it didn't work."

The way she said it sounded like she was praising me. I looked at her, pointing my light right at her face, and she was smiling. I'd impressed her, and I felt proud of myself. There was a lot we could have said right then, but both of us got quiet. I think the burden of all this was bearing down on us, yet we marched on with such purpose.

Katie and I had been walking side by side for a while, and the cadence of each step was in perfect harmony.

I asked, "Did we talk in that timeless realm, did we communicate?"

"What are you getting at? You mean, did we make a plan?"

"Yes. Did we agree to this? What we're doing right now. This."

She didn't say anything.

I said, "I'm asking because it feels like we did. It's the only thing that makes any sense. I mean, in that place, I could see everything, like forwards and backwards in time, feelings, truths, everything, and you were there, and I gotta think you could see and feel it, too. And now we're doing this."

She said, "I'm doing this because they can't have what's down there."

"I feel that, too."

She said, "And I don't think either of us can do it alone."

"I know."

She was beside me, walking with her head down, pointed at the sand.

I said, "Look, we are on our way. We're getting closer with every step, and we are going to do it, and I don't know what that means, but I'm fully committed."

She straightened up a little and said, "I am, too."

I thought about everything that had been happening, the intensity of it, and the power of it. And how it led us to this point, where we were marching together in that dark corridor.

I asked, "What happened when you were in the motel for those days?"

No response. She walked in silence.

I said, "It would help me if I knew a little bit."

"I don't remember anything."

"Do you remember the three men?"

I surprised her, and she asked, "How do you know about them?"

"The pilot told me."

"There's no way he would have told you that. It simply isn't done."

"He did. He flew them in and out of the valley, and he didn't like them. I think they scared him. That's what he told me."

"It doesn't make sense. He would never share that."

"It makes sense to me."

"What am I missing?"

"You made him tell me. Whatever it is that you do, you did it to him, and he came in the shop and unloaded on me. He told me a lot. I mean, like, *a lot*."

I could tell she was thinking, trying to put a puzzle together.

She said, "I didn't. I would know if I did."

"But you don't know what happened in the motel for those days, and that scares me."

She whispered, "It scares me, too."

"The pilot called them interrogators, and he said they were serious, and he thought they might have used hypnosis and drugs on you."

"John—stop—please."

"We're here, on our way, we're doing this. But I need to know why they were here. If they left, they must have gotten what they wanted."

"Stop. This is killing me."

I couldn't. I went on, "You said the people you work with came down the alley and didn't know where I went. You remembered that."

She let out a pained whimper. I wanted to stop, but couldn't. I said, "Look, I'm part of this. I don't understand how or why, but I am. And you know it, and they know it."

She didn't say anything, and I asked, "Those three men, did they ask about me?"

"Oh, John, they asked, but I didn't tell them anything."

"How do you know?"

"Because I wouldn't."

There was another drop-off, and I was close behind her when she stepped down to the next boulder. The slot was narrow, and she steadied herself with one hand on the wall.

I said, "Look, I'm not hiding anything from them, and I don't care what you told them, I really don't. But if they could access that timeless place, they would know everything, and not just about you and me—they would know *everything*."

"How could they?"

I cried out, "Through you!"

"But how?"

"Katie, they've been in your life since you were ten."

She stepped down lower, like she was trying to get away from me, and said, "John, stop."

"They could have used hypnosis, or drugs, or—"

"Or what?"

"Or torture."

She stepped lower and groaned, "Or a ritual."

I slipped and slammed into her, and everything was instantly dark. It happened fast, and I ended up on my side, with my head lower than my feet. My first thought was that I would tumble down further, but I was pinned between rocks I couldn't see.

I called out, "Katie?"

I'd lost my headlamp and couldn't tell up from down. Her lamp must have been off, too, and I pushed and squirmed and got to my knees.

Then Katie's voice rang out in the black void. She cried out, "John, I'm so sorry. If something bad happens, it needs to happen."

It was her, and she was close, but it wasn't her usual calm self. It was her voice from childhood. She sounded small and anguished.

I said, "Katie, are you okay?"

She didn't answer. The only sound was my own heavy breathing.

I could see a thread of light. It was above me, the only thing in the blackness. One of the headlamps had dropped into the rocks.

I said, "Katie, where are you? Answer me."

I worked my feet into spots that seemed stable, and felt along the cool sandstone with my hands. I stood up slowly.

"Katie, talk to me. Please."

She said, "I'm here."

She was below me. Her voice was further away than what I heard before. I asked, "Are you okay?"

She said, "I'm fine. I landed in sand. I'm not hurt."

"Thank God. I'm above you and don't want to kick off any rocks. Can you move away some?"

"Yeah, I can. Gimme a second."

I was hearing her adult voice, steady and husky. Her other voice, her child voice, had been much closer, almost like she whispered in my ear.

She said, "I moved. I think I'm far enough away."

I asked, "Do you still have your headlamp?"

"No, I lost it when I fell."

There wasn't much to see, only a crooked glow above me. I said, "One headlamp is still on. I need to figure out how to get it."

She told me to be careful, and I said I would. I needed to feel around and inch my way up. It took a while, but I got to a spot where I could reach down between the rocks. It was pointed into the sand, so most of the beam was blocked. I pulled it out and put it on my head. I said, "I got it."

I turned and looked down the slot. Katie was sitting on the floor with her arms wrapped around her knees. She looked fragile and cold.

I saw where she fell and where she landed. It wasn't very far, and I was relieved she wasn't hurt.

She asked, "Do you need help?"

I said, "I'm fine. Stay there and let me find your headlamp."

I stood and scanned the rocks and sand below me. I was focused on the rocks around my feet when she shrieked. It was loud, and the echoes boomed around us.

I looked up and yelled, "What happened?"

She cried out, "Something's here!"

I hurried down to the floor, and she was standing when I got to her. She pointed down the slot and said, "Aim your light there."

I did, but there was nothing to see. I put my hand on her shoulder and she was shaking. The narrow canyon turned about twenty yards from where we stood, right at the edge of the glow of my lamp.

I asked, "What did you see?"

"My guardian angel."

I ran to where the corridor turned, and stopped. I knew Katie was watching me from the darkness, and I walked slowly for a few steps. It was no different than the rest of the canyon. I took another step forward and saw two tiny footprints in the sand. They were smooth and didn't look like they were made by shoes. They weren't from a barefoot child either. I looked around and there were no other prints, leading here or walking way.

Oh God, my heart sank. I was seeing something that I didn't want to be true. I approached the little footprints and carefully smeared them away with my shoe. Then I stood where they had been and turned around. Katie was in the same spot, and I could barely see her off in the darkness.

I called out, "There's nothing."

That was a lie. Our daughter had stood right here.

47

WALKING BACK TO KATIE was further than I thought. I kept my head tilted low and off to the side, not wanting to shine my light in her eyes.

When I got to her, I said, "Let's go find your lamp." And I led her back to the bottom of the drop-off. She waited quietly as I searched.

I expected to see it right away, but didn't. I carefully looked around the smaller rocks, and ran my hand down between the bigger ones. I moved to look at other rocks, and I felt something through my shoe. Her headlamp was under the sand, shallow enough to feel. I dug it out with my fingers, and didn't know how it got there. It was off, and I turned it back on and handed it to her. She thanked me and put it on her head.

We walked side by side toward the river, and Katie slowed as we approached the turn in the corridor where she saw the skinny being. She stopped exactly where I'd stopped, and focused her headlamp beam on the spot where the footprints had been.

She said, "John, I understand you want to protect me from the emotions of all this. But, here's some advice, don't try to hide anything from a psychic."

I didn't say anything.

She said, "You did something with your foot. You were pretty far away, but I saw you. What was here?"

I said, "Footprints."

"You said there was nothing. Why did you lie?"

I needed to think because I didn't really know. I said, "It was like a reaction, or reflex. Seeing them scared me, but that was only part of it."

"What's the other part?"

"It's hard to put into words. It was the only thing I could say. I don't think I had a choice."

She knelt down and touched the sand, and asked, "What did they look like, the footprints?"

"They were tiny. Like a small child's. There was nothing else, just two small prints, facing up the slot, back that way." I turned and looked back to where she had been standing alone in the dark. Then I said, "They were pointed at you."

"Anything else?"

"They weren't like shoe prints, more like moccasins or socks. Or maybe those little kid pajamas with the sewn-on feet."

She pressed her hand flat on the ground and whispered, "She was here."

It sounded like she said that to herself and not to me. Then she leaned down and gently kissed the sand. I stayed still, in awe of her tenderness, and when she stood back up, she asked, "How much further til we get out of this?"

I said, "Not too long. We're close."

She walked away, and while her back was to me, I bent down and touched the sand, too, then hurried to catch up. I stayed next to her. The floor was tipped down at a slight angle, so walking was easy. There were no more drops and no obstacles, only a wide stone hallway, pulling us to the river.

I cautiously said, "That voice in your dream, your angel, she said 'bond us.' I think she was talking about you and me."

"I know. Seems our daughter was trying to tell me something."

Her reply was calm and steady, and I wasn't sure what to say, or even think. Then she stopped. I stopped, too, and she said, "Now I smell it. We're getting close to water."

I said, "Yes, and green things. Grass and trees. And it's gotten a little bit colder."

She walked faster. There was an urgency in her pacing. I stayed alongside, then watched her slow down and stop. She turned to me and said, "This is it."

She moved ahead with intent. I saw her as a black and white Dorothy, approaching the door to a Technicolor Oz. The corridor pinched for the last few yards, and I got behind her.

Then we were out. It happened in one step, and everything changed. We'd gone from a barren orange canyon to a tangle of leaves and branches. It was like a jump-cut between dreams. With all the leaves up close to our faces, the headlamps seemed way too bright. I stayed close as she pushed her way through willows and alders. Her movements were steady and deliberate, carefully moving a single branch, then easing past.

We moved out from the dense undergrowth and into the open. Then we walked through tall grass, then gravel, then sand, and then we were at the water's edge. I stood beside her as she snapped her head from point to point, searching with her light. I couldn't see her face, but I could tell she was amped up.

The beam of her lamp darted around, and she asked, "Is this where the helicopter landed, near here?"

I pointed behind us and said, "Yes, right there in that open spot."

"Oh my God, it feels so different with these little lights."

Then Katie was steady. She faced the river and kept her beam fixed out on the water. She said, "When I saw you out there, walking out of the darkness toward me, I knew it was you right away—your sparkly blue eyes."

I said, "I moved slow out there. I was worried I would scare you."

Katie turned and touched my heart, and for a flash, I saw her as a girl again, my steadfast friend from across the years and across the street.

She asked, "What do we do now?"

I took off my pack, got an empty bottle, and walked into the water. I didn't care about getting my shoes wet. The water was a little above my ankles, and I leaned over and filled the bottle, then walked back and gave it to Katie. She gulped down close to half of it, and gasped, "Oh God, that's so good."

She tipped her head back, took another swallow, and said, "The sky, wow."

I looked up, and there was an arching stripe of bright blue-violet, packed with stars and framed in absolute blackness. It was impossible to make sense of the giant walls in the dark, like my mind wasn't allowed to take in anything so mighty.

She handed back the bottle, and I drank the rest. She asked again, "What do we do?"

I pointed into the darkness and said, "I don't know, but whatever we're here for, it's gonna happen on that island."

She looked out at the water, but there was nothing to see. When she was here before, the lights on the helicopter lit everything with a fury, and now we couldn't see the other side of the river.

She asked, "Where is the island?"

"It's out there. It's close."

She asked, "Should I take my shoes off?"

I said, "You could. It's all sand, the river bottom and the island."

She took off her pack and sat down. I thought about leaving my shoes on, but when I saw her undoing her laces, I sat next to her, both of us facing the water.

She tugged at the knot on one shoe, and her hands were shaking. I asked, "Are you cold?"

"No. I'm—I'm—" Then she held her head like she was concentrating, or in pain.

"Katie?"

She leaned forward, hugged her legs and touched her forehead to her knees, and said, "John, I'm scared."

I put my hand on her back. She was trembling. I wasn't sure if she was shivering from the cold or the enormity of what brought us here.

I put my arm around her, pulling her close, and said, "We came here to do something impossible, and I know we can do it."

She leaned into me and whispered, "I hope so."

"Katie, you started driving west the same morning I walked away from my home. We were both being led here, to this spot, to that little island."

I reached over and pulled the rolled up sleeves of her jacket down over her hands. I said, "You're acting cold. Hug yourself, put your hands under your arms."

She moved her hands in a paltry effort, and I said, "C'mon. Really do it. Stick 'em right in there and squeeze."

With that, she put her hands tight under her arms, and I held her close. I said, "I don't have any doubts about this."

She wiggled in against me and said, "Neither do I."

We sat like that for a while without saying anything. At some point, I got up and pulled another jacket from my pack. I draped it over her shoulders and snugged the collar around her neck.

She said, "Thank you, but I'm not really that cold."

"Okay. I wasn't sure."

"I'm kinda freaked out." She pointed her light out across the water and into the darkness, and said, "But I'm doing this."

I knelt before her and said, "I am, too."

She shifted her shoulder and pulled the jacket tighter, then said, "This feels nice. I'm warmer."

I said, "*We're* doing this."

I started untying one of her shoes, and I expected her to protest, but she let me. I loosened the laces, slid it off and set it near my knee. Then I started pulling her sock down. It was damp from all the walking, and when it was off I rolled it loosely and put it in her shoe.

When I started undoing the laces of the other shoe, she said, "Thank you for everything."

I said, "What have I done?"

"You listened to me, and you understood."

"Well, that was easy."

I took off her other shoe and sock, then put the sock in the shoe and set them together. I held her feet and asked, "Are they cold?"

"No."

I set her feet in the sand and sat beside her, facing the water. I pulled off my wet shoes. Both socks seemed sticky, and it took some tugging to peel them off. I pushed them in my shoes and set them next to hers.

I looked at our shoes, side by side. The sand reflected little sparkles from the glow of our headlamps, and something about this simple sight seemed so terribly sad.

48

SHE LOOKED UP AT ME AS I HELD OUT MY HAND, and we both knew what this meant. I didn't say anything, and neither did she. I tried to read her face as she studied mine, and for that quiet moment both of us marveled at the other. After a bit, she took my hand, and I helped her stand up. I didn't help much, but my gesture was honest.

She asked, "We just leave our shoes here?"

"I don't think we'll need them."

"What about our packs?"

"We won't need them."

I walked into the water, then turned around and waited. She took off both jackets and dropped them on her pack. Then she approached the water, and her body language changed as she stepped in. She calmed down and walked out to me. She said, "Oh my God, this is so nice. The water isn't as cold as I thought it would be."

We moved further into the stream. The bottom was smooth, and the water wasn't much above our knees. There came a point when our lights no longer reached the spot where we'd been sitting, but we hadn't seen the island yet.

Katie said, "Wow, it's weird out here."

She was right, it was terribly weird. The river was wide enough we couldn't see either shore in the darkness, and she walked around and around me like a nervous cat. She was uneasy, but I think she was only trying to get her bearings.

She said, "John, I didn't expect it to feel so strange."

"Yeah, the night can mess with you."

"No, it's more than that. I feel something."

I felt it, too, and said, "Don't worry, the island is close."

Looking downstream, our legs left little ripples in the lazy current, and these sparkled in the light of our headlamps. But when

I faced upstream, the water was flat as glass in a way that seemed remarkable.

I said, "Katie, please, turn around. Face this way."

She walked around and crossed to my right, closer to the island. Now we were both looking upstream, toward the spring at the head of the canyon. She stood close to my side. I reached up and found the switch on my headlamp, and shut it off.

I whispered, "Turn off your light."

She did, and in that instant we were vaulted into another world. The blackness around us was absolute. Looking up, the stars were electric, and there was nothing else to see.

Looking down meant seeing the stars below us. They shone flawlessly in the mirror surface of the water. The canyon was probably a thousand feet deep, so we were looking another thousand feet further down at the stars shining under us.

Katie let out a sharp gasp, then sighed, "Oh God."

I replied quietly, "I know."

I had never experienced anything this powerful—*ever*. The stillness was overwhelming, like a buzzing without sound. I asked, "Katie, you doing okay?"

She answered, "This is disorienting." And I could hear the wonder in her voice.

I was floating, and I tried to look at her, but the night was absolute, and there was nothing. I could see her black outline in the stars below her, like she was hanging upside down in the water, as if there were two of her.

We hovered at the exact halfway point between the two perfect doors to the heavens. The sky was a deep indigo with a riot of cold diamond stars, above and below. Nothing held us. We were nowhere, surrounded by the deepest black, an infinite void held between the mirrored opposites.

Katie was close, and I tried to look at her, but there was only infinity. Yet there was something, a faint blue glow beyond her in the darkness.

I wanted to focus on it, but it was flitting in and out of view, and the harder I tried to look at it, the less it seemed to be there. I looked up at the sky, then down at the sky, then tried to find Katie, but couldn't, and now the hovering light was a little bit clearer.

It had a shape, a cold ball floating in nothing, and it seemed to be growing. There was something more, something distressing—it wasn't reflecting in the water. The shape was getting brighter, and it should have been lighting up the canyon walls, and the tree, and the sand on the island. But it wasn't, and this didn't make sense.

Then the tree was there. It was like some misty neon glimmer, but I wasn't seeing the tree, I was seeing its aura. The twisting branches reached up like an illuminated sea creature from the bottom of the ocean. And then the roots emerged. I could see them, too, hanging in space, all vibrant and warm.

I was seeing my dream. This is what I tried to paint, what I fought to capture, this ethereal vision. The branches, the roots, the radiant blue ball of light.

And I saw Katie, too, yet it wasn't her. It was a hazy glow, her essence. She was right next to me, but something was wrong. She seemed lost and haunted.

She wasn't aware of the light. She was looking away at nothing. I could see her, but it was only a shimmering outline. The orb kept getting stronger. The blue was blazing hot, but she ignored it. I didn't say it, but my mind was screaming, *why doesn't she see it?*

Katie replied, "I do see it, I do!"

I heard her vibrant voice, but her outline was frozen. It was her, yet it wasn't. I heard her child voice—my friend from across the street.

She was so close to me, and her present self, her normal self, stood tall and steady, but she was shattered. The blue light was blinding me, but it didn't hurt my eyes, and I couldn't look away. She was right next to me, and the orb was in line with her, and I should have seen her silhouette, but it wasn't like that.

It was like looking into a prism, like a zone of twisting crystal, refracting and distorted. I was close to Katie, but something was terribly wrong, I could feel it. There was something else, a quick movement in the water, a child in a white gown, looking at me, and at the orb, and at me. Snapping back and forth. There were two Katies, wavering, sliding apart, then overlapping.

They were one thing, but they were two, and they weren't the same.

The bush was on fire, blue electric flames, stretching up, up, up—into the orb, feeding it. And the roots reached down, down, down, hot wet roots, pulsing deeper and deeper.

The tall Katherine didn't move, but the smaller Katie was frantic, looking back and forth, between me and the fiery orb.

One Katie was the girl I knew so long ago, it was her, and I loved her. And the other was something else, it wasn't Katie, it was some splintered shadow, and I loved her, too. Even more.

Everything was silent, like an oppressive roar.

I looked down at the Katie I knew, and she was panicky, pleading somehow, warning me. Then the tall outline slowly turned to me, facing me, and she spoke, clear and plain, "The three men told me there needs to be a ritual."

Then her hand lurched to her forehead, and light hit my eyes. Katherine's lamp was on. A white hot eye, staring at me.

She hissed, "A sacrifice."

I was blinded and couldn't see her face, but I could see the younger Katie. She was obscured, partly hidden behind her other self, and she was watching me. I moved closer, and there was a noise, not much more than a quiet snap, and I felt it pass through me.

The blue light was gone, and there was a hole in my heart. It happened, and I knew this with a certainty. She reached out to steady me, gripping my shoulders. I tried to inhale, but couldn't.

"Forgive me."

She never said it, yet I heard it plainly in my head. It was her voice, steady and true.

I looked down at myself. My white shirt had a line of red running from my chest. I looked up at her, but the glare hid her face.

I stared into the blinding light, and gasped, "*Ka—hathor—ine.*"

That was my last breath, her name, my last chance to exhale. There was no more air. The broken Katherine was blind to me. But the hidden Katie spoke. I heard her confident voice. She told me, "Oh, John, we did it. They can't have it."

I tried to stay standing, and I managed for a bit. Then my legs gave out, and I dropped to my knees in the water—that glorious water. My friend, the child, this beautiful glow, stepped closer. She was my height now, and I could look into her eyes, and she held me.

I felt her arms around me, and I tried to talk but couldn't. I heard her sweet, calm voice close to my ear, "You did it. This needed to happen. You did it!"

I slipped away from her, and settled into the river. I could hear the water around my head, and then a horrid shrieking. It was Katherine. She was in agony.

She screamed, "You said you would kill *me!*"

I heard her, but there was nothing I could do. The gentle current swirled around me. There was a tugging. I was being pulled downstream, twisting and dragging along the sandy bottom.

Then I was looking down at Katherine. She was still screaming. Her agony filled the canyon, and I wanted so deeply to help her. I tried to console her, to hold her. I was right up close as she screamed, but couldn't reach her. I was totally confused.

I could see her, and I could see myself, both at the same time. I was drifting away. Gently rolling, slowly emerging, then sinking in the water. I was seeing it all from above. It was dark, and I could see everything clearly, and it wasn't the light from her headlamp. I could see above and below, all around me. All of it.

The river was under me, and I saw myself slowly gliding downstream with only my head above the water. My eyes were open but blank, and I was ringed by ripples. It looked like my head had been carefully centered on a plate.

I heard Tim call out to Katie. He was moving out of the tall grass, heading to the shore. He dropped a rifle on the sand, and I could see he wore big goggles, and I knew these let him see in the dark. This was something I could do, too, but the darkness meant nothing to me. I had a new freedom to see everything.

I watched Tim pull a flashlight off his belt. He turned it on and yanked the goggles off his head, then ran into the river. It was all so simple, like children having a tea party. They have their little cups, and a little teapot, and they pour it for each other, and pretend to drink. They act out a drama, but beyond the joy of playing, it means nothing.

Katie screamed at Tim, "You said you would kill *me!*"

Tim trudged closer and bellowed, "Stop your yelling."

She was unhinged with rage and cried out, "You were told to kill *me*—Not *him!*"

Tim walked right up close and faced her. He commanded, "Look at me. Katherine, look right at me. Stand up straight. Breathe deep for me."

She stopped screaming. I was further away now, but I could see her shaking, her face wet with tears.

She stammered, "It was supposed to be me. What happened?"

Tim said, "The team thought this was best. The plan changed."

I was drifting away, but I could see her face, and the horror in her eyes was awful. I yelled out, "Hey, that was me. I did that! I changed the plan!"

But I had no voice. She couldn't hear me. I was proud of myself, and so proud of us. I told her, "I'm free, Katie, it's all fine. It all happened. We did it."

I wanted to get closer but couldn't. I could see her, and my body. I was in a shallow spot downstream from where they stood. My head tipped and bobbed. I was stuck on a shallow spot in the sand.

Tim said, "Katherine, you did good."

She stammered, "He's leaving—he's gone. Oh God, he's gone."

"Yes, he's gone."

It's funny, they sounded so clear. I guess I was far away, but it felt like I was almost touching them. Their voices were easy to hear, like someone had adjusted the volume perfectly.

Katie asked, "Will somebody get him?"

"Yes, we'll get him."

I knew he was lying. Nobody was going to get me. She aimed her headlamp at me, and if I were any further downstream she'd see nothing but the river and the darkness. She shuddered and started crying again. Tim commanded, "Katherine. Stop! You will not be doing that."

His voice was ugly and stern. From where I was above them, I could see her buckle over in grief. Her sobs were dammed up, like she was choking.

He barked, "Stop that—now!"

That was an order, and she switched off. Her face went blank, and she stood steady. Then she wiped her eyes in a cold, ordinary way.

I was aware of so much from this new place. I knew things I never could have from down there, where they were. I wanted to tell her I understood and that I cared, but that was impossible. I was leaving.

Tim took her arm and led her toward the shore. And I saw my own head one last time, bobbing in the black water. I watched myself break free of the sand, and slowly disappear around the final bend in the canyon. The shell that once held me would soon be drawn down into the spiraling hole at the end of the river, surrendering to its seductive pull.

I looked down at the island and saw the tree, my old friend. It shone blue, smoldering in slow gentle swirls, but all that would end soon. I had slept there twice, under its branches, and each time, magic happened. I woke in the sun and found a way out of this canyon. And I woke to Katie stepping out of a helicopter. Both were miracles.

I knew Tim never saw the tree, even though it was roaring with energy. And Katherine didn't see it ether, but little Katie did. And I could see her in the water, splashing and playing a few steps behind them. She understood, much more than I did.

She looked up at me and smiled, just like when we ran off the dock, holding hands, leaping into the deepest part of the frog pond. Her smile was bold and confident, urging me to be my best shining self.

Katie waved joyously. She said, "John, you inspire me. You always have."

It was barely a whisper, her sweet small voice, but I heard her perfectly. She ran to Katherine and merged. And now there was only her tall broken self, but I knew she was still there. Waiting, with all that courage.

The sandstone walls quietly sank, as if the world around me was easing away. Everything was slowly sinking. I marveled at the beauty and the magnitude as I rose up along the graceful swirling overhanging walls.

I had ascended this canyon once before, with the roar of the rotor and Katie by my side. Now it felt so quiet and lonely. And there was no sense of motion. It felt like I was perfectly still, held in place, and the world was sinking around me.

I looked up at the rim, at a jutting prow of rock hanging over the void, and at the very tip were two small faces looking down at me. They were peering over the edge, watching me glide up toward them.

I was at the pulpit, the stone platform where I, too, had peered over the edge and looked into this glorious canyon. I gradually approached, and I knew passing that corner meant leaving.

I slowed but didn't stop. A boy and girl lay flat on the rock, staring at me as I rose in front of them. It was Katie and me, and I locked eyes with myself. For that brief instant, we got trapped in a kind of echo chamber, feeling each other's thoughts. I felt his worries and fears, and I tried so hard to convey what I knew, to impart a joyous release, my total peace.

Katie looked at me as I passed, and said, "John, it's you. You're leaving."

She was confused and horribly sad. I could hear it in her voice. She had expected to see herself, the essence of her adult self, rising up from the river. I surprised her, this was different, something had flipped.

Myself, my child self, stopped looking at me. I was forgotten. He was now fixed on Katie, completely. I was above them, and her white nightgown shone bright in the starlight. They were both on their stomachs, their fingertips wrapped around the edge of the abyss. I could feel the emotions and confusion in their lives ahead of them. In her and in me.

I was now far above the rim, and the sudden openness was glorious. I couldn't stay. They were receding. I was leaving Katie and myself, leaving them alone in that huge, empty landscape. They shrank away below me. The stars above and the rolling sandstone seemed endless. The enormity of it, all of it, all around me, it was so familiar, and I welcomed it.

There was a tiny dot way off in the distance, sliding a bit above the horizon. There were no lights, but I could hear the steady whump-whump of the helicopter rotor. And I could feel the thoughts of my friend, the pilot. He'd been waiting all night for the call to come get his teammates, and now he was on his way, alone above the valley. He didn't know, but this would be his final flight.

There was no moon, and it should have been perfectly dark, but I could see everything, and the silence and calm ran through all of it. The canyon and the sagebrush and the stars were all so perfect. It's not like I was seeing all this, *I was all this.*

49

THEN THE STARS WERE GONE, and I was back in the limbo room. I stood in its dazzling whiteness, and it all felt so familiar.

The little girl stood facing me, and she wasn't wearing a hat. I could see her clearly. She had long red hair and freckles, and she smiled. This was our daughter.

The pride welled up, grand and eternal. I tried to walk closer, but it wasn't like walking, it was something else. I floated closer, but her head was too large, and her eyes were too big. She was so skinny, and I tried to understand.

It was like she was ugly. I could see it, but I didn't feel it. She was family. My family. Our family. Everything glowed with love and peace. I felt light and unchained, free of that place of heaviness and sorrow. I was home.

"Everything is all right. I'm here to help you." I heard her, that same clear voice.

I tried to move closer, but she was changing. It was like she began to shine, bright from her heart, and the brightness matched the room. I thought she was leaving, but it wasn't like that, she was becoming something. She was everywhere, and I wanted to follow her.

She heard my thoughts and said, "Not yet, there's more you need to do."

I heard the words, but I didn't want to believe them.

She was made of brilliant white light, and I bowed my head. I did it out of reverence, and looking down I saw my legs. And then my arms. I expected to see my Wranglers and my pearl snap shirt, but they weren't there. My arms were skinny, too skinny, like the legs of a spider. I was wearing some kind of uniform. It was shiny and tight. I held up my hands, and my fingers were too long. I turned them from the palms to the back, and they moved in quick jerky motions.

I should have been shocked, but I wasn't. It was all fine, and I asked, "Is this me?"

She calmly answered, but not with her voice, "This is but a part of you."

I didn't want to see myself. I dropped my arms and looked around. I spoke without words, "I'm going back, aren't I?"

Our daughter said, "Yes, you are."

I cried out, "No! I want to stay here. I'm finally back and I want to stay!"

And I felt it again, the sadness. I understood. I knew what was happening and knew it was important. And she knew that I knew, and there was a powerful connection. Our thoughts were one. Nothing was separate, there was only one clear thought reverberating between us, and this grew and strengthened into an unbearable knowing.

Then I heard her voice, inside me, telling me, "There is more you need to do. You agreed to this."

I told her I didn't remember, and she said, "We know. It's supposed to be that way."

I was about to howl. I wanted to cry out, but there was someone behind me, and he said, "Go ahead, scream."

It was Donnie, and I spun around but couldn't see him. My daughter watched me twist and pivot. I could see everything, in all directions all at once, but I couldn't see him.

Donnie said, "Look at yourself again."

I spun back, trying to find him, but there was nothing.

He laughed and said, "C'mon, look!"

His voice was so close, like he was right behind me. I put my hands up in front of my face, and there was only shimmering energy. I looked at my body and it was all the same thing, a kind of light. I asked, "Is this me?"

Before I finished asking, the answer was in my mind, "This is but a part of you, and it is closer to the true you."

It was her voice again, calm and steady.

I was ablaze in this white realm, looking down at my glowing white body, as it somehow showed itself, allowing me to see it. My lustrous mitten hands were at the end of sparkling arms, morphing and swirling to match my thoughts. It was glorious, and I got drawn into the wonder of it. My gossamer body was melding with the enormous limbo room, which was connected to everything—everywhere.

I think I cried out, "Wow!" Or I might have only thought it. I'm not sure, but that's how I felt.

Donnie laughed at my innocence, "You've always been this, but you don't know it."

This snapped me back, and I blurted out, "Will Katie be okay?"

The girl put words in my mind, "She has always been okay. And always will be. Just like you."

There was a rush of emotion washing through me. The love was perfect and infinite and overwhelming. I felt held, embraced, and there was nothing else but this endless sensation.

I wanted to stay here, but I knew I couldn't. I asked, "Why did it have to be so hard, my life?"

She didn't answer in words. Instead I was awash in sympathy, complete and pure. I was unable to change anything, and I understood this was all correct. A perfect endless knowing rushed through me.

Then there was this unexpected weight, like I was heavy.

I sat up and pulled the sheet off my face and saw those men in hospital uniforms. I saw their expressions, and I knew they were scared.

50

THE DOCTOR LOOKED AT ME FOR A LONG TIME, then asked, "And that's when you woke up here?"

I nodded and said, "Yep."

Neither of us said anything. We simply sat there and stared at each other. He looked exhausted, and eventually said, "I need to understand one thing. Katie used you somehow, at the bottom of the canyon. She set you up. Do I have that right?"

"Yeah, pretty much."

The doctor said, "And she had you killed?"

I smiled and said, "Well, yes, but it didn't work. I'm still here."

He seemed annoyed and asked, "Aren't you angry?"

"Not at all. I walked into the desert to die. She gave me what I wanted."

He gave me a doubtful look, and I could tell he wasn't buying it. He slumped back in his chair, drained from all I'd put him through, but I felt pretty good. It was a relief to unload my story.

He shuffled through his notes like he was looking for something, but I think this was a way to stall for a little time to think. It was dark out now and still raining. There was only one small window, and everything in this room felt different now that the sun was down.

He stared at his pad, then looked up and asked, "Did you go willingly down that canyon to your death?"

I thought for a moment and said, "That's a good question. I mean, I knew everything in the universe, at least for a little while, and I would've seen my own future. So I must have known."

He asked, "Did she knowingly deceive you so they could kill you?"

"Knowingly? I don't think it was like that. She truly believed we would escape somehow."

He said, "But some part of her knew what would happen, and allowed it to happen."

"Well, that means some part of me knew it would happen, too. So we were both in on it."

He thought for a bit, and said, "So there was a surface reality and a deeper reality within both of you, and it was influencing both of you?" He said it plainly, but it came out as a question.

I said, "Look. She and I decided to escape, to run away, to get to the bottom of the canyon, and to the river. She was sincere and I know that. We needed to run. She knew what we were doing was important. We both believed we could pass through that portal, or change it somehow."

He said, "Yet for me, hearing your story, it seems like she set you up."

"Katie didn't know this was going to happen. She didn't know Tim was waiting there for us. But Katherine knew."

He asked, "Why do you believe that?"

"The Katie I was with, that I descended that canyon with, she was honest. She desperately wanted and needed to get to that island. To escape."

"Escape? You mean escape from the people at the motel?"

"Yes. She hated what she had become."

"And you believed her?"

"Completely."

He seemed annoyed, like I was some naive child, and he grumbled. "I'm having a hard time understanding why."

I said, "Because I know what it means to believe in something, even if it's impossible."

He was in a bad mood. I could see it and hear it in his voice. He wanted to get me to clarify things in a story that clearly baffled him, but I don't think he liked my answers.

He looked at his watch, and that was the first time he'd done that since he sat down this morning. Then then asked, "Do you feel sane?"

"Who are you asking, me or Daniel?"

"Well, let's start with Daniel. Do you feel sane?"

I shrugged and said, "Well, that's your job, isn't it? To assess me, whether I am or not. So does it matter what I say?"

"Okay, let me ask this, how did you, or Daniel, feel a week ago, before you tried to kill yourself?"

"As Daniel, I did kill myself."

"Yes, but how did you feel then?"

"I was trapped in hell."

"And as John, how do you feel now?"

"Well, I'm trapped in this room."

He sat there.

I said, "Look, I'm not worried about you believing me. When you walk out that door, you can make some phone calls, and you'll find out an artist named John Wilson went missing. He disappeared in the desert."

He said, "This was a long day, and I appreciate your willingness to share so much. You gave me a lot of information. I'll be back tomorrow."

He carefully flipped the pages of his yellow pad around so all his notes were in order. Then he set his briefcase on the table. He organized his pens and some folders, putting each item in its precise spot.

His face was empty, and he asked, "How did you end up here, in Daniel's body?"

I said, "I really don't know how it happened. The girl told me I couldn't stay, that I didn't have a choice. She said there's more I need to do. So maybe she made it happen—or they did."

He asked, "Then *why* did you end up here?"

I thought for a little bit before speaking, "All of this, from seeing the girl down the street from the gallery to right now, it's all felt important. There's this urgency, I've felt it so strongly. But, if there's a reason I'm here now in this body, I don't know what it is."

He nodded and turned off the little tape recorder. Then he put it in his briefcase and snapped it closed.

The doctor stood up and tapped on the door. The latch made a loud click, and the guard opened it. He said goodbye to me, and the door closed and clicked again.

I folded my arms and put my head on the table. I lied to the doctor. I *did* know why I ended up here.

51

I HEARD THE LATCH AND SAT UP. The guard opened the door and asked if I was all right, and I said I was fine. He explained that I'd missed both lunch and dinner during the day with the doctor, and the kitchen was closed but he could get me something. I thanked him and said I was okay for now.

Then I asked if he'd overheard anything during the hours the doctor had been in the room with me, and he said he hadn't.

He stepped in and closed the door behind him. The only way to lock it was from the outside with a key, so it wasn't latched shut. He stood by the door without saying anything, and it seemed like he was waiting.

I asked, "How long did you know Daniel?"

He answered without any emotion, "I knew Daniel for sixteen years. I've known you for three days."

I didn't say anything.

He said, "You walk different, you sit different, you talk different. I'm not sure if any of the doctors see it, but I do."

I asked, "How well did you know him?"

The guard said, "I got to know him as well as anyone could in this awful place. I know what he did to end up here, yet there was a kindness in him. And a pain too."

I nodded. I understood this and said, "That pain is gone. Wherever Daniel is now, I'm certain he's free of it."

He seemed to want to talk, and I asked if he'd like to sit. He took the few steps from the door to the chair, moving slow and steady, then sat across from me, just as the doctor had done. Daniel had seen him plenty in the years he spent here, but I hadn't, and there was something about the way he moved that got my attention.

I said, "I don't feel that pain, not really, but there's an echo of it in me."

He shifted in his chair in the drawn-out way a giant tree sways in the wind. He said, "Daniel was in a dangerous place when he arrived here. He was suffering. He'd been using drugs and drinking to keep the demons at bay. His first years here were pretty bad. He didn't do well on any of the medications, and in a place like this, there comes a point where the doctors give up. They keep someone like Daniel doped up, enough that they aren't a burden on the staff."

I said, "I know all that. But it helps to hear it from another perspective. It feels a lot more mixed up having lived it."

"I wasn't sure what you knew, or remembered."

"I remember all of it. The fears and how irrational it was. Now it's sort of behind a wall, the severity of it, and I'm grateful for that wall, but it seeps through."

He said, "His struggles lessened at times, but they never truly left him, not that I saw."

Everybody here had asked about this, if I was still struggling. I tried to tell them Daniel was gone, but nobody listened. This humble guard treated me differently. He seemed to understand.

I said, "He was strong, wasn't he?"

"Yes, he was. I had to restrain him—many times—and that wasn't easy."

I asked, "Your nose, he did that?"

He touched his crooked nose and smiled, "Yeah, he did, and it hurt like hell."

I looked down at my own hands, my new hands, and said, "Sorry about that."

He shrugged and said, "Don't worry about it."

I thought for a moment and said, "I have his memories. His whole life is here." I tapped the center of my chest. Maybe I should've tapped my head, but that's not how it felt. I went on, "It's all in me, but it's not my story. I remember hitting you, I remember that rage. I can feel it. I remember killing the girl. It's a terrible dark thing that I have in me."

We were quiet for a long time. I could tell he was curious about the change, from Daniel to me, but his interest was something much different than what the doctors were trying to figure out.

I asked if he should be out in the hall making rounds right now. He said, "No, I've been assigned to watch you."

That surprised me, but given everything that had happened, it made sense. I asked, "The doctor who was here all day, did he ask you to talk with me, to learn anything?"

"Well, he asked me to check in on you. He's aware I know you better than most of the other people on staff here."

"Have any of the doctors here asked you much?"

"Not really. I found you. And they pressed me on how I determined you were dead, where I checked for your pulse, that kind of thing."

"Did they imply you were too hasty in declaring me dead?"

"Well, yes, but they had a pretty good reason to feel that way."

"Do you have any doubts?"

"No. You were dead." He said it plainly, a statement of fact.

I asked, "Were you ever a cop?"

"For a while, yes."

"Then you would have had some experience dealing with dead people."

He didn't say anything. I thought about the way he walked from the door to the chair, and asked, "Did you work in Wisconsin in 1979?"

He moved his head back about an inch. His expression didn't change, but I knew he was listening.

I asked, "Were you ever called to search for a girl? It would've been at night, and she would have been missing from her home."

"Why are you asking?"

I said, "I'm not sure."

I watched him size me up. He didn't know what I was getting at and was chewing over how to answer.

He spoke slow and restrained, "We got called to a house, and the parents said their twelve-year-old daughter was missing. It was late, and she wasn't in her room, and they were very upset. We did an initial search, all of the upstairs rooms, the windows, and the yard. My partner and I assumed she had snuck out, maybe to meet a boy. After searching, we were talking with the parents on the first floor when she came down the stairs. She wasn't missing anymore, so we left."

I asked, "Okay. Anything else happen that night?"

He was stone faced, and said nothing. I asked, "Do you remember the girl's name?"

He nodded and said, "We wrote the report as Katherine, but her mother and father both called her Katie."

"That was thirty years ago, and you remember her name?" I said that as a sort of challenge.

His eyes narrowed, but he was looking past me. I asked again, "Did anything else happen that night?"

His was the cold face of a cop, and he wasn't showing any emotion. He looked at me for a long time, and I could tell he was trying to decide if he should say anything.

He spoke slowly, like he was recounting a dream, "She was wearing a white nightgown. She came out of her room and came downstairs, and we talked with her. We tried to ask her questions, but she didn't know what happened. She was visibly confused, and her nightgown was dirty. The front was covered in some sort of red dust."

I understood this so well, and said, "Tell me more, please."

"Her mother was shocked, and told her she couldn't wear that dirty thing. They went back into the bedroom, and my partner and I tried to talk to the father, but he was too scared to say much. When they came out, she was wearing a sweatshirt and pajama bottoms, and the mother ran down to the basement and put the nightgown in the washing machine."

"Okay. Anything else?"

Now he sounded upset, "Look, we were cops, and we let that girl's mom wash what might have been evidence in a crime. We stood there and let it happen. Neither of us would've done that, but we did that night."

He was no longer able to hide his emotions. It was like he was right back in that house, and I asked, "What aren't you telling me?"

"As a cop you see people in terrible moments, but this was different. The girl was scared about something, and it wasn't about being caught sneaking out at night. It went way beyond that, and it broke my heart to see someone so young suffering with that kind of terror."

His voice seemed far away, and he kept talking, "I could feel the fear. I felt it in her, all the anguish. Enough didn't make sense that I wanted no part of it. So if she was back, it was no longer a police matter. Maybe there wasn't any crime, but something happened."

I said, "Yes. Something did happen."

I waited and didn't push him. Eventually he took a deep breath and said, "My partner felt it, too, but I felt it worse. Something wasn't right. We lied in our report. We wrote it up so it didn't sound so strange, and we never talked about it again."

I asked, "What happened after that?"

He said, "My life fell apart. I drank too much, I lost my job, I got divorced. After a while, a lot of years I guess, I straightened out enough that I could do security work, and I've been here for over twenty years."

"Because of that night?"

He didn't answer, and stared off at nothing. I said, "You aren't telling me something."

He spoke slowly and cautiously, "Later that night, I drove home from the station. At the time I was living with my wife a ways out of town, and it was late and the roads were empty. I was really upset about everything that had happened at the house. And—I was driving. Then I—I came around a corner—and—"

His hands were on the table clenched in tight fists. He stammered, "I came around the corner—and—and I saw an owl in the road. I had lived in that area for years and had never seen an owl. I stopped the car. It seemed normal, maybe big—but I don't know, I got a really strange feeling—something wasn't right."

He stopped. I could see he was shaking. I urged him, "Please, go on."

"I wasn't in the car, I was standing in the road, I didn't understand how I got there. I was in my car—and then I was out on the road. It didn't make any sense. The owl was gone, and there was nothing, but—but—I could feel—something near me—a presence. I couldn't see it—but—it wasn't—a person. It was—it was—something else."

He was shaking so hard I thought he might break down. He gripped the table to steady himself, and said, "Then I was pulling into my driveway. I was home, and the sun was coming up. I should have been there a lot earlier. It should've still been dark."

Something was revealing itself, like the script of my life had been set out before me, and I was reading the lines that had been written and waiting for this moment.

I asked, "That night, who was in the road with you?"

"I don't know. It's not like I saw anything. It was a presence, or some kind of being."

"Did the being say anything to you?"

He looked at me with a kind of haunted acceptance, then he whispered, "Yes."

"What did it say?"

"It said, 'There will be a day when you will help the boy.'"

I took a deep breath and let it out slowly. My voice was steady when I finally spoke. I said, "This is that day."

He stared at me without blinking, and I said, "I talked to you that night. I was the boy."

Hearing this, he stiffened. He said, "By the fence, in the dark, after she returned."

"Yes."

"Oh, dear God, you were *very* upset."

"Yes, I was. You told me she was back, and I was so relieved. You being there and telling me that, you calmed me."

He leaned forward a little. He was concerned. It was the same way he'd been that night. I said, "I was looking up at her window, and I felt so helpless."

He asked, "Why were you there?"

"I was trying to protect her, but couldn't."

This big man looked at me with such empathy. We shared something that until this moment, neither of us could accept.

I said, "I need your help."

He was now deadly serious, and we talked about what needed to happen. I would need his clothes, his wallet, his staff keys, and the passcodes to any doors or gates. And I would need the keys to his car. He said he would stay in my room until the morning guard opened the door with my breakfast. Our tone was as ordinary as if we were chatting about a recipe for cupcakes.

He sat facing me with his back to the door, and I faced him with my back to the one little window in the room. He looked past me and I watched his eyes widen. I turned around in my chair and looked behind me, but there was nothing.

He said, "An owl, it just flew off. I don't know why I didn't see it before. It was in that bush against the window, looking in at us."

I got up, went to the window, and peered out through the heavy wire. There was nothing to see. It was still raining, and everything was wet and terribly lonely. I didn't say anything.

I had my back to him when he said, "What you are about to do, it's going to be hard."

I said, "I know that."

When I turned around he stared at me in an odd way, and I asked, "Why are you looking at me like that?"

He said, "Your eyes are different. They are a lighter blue."

I looked down at the floor for a few seconds, then faced him.

He said, "That night, the little girl was scared in a way I didn't understand. It was crippling fear. And I saw it in you, too, the same awful intensity. It was brutal for me, your pain. I was helpless."

I sat back down, and we talked it all through. His pass card would get me into the staff locker room, and there wouldn't be anyone there at that time of the morning. He wrote down the combination to his locker in crayon on a piece of the brown paper. I could put on his raincoat and his hat, so that's all any of the cameras would see.

He explained it would be best if I passed through the back loading dock then into the east parking lot. This should happen a few minutes after 3:30. This was when he normally left, and the next guard would be starting his morning rounds on the other end of the complex. The guy who monitors the video feeds would only see me as someone with a raincoat, and using his card. This would get logged in that he was leaving through the door to the staff parking lot. This was routine, and nobody would notice anything.

All this was orderly and simple.

We changed clothes. He kept his white undershirt on, and put on my denim patient pants. His guard pants were baggy on me, and mine barely fit him. But his shoes fit me perfectly, and when I put them on I said, "Cinderella," and we both laughed.

We sat across from each other again. He set his keys and wallet on the table and started to explain what I would need to do and the route I would need to take to get through the garage and out of the building. Where to fill up with gas, and what credit card to use. He handed me his watch, and I put it on. We had over an hour before I needed to walk out.

He was carefully explaining how to drive away from here, what route, and what to expect, when I interrupted and said, "You'll lose your job, won't you?"

"Yes."

I asked, "Will you go to jail?"

"Yeah, but hopefully not for long."

There was nothing I could say. I was leaving, and he was going to help me, and we both knew it.

He said, "The cops will know I helped you. They'll figure it out. They're gonna know I gave you the combination and that I told you the time I leave. I might be able to stall them for maybe a couple of hours, but not much more. You need to get as many miles away as you can, as quickly as you can."

He said his car would need gas, and I should deal with that early. He asked, "Have you used a credit card recently?"

I said, "Yes."

"You've been in here for sixteen years."

"Daniel has been here that long. I know how to use a credit card." I said this plainly.

Then I asked, "The night at the house. Did you see blue lights? They were all around me in the backyard."

He replied without thinking, "That was our patrol car. It had those blue blinking lights. They were bright and good for traffic work. I hated them, but my partner wanted them on when we arrived on a scene. He loved the show of it."

We talked through everything. He explained what halls to take, what doors, and where all the security cameras were. We talked and talked and talked. It felt like every detail had been discussed and scrutinized, and there wasn't much to worry about.

I said, "The girl from that night. I was with her before I arrived here."

He looked at me and said, "What are you saying?"

"We were together right before I sat up in the morgue. We met up again and talked, not how you and I are talking now, it was something different."

I could see him struggling to understand.

I wanted to tell him about the timeless realm behind the school, but I knew there wasn't any way to describe it, so I said, "We were together in a dream."

That was sort of true, and I said, "I was with her in the wilderness. She told me she wasn't happy at what her life had become, and the only way out was to give herself up to something."

He asked, "What do you mean about her giving herself up?"

I said, "She was planning to die for something. She explained it all, and I understood and I agreed. This was important, and when we left that dream, we forgot all about it, or it seemed like we did, at least on some level, but deep down we both knew."

He said, "That sounds awful."

"Oh, no, not at all. It was joyous."

He looked baffled. The joy was connecting with her in that timeless realm, the endless spiraling magic of it.

I said, "There were some bad people, and they wanted something, a treasure. This treasure would give them magical powers. Together, me and Katie, we had a sort of key to the treasure, but without the other, it would stay locked away.

"She wanted to die, to end the terrible work she'd gotten tangled up in. But she really wanted me to live, so I could draw and create. We made a plan in the dream. I agreed to all of it, but I knew I'd never let it happen, not the way she wanted it.

"So I changed things, I talked to some people, influenced them, and this all happened under the radar, so to speak. She showed me how to do this, to change those people. She didn't know, those bad people didn't know, and I didn't know either. These people were the important pieces on the chessboard, and I did all these things from a deep, hidden place. I didn't realize I was doing any of these things, but I understand it now. I was tapping into those people, and way deep down, I controlled them.

"Those bad men never got their treasure. And my friend, the girl you met with the red dust on her gown, she's still alive."

He said, "But you died."

I said, "Yes, but it's not like that. I'm here now."

"This other person, John, he died in her place?"

"Yes."

"You gave your life for her?"

I smiled and said, "Yes. Gladly."

I'm not sure he understood completely, but I could tell he felt the power of it. I expected him to ask some questions, but he didn't. He helped me tear the bed sheets into long strips, and I would use these to tie him up.

As we worked, I asked, "Should I hit you or something?"

He said, "You mean so I look beat up when they find me?"

"Yeah. Maybe."

He thought for a bit and said, "I don't think so. This isn't a TV cop show. They're gonna figure out I helped you no matter what you do. It might give you a little more time before they know, but not much."

Tying him up was awful. I didn't want to pull the knots tight, but it still needed to seem real. He explained it would be the guy pushing the morning breakfast cart who would find him and untie him. I bound his hands behind his back, his elbows, his knees and his feet.

He was sitting on my bed as I wrapped a strip of torn sheet around his wrists. He needed to twist around so I could tighten the knot behind his back. After it was tied he sat up and said, "I'm not sure, but it might be a good idea if you did hit me."

Then there was a loud crack, and his head snapped to the side.

He was drooped over, and I didn't know what had happened. It took a few seconds to realize I'd hit him in the face—and hit him hard.

I gasped, "Oh God. I'm sorry, I'm sorry. I don't know what I did."

Then I helped him straighten up, and he blinked a few times. His nose was bleeding, and he looked up at me and said, "Daniel is still in you."

He grimaced and shook his head a little, then added, "Daniel hit me more than once over the years, and that's what it felt like."

Oh God, I didn't like hearing that.

The radio on my belt clicked loud, and a voice said, "People are reporting a girl in the west side of the facility. They're seeing her in the halls."

The voice was panicky, and the guard said, "I need to respond to that."

He was all tied up, and he told me to take the radio off my belt and what button to hold. I held the little walkie-talkie close to his mouth, squeezed the button, and he said, "I'm on my way."

I let go and put it back on my belt, and he said, "Don't go to the locker room, just leave. Hurry."

I helped him ease back so he was lying down, and I tied his ankles to the metal rail on the foot of the bed. I took one long strip and tied it to the head of the bed, then rolled him on his side and lashed it around the knots at his elbows. I pulled it tight enough that it must have hurt, but he didn't say anything. He wouldn't be moving much, but it should seem convincing to whoever found him.

Then he told me what key to use to lock him in. He'd already said it earlier, but I let him tell me again. I wadded up another strip of the sheet into a ball and said, "I don't understand what's happening, but I know it needs to happen."

He reassured me, "It's okay. Good luck."

I pushed the ball into his mouth, and wrapped his face with the last strip of the sheet. Then I put my hand on his shoulder and said, "Thank you, my friend."

I stood up and was about to leave when Daniel turned around and hit him again. My fist hurt and blood splattered all over that awful mattress. He looked up at me, and I could see he was scared.

52

I LOCKED THE DOOR FROM THE OUTSIDE and started down the hall. There was a map in my pocket drawn by the guard with a crayon, but I didn't need it. I knew where to go.

A voice cracked, "Hurry, something's up, the patients are freaking out."

I pulled the radio off my belt and replied, "On my way."

I said it a little too loud with the mouth a little too close to the mic. I wanted my words distorted enough that no one listening would suspect anything, but I didn't need to worry. Katie's guardian angel was walking the halls of this hell, and every guard in the building was running to find her.

The staff was preoccupied, and my escape would be easy. I walked down some empty halls. I passed through some doors, and then I was outside.

It was the simplest thing. I was free.

I walked through the parking lot. It was raining, and the wind was at my back. The smells and richness were sumptuous. I was outside again. A part of me had been sleeping under the stars, but another part had been locked in a cell. I was so grateful to be breathing this clean wet air, but whose relief was I feeling?

I kept moving. There were hardly any cars in the lot, and his was right where he told me it would be. As I crossed the wet asphalt, a tiny spec of paper skittered out ahead of me, and I followed it all the way to the car. It stopped in a puddle under the driver's door. It floated there, turning slowly at my feet. I picked it up before getting in.

I sat in the driver's seat and started the engine. I turned on the dome light and looked at the fleck of paper, but I didn't need to. I already knew what it was. I held a tiny bit of the map I had torn up in the desert.

I rolled it in a little ball and dropped it on the floor. I pulled out of the lot and onto the empty highway.

They would find him in a few hours, and every cop and every trooper would be looking for his car. A murderer had escaped from an insane asylum, and the news would be on fire with such a lurid story. I needed to put some miles behind me before all hell broke loose. It was raining lightly, and the winding highway was a tunnel of giant black trees. It took a little bit to set the wipers on intermittent, and to figure out how to defog the windshield. The sun wouldn't be up for a while yet, and I was driving fast.

Holding the wheel, I rubbed my knuckles with my other hand. I didn't expect to hit the guard, and I didn't understand it. But this wasn't the time to think about any of that.

I had to tell the doctor everything, because when he finds out I'm gone, he'll start asking questions, and it won't take long before the team finds him. They'll do whatever it takes, and eventually have all the tapes of my story.

I probably told him too much, but I needed the things I said to get back to them. I needed to say enough that they wouldn't do anything to Katie. She hadn't done anything against them, not really. She tried to deceive me—at least that's the way I hoped they'd see it. I didn't know what happened to her after I left, and not knowing was like having my guts ripped out. All this might have gone terribly wrong, and she could be in danger.

I passed a yellow sign for a T-intersection ahead and took my foot off the gas. I wasn't sure which way to turn, so I reached under the driver's seat to get the road atlas. It was right where the guard told me it would be, and I set it on the passenger seat and stopped. But I ignored the map.

I sat frozen, staring straight ahead. The stop sign faced me, and at the base of the signpost sat a handsome red fox. It was lit beautifully in the high beams, and sat attentively, like it had been waiting for me. It had strange yellow eyes, and they stared back at me, unblinking. We both sat still and looked at each other. After about a minute it stood up, yawned and shook itself. The rain exploded off its fur, sparkling in a shower of electric diamonds. Then it turned around, calmly slipped into the grass, and was gone.

I sat for a long time with my hands on the wheel, focused on the wet grass beyond the signpost. The rain and darkness made me doubt everything.

Then I heard a voice say, "Turn left."

It was Donnie, taunting me like he always had, just like in that lonely canyon a lifetime ago.

I turned the wheel and drove into the night.

I have a new life, with only one purpose. I need to save Katie.

the end

About the author

Mike Clelland has spent over a decade researching the mysterious connection between owls, synchronicities, and contact events. His firsthand experiences have been the foundation for these comprehensive studies.

His 2015 nonfiction book, *The Messengers* was met with high praise. This is a collection of narrative accounts in which owls manifest in highly charged moments within people's lives. The strangeness and power of these stories defy simple explanations. *The Messengers* is also a deeply personal memoir, as the author grapples with his own owl and paranormal encounters.

The Unseen is his first work of fiction.

Mike is an artist and a recognized expert in the skills of ultralight backpacking. His website is MikeClelland.com.

Made in the USA
Las Vegas, NV
15 February 2024

85847486R00197